Outlandish English Subjects in the Victorian Domestic Novel

Outlandish English Subjects in the Victorian Domestic Novel

Timothy L. Carens
English Department
College of Charleston

First published in 2005 by
PALGRAVE MACMILLAN
Houndmills, Basingstoke, Hampshire RG21 6XS and
175 Fifth Avenue, New York, N.Y. 10010
Companies and representatives throughout the world.

PALGRAVE MACMILLAN is the global academic imprint of the Palgrave Macmillan division of St. Martin's Press, LLC and of Palgrave Macmillan Ltd. Macmillan® is a registered trademark in the United States, United Kingdom and other countries. Palgrave is a registered trademark in the European Union and other countries.

ISBN-13: 978–1–4039–4650–8 hardback
ISBN-10: 1–4039–4650–7   hardback

This book is printed on paper suitable for recycling and made from fully managed and sustained forest sources.

A catalogue record for this book is available from the British Library.

Library of Congress Cataloging-in-Publication Data

Carens, Timothy L., 1965–
    Outlandish English subjects in the Victorian domestic novel /
Timothy L. Carens.
        p. cm.
    Includes bibliographical references (p.) and index.
    ISBN 1–4039–4650–7
        1. English fiction – 19th century – History and criticism. 2. Race in literature. 3. Domestic fiction, English – History and criticism. 4. Difference (Psychology) in literature. 5. Human skin color in literature. 6. Imperialism in literature. 7. Colonies in literature. 8. Aliens in literature. I. Title.

PR878.R34C37 2005
823'.8093552—dc22   2005048760

10 9 8 7 6 5 4 3 2 1
14 13 12 11 10 09 08 07 06 05

Printed and bound in Great Britain by
Antony Rowe Ltd, Chippenham and Eastbourne

For Betsy

Contents

Illustrations

Acknowledgments

Many colleagues and students have assisted the progress of this book. Those whom I credit below have been especially helpful, but many others have given me the benefit of their insights and questions. I wish that I could specifically thank all who have prodded my thinking in off-hand comments made in classes, at conferences, and in email exchanges. I can only hope that the pages to come do some justice to their collective intelligence.

Through every stage of the development of this book, John Maynard has provided thoughtful criticism and kind encouragement. I could not have asked for a better mentor, and I am profoundly thankful for his ongoing guidance and friendship. Carolyn Dever, Perry Meisel, and Jeffrey Spear also gave crucial assistance at early stages of the manuscript. The members of my reading group at NYU – Sarah Blake, Peter Chapin, Anjali Gallup-Diaz, Allison Pease, Bill Tipper, and Anne Wilson – assisted me with keen intelligence and friendly support. My colleagues at the College of Charleston have proven equally helpful. Rich Bodek, Terry Bowers, Joe Kelly, Simon Lewis, and Bill Olejniczak have graciously found time in their busy schedules to read my work, and they have proven to be a challenging and sympathetic audience. Peter Chapin and Terry Bowers deserve special thanks for their comments on Chapter 5. I was lucky to have a graduate research assistant as smart and efficient as Nicole Fisk.

I could not have accomplished the archival research on which this book relies without the assistance cheerfully supplied by the librarians and staff of the British Library, Dartmouth College library, the Houghton and Widener Libraries at Harvard, the New York Public Library, the UCLA Department of Special Collections, and the Perry-Castañeda Library at the University of Texas Austin. Michael Phillips and his staff at the College of Charleston Interlibrary Loan Department diligently pursued my many requests.

A number of funding agencies at the College of Charleston supported stages of my research and writing. I am pleased to thank the Faculty Research and Development Fund, the English Department, and the Summer Undergraduate Research program. The latter agency afforded me the pleasure of working with Kirk Sladic and Meghan Brinson, undergraduate English majors who assisted me with unflagging good-humor and keen eyes for useful material.

Earlier versions of several chapters have appeared in other publications. Chapter 4 is reprinted from *Dickens Studies Annual* 26 (1998) by arrangement with AMS Press, Inc. Chapter 5 is reprinted from *Reality's Dark Light: the Sensational Wilkie Collins*, edited by Maria K. Bachman and Don Richard Cox (copyright © 2003, University of Tennessee Press). Chapter 6 is reprinted from *SEL Studies in English Literature 1500–1900* 41.4 (Autumn 2001). I thank the editors of these publications for granting permission to reprint.

I have received extensive encouragement and assistance from my family. My father, James F. Carens, continues to inspire me by his scholarly achievement. I am grieved that he did not live long enough to see the culmination of work that he graciously commended in its early stages. In her role as my mother, Marilyn R. Mumford has been unfailingly supportive. In her role as scrupulous editor of my prose, she has been as generous with her time as with her red ink. My brother, Geoff Carens, has on many occasions come to the rescue with obscure material wrested from the bowels of Widener library. Maddy and Ben Carens have always done their utmost to provide rambunctious diversion from the keyboard. I cannot now imagine a working life unrelieved by their delightful uproar. In too many ways to recount, Betsy Van Pelt has made this project possible, and my life fuller and richer than it could have been without her. My deepest gratitude goes to her.

1
Crossing the Divide

Abundant evidence suggests that Victorian writers perceived clear distinctions between themselves and those dark-skinned subjects they presumed to govern in distant colonies. In an 1848 *Examiner* article, for example, Charles Dickens asserts that "between the civilized European and the barbarous African, there is a great gulf set," adding for good measure that there is "a broad dark sea between the Strand in London, and the Niger" (533). In *British Rule in India* (1857), Harriet Martineau gestures to the "bottomless chasm which yawns between the interior nature of the Asiatic and the European races" (296). Significantly, both comments arise in the context of challenges to British imperial authority. Dickens writes in response to the disastrous Niger expedition of 1841, on which malarial fever defeated an attempt to found a civilizing colony on the upper reaches of the river. Martineau writes in the midst of the Indian uprising of 1857, the "present calamity," as she phrases it, facing "the English people" (2). Imperial crisis leads both writers to smooth over differences at home – to be English is also to be British and European – and accentuate them in relation to colonial otherness. Both writers intimate a vague connection between cultural and biological differences. For Martineau, it is the "interior nature" of the opposed "races" that counts. For Dickens, the mission to colonize the Niger fails because "the air that brings life to the [barbarous African] brings death to the [civilized European]" (533). Both writers accentuate differences by adopting geological figures that convey a sense of an essential, permanent, and unbridgeable divide between English and colonial subjects.[1]

Arguments dedicated to the analysis of such figures are particularly useful for discriminating the confident voice of Victorian imperialism, the voice in which English writers proclaim themselves the lords of human kind, invest themselves with the attributes of progressive and humane civilization, and pronounce their right to explore foreign ground and conquer and reform its inhabitants.[2] Such voices confirm the geographical, racial, and ethnic antitheses of imperial rhetoric decoded by Edward Said in *Orientalism* (1979), a text that still occupies a central place in debates about Victorian imperial culture.[3] The passages cited above certainly correspond to Said's definition of Orientalist discourse, offering a "political vision of reality whose structure promoted the difference between the familiar (Europe, the West, "us") and the strange (the Orient, the East, "them") (43). As many critics have observed, however, the very need to assert distinctions so loudly and so frequently implicitly indicates the presence of misgivings and self-doubts that noisy proclamations of supremacy and difference could not drown out. Certain novelists and social critics focused attention on social conditions and modes of thought and behavior that connected cultures and subjectivities located, supposedly, on different sides of a racial and cultural divide. In novels and essays governed by their skeptical view, subterranean tunnels cross the "broad dark sea" between London and Africa and bridges span the "bottomless chasm" between England and India.

Seeking a theoretical model that accounts for such ironies, a number of postcolonial critics have turned to "The Uncanny" (1919). Early in this classic essay, Freud suggests that the German words *heimlich*, homely or familiar, and *unheimlich*, unhomely or strange, are not quite as distinct as their antithetical construction implies. In addition to meaning "what is familiar and agreeable," *heimlich* also signifies "what is concealed and kept out of sight," while, according to one definition, *unheimlich* means that which "ought to have remained secret and hidden but has come to light" (17: 224–5). To Freud, the surprising proximity of meanings corresponds to a psychological dynamic through which certain aspects of the self that "ought to have remained hidden" disconcertingly "come to light." The sense of strangeness provoked by certain experiences is thus superficial and deceptive, for the ego seeks to protect the conscious mind from the knowledge of primitive impulses by forgetting them, allowing them to lapse into forms that then *appear* to be foreign to the self. The uncanny, he argues, is "in reality nothing new or alien, but something which is familiar and old-established in the mind and which has become alienated from it only through the process of repression" (17: 241). The distress caused by uncanny experiences represents the trace of a subconscious recognition; it signifies a repossession, however reluctant and partial, of the primitive "other" within.

In the Victorian period, imperial ideology functioned as a repressive mechanism that strategically estranged certain impulses and behaviors by projecting them onto the "lower races" inhabiting colonial locales. As Homi Bhabha (1990) observes, nationalist and imperial discourses set in opposition the "*heimlich* pleasures of the hearth" and the "*unheimlich* terror of the space or race of the Other" (2). As his use of Freud's vocabulary suggests, he emphasizes the instability of the distinction. He asserts, indeed, that the " 'locality' of national culture is neither unified nor unitary," that the " 'other' is never outside or beyond us" (4). Although I will return to the uncanny in the next chapter, in which I discuss the extent to which the doctrines of Victorian Evangelicalism and anthropology fostered a partial awareness of otherness within, I want to establish from the outset its compelling instrumentality. It offers such an effective approach to Victorian imperial discourses because it not only recognizes the construction of differences that serve to define Englishness and justify empire, but also explains its ambivalent uncertainty.

I hope in this book to advance understanding of the extent to which Victorian assertions of English difference and supremacy were always shadowed by the fearful suspicion that colonial otherness was not nearly other enough. The chapters that follow study how Victorian imperial culture expressed this suspicion in novels that narrate a collapse of clear distinctions between the familiarity of the English nation and character and varieties of strangeness associated with the colonial periphery. Toward the end of the nineteenth century, writers such as Haggard, Stevenson, and Conrad develop this irony in increasingly explicit forms in stories that depict the precariousness of civilization on the colonial periphery, the susceptibility of its agents to the savagery that England proposed to reform. This book focuses rather on what Dickens terms in *Bleak House* (1852–53) "home-made" savagery, the more intensely uncanny forms of colonial otherness that crop up in England itself, unbidden by the seductive appeal of the jungle.

In her discussion of the process of "crafting a sexual position," Judith Butler (1994) observes that the process of exclusion "always involves becoming haunted by what's excluded. And the more rigid the position, the greater the ghost, and the more threatening it is" (34).

The process of crafting Englishness in the age of empire leads to a parallel irony. The stakes are greater, the ghosts more fearful, when they arise at home, within the borders of the nation and, more disturbing still, within the borders of English subjectivity itself.[4] The uncanny return of colonial otherness represents a predictable side effect of "[t]he classical relationship," as Balachandra Rajan (1999) describes it, "in which a dominant self defines a subjected other and then defines itself by the exclusion of that other" (3). Indeed, at the start of the book that largely initiated appreciation of the antithetical structure of imperial rhetoric, Said observes that "European culture gained in strength and identity by setting itself off against the Orient as a sort of surrogate and even underground self" (3). *Orientalism* does not elaborate the significance of this subterranean link that apparently survives or inhabits rhetorical strategies of differentiation.[5] It seems likely, though, that Said cryptically refers to the ironic consequence of the process described more fully by Stallybrass and White (1986) as "the production of identity through negation, the creation of an implicit sense of self through explicit rejections and denials" (89). Said's "underground self" corresponds to what they call a "new domain" that the self creates within itself "by taking into itself as *negative introjections* the very domains which surround and threaten it" (original italics, 89).

Postcolonial studies of the Victorian novel have only just begun to detect the colonial ghosts that haunt stories about English romance and domesticity. Despite the extent to which the field has generally accepted the theoretical instability of imperial dichotomies,[6] the treatment of domestic novels has continued to emphasize the extent to which they are upheld. In *Culture and Imperialism* (1993), Said seeks to establish the "connection between the pursuit of national imperial aims and the general national culture" in part by demonstrating that depictions of romance and domesticity in England participate in the consolidation of imperial power (13). In a reading of *Mansfield Park* (1814), for example, he argues that a character's inheritance of an Antiguan plantation reveals Austen "to be *assuming* ... the importance of an empire to the situation at home" (original italics, 89). Of course, one need not even refer to a plot in which an English family explicitly reaps financial rewards from a distant plantation. Most references to imported colonial products intimately associated with middle-class luxuries – tea, sugar, coffee, etc. – might be said to assume on a basic level the fact of imperial trade and imperial power, the prerogative of English subjects to consume the fruit of colonial labor, the right of English merchants to profit from exploitative economic arrangements.[7] Even before the publication of *Culture and Imperialism*, Said's general point was advanced by postcolonial feminist critics who argued that Victorian domestic novels shore up imperial ideology as they debated and reshaped gender roles at home. In an influential essay on *Jane Eyre* (1847) and other "women's texts," Gayatri Spivak (1985) argues that the proto-feminist effort to adjust the distribution of power between the sexes is advanced in England at the expense of the colonial subject, and the novel thus affirms the "active ideology of imperialism" (247). In *Reaches of Empire* (1991),

Suvendrini Perera offered the first extended critical treatment of domestic novels from this approach. Through compelling readings of works by Charlotte Brontë, Dickens, Thackeray, and others, she argues that domestic novels consistently rely upon certain "key tropes of empire" – such as "abolition, interracial coupling, migration and transportation, mercantile 'adventuring', orientalist visions of sati and polygamy, 'thuggee', and the opium trade," – as they variously participate in the "organization of gender at home" (12). These tropes furnish the romantic plot with figurative devices, and as they do so they endorse assumptions about the oppression and injustice supposedly inherent to the colonial periphery and the ethical superiority of English culture. No less than novels about imperial conquest and governance, Perera contends, English romantic plots "prepared for, or made possible a climate for receiving or accommodating, empire" (7).[8] Perera has been followed by other critics whose projects differ, certainly, but who all generally confirm the point that representations of domestic affairs function collaboratively with imperial ideology.[9]

This conclusion is often grounded in the argument, elaborated by Said in *Orientalism*, that imperial discourse promotes a sense of clear differences between imperial self and colonial other (13). Perera argues, for example, that the " 'domestic' was most often formulated, sustained, and tested by its definition through and in opposition to the 'external', the 'foreign', and the 'other' " (8). Inderpal Grewal (1996), who analyzes the specific role of the harem in this process, likewise observes that the image of the "woman 'caged' in the harem, in purdah, becomes the necessary Other for the construction of the Englishwoman presumably free and happy in the home" (54). An emphasis on dichotomies has enabled persuasive readings of domestic novels that have collectively demonstrated the extent to which books apparently concerned only with romantic and class problems at home are also deeply invested in imperial ideology.[10] Unfortunately, though, this approach has also tended to obscure the extent to which domestic novels disrupt and challenge the dichotomies they also paradoxically affirm.[11] It has not helped students of Victorian literature and culture to perceive the extent to which domestic novels countered the logic of us versus them, familiar versus strange, home versus harem, by disclosing disturbing affinities and correspondences between English and colonial subjects.

Domestic autoethnography

Certain domestic novelists and social critics articulate this counter-logic through a satiric device that compels readers to confront the extent to which English imperial culture is infected by uncanny colonial otherness. This device subverts consoling assertions of difference and superiority by adopting the language and narrative structures of colonial ethnography in order to describe the domestic social scene. For the purpose of this study, the term *ethnography* broadly denotes metropolitan writing about colonial cultures and territories. It encompasses descriptions of colonial sites such as Asia, Africa, and the Americas produced by missionaries, travelers, imperial bureaucrats and soldiers, and unofficial Western travelers.[12] (The examples treated in the following chapters emphasize ethnographic description of India and Africa, which figured more largely than other colonial sites in the Victorian imagination.) Most nineteenth-century ethnographers make no effort to describe colonial cultures with the sympathetic understanding to which contemporary anthropological writing aspires. The missionary who dismisses indigenous religion as blind superstition provides a clear case in point. Most Victorian ethnographers in one way or another reveal the cultural biases that shape their colonial encounters. As ethnographic idioms gain currency in England, they often degenerate into the sort of derogatory caricatures that Thackeray and Dickens deploy in the examples discussed below.

The appropriation and redirection of colonial ethnography may usefully be termed "domestic autoethnography." Readers of *Imperial Eyes* (1992) will recognize that I have borrowed and modified a term that Mary Louise Pratt uses in her influential analysis of writing in the colonial "contact zones," those "social spaces where disparate cultures meet, clash, and grapple with each other, often in highly asymmetrical relations of domination and subordination" (4). In her use of the term, Pratt seeks to recapture a cross-cultural dialogue that begins with European description of territories and cultures undergoing the process of colonization. "If ethnographic texts are a means by which Europeans represent to themselves their (usually subjugated) others," Pratt explains, "autoethnographic texts are those the others construct in response to or in dialogue with those metropolitan representations" (7). In her introduction, she offers as an example of autoethnography the *New Chronicle and Good Government and Justice* (1613), a long and complicated letter written by Andean writer Guaman Poma to King Philip III of Spain. Poma takes the opportunity to rewrite "the history of Christiandom to include the indigenous peoples of America," to describe Andean culture in great detail, and to supply a "revisionist account of the Spanish conquest" that brings to light the "exploitation and abuse" suffered by his people (2). This example is somewhat idiosyncratic in a book that focuses largely on eighteenth- and nineteenth-century English travel writing, but it clarifies two important points about Pratt's use of the term autoethnography. First, the topic of autoethnography is the colonial space and culture subjugated by Western imperial power. Second, the figure who crafts the autoethnographic response is a representative of that colonial space and culture.

My use of the term differs on both these counts. The topic of *domestic* autoethnography is the space and culture of the imperial nation. The novelists and social critics who employ it are themselves middle-class English subjects. Despite these crucial differences, Pratt's description of the formal properties of autoethnography remains highly relevant for an analysis of a dialogue that occurs within the borders of Victorian imperial culture. For Pratt, autoethnography is an intriguing and complex form of discourse because it "involves partial collaboration with and appropriation of the idioms of the conqueror. Often, ... the idioms appropriated and transformed are those of travel and exploration writing, merged or infiltrated to varying degrees with indigenous modes" (7). Domestic autoethnography reveals a similar rhetorical dynamic of appropriation, transformation, and infiltration. Victorian writers produce an alternative and equally intriguing response to imperial travel and exploration writing as they appropriate ethnographic idioms and merge them into "indigenous modes" of writing such as the domestic novel and social criticism.

The fact that they generally do not challenge the veracity of the original application of those idioms registers the extent to which the perspectives of domestic and colonial autoethnography differ. The writers featured in the following chapters "collaborate" extensively with the ethnographic idioms they appropriate, indeed assuming and reconfirming their representational authority in relation to colonial subjects and space. They do, however, contest the geographic boundaries implicitly placed on them, disputing the notion that one must travel to the colonial periphery in order to discover appropriate referents. By asserting the truth of their application *within England as well*, they produce a domestic autoethnography that frays the network of oppositions promoted by imperial ideology. Applying the idioms of colonial otherness to Victorian domestic culture, these writers belie the naive assumption that familiar England can be disentangled from strange colonial otherness.

The writers who practice domestic autoethnography draw upon certain broadly circulating idioms of colonial otherness. Victorian imperial culture frequently affirmed its superiority and difference by expressing contempt for the colonial "heathen" who "in his blindness / Bows down to wood and stone!" as Bishop Heber (1819) phrased it in a popular hymn. Yet Macaulay, Carlyle, Ruskin, and many other Victorian writers discover a broad array of false religious commitments within English culture. They register the point by merging idioms of idolatrous otherness with description of practices and beliefs perceived as central to English life and thought. The works of novelists and social critics of the period reveal an extensive catalogue of English idolatries, replete with false gods, blind illusions, vain self-sacrifice, and acts of degrading self-abasement. In *Pendennis* (1848–50), for example, the prospect of the exhausted Major Pendennis, enduring "silent agony" in order to make an appearance at an exclusive party, prompts the narrator to observe that "the negroes in the service of Mumbo Jumbo tattoo and drill themselves with burning skewers with great fortitude; and we read that the priests in the service of Baal gashed themselves and bled freely" (578–9). The Major, who embodies imperial military conquest and discipline as well as snobbish debasement, falls in line with ancient and contemporary idolaters who punish the body in service to the "best thing they know" (579). In *Little Dorrit* (1855–57), Dickens uses the figure of African fetishism to critique the over-valuation of wealth. The narrator observes that those who cravenly worship the wealthy Mr Merdle "prostrated themselves before him, more degradedly and less excusably than the darkest savage creeps out of his hole in the ground to propitiate, in some log or reptile, the Deity of his benighted soul" (611). Victorian novelists and social critics thus appropriate and reapply ethnographic idioms of heathen blindness, compelling readers to confront the uncanny otherness that dwells within their own culture.

As these examples begin to show, domestic autoethnography functions as a historically specific mode of satire. This point deserves extended consideration, because it might be mistaken as grounds for dismissing its relevance as a measure of the fears and anxieties that ran beneath the ethnocentric certitudes of empire. It is of course important to note that the satiric device relies on the sort of ethnographic caricatures that functioned throughout the Victorian period to sharpen distinctions between Englishness and colonial otherness. Dickens's figure, for example, confirms and embellishes his culture's disdainful stereotype of heathen fetishism, which was perceived as the lowest and most degenerate form of religious practice.[13] As much animal as human, his version of the "darkest savage" inhabits a "hole in the ground" from which he "creeps" when moved to worship. The arbitrary choice of a base fetish object, "some log or reptile," underscores a sense of religious delusion on the part of the "benighted" worshipper. A studied disregard for cultural and geographical specificity shores up the repudiation of religious error. Although Dickens and his readers would have associated such practices with sub-Saharan Africa, the narrator evokes a distinctly generic savage who practices an indefinite form of worship. From Dickens's perspective, to describe more particularly would be to validate anthropological curiosity and thereby confuse the central objective. The narrator very clearly regards the domestic problem, the corrupting influence of wealth in England,[14] to be more worthy of notice than the rites practiced by the "darkest savage," who is evoked only to establish a standard of heathen darkness. These initial examples establish an important general point about domestic autoethnography: while the colonial periphery supplies the imagery and a comparative base, in most cases it does not rival the importance of the metropolitan culture as a topic.

It is also important to note that the comparisons at the heart of domestic autoethnography rely on deliberate exaggeration. The "tired, oh, so tired" Major Pendennis endures the pain of "weary feet burning in his varnished boots," but his self-punishment does not descend to the level of actually drilling his flesh with "burning skewers" (578–9). The very nature of comparison, moreover, leaves certain unstated differences implicitly intact. Unlike the "darkest savage," who can only ever embody savage darkness, those who bow before Merdle conform to standards of English civilization in other aspects of their lives. By developing an exaggerated point of similarity, it might be argued, such jibes purchase amusement and derision at the expense of credibility. They bear the mark of rhetorical intention, and cannot therefore be taken as a trustworthy register of cultural anxiety.

In the context of a broad and recurring pattern of comparisons, however, it would be a mistake to dismiss any instances of domestic autoethnography, even those apparently intended only to prompt a laugh. Satire, after all, has complex effects. The exaggerations it constructs cannot be rejected as merely absurd because they serve to uncover vexing truths. Satire thus provokes dismay and contempt as well as laughter. As Gilbert Highet (1962) observes, the satirist "intends to shock his readers. By compelling them to look at a sight they had missed or shunned, he first makes them realize the truth, and then moves them to feelings of protest" (20). This traditional point about satire charts a provocative connection between the satiric disclosure of colonial otherness at home and the uncanny discovery of that which "ought to have remained secret and hidden." Indeed, Freudian theory offers a forceful rejoinder to those who might be inclined to dismiss the sort of comparisons constructed by Thackeray and Dickens as merely instances of humorous exaggeration, irrelevant to an analysis of the anxieties of imperial culture. Rather than being slighted as nothing more significant than jokes, such examples of domestic autoethnography should be analyzed as nothing *less*. In *Jokes and Their Relation to the Unconscious* (1905), Freud argues (in language that anticipates his description of the uncanny) that jokes are relevant to his discipline because they "bring forward something that is concealed or hidden" (8: 13–14).[15] Although I do not mean to equate domestic autoethnography with the Freudian joke (to begin with, many instances of the former are not humorous), they share the property of disclosing ideas "shunned" by prevailing codes of propriety. Further consideration of Freud's essay will help to defend the assumption that the satiric discourse of domestic autoethnography provides occasions for the expression of ideas generally repressed by imperial ideology.

Like jokes, the subversive potential of domestic autoethnography is located in its form. Among the different forms of jokes he considers, Freud discusses the "joking analogy," which he describes as a "case of unification, the making of an unsuspected connection" (8: 83–4). Such connections are humorous because they "are to a great degree 'debasing' "; they function by "juxtapos[ing] something of a high category, something abstract ... with something of a very concrete and even low kind" (8: 85). This definition parallels Bakhtin's analysis of tropes that subversively jumble hierarchical categories. According to Stallybrass and White, for example, the Bakhtinian grotesque "is formed through a process of hybridization or inmixing of binary opposites, particularly of high and low, such that there is a heterodox merging of elements usually perceived as incompatible" (44). Domestic autoethnography represents a specific type of Freud's "joking analogy" and the Bakhtinian grotesque. Within the context of Victorian imperial culture, the presumably high category of English civilization suffers debasement when satirically juxtaposed to or merged with colonial otherness.[16] Dickens imagines a quite literal form of debasement as he compares the Londoner who admires wealth and power to the savage who "creeps out of his hole in the ground" to propitiate a lifeless god. Despite the fact that such comparisons are manifestly designed to amuse, they repay careful study because they "bring forward something that is concealed or hidden," fears that persistently inhabited the political unconscious of imperial culture. Predominantly committed to the binaries and hierarchies that justified its rule, Victorian England could not shake the suspicion of an underlying hybridity, a heterodox merging of itself with abhorred colonial otherness.

For Freud, jokes are relevant because they provide glimpses of the side of the mind that refuses to respect the inhibitions that structure the surface of conscious life. He draws a distinction between "innocent" jokes, which rebel against reason with word play and nonsense, and "tendentious" jokes, which rebel against propriety by giving vent to libidinal impulses of violent aggression and sexual desire. Tendentious jokes are either "hostile," using humor to attack or defend, or "obscene." A hostile joke "will allow us to exploit something ridiculous in our enemy which we could not ... bring forward openly or consciously; once again, then, the joke *will evade restrictions and open sources of pleasure that have become inaccessible*" (original italics, 8: 103). In one of the essay's least developed passages, Freud considers a specific type of hostile joke that corresponds closely to the discourse of domestic autoethnography. "A particularly favorable occasion for tendentious jokes is presented," he argues, when "criticism is directed against the subject himself, or, to put it more cautiously, against someone in whom the subject has a share – a collective person, that is (the subject's own nation, for instance)" (8: 111). Major Pendennis and those who idolize Mr Merdle might be considered to be "enemies" of Thackeray and Dickens respectively, but in a broader sense both authors and characters together embody the "collective person" that is the imperial nation. "[I]n the service of cynical and sceptical purposes," Freud later remarks, a joke "shatters respect for institutions and truths in which the hearer has believed" (8: 133). If Thackeray and Dickens do not definitively "shatter" respect for England and the "truth" of its difference and superiority, they do call into question the *extent* to which it differs from colonial otherness. And they are joined, it is important to consider, by many other novelists and social critics who similarly transgress inhibitions imposed by ethnocentric and imperial attitudes. According to Freud, tendentious jokes in particular "run the risk of meeting with people who do not want to listen to them" (8: 90). The discourse of domestic autoethnography no doubt ran that risk in its own day. To listen thoroughly to it from our historical remove, it is necessary to hear the anxious notes of skeptical reappraisal that sound below the more prevalent strain of humorous exaggeration.

Freud's discussion of jokes cannot, however, finally account for the motivation of domestic autoethnography, which attacks the institutions and truths of Englishness not in the service of libidinal rebellion but in defense of ideals that, it tells itself, still exist, even if they have been corrupted. The narrator of *Little Dorrit* despises those who bow before Merdle because they have transgressed religious and ethical codes of

Englishness, but the act of transgression indicates the presence of a border that the novel implicitly defends and affirms. Dickens takes for granted the superiority of Christian faith and of the nation that it should, ideally, permeate and sustain. The criticism that the discourse calls down upon the collective person of the nation bears the hostility of the super-ego, enacting, as Freud writes in *The Ego and the Id* (1923), the "self-judgement which declares that the ego falls short of its ideals" (19: 37). As it denounces notions and practices that compromise the nation's treasured image of itself as superior to and different from colonial otherness, domestic autoethnography articulates the vindictive conscience of the imperial nation. The collaborative relationship between the production of ideal self-image and satiric punishment helps to explain what appear to be ideological paradoxes in the work of writers who alternately affirm and attack the illusion of difference and superiority. Dickens, for example, maintains on one page that a "great gulf" separates civilized and barbarian peoples and, on another, devises comparisons that prove the contrary. The satirists discussed in the following chapters also tend to endorse English imperial projects while at the same time discrediting the rhetoric that justifies them. Such paradoxes are resolved in the persistent fantasy of a nation purged of the taint of colonial otherness and therefore justified to conquer and govern those who embody it.

The fact that domestic autoethnography remains committed at some level to the very distinctions it challenges does not, however, cancel the anxieties that it expresses and intensifies. If the self-critical conscience works alongside self-idealizing fantasy, the two do not necessarily work with equal strength or conviction.[17] The authors considered in the following chapters spread doubts much more effectively than they soothe them. Dickens indicates that the superiority of the imperial nation is precariously staked on religious and ethical codes that have failed, and failed broadly. The consciousness of swiftly deteriorating borders explains why the narrator's contempt for benighted heathen worship gains strength as it boomerangs back to England. The narrator indicates that heathen English subjects who have abandoned the true God and prostrated themselves before an image made of the "commonest clay" have surpassed the superlative standard of benighted degradation (611). They practice a *more* degraded and *less* excusable form of worship than even the "darkest savage." To make matters worse, it is unclear how many prostrate themselves before the English "Deity" of wealth and power. The narrator only observes that the "famous name of Merdle" becomes more famous each day, that a large and increasing number of English Christian subjects prostrate themselves before him (611).

This darkest of English idolatries is alarmingly widespread and the ideals professed by the imperial nation are unable to thwart the degrading otherness that spreads like contagion.

Ethnographic pre-texts and the civilizing project at home

Although the isolated figures discussed thus far exemplify the basic satiric strategy of appropriation and redirection at the heart of domestic autoethnography, they do not convey the force and complexity of extended instances. The novels treated in the following chapters demonstrate an acute awareness of very specific ethnographic discourses – and in some cases particular texts – through which imperial missionaries, travelers, soldiers, and bureaucrats comment on the outlandishness of colonial locales and cultures. As they build their novels, Dickens, Charlotte Brontë, Collins, and Meredith appropriate certain ethnographic "pre-texts," extracting from them elaborate narratives complete with plot, characters, and symbolic structure. Embedded within or merged into representation of the familiar domestic scene, these ethnographic discourses serve a new and intensely ironic purpose.

Late in the century, "General" William Booth, founder of the Salvation Army, furnishes a particularly clear example of the recontextualization of ethnographic discourse. His Evangelical social reform tract *In Darkest England and the Way Out* (1890) begins with the observation that "the attention of the civilised world has been arrested by the story which Mr. Stanley has told of 'Darkest Africa' and his journeyings across the heart of the lost continent" (9). Booth devotes several pages to a detailed summary of the section of *In Darkest Africa* (1890) in which the "intrepid explorer" describes penetrating the "great Equatorial forest" (9). This summary demonstrates the process through which Booth appropriates idioms of dark colonial otherness from a specific ethnographic text. He then deliberately reapplies those idioms to England. "May we not find a parallel at our own doors," he asks, "and discover within a stone's throw of our cathedrals and palaces similar horrors to those which Stanley has found existing in the great Equatorial forest?" (11–12). The rhetorical question commences an elaborate series of analogies that disclose the "horrors" of savage life in London, where Christian light has receded before a tide of heathen darkness and social depravity:

Hard it is, no doubt, to read in Stanley's pages of the slave-traders coldly arranging for the surprise of a village, the capture of the inhabitants, the massacre of those who resist, and the violation of all the women; but the stony streets of London, if they could but speak, would tell of tragedies as awful, of ruin as complete, of ravishments as horrible, as if we were in central Africa; only the ghastly devastation is covered, corpse-like, with the artificialities and hypocrisies of modern civilisation. (13)

The procedure of appropriation and infiltration of ethnographic material is particularly overt in this case. Booth identifies the ethnographic "pre-text" on which he relies and carefully explains to the reader how and why he projects the African imagery drawn from that text onto the "stony streets of London." Not one to leave unannounced the irony generated by the formal merging of strange and familiar locales, he pro-claims, "What a satire it is upon our Christianity and our civilisation, that the existence of these colonies of heathens and savages in the heart of our capital should attract so little attention!" (16).[18] *In Darkest England* carries readers through the steps of constructing domestic autoethnography, explicating in clear stages the satiric procedure through which idioms used to describe "heathens and savages" come home to roost.[19]

A similar process occurs in much more subtle and intricate ways in the novels discussed in the following chapters. Because they do not adver-tise the ethnographic texts on which they rely, it becomes necessary to recover the forgotten origins of the outlandish stories that uncannily resurface within representations of the familiar domestic scene. Chapter 3, for example, traces the journey of the idol of Juggernaut from English writing about India into Victorian domestic novels. The chapter begins with a comparative analysis of two competing narratives about this spe-cific idol, one produced by Evangelical missionaries, the other by official agents of the East India Company. Although these narratives differ widely in tone and resolution, they share disdain for the idolatrous cere-monies they describe, and both broadly manifest the assumption of English superiority and difference. Charlotte Brontë and George Meredith both embed Juggernaut narratives within their marriage plots, providing fascinating case studies of a major cross-current in the rhetorical system that sought to oppose Protestant England to heathen colonial otherness. Both authors discover an alarming affinity between the despised Hindu cult and English patriarchal culture. Both suggest that the Juggernaut of male authority threatens to crush women who bow before it. Crucial dif-ferences between their visions of reform, as well as the ironies that cast the efficacy of those reforms into doubt, only come into focus after first recovering the distinct narrative structures of the ethnographic discourses each appropriates and satirically reapplies.

Chapter 4 considers an example of the Africanization of London that precedes *In Darkest England* by several decades. Long before Booth's text appeared, social critics of a previous generation detected alarming eruptions of African darkness in London and other industrial cities. In *Chartism* (1839), Thomas Carlyle leads the "Upper Classes and Lawgivers" of England to "the shore of a boundless continent" of working-class misery and asks them "[w]hether they do not with their own eyes see it, the strange symptoms of it, lying huge, dark, unexplored, inevitable; full of hope, but also full of difficulty, savagery, almost of despair?" (197). Alongside the nineteenth-century "genealogy of the dark continent" traced by Patrick Brantlinger (1988) developed this ironic counterpart in discourses concerned with the condition of England itself. In *Bleak House* (1852–53), Dickens contributes to the genealogy of the dark continent at home, describing London with language drawn specifically from recent accounts of philanthropic explorations in the Niger River delta. *Bleak House* depicts an English landscape awash in mud and replete with disease, decay, and hopeless death. Dickens extracts this symbolic cluster from *A Narrative of an Expedition Sent by Her Majesty Government to the River Niger in 1841 under the Command of H. D. Trotter* (1848), a book that to his mind dramatically depicts the folly of attempting to civilize Africa before attending to poor and middle-class English "savages." Like Brontë and Meredith, Dickens associates the collapse of distinctions with misalignments in the power structure of sexual relations. While they identify patriarchal despotism as the source of the problem, he lays blame at the feet of women who betray English civilization by pursuing pseudo-professional careers at the expense of the nation and its domestic spheres. Dickens particularly faults Mrs Jellyby, whose philanthropic scheme misdirects concern to the Niger delta while hastening the Africanization of London. He devises reforms intended to repair distinctions both between the imperial center and the savage periphery and between female and male responsibilities.

Chapter 5 turns attention from the savagery encroaching upon the English landscape to forms of savagery inhabiting the English self. As the domestic forms of Juggernaut worship examined in Chapter 3 suggest, those English subjects who presumably represent civilization in its fullest sense ironically encompass sites of savage resistance and rebellion. Indeed, Victorian novels are full of characters who give vent to ungovernable desires, irrepressible rages, superstitious worship, and other impulses associated with colonial subjectivity. Many writers thus employ the trope of the unrestrained colonial self as they work to diagnose unwelcome eruptions of what Charles Kingsley calls in *Yeast* (1851) the "savage and spasmodic self-will" (5: 328). Chapter 5 discusses Wilkie Collins's novel *The Moonstone* (1868) in light of the prevailing assumption that Indians were ungovernable, which gained force in the wake of the Indian uprising of 1857. Ethnographic writing that emerged in the years following the "Mutiny," as it was termed in England, interpreted the outbreak of violence as the effect of unrestrained colonial subjectivity. While Collins does not directly contest the prevailing explanation, he does question the extent to which the English character differs from its supposedly ungovernable colonial counterpart. The arrival of a large Indian diamond in Yorkshire occasions the release of the same sort of fanaticism and idolatry among the English characters as post-mutiny narratives routinely attribute to Indians in thrall to base passions and false gods.

The final chapter focuses attention on another figurative connection between England and India. In his seldom-read late-century novel *Lord Ormont and His Aminta* (1894), Meredith seeks to contain and control the outbreak of native English savagery that Collins perceives as inevitable. Through an elaborate analogy between the heroine and India, the novel in part registers the extent to which the political status of both English women and India had advanced by the last decades of the century. Their potential for self-government and independence had become a question that could not be avoided. Rather than advocating independence for either, however, Meredith seeks instead to fashion an English male administration equipped to facilitate further reforms. He justifies this response by adopting the late-century liberal view of India as an inadequately, unstably reformed colony. The sequence of the heroine's romantic relationships corresponds to the progressive imperial history envisioned by Wilfred Scawen Blunt in a series of essays published in *The Fortnightly Review*, "Ideas about India" (1884–85). Paralleling the argument developed in Blunt's essays, Meredith calls for an end to autocratic control, but withholds endorsement of colonial self-rule abroad and female self-rule at home. In keeping with the late-century liberal reform discourse about India, he stakes the progress he envisions on the ability of male government to resist a seductive appeal for violent conquest that emanates from the female colony. This ability in turn confers the right to reform the still somewhat savage woman-as-India.

It is notable that the novels discussed in the following chapters use domestic autoethnography in order to satirize figures, institutions, and ideas perceived as synechdoches of Englishness. Varieties of colonial otherness infiltrate and estrange representations of the country gentleman, the Evangelical minister, the self-sacrificing middle-class woman and her more privileged sisters. They contaminate proper country estates as well as the streets and homes of London. Relations between the sexes in the spheres of romance and domesticity routinely manifest a strange otherness. This is perhaps most ironic of all, given the fact that Victorians particularly staked English superiority and difference on the civility of its chivalric code. The novels I foreground thus strike particularly disconcerting chords as they subvert the racial and cultural distinctions that undergird imperial ideology.

Practitioners of satire have of course traditionally justified their art by claiming that it exposes abuses and failings in order to correct them. This logic certainly arises within the novels analyzed in the following chapters. Domestic autoethnography, like its colonial counterpart, often serves the interest of plots that envision the reform of "savage" customs. Novels that recontextualize the idioms of colonial otherness to describe the English state and subject also then evoke what may be described as the meta-narrative of nineteenth-century imperialism, the civilizing mission. This term denominates the ideologically useful narrative that justifies colonial governance as a mechanism of benevolent improvement, endowing imperial civilization with the epistemological, political, spiritual, and technological tools with which to correct the many defects of colonial otherness: its ignorance, despotism, superstition, primitiveness, etc. Although a full analysis of the civilizing mission falls beyond the scope of this book, its history and theory warrant brief consideration, since the reform of "home-made" savagery emerges as an overarching narrative structure in many of the novels I discuss.[20]

Until the end of the eighteenth century, England perceived its colonies almost exclusively as money-making ventures.[21] At that point, however, Enlightenment confidence in the universality and perfectibility of human nature converged with the Evangelical movement's emphasis on missionary work to burden imperial expansion with a philanthropic imperative. The first vigorous proponents of civilizing responsibility were Evangelical figures who called the nation to task for treating indigenous people as commodities rather than seeking to enlighten their souls and improve their material condition. In the last two decades of the eighteenth century, the Evangelical Anglican group known as the Clapham Sect (which included William Wilberforce, John Venn, Charles Grant, John Shore, Zachary Macaulay, and others) sought to fulfill what they perceived to be the ethical mandate of imperial power by campaigning against slavery and founding the Society for Missions to Africa and the East (later the Church Missionary Society).[22] Members of the Clapham Sect used their substantial political influence to help pass the law outlawing the slave trade (1807) and to overturn the East India Company prohibition on Christian missionary work (1813).[23]

Although the Clapham sect placed a priority on religious conversion, they believed that the spread of Christianity should occur as part of a broader process of cultural transformation. In 1813, during the campaign for the right to proselytize in India, Wilberforce articulated what Eric Stokes (1959) calls the "full-blooded doctrine of assimilation" (35):

> [L]et us endeavor to strike our roots into the soil by the gradual introduction and establishment of our own principles and opinions; of our laws, institutions, and manners; above all, as the source of every other improvement, of our religion, and consequently of our morals. ... Are we so little aware of the vast superiority even of European laws and institutions, and far more of British institutions, over those of Asia, as not to be prepared to predict with confidence, that the Indian community which should have exchanged its dark and bloody superstitions for the genial influence of Christian light and truth, would have experienced such an increase of civil order and security, of social pleasures and domestic comforts, as to be desirous of preserving the blessings it should have acquired; and can we doubt that it would be bound even by the ties of gratitude to those who have been the honored instruments of communicating them? (qtd. in Stokes 35)

Over the course of the long nineteenth-century, the civilizing mission took many distinct shapes. Different factions predictably advocated different varieties of reform. Utilitarians such as James Mill placed priority on legal codes and governmental authority. Free Traders championed the transformative power of capitalism. In his "Minute on Indian Education" (1835), Thomas Babington Macaulay famously asserted the efficacy of the study of the English language and literature for carrying forward the "intellectual improvement of the people" of India (240). Different priorities sometimes occasioned bitter debates about the best way to effect change in colonial locales, particularly between religious and secular reformers. Nonetheless, proponents of civilizing assimilation generally shared assumptions about the "vast superiority" of English culture and the desirability of reforms it might export to colonial locales. These assumptions helped to produce a compelling narrative in which the imperial nation would benevolently foster the growth and progress of its colonies, winning "gratitude" in return for paternalistic care. As C. C. Eldridge (1984) observes, even those "who did not accept that the empire added either politically or economically to Britain's power, influence, and prestige" generally subscribed to the "moral view of empire that Britain had an obligation to bring civilization to the backward parts of the world" (183).

This "moral view" was so appealing in part because it functioned to repress suspicions that contradicted the notion of benevolent superiority, perhaps not least the nagging sense of identification with presumably inferior colonial subjects. The presumption of civilizing authority becomes highly ironic in the context of narratives in which ethnographic idioms form the basis of anxious and skeptical reassessments of England's "vast superiority." The irony is not dispelled by the fact that Victorian domestic novels express the impulse to reform the strange colonial otherness that has infected and distorted the nation's own "social pleasures and domestic comforts." For if they satirically expose multiple sites of "home-made" savagery in order to reform them and thus recapture England's "vast superiority," it would be inaccurate to assume that they achieve their aim. The civilizing missions enacted at home sometimes fail. When they do "succeed," they display the ideological duplicity on which they rely. The novels that seek to contain eruptions of English savagery ultimately only exhibit the limitations, deceits, and buried fault lines of civilizing rhetoric.

Novels by Brontë and Meredith, for example, both ultimately reveal the intransigence of the power relation that links Victorian patriarchal culture to the abhorred cult of Juggernaut. Jane Eyre remains susceptible to self-destructive fanaticism until the very end of the novel and is only rescued from idolatrous suicide by miraculous intervention. Although the heroine of *The Egoist* refuses to idolize her Juggernaut fiancé, she escapes his grasp only to prostrate herself before another male idol. Dickens seeks in *Bleak House* to redirect the reform energy wasted on the invincible savagery of Africa to the streets and domiciles of London, but the metropolis proves to be just as resistant to civilizing intervention as the deadly tropical jungle. The happy ending of the novel depends as much on a retreat from London and its social problems as the effort to engage those problems depends on a retreat from Africa. Collins propagates the disturbing knowledge that, as he observes in *The Evil Genius* (1886), "our ancestor the savage" broods within all English subjects (264). In *The Moonstone*, he cultivates a broad anxiety about the universality and irrepressibility of savage passions and calls into question the possibility of maintaining a stable civilized community. Although Meredith shares Collins's conception of the universality of savage instincts, he seeks in *Lord Ormont* to imagine more fully a progressive narrative in which they are brought under control. He constructs an English male colonial authority equipped to restrain his own savage instincts and thus exert a civilizing influence on the less responsible heroine. Ironically, however, Meredith must effectively abandon the figure of colonial progress in order to ensure that the hero retains colonial authority. His novel unwittingly exposes the false promise of civilizing rhetoric.

Given the fact that these novels not only expose the presence of "home-made" savagery but also indicate its recalcitrance, the hypothesis that Victorian domestic novels advance imperial aims requires careful reassessment. The notion that they do so by affirming and maintaining the opposition of familiar imperial self and strange colonial other is simply untenable. It is true that English domestic novelists often express the *urge* to purify national identity. The very fact that they rely on ethnographic language to describe the domestic social scene indicates the strength of the desire to believe that the familiar problems they describe are in some way foreign to English culture and character. Despite the strength of this desire, though, it is evident that they cannot dispense with the vocabulary of colonial otherness as a tool of satirical self-analysis nor dispel the problems that admit the necessity of using it. Perhaps Victorian culture did find it possible to imagine a national identity clearly and cleanly opposed to colonial otherness. Tony Claydon and Ian McBride (1998) rightly observe that "[i]dentity is constructed as much through objectives as through perceived achievements" (28). Still, to read the works of Charlotte Brontë, Dickens, Collins, Meredith, and many other domestic novelists is to confront the fact that this identity could only exist in the form of a distant, fragile, and ultimately mocking ideal. This point supports recent discussion of satire that has called into question the extent to which the genre is really invested in the reform of the abuses it decries. Dustin Griffin approaches satire as a "rhetoric of provocation" that is "designed to expose or demolish a foolish certainty" (52). Satire, he argues, provokes readers "by holding up to scrutiny our idealized images of ourselves – forcing us to admit that such images are forever out of reach, unavailable to us" (60). The Victorian domestic novels that employ the satiric discourse of domestic autoethnography generally confirm this argument as they enact a recurring, unresolvable clash between faith in the "vast superiority" and vast difference of Englishness and the disconcerting knowledge that the nation cannot attain its image of itself as clearly distinguished from debased colonial otherness.

2
Strange Relations: The Evangelical and Anthropological Roots of Imperial Anxiety

In their discussion of the ironies of Englishness, both Ian Baucom (1999) and Simon Gikandi (1996) trace a historical trajectory that culminates in the twentieth century. Granting that "it has never been clear where the identity between colonizer and colonized ends and the difference between them begins," as Gikandi puts it, both critics characterize postcolonial culture as the moment in which the overlap reaches its clearest expression (2). Gikandi speculates that the "loss of empire has forced the imagined community [of Englishness] to unravel" in a particularly visible way (31). From this perspective, Victorian culture might be misunderstood as a prefatory moment during which the nation imagined itself as a 'deep horizontal comradeship' set in opposition to dark-skinned colonial otherness.[1] The 'Englishness of the past', as Robert Young (1995) points out, "is often represented in terms of fixity, of certainty, centredness, homogeneity, as something unproblematically identical with itself" (2). Neither Gikandi nor Baucom promotes this misunderstanding, but the extent to which Victorian culture anxiously perceived forms of colonial "otherness" built into the framework of English identity requires further study.

The following chapters undertake this project by analyzing instances of domestic autoethnography, novels in which ethnographic language and narrative structures infiltrate description of the English state and subject. In this chapter, I investigate broad patterns of nineteenth-century thought that fostered the convergence of domestic and colonial narratives. My strategy here runs somewhat counter to the current predilection for arguments that perceive literary texts as responses to highly specific historical events. For example, in his admittedly absorbing discussion of representations of the urban metropolis in late-Victorian and modernist texts, Joseph McLaughlin (2000) argues that the trope of the "urban jungle" reflects metropolitan concerns generated by two material trends in the turn-of-the-century English city: immigration and the "intensification of an increasingly global commodity culture" (16).[2] McLaughlin is admirably sensitive to the process through which English writers appropriate ethnographic language and project it onto the domestic social scene, and our studies are in many ways complementary. It is important to consider, however, that English writers and social critics discover patches of "jungle" at home much earlier in the century, in rural as well as urban locales. In light of this fact, it seems likely that the socio-economic shifts McLaughlin identifies provided occasions for the expression of misgivings propelled by longer-standing and wider-spread sources of anxiety.

Broadly circulated religious and secular discourses certainly played a central role. Evangelical Christianity, which reached the peak of its influence in the 1820s and 30s, and evolutionary anthropology, which reached the peak of its influence in the 1860s and 70s, were both profoundly invested in conceptions of the relationship between English and colonial subjects. Both discourses disrupted assumptions about the superiority and difference of Englishness by maintaining strong theoretical commitments to the common origin of mankind. Rather than viewing colonial subjects as essentially alien and inferior, both fields perceived them as members of the same human family, degraded and distant relatives, perhaps, but relatives nonetheless. The subversive potential of this perspective was generally held in check by the tendency of both fields to accentuate differences of degree, if not of kind, between branches of the family. Still, the notion of a universal human family established a theoretical context in which estranged "relatives," those impulses, beliefs, and practices associated with inferior colonial otherness, might arise within the walls of the English family home, asserting consanguinity in the face of disavowal.

Homely materials

Although this chapter is devoted primarily to an analysis of the language of Victorian theology and social science, I would like to begin by briefly considering a novel that illustrates the sort of ironies generated within a text when the dichotomies of empire clash with the universalist assumptions promoted by Evangelicalism and anthropology. Toward the conclusion of Emily Brontë's *Wuthering Heights* (1847), Mr Lockwood makes a foray to the eponymous household. Upon arriving, he inquires "if Mr. Heathcliff were at home?" (299). The apparently simple inquiry taps into an issue fraught with ambiguity. Heathcliff acquires the deed of Wuthering Heights only by swindling Hindley Earnshaw, a member of the "old family" that has inhabited it for centuries (124). Beyond the moral and legal issues that shadow his acquisition of the house lies the more perplexing matter of his racial and ethnic identity and its relationship to an English domicile. Throughout the novel Brontë identifies Heathcliff as an alien intruder, a dark-skinned "stranger" who cannot be "at home" in a structure intimately associated with a native English family and locale (35). Yet a symbolic correspondence between Heathcliff and the structure he acquires in turn reinforces the possibility that the outsider has been "in" long before his actual arrival. Although the events of the plot transpire in a Yorkshire setting apparently far removed from colonial locales, the novel is deeply concerned with the possibility of drawing clear distinctions between English and colonial subjects. As the novel probes the uneasy relationship between Heathcliff and his house, it brings into sharp focus the instability of national identity grounded in race and place.

The tumultuous story is set in motion when Mr Earnshaw finds the child Heathcliff wandering on the streets of Liverpool and determines to bring him home. His generosity is complicated by an inclination to interpret the waif's dark skin as a sign of evil. "[Y]ou must e'en take [the child] as a gift of God," he admonishes his wife, "though it's as dark almost as if it came from the devil" (34). His equivocal appeal to charity falls on deaf ears. Mrs Earnshaw scorns the "gypsy brat" (35). Heathcliff's racial and ethnic identity remains uncertain – accruing a broad range of mostly Orientalist associations – but highly visible. When Lockwood first encounters his landlord he observes that the "dark-skinned gypsy" strikes a "singular contrast to his abode" (3). The novel repeatedly emphasizes a contrast between racial otherness and native English architecture, associating Heathcliff's acts of transgression with his dark skin.[3] When, for example, the Lintons discover him and Cathy peering in their window, they make a clear distinction between the familiar girl and her "gypsy" companion, whom they describe as a "strange acquisition ... quite unfit for a decent house" (48–9). Years later, Nelly calls him "the black villain" when she catches him kissing Isabella Linton in the courtyard of Thrushcross Grange (111). Still later, Isabella relates how, after she has refused to admit him to Wuthering Heights, Heathcliff bursts through a window and thrusts his "black countenance" into the room, baring his "sharp cannibal teeth" (176).

Wuthering Heights thus symbolically narrates a story of racial exclusion and retaliatory transgression, a nightmarish inversion of idealized colonial order. Rather than laboring dutifully in a distant land, acquiescing obediently to the civilizing regime of a just colonial government, the dark-skinned stranger crops up in Yorkshire, where he violently enters decent English homes, devastates the families who inhabit them, and ruthlessly acquires their leases.[4] In this inversion of colonial order, the novel expresses the deep fear of weakness and vulnerability that attended the expansion of imperial power. Narratives such as *Wuthering Heights* imagine what Nigel Leask (1992) terms a *"suspension* and dislocation of cultural sovereignty"* (his italics, 7). If Heathcliff's malevolent ascendance contests metropolitan sovereignty, it leaves intact, or even strengthens, a more fundamental principle of imperial ideology. Regardless of the extent to which Heathcliff disrupts the power relations of empire, he remains an outsider to the micro-culture he comes to dominate, a dark racial other who strikes a "singular contrast" to the abode he owns. He may well proclaim, "I'm not a stranger!" but he can never shed the "gypsy" complexion that attests the contrary (92).

If the representation of Heathcliff as a "dark-skinned gypsy" in contrast to his abode confirms the logic of "us versus them," the novel also ironically subverts that logic. Most obviously, the tempestuous love between Heathcliff and Cathy broadly challenges categories of identity based on race, ethnicity, and geographical or national origin, as well as those of class and gender. "I *am* Heathcliff," the English heroine memorably declares (original italics, 82). The murderous hatred that Heathcliff and Hindley feel for each other indicates another violent passion that paradoxically links the outcast to the old English family. Heathcliff and his foster-siblings display varieties of passionate excess that cut across what ultimately appear to be superficial differences of complexion.

The novel subscribes to two related forms of knowledge, both of which cast doubt on the antitheses of imperial ideology with a universalist approach to human nature. The first of these is supplied by Evangelical Christianity, which had an extensive influence on Emily Brontë and her sisters.[5] According to a central belief of the Evangelical movement, all humans, regardless of age or social position or race, are spiritually corrupt. Just before he dies, Mr Earnshaw asks his daughter, "Why canst thou not always be a good lass, Cathy?" (41). She laughs and replies, "Why cannot you always be a good man, father?" (41). Her rejoinder vexes him because by calling attention to the sinful nature they share she destabilizes the hierarchical relationship between master of the house and wayward daughter. The universality of sinful passion has the same effect on the racial hierarchy that justifies the exclusion of Heathcliff from Wuthering Heights. When Catherine insists that "[w]hatever our souls are made of, his and mine are the same," she tests the romantic potential of Evangelical racial doctrine (albeit transmuted into a demonic register) (80). From the theological vantage of Evangelical Christianity, it makes perfect sense that the dark-skinned other and his English opposites meet in Wuthering Heights, an "infernal house" (65).

The novel also reflects the universalist assumptions of early Victorian anthropology, or, as it was generally known when the novel was published, "ethnology." Before evolutionary theory transformed the field, most nineteeth-century ethnologists approached human biological differences within the framework of biblical history. Rejecting the "polygenist" assertion that different races belonged to distinct species, James Cowles Prichard (1836–47) affirmed that all human beings descended from a single family that gradually dispersed and diversified after the biblical flood. As a result, all humans shared the "same mental endowments, similar natural prejudices and impressions, the same consciousness, sentiments, sympathies, propensities, in short a common psychical nature or a common mind" (qtd. in Stocking 1973 lxxxiii). Prichard and others who held this theory believed that environmental factors of climate and culture shaped human subjectivity much more than race. In the "Editor's Preface" that appeared in the second edition of 1850, Charlotte Brontë seeks to explain the extraordinary characters who appear in her sister's novel by emphasizing the imprint of their environment. Hoping to appease readers offended by her sister's "rude and strange" novel, Brontë offers what amounts to an ethnological sketch of the "inhabitants, the customs, [and] the natural characteristics of the outlying hills and hamlets in the West-Riding of Yorkshire" (367).[6] Although she eventually singles out Heathcliff as the most depraved character and does mention his racial difference in passing, she primarily fosters an understanding of his character that grounds him in the "alien and unfamiliar," but decidedly English, locality, where "harshly manifested passions, ... unbridled aversions, and headlong partialities" represent customary forms of behavior (367). The novel and its characters are "hewn," as she puts it, in "a wild workshop, with simple tools, out of homely materials" (370). As Charlotte perceives, Heathcliff is a wild alien from distant shores who lands in a fittingly wild and alien district of England. The novel anticipates the work of late-century evolutionary anthropologists who discovered multiple connections between the "outlying hills and hamlets" of England and primitive locales on distant colonial ground.

The ideas developed by Victorian Evangelicalism and anthropology help to explain the striking symbolic correspondence between the dark stranger and the "old and dark" English house he inhabits (205). When Lockwood first describes "Mr. Heathcliff's dwelling," he observes that "the architect had foresight to build it strong: the narrow windows are deeply set in the wall, and the corners defended with large jutting stones" (2). Although Lockwood perceives only a contrast between the dwelling and its master, the novel repeatedly suggests a family likeness. Just as the "low-browed lattices" of the house shade its "deeply set" windows, Heathcliff greets the world with "brows lowering" and "eyes deep set and singular" (206, 92). Nelly reinforces the point by adopting architectural terms to describe his face to himself: "Do you mark those two lines between your eyes; and those thick brows, that instead of rising arched, sink in the middle; and that couple of black fiends, so deeply buried, who never open their windows boldly, but lurk glinting under them, like devil's spies?" (56). The dark stranger is apparently very much at home in Wuthering Heights. Declaring on its face the familiarity of the intruder, the house at the center of the narrative reflects the universalist assumptions of Victorian Evangelicalism and ethnology. It is an uncanny symbol of colonial otherness at home that indicates the failure of an effort to exclude the otherness of Heathcliff from the English family, locality, and nation.

This brief analysis of *Wuthering Heights* has, I hope, begun to respond to Balachandra Rajan's call for a critical approach which recognizes that canonical literature is simultaneously "a stronghold of the imperial presence" and "a principal interlocutor of that presence" (20). Rajan has asserted that "the tableau of a monolithic self that is Europe confronting a uniform other that is the Orient is not particularly difficult to discredit," and certainly Brontë's novel offers some fairly explicit challenges to the imperial dichotomies that it also seems to endorse (19). To fully understand the ideological clash that Rajan perceives, however, it is necessary to trace the paths of discursive influence, attending especially to the origin of ideas that call the "imperial presence" into question, which have received much less attention than those that sustain it. The rest of this chapter focuses specifically on Evangelicalism and evolutionary anthropology, both of which fostered an uncomfortable awareness of the extent to which the English state and subject harbored traces of colonial otherness.

Imperial universalism

I do not intend to represent Evangelicalism and evolutionary anthropology as clear-sighted and distinct alternatives to the sector of imperial affairs; to do so would be to turn a blind eye to an extensive field of overlapping historical events and ideological trends. It is important to note from the start that both disciplines were shaped by and frequently reconfirmed notions of English imperial supremacy. Evangelicals generally represented England's imperial power as a divinely sanctioned instrument for the extension of the gospel.[7] Church of England clergyman Anthony Grant (1844) declares at mid-century that "God has now made England the Empress of the Sea" (11). "[T]hough the least among the nations," he continues, "she has surpassed them all in the wide spread of her influence, and the amount of her responsibility; and in all this we cannot but feel that the finger of God ... is upon her" (11–12). Like many Christian apologists of empire, Grant perceives providential design in the acquisition of imperial power. England's "wide spread of influence" should not, however, be interpreted as an end in itself, nor primarily as a means for economic profit. Rightly understood, it signifies a mark of approval and conferral of responsibility. For Grant, God has chosen the English Church as a "commissioned converter of the Heathen" (10). Evangelical clergy often denounced forms of violence and exploitation – slavery being the central example – carried to the colonial world by English imperial power. Grant, for example, censures England for the "unhallowed influence" it has already exercised and worries that the nation may become an even more destructive "curse to the pagan world" (xvi). Such critiques did not condemn imperial expansion as such, but rather insisted that it be reformed by being conducted under the banner of religious conversion. As Anna Johnston (2003) argues, "missionary proselytising offered the British public a model of 'civilised' expansionism and colonial community management, transforming imperial projects into moral allegories" (13).[8] The Evangelical missionary movement was driven by an unquestioned faith in the superiority of Christianity and a concomitant sense of responsibility to convert the heathen.

Evolutionary anthropologists sought to study rather than convert colonial subjects, but they were by no means cultural relativists.[9] They believed that colonial subjects represented early stages in the line of cultural progress that had thus far reached its fullest expression in northern Europe. Their works are full of references to the "lower," "backward," "brutalized," and "savage" races of Asia, Africa, and the Americas. Even as they traced disconcerting connections between the "civilized" and "savage" mind, Victorian anthropologists deferred to popular sentiment by granting wide differences between the two. In *Researches into the Early History of Mankind and the Development of Civilization* (1865), for example, Edward B. Tylor perceives a "vast interval" of evolutionary time stretching between the "mental confusion of the lowest savages of our own day" and the clear and logical standard of civilized cognition (126). In *The Origin of Civilisation and the Primitive Condition of Mankind* (1870), John Lubbock observes that the "whole mental condition of a savage is so different from ours, that it is often very difficult to follow what is passing in his mind" (3). While Victorian anthropologists promoted the intellectual benefits derived from the study of "savage" customs, they made no effort to conceal their disgust for the "abhorrent" nature of the habits they described (Lubbock lxvi).

If the emerging discourse of anthropology confirmed racial and cultural bigotries, it also provided intellectual support for imperial conquest as a catalyst for civilizing progress. In an admittedly "schematized outline history of the relationship of anthropology and colonialism," George Stocking (1991) argues that during the "expansive phase of Western colonialism, evolutionism in anthropology was both the reflection of and the justification for the invasion, appropriation, and subjugation of the 'savage,' 'barbarian,' or 'semi-civilized' regions of the earth by the representatives of European 'civilization' – the actors being conveniently color-coded in racial terms" (4).[10] The extent to which evolutionary anthropology supported imperial enterprises is perhaps not surprising, given the fact that the field emerged in such close proximity to empire. Theorists such as Tylor, Lubbock, and McLennan relied upon data collected by colonial travelers and officials. In some cases, anthropologists sought to repay the debt, asserting the political utility of their findings. Lubbock begins his study by declaring that the "study of the lower races of men" possesses "direct importance ... in an empire like ours" (1).[11] Science, as well as God, seemed to affirm English superiority and point the nation toward the duties and responsibilities of empire.

Both fields explained English superiority as the result of a historical progress from a period of unity to a period in which England had gradually differentiated itself from colonial others. As one might expect, they emphasize different kinds of progress and chart them within differing interpretive frameworks. For Evangelical clergy, progress signified spiritual enlightenment. Their narrative, grounded in the Biblical account of creation and diffusion, begins with a series of general descents into darkness and sin. As the offspring of Adam and Eve multiplied and spread, they increasingly indulged the tendency to thwart God's will. The flood temporarily purged the world of sin, but was followed by another era of universal degeneration. William Carey, a member of the Baptist Missionary Society who established one of the earliest English missions in India, begins his *Enquiry into the Obligations of Christians to Use Means for the Conversion of the Heathens* (1792) with an account of this process. "One would have supposed," he remarks, "that the remembrance of the deluge would have ... perpetually deterred mankind from transgressing the will of their Maker; but so blinded were they, that ... gross wickedness prevailed ... [and] idolatry spread more and more" (4). In the pre-Christian era, significantly, England was not distinguished from the "pagan world" and its idolatry but rather exemplified the tendency of humanity in general toward "gross wickedness." After missionaries had carried word of the new Christian dispensation among the "barbarous Britons," however, England began gradually to purge itself of the "grossest ignorance and barbarism" that "prevailed in the world" (69). The progress of Christianity in England involved significant setbacks, including "episcopal tyranny" and "popish cruelty," but the Protestant Reformation enabled the nation to attain a position of relative spiritual purity (35). At the end of the eighteenth century, Carey declares the time ripe for England to spread the gospel among the "vast proportion of the sons of Adam ... who yet remain in the most deplorable state of heathen darkness" (62). The accelerated progress of enlightenment in England carried with it the responsibility to reacquaint benighted colonial brethren with forgotten spiritual truths.

In their largely secular approach to human history, evolutionary anthropologists subordinated religion to a broader range of cultural practices, but they too traced a gradual process of differentiation through which England attained a position of relative superiority. In the first half of the nineteenth century, the forerunners of evolutionary anthropology subscribed to the Biblical narrative.[12] As archeologists extended backward the span of human existence and the Darwinian hypothesis emerged and gained ascendancy, however, anthropologists began to dispute the Christian account of human history. In *Primitive Marriage: An Inquiry into the Origin of the form of Capture in Marriage Ceremonies* (1865), John F. McLennan quietly debunks the Christian theory of human genesis and degeneration. "[W]e have no evidence," he states, for theories based on a "declension from ancient standards of purity" (12) and "nowhere can tribes or nations be traced back to individuals" (107). By no means did all Victorian anthropologists treat Christian history as groundless mythology, but those who accepted the evolutionary paradigm generally argued that human beings, rather than descending into savagery, had gradually and unequally emerged from it.

Like Evangelical theologians, evolutionary anthropologists disputed the idea propagated by polygenists that colonial subjects were of a different species and conformed to a different set of natural laws. They did so, however, in order to assert a universal tendency toward more advanced social forms and habits of mind rather than to confirm a universal potential for spiritual redemption. Anthropologists believed that humans shared a common origin, albeit one obscured in the mists of time, possessed the same mental faculties and, as a result, advanced on the same developmental path. Lubbock articulates an axiomatic assumption when he observes that the "human mind, in its upward progress, everywhere passes through the same or similar phases" (192). Crucially, though, anthropologists believed that "upward progress" had occurred at different rates in different locales. If colonial subjects had not more thoroughly degenerated into "ignorance and barbarism" from an earlier state of purity, they had certainly lagged behind in the process of development.[13] Natural factors such as the climate combined with cultural factors such as despotic government to ensure that colonial subjects remained in relatively primitive states. Those conditions, on the other hand, had particularly favored the progress of civilization in England. Both Evangelical clergy and evolutionary anthropologists thus posited a universal process of human development – involving, respectively, spiritual enlightenment or cultural sophistication – in which England had for various reasons outpaced colonial cultures.

In an effort to conceptualize the relationship between English and colonial subjects, both disciplines favored the language of family. The Christian myth of creation affirms that all members of the human race are, as Carey puts it, "sons of Adam." Evangelical abolitionists applied this notion in the campaign to end the slave trade. The well-known emblem of the abolitionist movement depicted a shackled African who asks, "Am I not a man and a brother?" The motto appeals to a divinely sanctioned equality denied and offended by the institution of slavery. By the same token, however, the emblem holds in check the radical potential of brotherhood through the sentimentalized debasement of the shackled figure and the assumed agency of those to whom he appeals. Evangelical discourse frequently constructs a family relationship that even more effectively forestalls egalitarian implications. According to William Brown (1816), for example, effective missionaries to the heathen take "all that delight in their welfare and company, that a father does in the midst of his children" (2: 209). Such analogies grant the kinship tie while justifying an unequal distribution of authority.[14]

Evolutionary theorists similarly preserved a sense of English superiority while asserting the existence of a universal family. The recapitulation thesis, which held that the development of the human species corresponds to the development of a single individual, fostered a widespread analogy between colonial subjects and English children. As Peter Rivière (1978) observes, such parallels provided a "useful formula by which the notion of the unity of mankind and the distance between civilized and savage could be jointly maintained" (xlvii). In *Prehistoric Times* (1865), Lubbock observes that "[s]avages have often been likened to children, but so far as intelligence is concerned, a child of four years is far superior; although if we take for comparison a child belonging to a civilized race at a sufficiently early age, the parallel is fair enough" (qtd. in Rivière xlviii). It is no great surprise that imperial ideology easily assimilated the language of family ties into its representation of civilizing benevolence. To cite one of many possible examples, Henry H. M. Herbert, the Earl of Carnarvon (1878), envisions the "vast populations" of India "sitting like children in the shadow of doubt and poverty and sorrow, yet looking up to us for guidance and for help" (764). If the notion of family relations called into doubt the otherness of colonial subjects, the dismaying effect of that doubt could be controlled through an emphasis on paternalistic authority.

If Evangelicalism and evolutionary anthropology thus confirmed a sense of superiority and difference, the theoretical commitment to the existence of a single human family also produced unsettling moments in which family resemblances arose to subvert it. Freud explains the uncanny as an instance in which the mind subconsciously acknowledges ancestral ties to repudiated aspects of the primitive self. Evangelical and evolutionary theorists follow an analogous path backward in time, tracing the genealogy of the modern English subject back to a point of origin preceding racial and cultural differentiation. Like Freud, they also suggest that the strange primitive "other" – the "old Adam" or "original savage" – continues to abide within the modern self. According to Evangelical doctrine, the English Christian state and subject continued to harbor the same degenerate propensities given freer rein in tropical climes. Evolutionary anthropologists believed that the most progressive civilizations retained, in modified and hidden forms, primitive practices and beliefs. The uncanny offers a useful approach to Victorian imperial culture because widely influential discourses such as Evangelicalism and evolutionary anthropology anticipate Freud's conception of a development that does not efface primitive stages and, moreover, cannot prevent their disconcerting reappearance. Heathcliff, the racial other who asserts consanguinity, is intimidating enough. Yet the ghostly traces of otherness that arise within figures who are not visibly out of place in English homes are more threatening still.

Old temptations

In Evangelical theory, none of the "sons of Adam" can fully banish the common human inheritance of sinful propensities. This conviction overshadows any satisfaction taken in the assumed religious superiority of the imperial nation. In *The Law and the Gospel* (1833), for example, Disney Robinson begins his sequence of sermons with a typical expression of religious ethnocentrism. "It is undoubtedly the greatest blessing of our lives," he asserts, "that we were born in a CHRISTIAN land. ... The value of this blessing is greatly increased, by considering how many millions of our fellow-creatures there are, who are wholly ignorant of the true God" (1). Robinson reminds his readers, however, that "for a long season" the

> cultivators of that soil, which now gives back unto us the fruits of our labour, were also, in like manner, wholly ignorant of God; and, in their ignorance, worshipped men, animals, evil spirits, and things which their own hands had made, idols of silver and gold, of wood and stone! Yes, it is true, my Christian friends, that such darkness did *once* overspread this kingdom! (original italics, 1–2)

The sermon here strikes a balance between the disclosure of a scandalous family history and the distinction effected by the advent of Christianity in England. Yet Robinson increasingly draws forth the disturbing implications of England's dark past. "Remember then," he counsels his audience, "that but for [the blessing of Christianity], we, at this day, might have been Heathen; that is we might, yea more, *we should have been*, unacquainted with the gospel, wild, savage, uncivilized, cruel, hateful, and hating one another" (original italics, 2). The emphasis falls increasingly on the idea that English Christians and colonial heathen derive from the same spiritual substance.[15] Robinson thus stakes the entire distinction between the two on the national religion, and this fact could not afford complacent comfort. Affirming a universal propensity to sin that infects "Christian friends" as well as ignorant heathen, Evangelical ministers heightened awareness of the precariousness of the spiritual border between English Christianity and colonial heathenism. As Robinson gloomily observes, "Our disposition, by nature, being sinful, and our hearts corrupt, we are inclined to those things which are sinful and wicked, to go astray from God, and to follow after any thing rather than His favour" (3). The internal corruption of English subjects breaks down the clear opposition of Christian light and heathen darkness. From the Evangelical perspective, Christian faith is besieged from within the purported national stronghold of the faith by its own adherents.

Given that those "born in a CHRISTIAN land" can never shed their sinful disposition, Evangelical discourse represents Christian subjectivity as a microcosm of a world in which light and dark forces continually vie for supremacy. Anthony Grant (1844) foresees

> going on to the end of the world the same conflict of the kingdom of Christ with the powers of evil; the same alternations of advancing and receding light; the same victory and defeat, throughout the period of the mortal struggle that is carrying on, whether on the broad surface of the world by the Church militant, or by the individual Christian on the narrow stage of his own heart. (20)

The emphasis Grant places on the unpredictable "alternations" of this conflict adds tension to a spiritual drama whose final act is already set forth. Until the very "end of the world" no victory over darkness can be complete or secure. In an eighteenth-century text that remained popular through the first half of the nineteenth century, Thomas Wilson (1743) holds that "All Men have the Seeds of Evil within themselves" (12) and that the "best of Christians are Men of like Passions with others" (41). Projects intended to cultivate the soil of distant heathen ground represented an extension of and analogy for the ongoing effort to detect and uproot "Seeds of Evil" sprouting on ground already sown by Christian faith and knowledge.

Wilson describes those who populate the "Heathen World" as "Strangers to [God]" (216), but also stresses that human nature throughout the world is "strangely disordered" (53). His book, which purports to serve as a manual for missionaries to the heathen world, consists in large part of a series of "short and plain dialogues" between an earnest English missionary and an obliging Native American convert. Owing to the universality of evil, however, the text that sets forth a procedure for converting the heathen other proves just as beneficial at home. The twofold utility of the text is indicated in its lengthy title: *The Knowledge and Practice of Christianity made easy To the Meanest Capacities, or, An essay Towards an Instruction for the Indians: Which will be of Use To such Christians as have not well considered the Meaning of the Religion they profess; Or who* profess *to* know GOD, *but in* Works *do* deny *Him*. Wilson's uncanny catechism simultaneously addresses the manifest strangers of the heathen world and English subjects whose strange disorders hide beneath the guise of familiar Christianity. The missionary explains to his Native American convert that a Christian "is not one who has no Failings; but he is one, who … watches and strives against the Corruption of his Nature continually" (74). This speech captures the theoretical source of the racial and cultural ambivalence of Evangelical missionary discourse, which fostered a hyper-awareness of darkness within the imperial nation even as it imagined the effort to illuminate darkness in far-flung colonial locales.

Throughout the nineteenth century, Protestant theologians warned against susceptibility to idolatry, the "perilous tendency," as Archdeacon F. W. Farrar (1884) describes it, "which needs to be incessantly resisted" (770). The universality of idolatrous inclinations, lying as they do "deep in the human spirit," underscores the point that Victorian Evangelicals believed that their nation required the same sort of oversight as India or Africa (771). "We Christians have less excuse than all others for idolatry," Farrar observes, "yet we neither have been nor are exempt from the old temptation" (771). Earlier in the century, the author of "On the Worship of Idols" seeks to reverse the error of considering idolatry as "an object at the remotest possible distance from *us*; and the common inference … that there is nothing in *our* constitutions as Englishmen, no principle of *our* nature, or tendency of *our* passions, which might lead us to symbolize with the heathen in their worship of images" (original italics, 23). Protestant theologians frequently accused English Catholics of idolatry and were particularly distraught by "Romanist" leanings within their own church. The Reverend William Heber Wright (1890) warns against excessive attention to church decoration by reminding his flock of the "*peril* of idolatry" (original italics, 6). Although he associates idolatry primarily with Catholic ritual and symbol, he also appreciates the extent to which susceptibility to the "old temptation" links the presumably faithful in England to their benighted counterparts in colonial locales. His homily, he observes, "is no missionary sermon intended for the heathen" (6). The fact that it might be mistaken as such underlines the point that Christian English subjects, like colonial "heathen," require incessant reminders of the grave "danger of idolatry" (6).[16] Sharing the same dark impulses as those given free rein by dark-skinned colonial others, they could only be considered to be somewhat more conscious of the need to monitor and subdue the unregenerate forces of spiritual corruption.

The self-conscious process of watching and striving against internal corruption promoted a skeptical attitude toward the presumably Christian nation and subject. Evangelical theologians believed, as Grant asserts, that the gospel holds but a "doubtful sway" over "Christian countries" (21). Theologians often suggest that antithetical terminology has exaggerated or manufactured differences between Christian and heathen subjects. William Wilberforce (1797), a principal architect of the mission overseas, rails against English subjects for whom the title of Christian "implies no more than a sort of formal, general assent to Christianity in the gross, and a degree of morality in practice, but little if at all superior to that for which we look in a good Deist, Mussulman, or Hindoo" (77). Those "who bear the Christian name," Carey asserts, often exhibit "a very great degree of ignorance and immorality" (65). According to G. D. Hill (1845), "too many among us" are "[n]ominally Christians," but "really heathens and idolaters. They are blinded by heathen delusions. They are affected by heathen corruption. They are liable to heathen wretchedness and despair" (83–4). Evangelical clergy who organized and sponsored the effort to illuminate heathen darkness abroad were at the same time highly suspicious of rhetoric that confidently opposed Christian and heathen subjects.

For Evangelical social reformers, urban poverty particularly challenged the legitimacy of such distinctions. In *London and Calcutta, Compared in Their Heathenism, Their Privileges, and Their Prospects* (1868), Joseph Mullens discovers many distressing similarities. Sketching the spiritual geography of the English capital, he acknowledges that the "earnest, active spiritual life in London" is surrounded by a "broad border-land of 'respectable people,' … indifferent to vital religion, and ignorant of it," on the other side of which exists a territory characterized by "real heathenism, physically and socially degrading in the extreme; a heathenism widespread, involving myriads in its blackness" (17). Although Mullens eventually decides the "difference in favor of London," the comparison between London and Calcutta opens to view many "dark corners in the pleasant picture of Christian civilisation which England presents to the world" (94, 29). The idea that London and other English metropolitan centers have fallen into terms of comparison with such barbaric sites as Calcutta sustains a disquieting presence in fiction and social criticism throughout the latter half of the nineteenth century. In some cases, comparisons descend into full-blown paradoxes that proclaim the extent to which the "pleasant picture of Christian civilisation" is actually a grotesque landscape besmirched with "real heathenism." Although Dickens had slight sympathy for Evangelical piety, he shared the notion that urban industrial poverty produced a religious paradox. In *Bleak House* (1852–53), the street sweeper Jo, who remains "in soul a heathen" until the last moments of his life, functions as a shameful synechdoche for the "myriads" who dwell in metaphysical blackness, the "home-made" English savages of the slums (696). Later in the century, the Salvation Army galvanized support for its urban missions by accentuating the paradoxical distortion of the presumably Christian nation. In *Heathen England* (1891), George Scott Railton offers, as his subtitle declares, a *Description of the Utterly Godless Condition of the Vast Majority of the English Nation*. This is hyperbole, to be sure, but the sensational rhetoric expressed a genuine and widespread concern.

Firmly convinced that "All Men have the Seeds of Evil within themselves," Evangelical clergy maintained a wary lookout for social conditions favoring germination. As the examples above suggest, their gaze often focused attention on the urban slum; the Evangelical social reform discourse thus served the interest of middle-class hegemony. The novels considered in the following chapters demonstrate, however, that suspicion carried over to the middle class itself, in which more subtly disguised varieties of heathenism were practiced by those who inhabited the "broad border-land" of respectability. Within the framework of Evangelical discourse, England could hope to achieve only a relative degree of difference from heathen darkness "on the broad surface of the world," and could do so only by acknowledging and seeking to control multiple inposts of heathen darkness.

Evangelical anxiety about heathenism at home seeped into secular discourses such as the domestic novel and social criticism. The path of influence becomes particularly clear in the careers of social critics reared in Evangelical households. In *Praeterita* (1899), John Ruskin describes an early education grounded in the daily study and recitation of Bible verses. He numbers Exodus 20, which includes prohibitions against idolatry, as one of the chapters of the Bible that constitutes "the most precious, and, on the whole, the one *essential* part of all [his] education" (33, original italics).[17] Ruskin makes this remark decades after he had abandoned the religious beliefs of his childhood, acknowledging the persistent influence of Evangelical principles on his secular theories. His frequent use of the trope of idolatry confirms an argument recently made by Kathleen Vejvoda (2003), who argues that idolatry represented a "serious and compelling moral problem for Victorian culture" (241).

In the mind of Victorian Protestants, she rightly observes, idolatry "meant more than simply the worship of graven images: it became the privileged term for denoting any devotion to a person, thing, or idea that hinders or supplants one's relation to God" (241). In "Traffic" (1864), for example, Ruskin rails against the national idolatry of wealth or "Mammonism" in language that echoes the formulae of Evangelical suspicion. Conceding that "we have, indeed, a nominal religion, to which we pay tithes of property and sevenths of time," he asserts that "we have also a practical and earnest religion, to which we devote nine-tenths of our property, and six-sevenths of our time" (242). Only in name Christian, the industrial nation earnestly prostrates itself before the "Goddess of Getting-on" or "Britannia of the Market" (242). The essay culminates in iconoclastic fury as Ruskin denounces "this idol of yours; this golden image, high by measureless cubits, set up where your green fields of England are furnace burnt into the likeness of the plain of Dura" (249). The ethical principles that inform Ruskin's criticism of industrial progress thus reveal the imprint of his Evangelical upbringing.

Leslie Stephen, grandson of a prominent member of the Clapham Sect, also inherited the Evangelical propensity to ferret out modern English forms of the "old temptation."[18] In *The Cornhill Magazine* and other liberal journals, he practiced a variety of secular iconoclasm that trained the introspective gaze of Evangelical scrutiny on the national self-image. In "Idolatry" (1869), he begins by recalling an episode of *Robinson Crusoe* in which Crusoe encounters an outlandish sect that worships an "idol of wood" named Chim-Chi-Thaunga;[19] excited by "that intense disgust which we generally feel for other people's objects of worship," he attempts to destroy it (33). The reference to distant idol-breaking adventures prepares for an ironic return of iconoclasm in the domestic social field. Stephen confesses, "whenever I see a Chim-Chi-Thaungu in these islands – and there are a good many of them in different places – I feel a strong propensity to go and do likewise" (689). He offers the preeminence of Shakespeare as an initial example, but then proceeds to argue that the "modern things and poems which we place in our most sacred shrines … produce the more crying evils. The sects who pay them reverence are scattered through all classes of men, and all schools of thought" (691). Among these modern things, Stephen singles out the image of the British working man, before whom demagogic politicians bow the knee, and that "magnificent object of worship, the British Constitution," which, despite being lauded as the "pride and envy of the world," exists as a "rather vague abstraction" in those who uncritically sing its praises (692). Adapting the rhetoric of Evangelical reform to his critique of ethnocentric complacency, Stephen exposes an intense irony within the nation's self-approving regard. The native icons believed to confer superiority on England erode the legitimacy of the distinction between outlandish and familiar locations where "Chim-Chi-Thaungus" are idolized.

Persistent habits

Victorian evolutionary anthropologists viewed "modern civilisation" from a secular perspective, discussing religion as only one of several important measures of cultural progress. Yet a parallel conviction in the persistence of primitive elements of the self resulted in a similarly skeptical attitude toward clear-cut differences between English and colonial subjects. From an evolutionary perspective, human cultures generally progress, but the earlier stages through which they pass do not simply disappear. As McLennan observes, "customs tend to perpetuate themselves and die hard" (66). Even practices and ideas associated with abhorred savagery retain a hold on the mind, just as from an Evangelical perspective the "old Adam" retains a hold on the soul. As a result, modern civilization discloses many relics of earlier phases of development. Tylor and other anthropologists who adhered to this doctrine of "survivals," as he called the persistent relics of primitive life, conducted a comparative analysis of cultures in Africa, the Americas, Asia, and other supposedly primitive locales, in part to discover the ancestral origin of ideas and habits still visible, albeit in modified form, in modern England. "The explanation of the state of things in which we live," Tylor explains, "has often to be sought in the condition of rude and early tribes; and without a knowledge of this to guide us, we may miss the meaning even of familiar thoughts and practices" (1). The evolutionary scheme affirms the relative superiority of those who inhabit modern civilization; colonial others dwell in a time that England has passed by. Victorian readers, however, would have been more struck, and perhaps a good deal alarmed, by the extent to which Tylor's approach to culture traces still visible links between modern English civilization and primitive savagery. In even the most "familiar thoughts and practices" might lie undetected connections to abhorred strangers.

The books and essays published by evolutionary anthropologists in the 1860s and 70s detected such connections in many different spheres of presumably civilized life. In the *Early History of Mankind*, Tylor himself focuses primarily on habits of mind as illustrated through language, thought processes, and mythology. Discussing the evolution of communication, he charts a developmental path from gesture language, the most primitive and "natural" mode of expression, to picture writing, and, finally, to written language, the most sophisticated mode. The advent of each more refined mode of expression supplants the earlier stage, but not entirely. Tylor observes that physical gestures, the most primitive form of expression, have largely fallen out of English middle-class culture, perhaps because "we read and write so much" (37). Even the literary English, however, have not fully renounced physical gestures as a mode of communication. Tylor points out that blowing a kiss, snapping the fingers, shaking hands, and other gestures have survived the process of sophistication. "Cowering or crouching is so natural an expression of fear or inability to resist," he observes, "that it belongs to the brutes as well as to man. Among ourselves this natural sign of submission is generally used in the modified forms of bowing and kneeling" (39). By surveying "analogous gestures found in different countries," Tylor discovers the "intermediate stages between an actual prostration and a slight bow" (39). The evolutionary approach to culture thus fills in the "bottomless chasm" supposedly yawning between upright English subjects and their groveling primitive counterparts.

In the face of the most disquieting customs and beliefs, staunch advocates of cultural evolution sometimes betray the principles of their argument. Distaste for certain practices to which he alludes leads Lubbock into theoretical contradictions. He states, for example, that "religion, as understood by the lower savage races, differs essentially from ours; nay, it is not only different, but even opposite" (116). It is of course the notion of essential difference that cultural evolution clearly challenges. As Tylor argues, observable differences "in the civilization and mental state of the various races of mankind are rather differences of development than of origin, rather of degree than of kind" (232). Confronted by the "melancholy spectacle of gross superstitions and ferocious forms of worship," Lubbock briefly abandons this axiom (114). He later concedes, however, that "old beliefs" tend to survive the onset of "a higher religion," and "[w]e must therefore expect to find in each race traces – nay, more than traces, of lower religions" (118). He notes, for example, that the "old belief" in sacred wells still exists in Scotland and Ireland, which is not surprising given that "no race of men has yet entirely freed itself" from the fetishism of natural objects (169). Lubbock compares "our spirit-rappers and table-turners" to conjurers who exploit superstitious credulity in China and India (148–9). "We cannot wonder that savages believe in witchcraft," he observes, "since even the most civilised races have not long, nor entirely, ceased to do so" (148).

Victorian anthropologists tended to locate survivals among those sectors of the civilized world that, to their minds, functioned as preserves of primitive thoughts and habits. The recapitulation thesis led many to perceive childhood as one such preserve. Tylor argues, for example, that the "idol answers to the savage in one province of thought the same purpose that its analogue the doll does to the child" (94). In *The Mill on the Floss* (1860), George Eliot illustrates a similar point in the representation of Maggie Tulliver, who transforms her doll into a "Fetish which she punished for all her misfortunes" (78).[20]

Increasingly, anthropologically minded writers discovered surviving relics of earlier stages of development in the rural hinterlands of England and Scotland, sites analogous to the "outlying hills and hamlets" to which Charlotte Brontë refers in her preface to *Wuthering Heights*. In *Primitive Culture* (1871), Tylor asks readers to consider "the modern European peasant using his hatchet and his hoe, see his food boiling or roasting over the log-fire, observe the exact place which beer holds in his calculation of happiness, hear his tale of the ghost in the nearest haunted house" (1: 6). By focusing on such practices and habits of mind that "have altered little in the long course of centuries," he produces a picture in which there is "scarce a hand's breadth difference between an English ploughman and a negro of Central Africa" (1: 6). In a series of lectures entitled *The Past in the Present* (1881), Arthur Mitchell tests the assumptions of cultural evolution against materials discovered in rambles through the highlands of Scotland. "[M]y witnesses," he explains, "shall be chosen from objects and practices in the midst of which we live, even though their homeliness may at first seem a defect, and though near neighborhood and familiarity may, to some extent, strip them of the obscuring enchantment which remoteness and strangeness often lend" (30). This Wordsworthian formula recalls attention from exotic distance to the strangeness disguised by familiarity at home. In the rude technologies and superstitions that cling to rural districts, evolutionary anthropologists discover a rich vein of homely primitivism.

More than any other Victorian novelist, Thomas Hardy took this anthropological perspective to heart. His rural English landscapes are dominated by barrows and tumuli that arch into the sky, symbols of a primitive past that is at once concealed and obtrusive. In *The Return of the Native* (1878), Hardy decodes the text of the rural landscape in a passage fully informed by the doctrine of survivals. When the heath folk celebrate the arrival of spring with "May-revel" fertility rites, the narrator comments that the

> instincts of merry England lingered on here with exceptional vitality, and the symbolic customs which tradition has attached to each season of the year were yet a reality on Egdon. Indeed, the impulses of all such outlandish hamlets are pagan still: in these spots homage to nature, self-adoration, frantic gaieties, fragments of Teutonic rites to divinities whose names are forgotten, seem in some way or other to have survived mediaeval doctrine. (452)

Fascinated by the cultural contradictions implicit in the concept of anthropological survivals, Hardy takes every opportunity to reveal pagan impulses that still hold sway in the "outlandish hamlets" of England. In his thorough account of the influence of evolutionary anthropology on Hardy's work, Andrew Radford (2003) argues that novels such as *The Return of the Native* offer "striking contrast[s] to the complacent arguments of scholars who treated European culture as the capstone of human achievement, and who promoted the idea of progress as logically natural, universal and inevitable" (5).

Given his penchant for ironies subverting the "complacent arguments" of his day, it is curious that Hardy does not mount a full-scale direct attack on racial and geographical distinctions of imperial ideology. In *The Return of the Native* the narrator remarks upon the "sable features" (187) of the heath and observes that a character appears on the "dark ridge of heathland, like a fly on a negro" (183). The metaphor of the unreclaimed rural landscape as a black body links the surviving primitivism of England to African otherness. Such references are not frequent in his novels, however. For Hardy, the figure of outlandish England is intriguing primarily as an ironic commentary on temporal progress. The racial and geographical dimensions of the figure remain largely implicit in his work.[21]

Like Evangelical social reformers, Victorian anthropologists also frequently refer to the urban slum as another pocket of civilized society in which outlandish instincts and impulses may be detected. Asserting that "[s]avages are unrestrained by any sense of delicacy from a copartnery in sexual enjoyments," McLennan further observes that "in the civilised state, the sin of great cities shows that there are no natural restraints sufficient to hold men back from grosser copartneries" (69). The presence of savagery in English cities indicated to some observers a more disturbing principle at work than the "lingering" practices and habits of mind on view in rural locales; the "grosser copartneries" practiced by the sinful poor in the nation's "great cities" indicated a reversion to rather than a survival of outlandish habits.

Still, most adult middle-class readers would no doubt have been comforted by the fact that they themselves did not dwell within the special preserves of English primitivism. In general, anthropological treatises of the 1860s and 70s betray a tactful reluctance to apply their principles too directly to middle-class England. At the beginning of his chapter on marriage, Lubbock states that nothing "gives a more instructive insight into the true condition of savages than their ideas on the subject of marriage; nor can the great advantages of civilisation be more conclusively proved than by the improvement which it has effected in the relation between the two sexes" (50). On the other hand, McLennan provides the basis, at least, for a reassessment of this assertion. In *Primitive Marriage*, he argues that the institution of marriage began in acts of "capture." Compelled by the incest taboo to seek wives from other tribes, primitive men used brute force to overpower their chosen "brides" and carry them bodily away from their own tribes. Although forceful capture evolved gradually into forms of consensual agreement, modern marriage ceremonies symbolically recall the practice of "rude times" (24). Having surveyed many "barbaric" cultures in which symbolic forms of physical force accompany the marriage rite, McLennan observes that it is impossible "not to recall what Plutarch says of the ceremonies of Roman marriage, apropos of the Rape of the Sabines: 'It is a custom still observed for the bride not to go over the threshold of her husband's house herself, but to be carried over ... because the Sabine virgins did not go in voluntarily, but were carried in by violence' " (122). Although McLennan himself does not pursue the point, some readers might have reflected that Plutarch's words apply to contemporary English marriage ceremonies as well.

Of course, even those willing to acknowledge an ongoing link to "barbaric" practices might also console themselves with the notion that such customs hold the status of obsolete symbols, historical curiosities that reveal nothing significant about modern institutions or habits of thought. Lubbock, for example, justifies the "study of the lower races of men" by referring to the information it supplies about England's own past and present. He begins *The Origin of Civilization* by observing that

the condition and habits of existing savages resemble in many ways, though not in all, those of our own ancestors in a period now long gone by; in the second [place], they illustrate much of what is passing among ourselves, many customs which have evidently no relation to present circumstances, and even some ideas which are rooted in our minds, as fossils are imbedded in the soil. (1)

Lubbock at once acknowledges the persistence of "old" beliefs and practices and curtails the subversive potential of their presence in English culture. To his mind, surviving customs stand in ironic contrast to "present circumstances." Certain ideas have stayed "rooted in our minds," but they have been covered over by accretions of progress. Like "fossils imbedded in the soil," they were discarded long ago. They may be excavated and wondered at as artifacts of a brutal past without necessarily questioning the superiority and difference of those who embody civilization in its highest form.

Yet some who peered within the English mind in its most advanced forms discovered that "fossils" of savage belief systems might in certain circumstances be taken up again. Although the mind moved generally "upward" over the course of time, evolutionary theory did not deny the possibility of reversion or regression. Mitchell asserts, for example, that a superstitious practice "founded on a belief in the efficacy of doing something to propitiate a superhuman source of misfortune and evil is not necessarily pre-Christian and pagan. It might spring up, in a community professing Christianity, as the outcome simply of man's mental constitution" (163). From this perspective, ideas presumably at odds with civilization are less fossils "imbedded in the soil" than seeds lying dormant in a ground that, given appropriate conditions, might "spring up" into luxuriant growth. Although Mitchell approaches religion from a secular perspective, his figure recalls the Evangelical notion that "seeds of evil" lie dormant within all human souls. George Meredith, whose work, like Hardy's, is deeply influenced by anthropological theories, perceives the emergence of the primitive, in particular rapacious male desire, as a more violent process. He figures modern, civilized man as a "thinly-sealed volcano of our imperishable ancient father."[22] Such figures express an anxiety that progress, whether spiritual or cultural, was precarious and incomplete.

The anthropological notion that primitive ideas remain dormant in the mind also looks forward to the Freudian conception of the conservative economy of psychological development. Although Freud primarily uses the uncanny to explain the re-emergence of primitive thoughts on the narrow stage of the individual subject, he also applies the concept to the survival of culturally primitive habits of mind. Commenting on the animistic belief in the "omnipotence of thoughts," for example, he observes that "We – or our primitive forefathers – once believed that these possibilities were realities, and were convinced that they actually happened. Nowadays we no longer believe in them, we have *surmounted* these modes of thought; but we do not feel quite sure of our new beliefs, and the old ones still exist within us ready to seize upon any confirmation" (17: 247). From this perspective, the cultural progress of the human mind is never entirely secure. Like Mitchell, Freud emphasizes the suddenness with which the presumably civilized mind might revert to an imperfectly "surmounted" stage, "seiz[ing] upon any confirmation" of primitive beliefs.

Some Victorians who analyzed the structure of English society from the perspective afforded by evolutionary anthropology discovered that the supposed "fossils" of impulses and belief systems had never been discarded. In an article on the history and origin of gypsies (1866), a writer in *Blackwood's* undermines racial and cultural differences in a way that exemplifies the influence of anthropological theories. Like other Victorians who write on the subject, the author argues that gypsies did not originate in Egypt (as the etymology of their English name suggests), but rather in India. For much of the article, the author predictably emphasizes their racial and ethnic otherness, remarking upon their peculiar language and customs, odd dress and "swart complexion" ("Gypsies" 567). They are "strange visitants" (571), "waifs and strays who contrast so remarkably with our settled English habits and advancing civilization" (565). (Note the similarity to descriptions of Heathcliff, the "strange acquisition" who is called a gypsy by several characters.) The author frequently describes the gypsies and their customs as "curious"; as the article progresses, however, the term acquires a paradoxical complexity, bespeaking an interest in repressed aspects of the English self as well as in exotic otherness (575). "Everybody" in England has seen gypsies, he observes, and "most of us, in our younger days, have stopped and looked at the wayside tent and the circle round the fire with a kind of longing curiosity" (565). This "longing" to join the "circle round the fire" reflects a mysterious "magnetic attraction" for long-forgotten biological relatives and their customs (575). It is in truth a desire to *re*-join a family circle. Claiming that gypsies have in England intermarried much more extensively than commonly recognized, and moreover that "there is some remarkable virtue in the Romany blood ... which entirely overpowers, or assimilates ... all foreign admixtures," this writer entertains the "very frightful consideration [that] ... it is really very difficult to say which of us are not Gipsies" (575). The author then speculates that a commonplace English habit reveals another manifestation of the longing to re-join the gypsy circle. "It must have puzzled a good many philosophical inquirers besides ourselves," he declares,

> to account for the curious propensity of all classes of English people to rush out into the fields and woods at certain seasons to eat their meals. ... [I]t is the Egyptian blood – the habits of "the tribe" – strong enough to break through even the most stringent formalities of English life and going back ... to "the old thing." What but some overmastering impulse could urge the careful English mother forth with her daughters on these migrations, careless of sunburnt complexions or damp grass, or make an orthodox Briton act in the matter of dinner on no higher principles than a heathen Hottentot?

The extent to which this article advances a biological explanation for the endurance of "old" habits distinguishes it from the work of evolutionary anthropologists such as Tylor, who would be inclined to explain such phenomena as the result of persistent customs and habits of mind rather than the "admixture" of bloodlines. Still, the author has clearly absorbed from anthropology an idea that intrigues and frightens him, that "orthodox" English culture imperfectly restrains certain deep and lasting affinities to primitive otherness.

A still more skeptical social critic, John Stuart Mill adopts the principles of evolutionary anthropology to call into question the difference between English sexual relations and primitive otherness. In *The Subjection of Women* (1869), Mill asserts that the "relation between the two sexes" in modern England still very much carries the "taint of its brutal origin" (476).[23] From his perspective, one need not trace the origin of quaint customs such as carrying the bride over the threshold for evidence of links to an era of male force and brutality. By excluding women from rights and responsibilities and thus ensuring their dependence, the entire legal structure of English society proves the "great vitality and durability of institutions which place right on the side of might" (477). In this light, civilization does not simply contain isolated pockets of ideas and practices demonstrably antithetical to its values. Rather, civilization is itself fully paradoxical, still regulated by principles inherited from savage life. The laws and opinions that govern relations between the sexes in modern England, upheld by Lubbock as the clearest proof of the "great advantages of civilisation," represent to Mill's mind the most primitive of social rules cloaked in the obscuring language of civility. The "inequality of rights between man and woman," Mill declares, "has no other source than the law of the strongest" (476). The historical continuity of male force in

England calls into doubt the "great advantages of civilization" extolled by Lubbock.

It is crucial, of course, to appreciate the effect of "distancing devices," as Johannes Fabian refers to anthropological concepts that function to locate other cultures in the primitive past. But it is equally important to perceive the contrasting effects of devices that alarmingly narrowed the distance between English and colonial subjects. Like Evangelical Christianity, evolutionary anthropology facilitated a theoretical reappraisal of the "great gulf" or "bottomless chasm" that supposedly separated England from colonial otherness. Prominent theorists in both fields were much more likely to discover eruptions of savagery, barbarism, or heathenism at home within relatively contained pockets, especially rural or urban poverty. Yet the principles they upheld made it virtually impossible to perceive any sector of society as untainted by ideas and practices associated with colonial otherness. By affirming the universality of the human mind and soul, and, crucially, the instability of spiritual and social progress, the two fields together encouraged skeptical minds to perceive abiding affinities.

If Victorian culture took comfort from imperial ideology that proclaimed the difference and superiority of England, it could not banish the knowledge that English subjects had once been indistinguishable from those they now abhorred and, more disturbing still, that traces of the connection persisted. In *Primitive Culture*, Tylor observes that "[p]rogress, degradation, survival, revival, modification, are all modes of the connexion that binds together the complex network of civilization" (1: 16). Evangelicals held a parallel consciousness of the multiple ways in which Christianity remained imperfectly opposed to heathenism and paganism. In his treatise on idolatrous church ornamentation, Wright bemoans the fact that "[w]e are, alas! travelling *backwards not forwards*" (original italics, 14). Because of their commitment to a view of the human subject as a structure that clings to habits and modes of thought, neither discipline could afford much hope that England (or any other supposedly modern civilization) could heal its self-divisions by expunging traces of colonial otherness within. Old habits and temptations never release their grip on the mind or soul. They survive in a host of curious customs and instincts and, given the chance, will spring up anew, reviving long after their apparent demise. Taking advantage of new technologies and cultural preoccupations, they modify themselves and find new modes of expression. Both discourses promote a view of modern English civilization as a "complex network" that involves paradoxical forms of thought and behavior.

Despite extensive ideological affiliations with empire and ethnocentrism, then, Evangelical Christianity and evolutionary anthropology disseminated an anxious uncertainty about presumed differences between English and colonial subjects. By acknowledging affinities that bridge divisions of race, place, and culture, the two discourses lay the groundwork for the satiric method of domestic autoethnography. The many novelists and social critics of the period who project ethnographic language and narrative structures onto the domestic scene play upon and play up their culture's largely repressed fear that colonial "otherness" dwells within the English state and culture.

3
The Juggernaut Roles in England: The Idol of Patriarchal Authority in *Jane Eyre* and *The Egoist*

> It is considered a very meritorious act for Hindoos to commit suicide, either by drowning in some sacred stream, or by allowing the wheels of the car of Juggernaut to pass over them. But, where British influence prevails, these things are now prohibited.
>
> Thomas Hodson (1851: 59)

The word *Juggernaut*, which denotes any object, institution, or idea bearing destructive and inexorable force, is now a relatively familiar English term. In the nineteenth century, however, English readers and writers were acutely aware of its foreign origin. The word is derived from the Hindi *Jagannáth*, the name of an idol of Krishna, the most famous of which resided at a temple in Puri, India. Translated literally, the name means "lord of the world." At the turn of the nineteenth century, this idol became a widely recognized emblem of Oriental idolatry, a focal point of imperial concern, disgust, and amusement. It was remarked upon and described in Parliamentary debates, East India Company despatches, missionary tracts, and travel narratives. By turns sublime and picturesque, dangerous and ludicrous, Juggernaut functions throughout these texts as a vivid image of heathen idolatry.[1] By the 1840s, however, it also paradoxically served as a figure for varieties of destructive violence and idolatrous worship detected by novelists and social critics at home. As the word wanders from descriptions of outlandish India into descriptions of the domestic social field, it provides intriguing case studies of domestic autoethnography, compelling evidence of the Victorian anxiety that England had failed to distinguish itself from colonial otherness.

Early in the nineteenth century, the temple of Juggernaut became a frequent stop on Anglo-Indian tours of India. Colonial officials, missionaries, and travelers were particularly fascinated by the annual spectacle of *Rath Játrá*, the car festival, during which Juggernaut rode forth on an enormous vehicle through a vast crowd of votaries. Attempting to convey the "lofty and massive dimensions and clumsy architecture" of Juggernaut's car, Godfrey Charles Mundy (1832) calculates that it "is nearly forty-five feet in height, has a platform of thirty-five feet square, and moves upon sixteen wheels of solid timber" (254). Descriptions of the procession typically reflect intermingled awe and contempt. A. Stirling (1825) finds it "impressive" and "astounding," but also insists that it "excit[es] the strongest sensations of pain and disgust in the mind of every Christian spectator" (323). Emma Roberts (1837) describes the idol itself as "gigantic" and "hideously ugly" (260). English observers express particular disdain for idolatrous zealotry as they sketch a scene peopled with "20,000 frantic devotees" (Parks 382) pulling the car by ropes through a "fanatical multitude" (Mundy 254) of idolaters who gaze upon the idol "in stupid admiration" (Stirling 321). A recurring word tells much about English attitudes. In his *Lectures on India* (1851), Caleb Wright refers to Juggernaut as a "monstrous form" (106). For Fanny Parks (1850), it is a "monstrous idol" (382), for Mundy, a "monster deit[y]" (254). Roberts refers to Juggernaut's car as a "monstrous vehicle" (261). The word "monstrous" indicates an effort to convey the dimensions of the idol. It also expresses aesthetic distaste for the "hideous" image and religious disapproval of worship of an object constructed by humans. In a broad way, the word articulates the extent to which English observers perceived the grand idolatrous spectacle as strange, otherworldly, and unnatural.

Strangest of all to English observers were reputed incidents of idolatrous suicide. The word *Juggernaut* carries destructive associations owing to accounts of the festival such as the one furnished by Eliza Fay (1817), who, despite the fact that she was unable to view the procession herself, claims to be "credibly assured" that the idol "is taken out in an enormous car, with a great number of wheels beneath which his votaries prostrate themselves with the most undaunted resolution; firmly persuaded that by thus sacrificing their lives, they shall pass immediately after death into a state of everlasting felicity" (171). In *The Curse of Kehama* (1810), Robert Southey helped to popularize this image of fanatical self-sacrifice to the monstrous idol. The narrator sketches the scene at the temple of Juggernaut, where

> A thousand pilgrims strain
> Arm, shoulder, breast and thigh, with might and main,
> To drag that sacred wain,
> And scarce can draw along the enormous load.
> Prone fall the frantic votaries in its road,
> And, calling on the God,
> Their self-devoted bodies there they lay
> To pave his chariot-way.
> On Jaga-Naut they call,
> The ponderous Car rolls on, and crushes all.
> Through blood and bones it ploughs its dreadful path.
> Groans rise unheard; the dying cry,
> And death and agony
> Are trodden under foot by yon mad throng,
> Who follow close, and thrust the deadly wheels along. (147)

Seeking to lend credibility to this "dreadful" picture of "mad" idolatry in distant India, Southey supplements the poem with presumably authoritative accounts supplied by Western missionaries and scholars. According to Anna Johnston, "India proved to be a culture of such fascinating, although often abhorrent, difference from British experience that what could be defined as early 'ethnographic' narratives ... were readily produced by missionary observers and widely circulated and sold to the British reading public" (80). Southey's popular poem offers a case in point. In the decades following the publication of *Kehama*, reports of idolatrous suicide were received with increasing skepticism by Orientalist authorities. Nonetheless, the strange image of fanatical idolaters sacrificing themselves to the gigantic heathen idol took hold in English popular culture.

This was in part the case because "Christian spectators" at home and abroad were predisposed to revile Hinduism and happy to receive any information that confirmed its ill repute. In a document published periodically by Parliament, Charles Grant (1792–93; 1812–13) roundly condemned "its impure deities, its monsters of wood and stone, its false principles and corrupt practices, its delusive hopes and vain fears, its ridiculous ceremonies and degrading superstitions, its lying legends and fraudulent impositions" (79–80). The procession of Juggernaut seemed to gather and concentrate all of these negative attributes of Hinduism. The idol became a widely recognized symbol, a "gloomy type," as Roberts calls it, of the "hideous superstitions" of India (256). John William Kaye (1859) observes at mid-century that, "by reason of its gigantic proportions and its excessive monstrosity," Juggernaut has "always stood forth, in the sight of European nations, as the great representative of the idolatries of the Indies" (386–7). Indeed, the idol functioned in Victorian culture as a powerful and widely known synecdoche of colonial otherness.

Juggernauts of civilization

Soon after it came to be fixed in Victorian culture as a symbol of strange Indian idolatry, however, Juggernaut began to roll its destructive path in England. Appropriating the foreign idol as a rhetorical figure, novelists and social critics used it to depict and analyze domestic problems involving various forms of destructive force and vain self-sacrifice. In *The Book of Snobs* (1845), W. M. Thackeray perceives a connection between English "Snobs, and their worship, and their idols" and the self-destructive fanatics of India (143). The narrator fulminates against those who remain celibate for financial reasons, thus sacrificing natural impulses beneath the car of "Society," that "man-eating Juggernaut" (143). While Thackeray uses the figure to mock those who idolize "Society," later in the century Robert Louis Stevenson (1885) uses it to depict anti-social impulses. In one of his first appearances, Mr Hyde, whose wizened frame belies the "excessive monstrosity" of his destructive passions, "trample[s] calmly," like "some damned Juggernaut," over a young girl, whom he leaves "screaming on the ground" (31). The personification of the London gentleman apparently conceals forces as cruel and merciless as those associated with the Hindu idol.

The social turmoil produced by the Industrial Revolution led to a whole set of English juggernauts. This context is particularly ironic, since many Victorians perceived England's industrial might as evidence of racial superiority and an implicit justification for imperial rule. Samuel Smiles (1859), for example, celebrates the "commons of England" as embodiments of an "indomitable spirit of industry" that has "built up the industrial greatness of the empire, at home and in the colonies" (23). In an article in *Blackwood's* entitled "Our Rural Population and the War" (1855), however, a critic of industrial progress calls attention to the plight of the rural poor who, deprived of farm land by enclosures, have "gone to swell the pauperism and sink into the physical degeneracy of the factory-towns. A Juggernaut civilisation is crushing them beneath the wheels of its onward car" (736). The paradox of a "Juggernaut civilisation" succinctly captures a widespread anxiety about the collapse of distinctions between progressive English civilization and backward Indian idolatry. Unlike Smiles, this writer sees the "commons of England" falling prostrate before indomitable socio-economic forces. They are not energetic and active individuals invigorated, as Smiles says, by "free industrial energy" (23). They are a mass of enchained victims crushed into pauperism by relentless socio-economic and demographic forces. To his more cynical eye, England's vaunted progress does not, as one might expect, increase the distance between the imperial metropolis and its backward colony. English paupers remain as helplessly fatalistic as their Indian counterparts. The national idol that crushes them is as monstrously indifferent to human life as Juggernaut. The satiric application of the Juggernaut narrative to the industrializing metropole demonstrates the Evangelical and anthropological principle that human nature clings to old habits and inclinations. The growing "industrial greatness" of the imperial nation merely provides an occasion for the eruption of grotesque superstition in a form suited to modern England.

The comparison does not, to be sure, completely erase differences. Even as the figure of "juggernaut civilization" asserts a likeness, it recognizes underlying differences between the forces destroying English laborers and Indian votaries. But the figure does call into question the presumed *extent* to which civilized progress differs from backward idolatry. If this instance of domestic autoethnography does not erase the boundary between England and India, it significantly blurs it, indicating that supposedly civilized England cannot, as much as it would like to do, clearly and cleanly distinguish itself from its benighted colony.

The following illustrations graphically convey this point. The first (Figure 3.1), an engraving of the car festival by William Green, appeared as the frontispiece of Mary Martha Sherwood's *The Indian Pilgrim* (1818), a widely read imitation of *Pilgrim's Progress* set in India. Early in the narrative, Goonah Purist, the allegorical figure of the Hindu convert, finds himself at the temple of Juggernaut. The illustration and accompanying text together offer an account of the festival which is in many ways typical, if somewhat more sensational than most. Sherwood particularly stresses a reciprocal relation between idolatrous rites and bestial consumption. A vulture hangs in the air at left, and the human bones in the right foreground show the aftermath of a scavenger feast. At lower left, as the narrator observes, "mothers cast their infants into the mouths" of "sharks and alligators" and "sons and daughters plung[e] their aged parents into the lake, as an offering to its insatiable inhabitants" (26). Struck with "horror and amazement," the narrator describes the scene depicted at center, the appearance of the "enormous car, of a pyramidal

Figure 3.1 William Green. Frontispiece. Mary Martha Sherwood, *The Indian Pilgrim* (1818). Image provided by the President and Fellows of Harvard College.

form, … the noise of whose many rumbling wheels was like the agitation of the earth" (26). The body of an "infatuated" idolater is visible beneath the "car of Jugunnathu" (23). Sherwood expected that the representation of such scenes would serve to reconfirm the faith of "European pilgrim[s]" by affording them "an opportunity of comparing the reasonable services of Christianity with the superstitious vanities of heathenism" (4).

The next illustration (Figure 3.2), however, demonstrates how Victorian satire discovers an opportunity to consider the "superstitious vanities of heathenism" without removing attention to distant India. The spatial composition of this cartoon from *Punch* (1845), which compares foolhardy English railway investors to suicidal idolaters in India, suggests a deliberate parody of the frontispiece of Sherwood's well-known text and an effort to satirize and question the religious and intellectual antitheses she takes for granted.[2] Depicted in the same position as its Indian counterpart, the enormous railway car, with its smokestack and descending plume of steam, appears as a "pyramidal form" moving from left to right with overbearing force on "many rumbling wheels." The devil of venture capitalism sits astride the engine in the place occupied by the heathen idol in India. Since the steam-powered train does not require human assistance, the idolaters who pull the car in Sherwood's illustration make room for more sacrificial victims. The outstretched arms of the middle-class investors who hurry to cast themselves and their wealth beneath the oncoming train mimic the gesture of fanatical worshipers to the left of the car in Sherwood's illustration. The discarded hat at right, which replaces a human skull, indicates that a frantic investor has, symbolically at least, lost his head. The woman in widow's weeds at center right does not, like her Hindu sister, sacrifice her children, but she does enthusiastically surrender the cash on which their lives depend. The alligators, who in Sherwood's text wait for their "accustomed prey with wide-extended jaws," wear the wigs of voracious lawyers in the *Punch* cartoon (26). The hooked "beaks" of the vultures at upper right, a doubled and transposed element of the original illustration, suggest an anti-Semitic reference to pawn-brokers who hover above irresponsible speculation, eager to scavenge any scraps of cash left by the lawyers. In the cartoon, the dome of St Paul's Cathedral is just barely visible at center right, a dim reflection of the towers of the temple of Juggernaut foregrounded in Sherwood's illustration. The obscurity of the Christian architecture indicates that the belief system on which Sherwood stakes the cultural distinction between England and India has been almost entirely displaced by a superstitious idolatry of industrial capitalism.

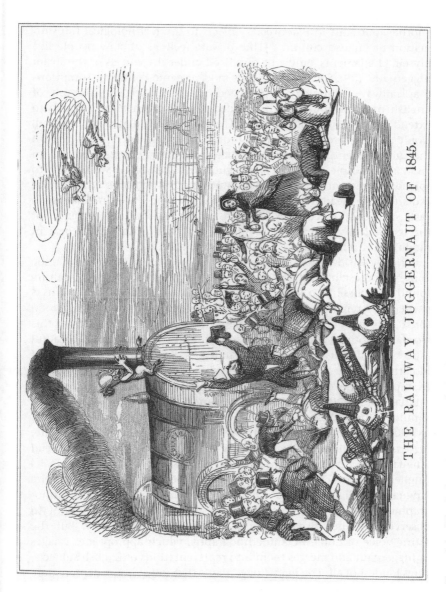

THE RAILWAY JUGGERNAUT OF 1845.

Figure 3.2 "The Railway Juggernaut of 1845." Cartoon. *Punch* 19 (July–Dec. 1845). Image provided by the President and Fellows of Harvard College.

The satiric comparison of the railway train to Juggernaut was not unusual. In an article entitled "The Barbarisms of Civilisation" (1861) another journalist in *Blackwood's* objects to the technological transformation of English culture. "[T]he private feelings of slow people like myself," he laments, "must be sacrificed under the wheels of the steam Juggernaut" (89). Such comparisons mock the mid-century assumptions that railway technology symbolized the technological triumph of English progress and as such afforded a practical means by which to extend colonial authority in India. The railway in India, it was believed, would at once strengthen British industry, tighten the military grip on the subcontinent, and spur the process of cultural transformation. In 1857, for example, *The Economist* argued that the railway would help to spread "English arts, English men, and English opinions" throughout India (qtd. in Headrick 1981: 182).[3] The nostalgic writer in *Blackwood's* casts such confidence in ironic light as he suggests that reverence for the technological achievements of English civilization only repeat in modified form the fanaticism associated with India.

I briefly consider these initial examples, drawn from different domestic contexts, to establish the general point that Victorian imperial culture found it impossible to separate the vocabularies of self and other. This is particularly remarkable in the case of *Juggernaut*, a word that "stood forth" as a symbol of heathen idolatry in the distant colony. Even this word, connoting as it did the most apparently distasteful and dreadful aspects of Hinduism, becomes an indispensable figure for varieties of idolatry at home. By the 1840s, indeed, it stands forth as a remarkable example of the discursive hybridity of English imperial culture. As Mikhail Bakhtin (1981) observes, "one and the same word" can "belong simultaneously to two languages, two belief systems that intersect in a hybrid construction" (305).[4] In the service of domestic social satire, *Juggernaut* provides an exemplary case of a word in which several languages and belief systems interact. Still faintly audible, even in its Anglicized forms, is the belief system of the Hindu pilgrim and the language of religious veneration. It is almost drowned out by the ethnographic voices of colonial rule, those that assert England's right to observe, describe, disparage, and ridicule colonial idolatry. But the satiric voice of domestic autoethnography, which appropriates images of Juggernaut and merges them into representations of English subjects, rings loudest of all. The many juggernauts that roll at home demonstrate that it is only the most naive who might credibly assure themselves that English imperial culture offers a pure alternative to colonial otherness.

Competing narratives of colonial authority

This chapter culminates in extended readings of *Jane Eyre* and *The Egoist*, both of which novels appropriate ethnographic representations of Juggernaut. It is necessary first to investigate in some detail an obscure early nineteenth-century debate between Evangelical colonial missionaries and secular bureaucrats of the East India Company. This debate is crucial both because it helped to introduce Juggernaut to the English public and, more specifically, because it produced two distinct narratives of colonial intervention that Brontë and Meredith reenact at home. It was within the specific context of the "pilgrim tax" controversy that these narratives took shape. In the eighteenth century, having begun to conquer and govern vast expanses of the subcontinent, the East India Company sought to finance its administrative operations and supplement trade profit by extracting tax revenue from the native population. It generated the greatest share of its revenue from taxes levied on land, but it also taxed religious festivals, following a policy established by the Moghul empire that it displaced.[5] Many of those who sought to attend the car festival in Puri paid a fee in order to be admitted to the temple. In return for this pilgrim tax, the colonial government paid for the upkeep of the temple and its idols and kept order during celebrations. The religious tolerance implied by this arrangement outraged Evangelical ministers and politicians who believed that England had the moral duty to reform idolatrous colonial subjects. They denounced the colonial administration for serving as "Juggernauth's churchwarden" and handling an "unclean thing" (Kaye 385, 381). As part of a successful campaign to gain the right to establish Christian missions in India (recognized by the 1813 Company Charter), they publicized the scandalous connection between a presumably Christian government and the monstrous Indian idol. The pilgrim tax itself was not abolished until 1833, however, and the rival factions continued to debate the issue through the middle of the century.[6]

Holding divergent notions of the objectives and responsibilities of colonial rule, Evangelical ministers and secular bureaucrats viewed the strange heathen idol from very different perspectives. They produced narratives that differ widely in plot, tone, and symbolic structure. As one might expect, the Evangelical narrative fits Juggernaut into a story of spiritual enlightenment effected by English missionaries.[7] In a speech delivered to Parliament on the eve of the 1813 Charter reform, William Wilberforce demonstrates the spiritual darkness of India by referring to the "obscene and bloody rites" practiced at the temple of Juggernaut, hyperbolically claiming that "the lives of 100,000 human beings are annually expended in the service of that single idol"; he then expresses "the most earnest wishes that we should commence, with prudence, but with zeal, our endeavours to communicate to those benighted regions, the genial life and warmth of our Christian principles and institutions" (qtd. in Howse 91). Juggernaut plays a crucial role in the salvation narrative that Evangelicals projected onto the colonial scene.

Evangelical accounts of Juggernaut relied heavily on Claudius Buchanan. In *Christian Researches in Asia* (1813) and other works, he presents the idol as an emblem of vain idolatry, moral darkness, and, above all, temporal and spiritual death, the antithesis of genial Christian life. Describing his 1806 journey to the car festival, Buchanan calls attention to the "squalid and ghastly appearance of the famished pilgrims" and emphasizes that many die before reaching their destination (19). The sand plain surrounding the temple is "whitened with [their] bones," a veritable "Golgotha, where the dead bodies are ... cast forth; and where dogs and vultures are ever seen" (19). At the epicenter of this "valley of death" is Juggernaut himself, whom Buchanan dubs the "Moloch of the present age," explaining that "the sacrifices offered up to him by self-devotement [sic] are not less criminal, perhaps not less numerous, than those recorded of the Moloch of Canaan" (19). He describes two incidents of "self-devotement" in grisly detail, noting that after one of them the crowd of worshipers raises a "shout of joy" to celebrate the "libation of blood" (23). For Buchanan, colonial India represents a new forum for the age-old contest between life-affirming Christianity and bloody idolatry.

Buchanan presents the erotic features of Juggernaut idolatry as further evidence of its spiritual depravity. He observes that the temple walls feature "indecent emblems, in massive and durable sculpture" and recalls with disgust "obscene stanzas" chanted by a priest (19). In his *Apology for Promoting Christianity in India* (1815), Buchanan discusses such indecency more explicitly. Some Western observers express admiration for a large stone pillar located outside Juggernaut's abode. Fanny Parks describes it as "elegant in form" (381). For Emma Roberts, the "pillar of black stone" is "beautifully proportioned and finely designed," the "only object worthy of praise" within the temple (257). Yet Buchanan, ever alert for evidence of obscenity, asserts that the pillar links the worship of Juggernaut to "Phallic ceremonies" (40). He insists that the lingam, or symbolic representation of the phallus, "is the daily, emphatical, primeval, and almost universal worship of the Hindoo people" (40). The "band of courtesans retained for the service of the temple" confirm for

Buchanan the lascivious and debased nature of religion at the temple of Juggernaut (47).

For Christian authorities, the "obscene and bloody rites" on view at the temple of Juggernaut reflected the inevitable result of heathen idolatry, the substitution of a lifeless material object for an immaterial and unrepresentable deity. To visualize the deity in material form indicated profound spiritual blindness. From the Evangelical perspective, the deplorable spiritual mistake is compounded by the base human passions, which steadily corrupt the act of worship until the idol only functions as a repository of projected violence and lust. For Buchanan, the objects worshiped at the temple of Juggernaut declare on their surface the multiple transgressions of idolatry. In *Christian Researches*, he denounces Juggernaut as a mere "block of wood having a frightful visage painted black, with a distended mouth of a bloody character" (21). In the *Apology*, he disparages Juggernaut idolaters for worshiping the lingam, "falling prostrate before a black stone, and that black stone an indecent emblem!" (45). Buchanan conveys to Christian readers the degenerate otherness of Juggernaut votaries by emphasizing that they have replaced the unrepresentable and true God with a greedy face of death and an indecent emblem of desire.

The representation of heathen idolaters in Evangelical discourse is necessarily two-sided, however, for the missionary project was driven by the confidence that degenerate heathen souls could be reclaimed. In her analysis of the generic conventions of missionary discourse, Johnston finds that "there is always an emphasis on positive Evangelical achievements" (7). Buchanan communicates disgust for the "infatuated and impure adorers" of Juggernaut much more effectively than he expresses hope for their salvation (27). Nonetheless, he does introduce a letter from another missionary that tells of an ailing man named Subhasingha who, hearing "something of the sufferings and death of Christ for the salvation of sinners," abruptly decides that "he would take Christ as his refuge, and instead of prosecuting his Journey to Juggernaut, would remain here to hear more of the word of God" (27). The notion that the essential truth of Christianity remained inscribed in all human hearts made it perhaps possible to credit such suspiciously abrupt conversion experiences. In *The Indian Pilgrim*, though, Sherwood attempts to capture the ambivalence of the conversion experience. Having awakened to a sense of his spiritual depravity, Goonah Purist sets forth on a spiritual pilgrimage. He first encounters a Brahmin priest, who directs him to the temple of Juggernaut. Although Goonah Purist witnesses the accentuated horrors of the car festival as depicted by Sherwood, he nonetheless manifests the indecision of a subject suspended between systems of belief, urged by inner light toward Christianity yet unable to renounce the idols and priests of his culture. Before the oncoming car of Juggernaut, he "hesitate[s], and look[s] this way and that way, not knowing what to do" (24). On the verge of sacrificing himself, he is like Subhasingha saved by an external agent, a voice that proclaims "with authority: – 'Cease, ye idolaters' " (24).[8] Goonah Purist's salvation experience extends over many chapters and involves many moments of agonizing indecision and doubt, but its triumphant conclusion justifies the Evangelical colonial mission by demonstrating that heathen subjects who open their souls to the Christian God might yet be saved, even within the especially benighted neighborhood of Juggernaut.

Riled by attacks on the pilgrim tax, secular officials of the East India Company dismiss Evangelical accounts of the car festival as "very exaggerated and unfounded" (Buller 597).[9] They represent the narrative of spiritual enlightenment in India as hopelessly naive and potentially dangerous. In an article published in the *Journal of the Royal Asiatic Society* (1833), F. Mansbach, a Company official responsible for collecting the pilgrim tax, discredits the missionary perspective by representing it as simply another variety of religious infatuation. "We have some missionaries down here," he cooly observes, "who, with the Bible in their hand and abundance of zeal, ... [expect] that their well-meant exhortations are to convert the heathen" (257). Only a zealot, he suggests, might hope to convert a zealot. Grounding their authority in rationality rather than in spiritual enlightenment, Company bureaucrats construct a narrative of colonial intervention that culminates in the institution of reasonable secular government. They emphasize the need to comprehend the Juggernaut pilgrims and the delusion under which they suffer, to protect them from the effects of their unshakeable superstition rather than attempting to reform them.

While Evangelicals depict the temple of Juggernaut as a stage on India's journey toward Christian light, secular Company bureaucrats perceive it as an unalterable feature of the cultural landscape.[10] They stake the legitimacy of their accounts on local experience and knowledge rather than transcendent spiritual truth. Mansbach introduces himself as a "person who for several years has resided" near the temple (253). Believing that his tenure as Company agent has afforded him a reliable "acquaintance with the native character," he makes general pronouncements about "the natives" (253). They are "the most inquisitive race upon earth" and "in general ... great idlers, especially the pilgrims at *Jagannát'ha*" (257). Throughout his report, Mansbach implicitly contrasts himself, a seasoned expert on the local form of Hindu superstition, to itinerant missionaries who swoop into the district for a brief and appalled glimpse of idolatrous monstrosity.

The peculiar customs on view during the car festival afford secular officials many opportunities to comment sarcastically on the irrationality of colonial superstition. Mundy, who like Mansbach defends the pilgrim tax, is amused to observe that priests constantly fan Juggernaut and his compatriot idols in order "to prevent the flies and musquitos [sic] from invading their sacred noses" (251). In their description of the procession of the idol, secular observers develop a comic contrast between the faith invested in the idol and its material existence. Mansbach wryly notes that the "infatuated pilgrims" do not seem to notice that the "manifest helplessness of the block of wood" belies the powers attributed to the idol (259). Several commentators derive particular amusement from the process by which Juggernaut is stationed in his car. As Mundy reports, the massive figure is "dragged 'neck-and-heels' down the grand steps, through the mud, and … finally hauled by the same gallows-like process" into its vehicle (253). This defilement captures, for secular bureaucrats, the absurdity of the entire spectacle. The pilgrims are too infatuated to understand that this comical result of the "helplessness" of their wooden god reveals the emptiness of their faith. Company officials perceive idolatry as the corruption of the intellect and reason much more than the soul. As they sarcastically diminish the monstrous idol and the ridiculous ceremonies meant to honor it, they implicitly display the rational and reasonable mind that equips them to govern.

Absurd and comic touches thus contribute to a very serious attempt to justify colonial governance. Because their vision is unclouded by the mists of idolatrous infatuation, secular Company officials can understand the true sources of idolatry and prevent its worst effects. James Mill, whose *History of British India* (1819) landed him an administrative post in the East India Company, explains idolatry as a system perpetuated by Brahmin priests who maintain their socio-economic power by fostering superstitious ignorance.[11] Company bureaucrats in India similarly deprecate the "crafty Brahmins" who, Mundy suggests, "doubtless secure to themselves a large share of the offerings paid at the shrine" (253). Having described the sumptuous feast prepared each day for the wooden god, Mansbach is careful to note that "the Rajah of *Khurda*, as high-priest of the temple, divides it with the priests" (255). Utilitarian *real politick* exposes the exploitative greed of corrupt native officials behind the artifice of ritual and faith.

The bureaucratic narrative culminates not in the salvation and conversion of benighted worshipers, but on the institution of a colonial government that protects them from unjust native authority. Company officials justify English involvement in the car festival by claiming that they serve to guard pilgrims "against the oppressions of their own rapacious priests and *Pandits*" (Mansbach 257). Mansbach emphasizes that this protection is compassionate; the "poor and indigent pilgrims" who travel to the car festival are "extremely well taken care of" (257). While missionary work threatens to spark rebellion, rational and humane paternalism, he is certain, wins political consent. "I can assure you," says Mansbach, that "the pilgrims are aware of, and greatly thankful for the liberality of Government" (257).

The insults and accusations traded by Evangelical missionaries and bureaucratic officials reveals an anxiety about the stability of the distinction between English colonial authorities and the deluded idolaters of Juggernaut. Buchanan indicts the colonial administration by accentuating its proximity to the darkest rites of India. The "blood of Juggernaut," he indignantly declares, "is shed at the very doors of the English, almost under the eye of the Supreme Government" (26). According to Mansbach, Christian missionaries are as irrational as those they attempt to convert. Their interference would be wholly comical if it were not also potentially dangerous. Although their criteria differ radically, both camps measure the legitimacy of English authority by the extent to which it rises above the condition of idolatrous otherness.

As they study relationships between men and women in England, Charlotte Brontë and George Meredith also express the anxiety that the distinction between English imperial subjects and Juggernaut idolaters has fallen into disrepair. Indeed, by detecting destructive false gods and vain self-sacrifice, spiritual corruption and exploitative priests, at home in England, they certainly intensify that anxiety. Although it remains uncertain whether or not either writer would have read the specific texts discussed above, *Jane Eyre* and *The Egoist* reflect basic familiarity with the plots, symbolic structure, and forms of colonial authority constructed within the Evangelical and bureaucratic Juggernaut narratives.

The patriarchal idol of Evangelical authority

> It is not the Persian alone, who adores the sun, or the Indian who falls down to the monstrous, obscene Idol at Juggernaut, that is an Idolater
>
> John Graham (1826: 24)

Jane Eyre (1847) is among the earliest of the many Victorian novels that incorporate the figure of Juggernaut worship. It is a particularly interesting case because it parodically responds to the Evangelical discourse that first introduced the prominent symbol of heathen idolatry to the imperial nation. Brontë, raised in the home of an Evangelical Church of England minister, was intimately familiar with the discursive conventions of the Evangelical colonial mission.[12] In *Jane Eyre*, she mimics the voice of Evangelical ministers who compare "professed" Christians at home to benighted heathens abroad. With devastating irony, she uses this same tactic to subvert the moral legitimacy of those who bear Evangelical authority. For Brontë, English men invested with religious authority wield a particularly dangerous variety of power. They are themselves human and fallible, but claim special access to divine knowledge and present themselves as instruments of God. Kathleen Vejvoda (2003) also discusses the novel in relation to idolatry, although she focuses specifically on figures based on Catholic rites and habits of mind. "Throughout the novel," she argues, "Brontë uses the Victorian fascination with Catholicism and idolatry to expose the more insidious forms of idolatry in her own Protestant culture, particularly in the gender politics of courtship and marriage" (243). The Victorian fascination with the "gloomy type" of Hindu idolatry furnishes insights that extend and complement Vejvoda's analysis of Catholic imagery in the novel. Brontë compares the rule of the Christian minister to the roll of Juggernaut, using the satirical discourse of domestic autoethnography to expose a particularly weighty form of Victorian patriarchal authority as a false and destructive idol.

Images of outlandish worship begin to infiltrate and estrange Evangelical male authority early in the novel. When Jane arrives at Lowood, pious Mr Brocklehurst disgraces her by exclaiming before the assembled school that "this child, the native of a Christian land, worse than many a little heathen who says its prayers to Brahma and kneels before Juggernaut – this girl is – a liar!" (69). Forging a comparative link between colonial and domestic forms of corruption, Brocklehurst fashions an imperial rhetoric of shame through which he exercises his disciplinary command. Yet the effort to disgrace Jane rebounds as the Juggernaut figure transmutes from his sermonizing denunciation into a subtler metaphor that encompasses the sources and ill-effects of the power he himself wields. After her humiliating punishment, Jane sinks "prostrate with [her] face to the ground," where she lies "crushed and trodden on" (71). This language certainly confirms the link between Jane and the "little heathen" who "kneels before Juggernaut," but it notably implicates the overbearing minister by figuring him as the brutal and destructive idol.

It is important to note that as Brontë appropriates the figure of Juggernaut worship from Brocklehurst she does not simply invert its gender politics, shifting blame from Jane to her male accuser. Rather, she uses it to expose a destructive dynamic that encompasses both men invested with authority and women who figuratively kneel before it. If Jane often rebels against tyrannical men, she also often reveals the impulse to submit to their authority and internalize their discipline. Late in the novel, she explains that she has never "known any medium" in her response to "positive, hard characters ... between absolute submission and determined revolt" (422). The Juggernaut figure specifically addresses her submissive impulse, representing it as a form of self-destructive worship. The Brocklehurst episode indicates that Jane need not be "crushed" by what she knows to be a false representation of her character, that by succumbing to humiliating discipline she effectively confers the power of a deity on her mortal and fallible accuser. Helen Burns finds it necessary to remind her devastated friend that "Mr. Brocklehurst is not a god" (72). This early scene indicates that the idol of patriarchal authority only treads upon those women who fall prostrate before him.

Although Jane comprehends this lesson, she nonetheless finds it difficult to control her submissive impulse. She comes perilously close to sacrificing herself to other overbearing men as well. Brontë extracts from the Evangelical account of Juggernaut its stark symbolic contrast between Christian life and light and idolatrous darkness and death. Her heroine's encounters with the patriarchal idols of England is, however, characterized by the ambivalence experienced by Sherwood's Indian Pilgrim. She replays the agonizing ambivalence of the "poor man" who, in the path of Juggernaut, "hesitate[s], and look[s] this way and that, not knowing what to do" (24). Like him, she only gradually and imperfectly internalizes Christian doctrine. Jane begins to acquire a sense of her degradation from Helen Burns, who plays the role of the colonial missionary by advising the benighted "little heathen" not to worship false idols. But she remains until the end of her narrative intensely divided, caught between the impulse to bow before false gods of patriarchal culture and the sense that she must follow the rigorous principles of her new-found faith.

This internalized struggle qualifies the general assumption by postcolonial critics that Brontë upholds cultural distinctions that serve the interests of empire. Since an influential essay by Gayatri Spivak, postcolonial readings of *Jane Eyre* have tended to argue that the novel defines the English heroine in clear opposition to colonial others.[13] Jenny Sharpe (1993) argues, for example, that the novel enacts a "national and racial splitting of femininity," awarding moral agency to the English heroine by "bind[ing] ambitions and passions to the West Indian plantation woman and female self-renunciation to the Hindu widow" (28). In a similar formulation, Deirdre David (1995) represents Jane as the "ideal Victorian woman of empire" (77) and contends that "Jane's values station her in direct opposition to what was seen as barbaric superstition in British culture" (92).[14] To a certain extent, interpretations that emphasize distinctions between Jane and colonial others offer a persuasive approach to the novel. Brontë certainly associates varieties of self-destructive femininity with the torrid colonial periphery. The novel seems to ensure that Jane charts a temperate middle course between Bertha Mason's violent rebellion against male despotism and the Eastern woman's degrading surrender to it.

Yet the line of argument pursued by Sharpe and David is complicated by the many contradictions that persistently inhabit the heroine. Jane is at once upstanding English woman and prostrate idolater. The problem the novel foregrounds is the great difficulty of *achieving* a "national and racial splitting of femininity" within a culture in which central institutions and prevailing ideas blur the line between metropolitan and colonial values, Christian and heathen forms of worship. David identifies self-sacrifice as the cornerstone of Jane's moral agency, the value that principally distinguishes her from colonial others and their barbaric superstitions. It is by enduring emotional and physical pain and deprivation that Jane is able to reform Rochester and thus define "the proper role of women in the empire" (97). Yet the paradox of imperial hybridity arises with particular intensity in the novel's representation of female self-sacrifice. It is this value that dangerously links the submissive attitude of women in English patriarchal culture to the heathen idolater's self-annihilation.

Like many other Victorian writers, Brontë idealizes a purified national identity. After leaving Rochester, Jane draws strength from the image of herself as a "village-schoolmistress, free and honest, in a breezy mountain nook in the healthy heart of England" (379). But it is crucial to note that this vision of an independent self and nation, uncontaminated by heathen degradations, offers a glimpse of a healthy and pure identity that the novel never fully attains on the level of subjectivity or culture. Jane in fact uses the image as a disciplinary ideal in order to recall her "wandering" imagination from dwelling on the pleasures of succumbing to her lover's overbearing desire by living as his mistress in a sultry "southern clime" (378–9). Part of her detests the thought of such dependence, which the novel associates with the slavery of the West Indies and the harems of the Orient. But that part must continually struggle against "southern" inclinations. The novel perhaps depicts admirable values as English and wayward impulses as "foreign," but still it constructs a hybrid heroine who encompasses both. If Brontë yearns to banish forms of colonial otherness from the "healthy heart of England," she also acknowledges that the cultural institutions that shape the deepest impulses of her narrator counteract the potential to do so.

Jane's tendency to worship powerful men vividly exemplifies a persistent wayward side of her character. Brontë frequently associates romantic affection with idolatrous inclinations. As a young women, she explained in a letter (12 Mar. 1839) to her friend Ellen Nussey that she had rejected her brother's marriage proposal because she did not feel for him "that intense attachment which would make [her] willing to die for him"; "if ever I marry," she asserts, "it must be in that light of adoration that I will regard my husband" (*Letters* 1: 187). As a novelist, she characterizes such impulses toward romantic subordination as a stubborn foreign element within the English Protestant woman's mind. In *Jane Eyre*, the process begins as the heroine falls in love and gradually loses the critical faculties that enable her to distinguish between true and false gods. "I was growing very lenient to my master," Jane recalls, "forgetting all his faults, for which I had once kept a sharp look-out" (197). This forgetful leniency eventually attains the status of full-fledged idolatry. She confesses, "I could not ... see God for His creature: of whom I had made an idol" (287). The fact that Jane abandons Rochester suggests that she never entirely forsakes her "sharp look-out" for the flaws of his overbearing nature or her own tendency to submit to it. He himself anticipates her capacity for controlling "lenient" impulses when, garbed as a gypsy woman, he reads her physiognomy. Her brow indicates that "Reason sits firm and holds the reins, and she will not let the feelings burst away and hurry her to wild chasms. The passions may rage furiously, like true heathens, as they are; and the desires may imagine all sorts of vain things: but judgment shall still have the last word" (211). Confirming the imperial paradox of Jane's subjectivity, Rochester describes an internalized colonial system in which presumably English and Christian faculties exert control over heathen passions and desires. He justifiably suggests the necessity for perpetual surveillance, a continual holding of the reins.

An ongoing tendency to bow before male idols conveys the persistence of the heathens within. Despite the early intervention of the missionary who warns her not to idolize men, Jane manifests the habit in most of her interactions with figures bearing patriarchal authority. The language she uses to describe powerful men suggests that her heathen passions readily transform them into "idols of wood and stone." Early in her acquaintance with Rochester, she admires his "granite-hewn features" (137). As she later stands beside him in the church where their marriage plans are frustrated, she observes that his "whole face was colorless rock" (303). While Rochester's defiance of Christian principles domi- nates the scene, this metaphor reveals the extent to which Jane has "made an idol" of her lover. If love unleashes the idol-making passions, so too does fear. Brocklehurst appears to young Jane as a forbidding "stony stranger" (33) and a "black marble clergyman" (69). Later, her perception of St John again suggests an idolatrous regard. She fully realizes the heroic nature of his character as she "look[s] at his lofty forehead, still and pale as a white stone" (413). The stony male face often attains the "gigantic proportions" of the bust of Juggernaut. Recalling her first terrifying encounter with Brocklehurst, Jane recalls that she "was very little" while "his features were large" (33). As she grows into an adult, the stony male face still looms above her. She observes with wonder "how like quarried marble was [Rochester's] pale, firm, *massive* front" (my italics, 303). She notes a likeness between St John and a "frowning giant of a rock" (426). Jane has very different relationships with these men, but she is at times in awe of them all. In fear and admiration, she transforms patriarchal authority figures into monstrous stone idols.

The "healthy heart of England" thus harbors a primitive idolatry of male authority similar to the abhorred superstitions of India. The connection is further suggested by imagery that recalls Buchanan's denunciation of "Phallic ceremonies." In the *Apology*, Buchanan invites his "Christian nation" to behold the degradation of "the Hindoo people," who fall "prostrate before a black stone, and that black stone an indecent emblem!" (45). *Jane Eyre* redirects this scandalized ethno- graphic gaze to the Christian nation itself. Jane falls "prostrate" after being punished by Brocklehurst, whom she first describes as "a black pil- lar," a "sable-clad shape standing erect on the rug" (32). St John later appears to her as a "cold cumbrous column" (414). Brontë uses this phal- lic imagery to uncover a repressed connection between the distribution of power in English sexual relations and the "indecent" superstitions of

India. Her novel thus offers a humorous response to the distaste with which Buchanan considers the "almost universal worship" devoted to the lingam in India. When the ethnographic images of phallic worship resurface in the metropolitan context, they expose the sexual basis of power held by Evangelical ministers and other middle-class men in England.

The section of the novel detailing the relationship between Jane and St John vividly demonstrates the extent to which the disguised primitivism of domestic life in England endangers middle-class English women. Patterned on missionaries such as Henry Martyn and Buchanan himself, St John plans to go to India in order to pursue the glorious mission "of carrying knowledge into the realms of ignorance – of substituting peace for war – freedom for bondage – religion for superstition" (394). Yet the conventional language of the colonial religious mission here provides a satiric measure of St John's conduct at home, where he helps to produce the very conditions he envisions reforming in India. Rather than freeing Jane from bondage, he "acquires a certain influence" over her which deprives her of "liberty of mind" (419). Rather than fostering her direct relationship with God, he appropriates her veneration to himself, holding her in the "awful charm" of his commanding presence (423). Once again, despotic control confuses distinctions between English patriarchal culture and colonial superstition.

The irony of the link between the figure of the Evangelical minister and the destructive force of Juggernaut intensifies in the representation of St John. Jane's pilgrimage toward him specifically parallels the miserable and dangerous voyage undertaken by the "ghastly" and "famished pilgrims" described by Buchanan. Jane "crawl[s]" through a landscape of green marsh instead of desert sand, but she too suffers the "pang of famine" (346). She too appears "ghastly, wild, and weather-beaten" (354). The English moors nearly become a Western version of the Indian "valley of death." On the point of collapse from starvation and exposure, Jane imagines dying on the heath, where "crows and ravens" would fulfill the office of Indian scavengers by picking the "flesh from [her] bones" (348). The weary pilgrim finds a dubious sanctuary at Marsh End, a house that wavers between Christian mission and temple of Juggernaut. Embodying the cultural paradox of Evangelical patriarchal authority, its master is at once the minister of Christian "life and warmth" and a "tall imposing figure" (429) as "inexorable as death" (376). Jane fittingly describes St John as "something uncanny," for his character brings home the destructive power of the heathen idol (418).

Although St John at first nurtures the independence which Jane associates with healthy Englishness, his campaign to marry her in order to acquire a subaltern missionary in India threatens to destroy her freedom and extinguish her life. His sister Diana ominously notes that he "will sacrifice all to his long-framed resolve" (375). Jane herself describes St John as a "great man" who "forgets, pitilessly, the feelings and claims of little people" like herself; she perceives that he would "trample them down" in pursuit of his goals (438). After first refusing his marriage proposal, she experiences first-hand the effects of his pitiless determination: he adopts an attitude of cold indifference that "crushe[s her] altogether" (433). Her relationship with this overbearing figure illustrates an ironic infiltration of the English marriage plot by Juggernaut discourse.

Brontë perhaps draws specifically on the Juggernaut episode of *The Curse of Kehama*, which she likely would have read.[15] There are at any rate certain striking parallels between the climax of the relationship between St John and Jane and the bizarre "marriage plot" that Southey imagines. Elaborating on the missionary account supplied by Buchanan (whose text he cites at length in notes to his poem), he creates a scenario in which priests of the idol convince Kailyal, a virtuous Hindu maiden, to "marry" Juggernaut. The towering platform transmutes into a bizarre "bridal car" in which at the side of the God

> Sate Kailyal like a bride;
> A bridal statue rather might she seem,
> For she regarded all things like a dream,
> Having no thought, nor fear, nor will, nor aught
> Save hope and faith, that liv'd within her still. (146)

Apostrophizing her absent lover, Kailyal appeals for aid, "Where art thou, Son of Heaven, Ereenia! where, / in this dread hour of horror and despair?" (148). A band of temple "harlots" then prepares Kailyal for her marriage ceremony, urging the "astonish'd" maid to "fill [the] longing arms" of her espoused, and a lascivious temple priest emerges to "to seize the prey" in the name of the idol (150–1). Southey enhances the Orientalist rape fantasy with supernatural details. The priest is struck dead by Arvalan, a demon who then inhabits the priest's corpse in order to "take [his] pleasure" with the virtuous maid (153). Kailyal frustrates his ghoulish desire only by setting the bridal bed and her demon lover on fire. "Freed from his loathsome touch" yet overwhelmed by dread, the "self-devoted" bride decides to commit suicide by casting herself into the flames (154). She is only stopped at the last moment when a "sudden cry withheld her, … Kailyal, stay!"; miraculously appearing, her father makes his way "unharm'd, through smoke and flames" to save her (155).[16]

Much of the machinery that Southey extracts from the Evangelical Juggernaut narrative and develops for sensational effect – the towering car, the hideous idol, the prostrate multitude, the band of harlots – does not of course re-emerge in the climactic scene between St John and Jane. The obvious differences between the two texts, however, should not obscure their striking parallels. Like Kailyal, Jane narrowly escapes marriage to an imposing figure who pitilessly tramples down the little people in his path. The paralyzing disorientation of Southey's heroine, who "regarded all things like a dream," is matched by the condition of her English counterpart, who stands "motionless" under St John's mesmeric influence as the "dim room" fills with "visions" (441). Jane is urged by her own sense of religious duty rather than a "harlot-band," but the morally transposed source of compulsion nonetheless prepares her for physical intimacy with a spouse whose touch she abhors. St John claims her by "surround[ing her] with his arm" (441). Although Kailyal ignites her demon lover, her impulse to cast herself on the flames of the bridal bed prefigures Jane's impulse to marry St John and accompany him to India, where she expects "to be grilled alive" in the tropical heat (438). Jane understands that accompanying the English Juggernaut to India would be "equivalent to committing suicide" (436).

Even as Jane comes to appreciate his merciless nature and the threat it implies, she remains in superstitious thrall. St John appeals forcefully to that side of her mind inclined to bow submissively before "men of talent" who "subdue and rule" (441). When he makes a final appeal, Jane experiences a "veneration so strong that its impetus thrust[s her] at once to the point [she] had so long shunned" (441). In an idolatrous fervor, she entertains the possibility of marriage to the inexorable minister and, appropriately enough, envisions "death's gates opening" (441). Just as Kailyal is held back from suicide only by her father's "sudden cry … Kailyal, stay!" so too is Jane rescued when she hears "a voice somewhere cry – 'Jane! Jane! Jane!' " (442). Although not entirely "unharm'd," Jane's savior is, like Kailyal's father, tested by "smoke and flames." The quiet English parsonage in which Jane nearly succumbs to suicidal idolatry could hardly be more different than the riotous and exotic scene sketched by Southey. The corresponding details suggest, however, that Brontë has appropriated features of the Juggernaut narrative and projected them onto the familiar domestic setting. The interweaving of the romantic English plot and the otherworldly fantasy produces a hybrid text that accentuates the danger for English women of succumbing to the imposing will of "men of talent" such as St John.

After Jane's near-fatal brush with the Evangelical Juggernaut, the novel seems to achieve a conclusion in which England cleanses itself of heathen idolatry. The relationship between Jane and Rochester depicted in the last pages of the novel transcends the idolatrous dynamic of over-bearing male power and female submissiveness. An earlier reference to Rochester as a "broken idol" anticipates the injuries that topple him from the enormous car of male authority and fracture his dominating influence (371). The "powerlessness of the strong man" enables Jane to assume a role in which she escapes the dangers and degradations of the prostrate votary (462). In Ferndean, at last, it is only the dog Pilot who need be "afraid of being inadvertently trodden on" by the man of the house (456). Yet the miraculous plot device of Rochester's call, without which readers must assume that the heroine would have sacrificed herself to her imposing suitor, illustrates an Evangelical doctrine that denies the possibility of purifying England of idolatrous otherness. Because all erring mortals, in England as in India, are beset from within by degenerate inclinations, none can hope for unassisted salvation. Jane is rescued from the self-destructive impulse she shares with her Hindu sister Kailyal not by her "judgment," which ultimately cannot hold the reins on the heathen passions, but by providential intervention. The very device that magically extricates her from suicidal submission and preserves her for domestic felicity concedes the impossibility of differ-entiating the English woman from the "little heathen" who "kneels before Juggernaut." Brontë can only effect a relatively happy conclu-sion, that is, by imagining a circumstance in which her heroine's hea-then passions are balked by miraculous rescue. The deep seclusion and "insalubrious" situation of Ferndean indicate that the novel can escape, but cannot finally cure, the idolatrous rites that have infected love and domesticity in the "healthy heart of England" (453). (The fact that Lucy Snowe, the heroine of *Villette* (1853), also prostrates herself before men she loves further demonstrates that Brontë finally perceives no easy rem-edy to the idolatrous subjection of women.[17])

Many postcolonial readings of *Jane Eyre* have objected to the apparently approving picture of St John in India with which the novel concludes. In her fascinating discussion of the novel in relation to biographical portraits of Henry Martyn, Mary Ellis Gibson (1999) traces the process through which missionary journals and narratives obscure the "violence implicated in the missionary endeavor – the spiritual conquest of the heathen" by dramatizing instead the "self-violence of renunciation" practiced by Christian heroes (424). In her account of St John, Gibson does suggest that Brontë exposes missionary brutality, but only within the sphere of English domesticity. St John "does violence not to the heathen but at home" (434). Yet the metaphoric pattern that subverts the authority of the Evangelical minister at home also casts doubt on the legitimacy of his colonial mission. Jane certainly obscures this irony by glorifying the Evangelical work undertaken by St John. Having escaped from his destructive path, she becomes generous to a fault, evincing no sympathy for the "little people" of a darker complexion unfortunate enough to trade their idol for the English Juggernaut. She rehabilitates his will to conquer by cloaking it in the language of Bunyan's spiritual allegory, imagining him in the persona of "the warrior Greatheart" as he "hews down like a giant the prejudices of creed and caste" (476). The moral clarity of her imperial allegory is clouded, however, by a disturbing half-echo of Juggernaut imagery surfacing even within the Protestant rhetoric. As colonial missionary, no less than oppressive suitor, St John appears in the character of a destructive giant willing to "sacrifice all to his long-framed resolve." In both phases of his career Brontë shows that Victorian culture confers devastating power on the Evangelical patriarch. She more thoroughly exposes the dangers of that power in the domestic context, but the novel closes with a disquieting glimpse of its effects on the colonial frontier.

Juggernaut gentility at Patterne Hall

Pausing in his derisive description of the car festival, Mundy reflects that "[m]any as notorious a *block*-head as friend Juggernauth ... receives – without the excusing plea of religious superstition – the obsequious homage and adoration of more enlightened idolaters" (253). Half a century later, *The Egoist* taps the comic potential of this same point. In the first sentence of the novel, Meredith defines a setting that would seem to prohibit such hybridity. The narrator announces that "[c]omedy is a game played to throw reflections upon social life, and it deals with human nature in the drawing-room of civilized men and women" (3). As played by Meredith, however, this "game" involves exposing primitive modes of thought and behavior. His comic procedure reflects the insights of evolutionary anthropologists who argued in the 1860s and 70s that vestigial forms of primitive habits survived within civilization. Willoughby Patterne, the egoist "who live[s] backwards almost as intensely as in the present," embodies this quirk of evolution (30).[18] Although those who subscribed to the evolutionary paradigm shared prevailing notions of European superiority, they also eroded a sense of clear distinctions between the imperial nation, where savage habits survived in hidden forms, and its colonial locales, where they remained extant.[19] As Lubbock asserts in 1870, the "condition and habits of existing savages ... illustrate much of what is passing among ourselves" (1). In *The Egoist*, this conviction informs the representation of human affairs in the civilized drawing-room at Patterne Hall, which is known, significantly, as the "Indian room" (14).

Indeed, Meredith overreaches anthropologists such as Lubbock in his understanding of the extent to which primitive thoughts and habits determine the shape of modern English culture. Lubbock characterizes primitive survivals as peculiar aberrations, "customs which have evidently no relation to present circumstances" and forgotten "ideas which are rooted in our minds, as fossils are imbedded in the soil" (1). For Meredith, however, central institutions of Victorian domestic life, particularly romance, still bear the imprint of primitive thoughts and customs. Fossilized ideas are paradoxically still very much in use. As a result, the comic novel must adopt hybrid terms and narrative forms in order to effectively describe English courtship or, as Meredith terms it, the "fair western-eastern" (35). This explains why he splices into *The Egoist* narrative devices of the bureaucratic report on Juggernaut. Like Brontë, he uses the figure of the "*block*-head" idol to discredit a particular type of oppressive patriarchal authority. In his novel, it is the country squire rather than the Evangelical minister who stands forth as a false and destructive god. Willoughby is perceived by himself and others as the very "picture of an English gentleman" (295). Yet Meredith demonstrates that the fortuitous intersection of nation, gender, and social status produces an ego of vast dimensions, a "monumental pride" cultivated by a circle of deferential women who give themselves to Willoughby as "votive offerings" (271, 292). Meredith depicts the colossal figure of English male gentility as a "carved-in-wood idol" at the center of a "national worship" that mimics the despised cult of Juggernaut (350). Echoing the derisive humor of the bureaucratic report, he represents the idolatry of English male gentility as an irrational and ludicrous example of primitive worship at home.

Juggernaut idolatry represents one element of an extensive network of colonial tropes used by Meredith to comment satirically on English patriarchal culture.[20] Despite this characteristic feature of his satire, critics of Meredith have in general dismissed the significance of imperial history and rhetoric to his work. Simon Gatrell (1992), who rightly stresses the importance of European internationalism to Meredith, argues that "even in his later fiction [he] was hardly interested in Imperialism" (76). Norman Kelvin (1961) provides a more measured assessment of Meredith's attitude toward the imperial affairs of his day, but does not demonstrate their impact on his literary work and decides, finally, that they "occupied a much smaller place in his thought than other questions relating to England's power" (64). Postcolonial critics have begun to assert that Meredith was indeed interested in imperialism, but have not yet supplied substantial treatment of his work. Edward Said (1993) numbers Meredith among those Victorian writers for whom it was "both logical and easy to identify themselves in one way or another with [imperial] power," but does not expand upon the ambiguous claim (103). In the Introduction of *Reaches of Empire* (1991), Suvendrini Perera refers to a passage from *The Egoist* that, as she rightly observes, vividly illustrates the mutually constitutive relationship between ideologies of empire and gender.[21] She advances her argument through readings of other novelists, however.

By drawing on Bakhtin's concept of heteroglossia, a recent book on Meredith establishes a theoretical basis for perceiving the presence and understanding the function of imperial discourses in his work. Neil Roberts (1997) identifies as a typical feature of Meredith's novels their tendency to "represent and enter into dialogue with – or set in dialogue with each other – the numerous voices of [their] ideological environment" (4). An extended analysis of the figure of Juggernaut confirms his theoretical point by demonstrating that Meredith was attuned to very specific voices of empire and appreciated the ironies of their dialogic interactions. Inflected by turns with accents of imperial ridicule, anthropological skepticism, patriarchal egotism, female surrender, and proto-feminist defiance, references to Juggernaut convey "numerous voices" of late-Victorian imperial culture. It is crucial to note, however, that Meredith does not convene the discussion merely to enjoy the clash of perspectives. Rather, he seeks to generate a satirical energy that serves a particular end. Throughout the novel, the Juggernaut dialogue exposes the superstitious power of the idol of English male gentility and documents its destructive effects. It serves to justify toppling an object of national worship.

Thus, on one level at least, it is necessary to distinguish Meredith's attitude toward the cult he describes from that exhibited by Colonial bureaucrats who, earlier in the century, represent Juggernaut idolatry as an unalterable feature of Hindu culture. Even as he acknowledges the conservative tendencies of human nature, Meredith professes confidence in its progressive development. Over the course of the novel, indeed, civilization seems to take a decisive step forward. The heroine Clara Middleton eludes the forces compelling her to sacrifice herself in marriage to the English Juggernaut and instead engages herself to Vernon Whitford, the progressive-thinking scholar who helps her to extract herself from the destructive romantic cult. A relationship in which the woman is expected to idolize male authority gives place to one in which she is encouraged to think and act independently. Yet the novel expresses a deep ambivalence about the progress it seems to advocate. To begin with, Meredith is uncertain about the ability of women to relinquish primitive subjection. Although Clara refuses to worship Willoughby, she ironically manifests the inclination to bow submissively before her new lover. Crucially, Meredith finds it possible to reconcile this inclination with the comic resolution, which suggests that he objects more to the quality of the patriarchal idol than to the subjection of female votaries. The apparent step forward is thus incremental and hesitant. The novel does not finally depict the eclipse of the idolatry of patriarchal authority, but rather shifts its location from the country gentleman's drawing room to the pedagogue's study.

This irony can only be fully appreciated in light of the narrative strategies designed to overthrow the current object of national worship. Meredith appropriates the satiric instruments used to diminish Juggernaut in Puri, finding them equally effective when applied to the monstrous ego of the English country squire. The narrator adopts the perspective of the seasoned colonial administrator who offers his audience a diverting account of the strange customs practiced in the "Indian room" at Patterne Hall, where "as notorious a *block*-head as friend Juggernauth," receives "obsequious homage and adoration" from a circle of female idolaters. He establishes his credentials by describing the peculiar customs practiced in this English temple. Willoughby's maiden aunts appear as priests who continually echo "one another in worship of [the] family idol" (200). At every opportunity, they take "to chanting in alternation" praises for the man of the house (374). Like the bureaucratic report, the novel exposes the comic irrationality of their Brahminic observances. Recounting the ascension of her god, Aunt Isabel recalls how as a child Willoughby "one day mounted a chair, and ... would not let us touch him, because he was taller than we, and we were to gaze ... It was inimitable!" (374). Her gushy veneration indicates that the English idol receives its own share of "stupid admiration."

The narrator distinguishes himself from the idolatrous cast of mind as secular officials in India do, by accentuating a comic contrast between faith that exalts the idol and experiences that degrade it. Early in the novel, the narrator observes that Willoughby affects the smooth "composure of Indian Gods undergoing worship" as "showers of adulation [drench] him" in drawing-room ceremonies (14). Willoughby achieves a greater triumph than his carved-in-wood counterpart, since he reposes "upon no seat of amplitude to preserve him" and must "continue tripping, dancing, exactly balancing himself" as he interacts socially with "his idolaters" (14). Although the narrator seems to praise Willoughby, he actually savors in anticipation moments when the English god loses his balance. Like Mundy, he relishes the defilement of the god as it is "dragged 'neck-and-heels' down the grand steps" of the temple and maneuvered unceremoniously "through the mud." The idol of English gentility suffers similar humiliation as the plot drags him down a series of bruising romantic rejections and finally deposits him in the mire of Clara's rejection. Willoughby learns to his dismay that his chosen priestess is just the sort of woman "to drag men" like himself "through the mud" (318).

Although at times a highly diverting spectacle, the procession of the idol through the comic plot nonetheless threatens to leave extinguished pilgrims in its wake. Laetitia Dale, the devoted woman Willoughby holds in reserve while seeking more desirable mates, offers her life as an idolatrous tribute. Thinking him "right in all his actions," she manifests a fanatical esteem that corresponds to the "ecstacy of the devotee of Juggernaut" (19). Although she does not annihilate herself in a single act, her self-sacrificing faith steadily compromises her health. Nourished only on patient devotion, she displays the "hollowed cheeks" of a famished pilgrim (25). Indeed, she acquires a "certain likeness" to "the dead" while striving over the course of years "to justify her idol for not looking down on one like her" (25). Willoughby, of course, thoroughly enjoys slowly crushing the life of this "woman who bow[s] to him" in a "passion of self-abandonment, self-immolation" (264). The monstrous ego of the English idol battens on the self-destructive worship of young women.

Like James Mill and the Company officials in Puri, Meredith explains the irrational behavior of female votaries as the inevitable result of a corrupt social system. As he demonstrates, a priestly class derives socio-economic advantages by actively promoting superstitious ignorance. The Patterne aunts, who live under the threat of expulsion from the Hall, work to secure their comfortable berth by schooling impressionable young women in the attitudes of idolatrous subjection. Brahminical self-interest becomes even more pernicious in those who are themselves invested with patriarchal authority. Willoughby easily tempts the epicurean Dr Middleton to enter the priesthood by admitting him to the "inner cellar" of the "sacred" Patterne wine vaults (157). There he cultivates the priestly arrogance of his fiancee's father, who quickly agrees that a sumptuous aged Port would be a "sealed book" to all "[w]omen" and "most men" (159). Intoxicated by esoteric privileges, Dr Middleton begins to imitate the "rapacious priests and *Pandits*" of India, purchasing his own comfort by ensuring the subjugation and misery of others. As a "fresh decanter" is placed before him, he exclaims, "I have but a girl to give!" (161). Having attained a position of subordinate authority within the cult of male gentility, he protects his perquisites by exploiting the disenfranchised.

In Meredith's version of the Juggernaut narrative, however, the disenfranchised do not always submit without resistance. Having engaged herself to Willoughby, Clara quickly realizes her mistake and almost immediately begins to rebel against the abject role fashioned for her within the sphere of upper-class domesticity. She does attempt to acquire the proper reverence, even encouraging the devoted aunts to "magnify the fictitious man of their idolatry, hoping that she might enter into them imaginatively" (83). The exercise fails, however. Clara too clearly perceives the discrepancy between Willoughby's "monumental pride" and his petty nature. She feels "contempt" for his aunts "for their infatuation" (83). Still, the effort required to obtain liberty appears to exceed her ability to resist the tide of social opinion and family coercion. In a spasm of self-abasement, she perceives herself as a "worthless creature" who "might as well yield to her fate" (102). Meredith introduces the possibility that even though Clara recognizes that she "cannot idolize," she might nonetheless marry the idol worshiped by others, casting herself in fatalistic self-surrender beneath the car of the House of Patterne (107).

Clara's ambivalence "might be mapped," as the narrator observes (165). He locates the heroine at a "well-marked cross-road," the intersection "where kismet whispers us to shut eyes, and instruction bids us look up" (165). Within a domestic culture characterized as "western-eastern," it is not surprising that Clara should find herself stalled at this psychological juncture. Even as he exposes the cultural "cross-road" within the mind of the English heroine, however, Meredith expresses the desire to believe that habits of thought are clearly designated, "well-marked" as western or eastern, familiar or strange. This assumption sustains the line of the novel committed to the progressive development of the heroine. The path of blind fatalism leads eastward to the condition of the Arab subject who bows before kismet and, just a bit further on, to the more degraded condition of the idolatrous suicide. The western road, the path of "look[ing] up," of critical awareness and self-assertion, presumably leads toward an independence the English woman has not yet experienced.

The fact that Meredith represents critical awareness as a response to "instruction" quietly introduces the point that Clara does not by herself possess the will or knowledge requisite for this westward journey. For secular bureaucrats in India, colonial government justifies itself by protecting the "poor and indigent pilgrims" it cannot hope to reform. Although Meredith notes the pathetic condition of Laetitia Dale, he attends with greater interest to the disgruntled pilgrim, the English woman who refuses to worship the national idol of male gentility. Clara clearly requires assistance in her bid to extricate herself from the idolatrous cult. In her desperation to escape Willoughby, she undertakes a series of "fibs and evasions" that includes a dangerous flirtation with the caddish Colonel DeCraye (204). Vernon Whitford steps into the plot as a pedagogical "guide" who instructs Clara in the responsibilities of independent thought and action (204). He encourages her to brave the persuasive tactics of those who strive to keep her in worshipful subjection, advising her to make and act upon a definite decision to break her engagement. "I wish you," he tells Clara, "to have your own free will" (224). More committed to the idea of liberal reform than Company bureaucrats earlier in the century, Meredith constructs a colonial authority equipped to lead the oppressed subject out of the cult of Juggernaut.

The romantic plot rewards Vernon for cultivating in the heroine a habit of mind and strength of character opposed to fatalistic self-sacrifice. In language that confers upon this variety of male authority the status of an evolutionary advance, Doctor Corney observes that Vernon is "*better adapted* for eminent station" than Willoughby, and "especially better adapted to please a lovely lady" (350, emphasis added).[22] Ironically, though, the phrase that predicts the triumph of the progressive man also reveals Meredith's reluctance to change the distribution of power he criticizes. If Vernon is "better adapted" than the "carved-in-wood idol" for social and romantic success, his superior traits function to justify *his* ascendance to "eminent station." Willoughby is tumbled from that position and forced to perform the especially "monstrous immolation" of his own monstrous pride by marrying faded and famished Laetitia (397). Yet patriarchal authority, in the form of liberal progress, arises from the mud to regain its lofty seat. Unable to take a step forward that decisively leaves idolatrous subjection behind, the romantic plot exemplifies a conservative counter-drift in Meredith's view of social evolution.

Crucially, Meredith blames Clara herself for the survival of idolatrous subjection. Early in the novel, Willoughby finds himself annoyed at dinner because Dr Middleton has captured the attention of the female audience. He reflects with exasperation that "young or youngish women are devotees of power in any form, and will be absorbed by a scholar for a variation of a man" (118). It is not surprising that Willoughby, who embodies in grand form the survival of primitive ideas and practices, confuses the language of idolatry with the language of evolutionary change. To his eye, the scholarly "variation of a man" merely represents another idol that threatens to "absorb" veneration properly directed to himself. What is more surprising is that the novel largely confirms his fear. Vernon, the scholarly variation of Patterne gentility, eventually replaces Willoughby as Clara's idol. The tendency of women to worship male power introduces an ideological paradox into the comic resolution: Clara idolizes Vernon *because*, as a new variety of male authority, he encourages her not to idolize male authority. In a final interview, she conveys her romantic interest by promising to accompany her father on a planned journey to the Alps, where he has arranged to meet Vernon. When he asks her to acknowledge that she understands the full implications of her decision, she replies, "Mr. Whitford, I shut my eyes and say Yes" (413). "Beware," he cautions, "If you shut your eyes ..." (413). Although Clara this time engages herself to a man who desires to foster rather than crush her "free will," she remains stalled at the cross-road where the voice of primitive fatalism "whispers us to shut eyes, and instruction bids us look up." In response to the instructive suggestion, she consents to "look up," but ironically does so with idolatrous esteem. Projecting the majesty of the Alps onto her new lover, she resists his effort to cultivate her progress. "[B]ig mountains," she declares, "must be satisfied with my admiration at their feet" (414). Clara refuses to prostrate herself before the patriarchal idol who threatens to obliterate her, but then does so before the one who bids her climb to new heights. She confers on Vernon the stature and inviolability of a god, perceiving him as an "inaccessible" figure who "tower[s] too high" above her lowly self (414).

Despite its commitment to the progressive development of the heroine, *The Egoist* thus settles for an incremental improvement, a variation in the idol of male authority. While Meredith attributes the survival of idolatrous subjection to Clara, it is he of course who fashions for her an idol apparently worthy of her admiration. Quietly committing a variety of the uncritical reverence it professes to despise, the novel again corresponds to the bureaucratic Juggernaut narrative. Mansbach attempts to distinguish himself from those he governs, but his exaltation of colonial "Government," a term he always respectfully capitalizes, suggests that the devoted "servan[t] of the Government" simply worships at a different altar (259). Under pains to exonerate the administration attacked by missionaries, he represents it as a perfect, all-powerful, and benevolent deity. "[N]othing is left undone by Government," he proclaims, to care for the miserable pilgrims (257). "[E]very precaution is taken by the authorities" to protect them from the effects of their infatuation (258). The representation of Vernon Whitford as an ideal alternative to Willoughby indicates a similarly ironic recurrence of the idolatrous cast of mind. Like the East India Company official who derides Juggernaut but sets up English colonial "Government" as a better god, the novel topples the monstrous country gentleman only to set up the progressive scholar in his place.

Etymological cross-roads

While many English words implicitly recall the long history of the invasion and colonization of England, the language acquired *Juggernaut* during England's own moment of imperial power. The earliest recorded instance in the *OED* dates to the fourteenth century, but it was only after the British East India Company began to annex and govern territory in India that the vast idol and its reputed victims became available for observation and description by the bureaucrats, missionaries, and unofficial travelers who popularized the word. Only then did an English readership became broadly acquainted with the festival and only then did the word become incorporated into English. So, one might argue, just as England exploited the material and human resources of India, so too did it enrich the coffers of the national language by expropriating words from colonial culture. One might perceive the word *Juggernaut* as a variety of imperial loot (and one might similarly perceive *loot*, another English word derived from Hindi).

To do so, however, would be to sacrifice the significance of the word as a register of the ironies that besiege assertions of imperial supremacy. Gauri Viswanathan (1989) argues that imperial educators sought to use English, as embodied in its great works of literature, as a "disciplinary branch of knowledge" and a "disguised form of authority" (10). Macaulay's "Minute on Indian Education" provides a well-known example of the belief that the language itself would help to transform India by providing access to enlightened alternatives to corrupt mythology and history. Yet the intention to use English literature to transform the colony finds an ironic rejoinder in the literature produced during the colonial era. The very presence of words such as *juggernaut* in the works of canonical novels furnishes proof of the extent to which the process of influence worked in reverse. If English literature transformed India, so too did contact with India transform English literature.

More significant still is the fact that the many disconcerting appearances of English juggernauts destabilize the ideologically crucial distinction between familiar imperial civilization and strange colonial otherness. According to many Victorian novelists and journalists, England itself harbors idols as degrading and ruinous as that which stands forth as an emblem of Hindu idolatry. If Brontë and Meredith thus expose the need for civilizing interventions at home, their works do not suggest the possibility of neatly resolved missions. The ironies that afflict the resolutions of the Evangelical and bureaucratic colonial narratives recur within *Jane Eyre* and *The Egoist*. English juggernauts prove as difficult to combat as their "gloomy type" in India.

4
Failed Colonies in Africa and England: Civilizing Despair in *Bleak House*

> Innumerable things our Upper Classes and Lawgivers might "do"; but the preliminary of all things, we must repeat, is to know that a thing must needs be done. We lead them here to the shore of a boundless continent; ask them, whether they do not with their own eyes see it, the strange symptoms of it, lying huge, dark, unexplored, inevitable; full of hope, but also full of difficulty, savagery, almost of despair?
>
> Thomas Carlyle, *Chartism* (1839)

> We are a great country, Mr Jarndyce, we are a very great country.
>
> Charles Dickens, *Bleak House* (1852–53)

In *Bleak House* (1852–53), Dickens mocks England's self-proclaimed reputation as the greatest and most civilized nation in the world. Like Carlyle, he questions the status of civilization in England by suggesting that a sector of the familiar nation has strangely lapsed into a dark and savage continent. While Carlyle figures working-class discontent as a "boundless" Africa within England, Dickens locates the metaphor in London, the imperial metropolis. As Alexander Welsh observes, the city as a "wilderness or desert" represents one of the "stock literary ideas" available to nineteenth-century writers who sought to satirize the city (13). In *Bleak House*, however, the stock idea acquires a high degree of historical specificity; the wilderness of London reflects mid-Victorian conceptions of the Niger river delta, the location that in the 1840s and 1850s represented African darkness in its most indomitable form. In 1841, the African

Civilization Society had conducted a highly publicized expedition to the region, intending to establish a model farm that would function as an outpost of civilizing progress on the upper reaches of the river. In 1848, several widely read narratives of the expedition gave the public a day-by-day account of its catastrophic progress. Malarial fever struck and incapacitated most of the European crew members and killed many of them. The model farm had struggled on for just a year, but its fields then reverted to jungle. Dickens, who reviewed one of these narratives, publicly criticized the expedition as a vain waste of resources needed in England itself. In *Bleak House*, he illustrates this point by appropriating imagery and other narrative devices from accounts of the 1841 Niger expedition and projecting them onto the landscape of London, the purported "heart of a civilized world" (691). Rejecting the effort to civilize the distant Niger delta, the novel redirects the ethnographic gaze to the public and private spaces of this dark continent at home.

In the novel, Dickens personifies the irony of misplaced philanthropic concern in the memorable character Mrs Jellyby. Borrioboola-Gha, the colony she plans on the Niger, is a thinly disguised version of the model farm planned by the African Civilization Society.[1] Mrs Jellyby functions as an efficient target of satire because she doubly offends the effort the novel undertakes to restrict and control humanitarian reform impulses. By focusing attention on distant Africa, her philanthropic initiative encourages the nation to ignore the savagery that has begun to encroach upon the English metropolis. She is even more culpable in Dickens's eyes for abandoning her duties as mother and wife, which in turn allows savagery to spring up within her own middle-class household. In an effort to correct the ideological disorder associated with the professional female philanthropist, the novel fashions a domestic policy that delineates appropriate gender roles for those who aspire to recapture distinctions between the Niger delta and London. As Esther Summerson and Allan Woodcourt compassionately attend to those who inhabit the dark continent at home, they respect traditional distinctions between male and female spheres of responsibility. Although Dickens endorses their mode of philanthropy, he does not indicate that it has much effect on the darkness of London. The ultimate irony of the novel is that the inadequately civilized "heart of a civilized world" proves as inimical to reform as the Niger delta itself.

The strange condition of England

Both *Chartism* and *Bleak House* contribute to the mid-Victorian debate known as the Condition of England Question. The socio-economic turmoil produced by the Industrial Revolution led many essayists and writers to take an anxious look at the state of the nation. Some, like Macaulay, perceived the progressive development of English civilization beneath the ferment of industrialization and urbanization. Less optimistic commentators, including Carlyle and Dickens, perceived forces of degeneration and decay that threatened to compromise the superiority and very identity of England. Both sides of the debate relied upon the concept of primitive African otherness. As Simon Gikandi has argued, nineteenth- and twentieth-century efforts to diagnose the condition and conceptualize the identity of the imperial nation frequently rely on the concept of racial and ethnic otherness. Particularly in moments of crisis such as the Industrial Revolution at home and imperial conflicts abroad, he argues, English culture strives "to assert its authenticity by negating colonial spaces and subjects as constitutive elements" of Englishness (50). Macaulay, for example, confidently opposes progressive and civilized England to static and barbaric lands such as India. Such acts of negation are haunted by fearful insecurity, however. Carlyle, Dickens, and many other writers imagine a dissolution of borders and differences, an England infected and estranged to various degrees by primitive darkness. As the most vivid and threatening symbol of this darkness, Africa often plays a prominent role in the disturbing transfiguration of England.

Novelists and social critics who take up the Condition of England Question often suggest that industrial labor and exploitation had reduced English working-class subjects to the condition of enslaved and exploited Africans. In *Sybil; Or The Two Nations* (1845), Disraeli imagines the racial defamiliarization of the English working class in a passage that depicts miners who have been literally blackened by coal dust. As "the mine delivers its gang and the pit its bondsmen," the

> plain is covered with the swarming multitude: bands of stalwart men, broad-chested and muscular, wet with toil, and black as the children of the tropics; troops of youth – alas! of both sexes, – though neither their raiment nor their language indicates the difference; all are clad in male attire; and oaths that men might shudder at, issue from lips born to breathe words of sweetness. Yet these are to be – some are – the mothers of England! But can we wonder at the hideous coarseness of their language when we remember the savage rudeness of their lives? … circumstances that seem to have escaped the notice of the Society for the Abolition of Negro Slavery. Those worthy gentlemen too appear to have been singularly unconscious of the sufferings of

the little Trappers, which was remarkable, as many of them were in their own employ. ... With hunches of white bread in their black hands, and grinning with their sable countenances and ivory teeth, they really looked like a gang of negroes at a revel. (178–9)

In this rich passage, which anticipates many of the concerns developed by Dickens in *Bleak House*, Disraeli expresses a series of intermingled anxieties about the confusion of distinctions he would prefer to uphold. In the coal fields, free market labor has become indistinguishable from bond slavery; white workers have become indistinguishable from the black "children of the tropics"; women have become indistinguishable from men; the condition of presumably civilized England has broadly deteriorated into "savage rudeness." Like Dickens, Disraeli finds a useful target for his anger in an institution that expends compassion on distant "negroes" rather than the oppressed and enslaved at home. The irony of misplaced concern is compounded by hypocrisy, since the "worthy gentlemen" who campaign for the "Abolition of Negro Slavery" them-selves benefit from the industrial system that has brought outlandish forms of exploitation and misery home to England.

Condition of England texts such as *Chartism*, *Sybil*, and *Bleak House* thus use tropes of racial and geographical confusion to register what Patrick Brantlinger (1988) refers to as the "reformist point that savagery or barbarism in the heart of civilization is as bad as anything" encoun-tered on the periphery (117). Dickens himself very clearly expresses this "reformist point" in a letter (9 July 1852). Responding to the Rev. Henry Christopherson, a reader of *Bleak House* who had objected to its satiric attack on overseas philanthropy, Dickens writes,

If you think the balance between the home mission and the foreign mission justly held in the present time – I do not ... I am decidedly of opinion that the two works, the home and the foreign, are *not* con-ducted with an equal hand; and that the home claim is by far the stronger and the more pressing of the two. Indeed, I have very grave doubts whether a great commercial country holding communication with all parts of the world, can better christianise [sic] the benighted portions of it than by the bestowal of its wealth and energy on the making of good Christians at home and on the utter removal of neglected and untaught children from its streets, before it wanders elsewhere. (*Letters* 6: 707)

Dickens here clarifies the effort to contain within the borders of the nation the mission to "christianize" and educate those suffering from what he later calls the "darkest ignorance and degradation" (*Letters* 6: 707). He constructs an imperial economy of compassion that would restrict humanitarian concern and philanthropic reform initiatives within England.

In *Bleak House*, Esther Summerson articulates what the novel offers as the theoretical antidote to the condition of England. She explains that she strives "to be as useful as [she] could ... to those immediately about [her]; and to try to let that circle of duty gradually and naturally expand itself" (154). Bruce Robbins (1990) argues that this figure of the gradually expanding circle privileges a proximate, amateur model of influence, in which "all action remains continuous with and answerable to its originary center," over Mrs Jellyby's attempt to reform distant problems through professional institutions and projects (215). He emphasizes that the novel's endorsement of "concentric gradualism" reveals an (inevitably imperfect) effort to replace systematic social reforms with "personal" responsibility (215).[2] The figure also provides a fascinating example of how, as Deirdre David (1995) formulates it, "writing about empire ... elaborates Victorian gender politics" (5).[3] Esther's theory of reform represents, like the satire on Mrs Jellyby that it complements, a rhetorical intersection of anxieties related to the location of philanthropic duties in the context of empire and the division of those duties into gendered spheres of influence. Although Dickens worries about the moral agency of middle-class rather than working-class mothers, he is as much concerned as Disraeli with the role played by "mothers of England" in the construction and defense of national identity. The figure of the gradually expanding circle insists that the civilizing mission begins "at home" for both the imperial nation and the middle-class woman. Mrs Jellyby at once symbolizes the negligent middle-class mother and Britannia astray, a motherland who seeks to nurture the benighted children of the tropics before attending to her own "neglected and untaught children." Particular conceptions of the proper way for a middle-class woman to extend her influence thus converge with the imperial economy of compassion.

This convergence comes into view with particular clarity in relation to endorsed reforms that defy the logic of the gradually expanding circle. Esther's rejection of distant colonial affairs finds interesting exceptions in the careers of heroic male characters such as Woodcourt and George Rouncewell, both of whom gain extensive experience on the colonial periphery before putting their altruism to work at home. As he seeks to correct the varieties of disorder introduced by the female philanthropist, Dickens maps two different and complementary paths toward national reform. The first, which restricts the compassion and reform initiative of middle-class women to the English home, offers a clear-cut contrast to Mrs Jellyby's "telescopic philanthropy." The second, which culminates as certain male characters enact compassionate reforms in the public sphere, qualifies the apparent rejection of distant activities. Dickens indicates that men acquire the very sort of experience and authority needed at home through imperial adventure and military service. Charity only necessarily *begins* at home for the middle-class woman.

The male path toward national reform underlines a crucial point about the imperial political vision that *Bleak House* affords. Although Dickens subjects England's imperial sovereignty to some sarcastic asides, he ultimately does not criticize imperialism itself. Rather, he hopes to readjust the imperial relationship so that it consistently benefits and strengthens civilization at home. Dark colonial elsewheres provide a useful service to England as a stage for the development and display of masculine force and initiative. They also, however, hold the dangerous potential of weakening the nation by vampirically sapping its compassion and reform energy.

Cultivation and decay on the Niger

For Dickens, the Niger river delta represents the paradigmatic case of this dangerous potential. A devoted reader of travel and exploration narratives, he was familiar with the gloomy history of British forays into the region. In *Travels in the Interior Districts of Africa* (1799), Scottish surgeon Mungo Park recounts the destitute and solitary journey on which he became the first British explorer to discover the headwaters of the Niger. On a subsequent trip, Park led 40 European companions to their deaths. Most perished from malarial fever; those who survived, including Park, were killed during an attack of indigenous people. Hugh Clapperton recorded a similarly tragic expedition in the posthumously published *Journal of a Second Expedition into the Interior of Africa* (1829). Clapperton's assistant, Richard Lander, survived the initial voyage, and soon returned to the region with his brother John. Their *Journal of an Expedition to Explore the Course and Termination of the Niger* (1832) describes their discovery of the Niger's termination on the Atlantic coast at the conclusion of a journey punctuated by disease and other crises. Lander returned once again in command of a well-financed venture that sought to capitalize on his geographic knowledge by trading for ivory in the interior. Thirty-nine European officers and men set out on two steamships. Only nine survived. Most succumbed to fever, although Lander himself died from a gunshot wound he received when his boat was attacked by river bandits. MacGregor Laird and R. A. K. Oldfield, a chief officer and junior surgeon, recount the grim details of this journey in the *Narrative of an Expedition into the Interior of Africa by the River Niger* (1837).

The African imagery that infiltrates and estranges the picture of London in *Bleak House* comes from the body of literature that recounts the next major attempt to explore the region, which was described in *A Narrative of the Expedition Sent by Her Majesty's Government to The River Niger in 1841 under the Command of H. D. Trotter* (1848) by Second-in-Command William Allen and medical officer T. R. H. Thomson. Chief medical officer Dr James Ormiston McWilliam, who also wrote the *Medical History of the Expedition to the Niger* (1848), contributes some chapters and appendices. Dickens reviewed the two-volume *Narrative* in an untitled article in *The Examiner* (1848), and he likely read other accounts of the expedition as well. The *Narrative* is a fascinating anthology of mid-Victorian imperial discourses. Like the accounts of previous explorations to the region, it expresses the desire to gather and disseminate scientific and ethnographic knowledge about a relatively unknown sector of the dark continent and the people who live there. The book includes many maps and illustrations, extensive description of the landscape, and commentary on curious manners and customs. Appendices include a geological survey, a polyglot glossary, and a catalog of flora and fauna (including principal ethnic groups). As in the accounts of previous forays, such knowledge is gathered with an eye to its economic utility. The Colonial Secretary, Lord John Russell, instructed the commissioners of the 1841 expedition to make the "commercial interests of Great Britain an object of ... constant attention" (1: 424).

As the *Narrative* makes clear, however, the effort to know the Niger delta and exploit its commercial potential was in this case subordinate to humanitarian objectives. Distinguishing their mission from those stimulated only by a "thirst for discovery, and the spirit of commercial enterprise," Allen and Thomson claim to have served "nobler ends than the acquisition of wealth" (1: 22). Although supported by public funds, the 1841 expedition aimed to advance an abolitionist scheme promoted by the African Civilization Society, a private philanthropy founded by the Quaker politician and philanthropist Thomas Fowell Buxton.[4] Like many British abolitionists, Buxton had been grieved to see that England's naval campaign to intercept slave-trading vessels and liberate their human cargo had not substantially diminished the transatlantic slave trade. *The African Slave Trade and Its Remedy* (1839) presents his conclusion that the only way to end slavery would be to radically transform African culture itself. With the endorsement of Prince Albert and many other prominent members of the African Civilization Society, he formulated an ambitious scheme to purchase a tract of land on the upper reaches of the Niger and there establish a permanent settlement and model farm. Buxton imagined that this philanthropic colony would serve as an outpost of enlightenment from which the Society might, as Allen and Thomson recall, carry forth the "deliverance of Africa" by "Impeding the Slave Trade, Establishing legitimate commerce, Promoting and teaching agriculture, and Imparting religious and moral instruction" (1: 24).

These "nobler ends" did not, alas, secure providential protection. While aware of high European mortality rates on previous Niger forays, Buxton optimistically believed that moral and physical regulations might "render life within the tropics not subject to very much greater hazard than in this country" (qtd. in Temperley 22). An unprecedented level of attention was devoted to safety and health concerns. Three iron steamships were specially constructed for tropical river navigation. An ingenious ventilation system was designed to protect officers and men from the climate that had proven so perilous to the European constitution. The expedition was nonetheless plagued by illness and accident. The *Narrative* traces a gradual descent from exuberant optimism into descriptions of prostrating fever aboard ship and chaotic failure on land. Despite the many safeguards, approximately one-third of the European officers and men eventually died from malaria and other causes. In his *Examiner* review, Dickens bitterly reviews the chronicle of "Death, Death, Death" (1848: 533).

Those who took part in the 1841 expedition acknowledge the insalubrity of the Niger delta, but their fear of the "fatal river," as Dickens unambiguously terms it, was offset by appreciation of its beauty and hopes of economic development (531). Allen and Thomson frequently describe picturesque vistas, and the *Narrative* includes many vignettes and full-page engravings based on sketches by Allen himself. The authors praise "splendid panoramic view[s]" and "magnificent park scenery" (1: 280, 375). Since the expedition planned to replace the slave trade with the "lawful" trade of raw materials, they also scanned the landscape for its economic potential. The *Narrative* includes a royal address "To the Chiefs and People of Africa" in which Queen Victoria herself sketches a prospect of economic development. In a passage wonderfully indifferent to the finer points of diplomacy and agriculture alike, she regally lectures the chiefs of Africa: "Now, you live in a country where everything grows very quickly out of the ground, and these are the things which we want. You must dig the ground, and raise cotton trees, indigo, coffee, sugar, rice, and many other things of the same kind; and while these are growing, you can collect elephants' teeth, gold dust, gums, wax, and other things of that sort" (1: 450–1). "[A]lmost without any trouble," she cheerfully adds (1: 451). Although Allen and Thomson discuss plans for commercial development somewhat more practically, their appreciation of the African landscape is certainly also inflected by the potential for trade in "things of that sort" enumerated by Victoria. One "exceedingly beautiful" view, for example, comprises shores "richly clothed with verdure, and many noble trees," as well as ample fields of staple crops (1: 266). "[R]ichly clothed" scenery promised lucrative trade. The *Narrative* demonstrates a particular interest in the variety and extent of cultivation, which indicated not just the fertility of the land but also the willingness of the indigenous population to "dig the ground." The plan to foster "lawful" commerce in natural products depended on both factors. Encouraged by the industry they witness on the banks of the Niger, Allen and Thomson note with satisfaction that "wherever man has been able to get a firm footing, he has cleared away a patch for cultivation" (1: 379). Such observations established auspicious precedent for a central objective of the mission, which was to displace the slave economy by "promot[ing] the extended cultivation of the soil of Africa" (*Narrative* 1: 432).

Members of the expedition did also perceive African nature with an acute sense of foreboding, however. Recalling their "anxiety for the future," Allen and Thomson register their sense of vulnerability in a "climate, which Almighty wisdom had adapted to constitutions so different to our own" (1: 313). As the expedition approached the Niger delta, Dr McWilliam (1848) carefully recorded weather that seemed full of ominous signs. Off the coast of a volcanic island, the ships were engulfed by a "cloud of a dirty brownish colour" (24). The next day was "hazy throughout," with "very heavy rains" (25). Another storm produces "more than ordinarily fearful effects": the "whole arch of heaven seemed enveloped in gloom … and the rain then poured in torrents" (28). As the expedition arrives at Cape Coast, where the British maintained a military garrison, "there were heavy fogs in the mornings and evenings" (40). Poised at the mouth of the river, the ships were prevented from crossing the bar by especially foul weather. Allen and Thomson recall "a great deal of rain" and "excessive gloom" caused by "low and dense clouds" that "hung over the prospect like an impenetrable veil" (1: 156–7). They comment specifically on a "peculiar condition of the atmosphere," known as the "Smokes," that "envelop[es] portions of the land" in the "form of a dense vapour" (2: 153). "Nothing could be more debilitating," they observe, "than the effect of these 'smokes' on European constitutions; and the feeling of unconquerable anxiety and nervousness was very distressing" (2: 154). In both the *Medical History* and the *Narrative*, the weather acquires symbolic significance as an obstacle to civilizing progress, depressing the spirits of the missionaries, blocking their vision, and gloomily foreshadowing disaster.

From the perspective of mid-Victorian medical science, the fogs, haze, and clouds of Africa also carried the very literal potential of disease. In 1841, the cause of malaria remained a mystery. Until the end of the century, when researchers discovered that mosquitos transmitted a parasite to humans, it was mistakenly assumed that the fever was caused by miasmas that rose from tropical swamps and marshes. The name of the fever, derived from the Italian *mala aria*, bad air, reflects this long-held view. If the hopes of the expedition were pinned on signs of industrious cultivation on high banks, its fears centered on low-lying areas where man had *not* been able "to get a firm footing." Allen and Thomson provide some commentary on causes and symptoms of malaria, but they refer interested readers to the more detailed discussion of the disease provided by McWilliam in his *Medical History*. Although he admits that chemists have as yet failed to "unfold the nature of pestilential gaseous emanations," McWilliam adheres to the theory that the disease was communicated by "[t]errestrial exhalations ... resulting from the decomposition of animal and vegetable matter, and the consequent formation of deleterious gases vitiating the air" (159). During the rainy season, he explains, the Niger floods its banks and begins to decompose the "animal and vegetable matter" with which it comes into contact. When the "rains cease" and the Niger falls, the delta becomes increasingly "pestilential" as "day to day a greater surface of muddy soil becomes exposed, and the organic matters, saturated with water, are ... powerfully acted upon by the sun, and gaseous emanations are abundantly evolved" (184–5). African nature seemed to guard itself from European cultivation with a "miasmatous poison" concocted from the basic elements of water, mud, and sun (179).

The *Narrative* includes a list of regulations intended to protect the crew from the deadly miasmas of the Niger delta. Drawn up by Dr McWilliam, the list provides extensive and precise guidelines regarding ventilation, clothing, exposure, and diet. Although he comments on the potential of quinine as a prophylactic (which was fully confirmed in the 1850s), the regulations only stipulate occasional doses at the surgeon's discretion. McWilliam seems to put as much faith in "a cup of warm coffee," which he directs should be "given in the morning to each European" to ward off the effect of "unhealthy places" (1: 456–7). He does not explain this prescription, but perhaps thought that the stimulating principles of coffee would counteract the "lassitude" and "idleness" produced by the "enervating effect of the climate" (*Narrative* 1: 371). The fever was believed to strike more readily those who succumbed to this "enervating effect." Allen and Thomson retrospectively suggest that such measures were futile, for the "climate gave rise to an indescribable languor and want of nervous energy, under which the strongest constitution must have yielded" (2: 165). Even when fortified by coffee, neither masculine vigor nor moral rectitude could resist the "enervating effect of the climate" and the deadly fever. Most of the English members of the expedition succumbed, and many eventually died. Gradually incapacitating and killing officers and men, the fever effectively vanquished the entire philanthropic scheme. One by one, the ships descended the Niger, full of sick and dying seamen. The model farm struggled on for a year, staffed by Africans brought from Sierra Leone and indigenous workers, but it was then abandoned.

A story intended to conclude with the triumphant cultivation of African nature and culture instead culminates with the deterioration and death of English men and a chaotic retreat from the site of their dreams. The African Civilization Society particularly hoped to encourage the growth of cotton, which might supply British textile mills with an alternative to the American slave-grown variety. Unfortunately, the cotton seed brought from home failed to grow, perhaps, as Temperley speculates, because it "had been damaged on the way out from England or because it was unsuited to African conditions" (156). The 1841 expedition finds its appropriate symbol not in a thriving model farm, a brave outpost of agricultural progress and cultural enlightenment, but in these dead seeds, planted only to rot in the "soil of Africa." Those seeds correspond to the many English bodies interred along the banks of the river (sometimes adjacent to the graves of those who had died on previous expeditions). Funeral rites were hastily performed since, as Allen and Thomson recall, "decomposition was rapidly going on" (1: 341). Rather than initiating the cultivation of the dark continent, the expedition only supplied more "animal and vegetable matter" for the Niger to brew into more "miasmatous poison." Perhaps as a warning to the next wave of optimistic English explorers, the sailors of the 1841 expedition dubbed the entrance to the Niger the "Gate of the Cemetery" (2: 328).

In his review, Dickens fixes on this grim metaphor as a perfect expression of the futility and waste of the overseas mission. His short article is broadly valuable as a vivid expression of mid-Victorian resistence to humanitarian colonialism. More specifically, it provides crucial insight into the origin of central patterns of imagery and metaphor in *Bleak House* and sheds further light on the process through which Victorian novelists produced the satiric discourse of domestic autoethnography. It begins to document how Dickens selectively extracts from ethnographic source material certain images of African nature and certain conceptions of English masculine heroism. It certainly begins to express his contempt for the philanthropic agents that he believed had staged a highly unequal conflict between the two. In his review, Dickens shapes the 1841 expedition into a colonial tragedy in which English men conduct a heroic but doomed campaign against African nature, "an enemy," as he calls it, "against which no gallantry can contend" (531).

As in *Bleak House*, Dickens holds female philanthropists to blame for this tragedy. Echoing *Macbeth*, the review begins with a disparaging portrait of "weird old women who go about, and exceedingly round-about, on the Exeter Hall platform" (531). The 1841 expedition was largely planned, of course, by the male organizers of the African Civilization Society, principally Buxton and his colleague Stephen Lushington, and government officials such as Colonial Secretary John Russell. Dickens does later identify these men, which makes it all the more striking that he first directs scornful attention to anonymous female philanthropists.[5] To Dickens, these unnamed predecessors of Mrs Jellyby are "weird" in multiple senses. The witches of Exeter Hall are more culpable in relation to fate (the Old English term for which, *wyrd*, represents the root of weird) than their counterparts in *Macbeth*, for they do not simply foresee the fate of the colonizers they send to Africa. They actually determine fate by cooking up the notion of the overseas mission. Their philanthropic concern is also weird in that it ignores proximate locations in favor of the exotic and outlandish world of the Niger delta. The First Folio edition of *Macbeth* twice spells the word *weyward* (I. iii. 33 and II. i. 20). Shakespeare seems to have associated weirdness with waywardness, and Dickens's condemnation of wayward philanthropy extends the connection.[6] The fact that female philanthropists occupy a public forum and engage themselves in colonial affairs indicates an additional source of weirdness, a strange distortion of feminine identity and duty.[7]

African nature functions as the engine of fate set in motion by the weird sisters of Exeter Hall. Turning a blind eye to the many passages of the *Narrative* that praise the delta for its picturesque beauty and fertility, Dickens only reproduces impressions of its threatening malignancy. He instinctively reviles African authority figures such as King Boy and King

Obi, but, in relation to the "fatal Niger," they play a passive role, deceptively agreeing to end the slave trade in their dominions while knowing that the climate will obviate the need to act upon treaties (533). "Can it be supposed," Dickens wonders,

> that on this earth there lives a man who better knows than Obi, leering round upon the river's banks, the dull dead mangrove trees, the slimy and decaying earth, the rotting vegetation, that these are shadowy promises and shadowy threats, which he may give to the hot winds? In any breast in the white group about him, is there a dark presentiment of death (the pestilential air is heavier already with such whispers, to some noble hearts) half so certain as this savage's foreknowledge of the fate fast closing in? (533)

Dickens, who later confesses a "painful interest" in the fever which "wrought such terrible desolation," appropriates the language with which McWilliam and his colleagues explain the evolution of malaria (533). In his scripting of the colonial tragedy, the nature of the Niger delta – the "slimy and decaying earth," the "rotting vegetation," the "pestilential air" – plays the role of a malignant and impersonal antagonist empowered to destroy men who collectively represent British masculine heroism.

The certainty of their doom intensifies the exasperation with which Dickens retrospectively views their story. The venture has proven once again that "all the white armies and white missionaries of the world would fall, as withered reeds, before the rolling of one African river" (533). Dickens is acutely sensitive to the implications of racial differences in relation to susceptibility to the fever. He sarcastically doubts whether African rulers have learned "respect for the British force" by witnessing "our perfect impotency in opposition to their climate, their falsehood, and deceit" (my italics, 531). An element of psycho-sexual frustration and embarrassment surfaces within the tragedy suffered by the male colonists and vicariously borne by Dickens. Rather than vigorously penetrating the dark continent, cultivating its soil and reforming its culture, the "British force" has pathetically withered. The seeds it has managed to plant have not prospered in the strange and hostile environment. Its heroic agents have been forced to display "perfect impotency" before the bemused gaze of African "potentates" (531). The vituperative energy with which Dickens conducts his satiric attack on African male authority figures suggests a rhetorical campaign to defend and recoup "British force."

Dickens discovers a source of redemptive consolation in the strength and resolve with which certain members of the expedition uphold the ideals of British masculine heroism. He particularly celebrates Dr McWilliam and his colleague Dr Stanger, who together guided one of the ships down the Niger when all their comrades were incapacitated by fever. Keen to offset the record of humiliating "impotency," he praises the "quiet courage and unflinching constancy of purpose" exemplified by the doctors, who to his mind deserve "memorable and honoured" places in the "history of truly heroic enterprise" (533). The fact that their compassionate heroism serves the interest of their white comrades rather than the hopelessly dark continent further redeems them for history. The review ends with another, broader gesture to British masculine virtue and heroism. Deploring the expedition itself, he nevertheless eulogizes with "a glow of admiration and sympathy" the officers and men who "sacrificed themselves to achieve its unattainable objects" (533). Their distant graves, he concludes, are "not to be ungratefully remembered, or lightly forgotten" (533).

The Africanization of public and private England

Bleak House, a novel that depicts a land immersed in rain, fog, and mud, that narrates efforts undertaken by valiant and compassionate characters to extend humanitarian relief within a strange and desolate region, and that returns obsessively to the "Gate of the Cemetery" where one selfless hero lies buried, proves that Dickens himself did not lightly forget. The setting of indomitable nature, tragic death, and heroic resolve has shifted, of course, from Africa to London. In response to the misplaced concern of the foreign mission, Dickens projects imagery and themes extracted from accounts of the 1841 Niger expedition onto the imperial metropolis. In his review of Allen and Thomson's *Narrative*, he briefly forecasts the irony that *Bleak House* develops at length. After reviewing the "short list" of the expedition's objectives, including the abolition of slavery and human sacrifice, an "improved system of agricultural cultivation," and the "diffusion among those Pagans of the true doctrines of Christianity," Dickens faults the African Civilization Society for hypocrisy as well as naive ambition (532). In a satiric aside, he takes a "retrospective glance at the great number of generations during which they have all been comfortably settled in our own civilized land" (532). Believing that measures of civilization remain highly unsettled in England itself, Dickens insists, in language that anticipates Esther's formula, that "[g]ently and imperceptibly the widening circle of enlightenment must stretch and stretch, from man to man, from people on to people. ... [N]o convulsive effort, or far-off aim, can make the last great outer circle first, and then come home at leisure to trace out the inner one ... [T]he work at home must be completed thoroughly, or there is no hope abroad" (533). By splicing the "sad story" of the Niger expedition into his domestic plot, Dickens illustrates the extent and importance of the civilizing work that remains to be done within the borders of the imperial nation (533).[8]

Mrs Jellyby, of course, expends her reform energy on a vain and "convulsive" effort to enlighten the dark continent. Early in the novel she announces that she and her cohorts "hope by this time next year to have from a hundred and fifty to two hundred healthy families cultivating coffee and educating the natives of Borrioboola-Gha, on the left bank of the Niger" (86). The few details the novel includes about this colonial scheme suggest a comic exaggeration of the 1841 expedition. While Buxton hoped to reduce mortality to an acceptable level, Mrs Jellyby hyperbolically proclaims that the Niger offers the "finest climate in the world!" (86). The members of the 1841 expedition failed to make inroads against the slave trade, but their novelistic counterparts are themselves nearly enslaved. Esther eventually reports that the colony utterly fails "in consequence of the king of Borrioboola wanting to sell everybody – who survived the climate – for Rum" (933).

The tragic end of Borrioboola-Gha indicates one disastrous effect of misplaced concern, but the novel focuses almost exclusively on unaccomplished work and unalleviated suffering at home. The inhabitants of London need not travel to the "left bank of the Niger" to experience the manifold discomforts and dangers imposed by ominous weather, for the "heavy fogs" and "smokes" and "dense vapour" noted by Allen and Thomson have drifted inconveniently northward. *Bleak House* begins with the memorable portrait of the imperial metropolis enveloped in "smoke" and "dense fog" (49–50). The mud of the African riverbank has also intruded upon the scene, and as a result the inhabitants of London find it nearly impossible to find "firm footing." Pedestrians continue to lose "their foot-hold at street corners, where tens of thousands of other foot passengers have been slipping and sliding since the day broke" (49). The mud that has encroached upon the metropolis indicates that civilization itself maintains a precarious balance. In *The Examiner*, Dickens characterizes African nature as malignant decay; he imagines with distaste its "slimy and decaying earth" and "rotting vegetation" (533). In *Bleak House*, this malignant nature has begun to deteriorate and overwhelm the monuments of civilized life. The "decaying earth" of

Africa becomes the "decaying houses" of England; the pavements and roads disappear beneath "crust upon crust of mud" (51, 49).

This picture of London indicates a perilous slide from familiar English city into strange Niger swamp. When Snagsby walks through Tom-all-Alone's, the novel's representative urban slum, Dickens emphasizes the unfamiliarity of the terrain. He walks along "a villainous street, undrained, unventilated, deep in black mud and corrupt water ... and reeking with such smells and sights that he, who has lived in London all his life, can scarce believe his senses" (364). The novel diagnoses the condition of England as a geographical paradox, a puzzling confusion of strange African nature and familiar urban civilization.

Just as it does in Africa, the "peculiar condition of the atmosphere" gives rise to disease in England. Dickens's references to the fever that infects several characters and kills some recalls the description of the Niger malaria that Dr McWilliam attributes to "pestilential gaseous emanations" or "miasmatous poison" produced by the "decomposition of animal and vegetable matter." Dickens describes Africa as a "pestilential land" in *The Examiner* (533). In *Bleak House*, however, it is London where "pestillential [sic] gas" rises from the muddy land to poison and sicken (683). The pestilence that has invaded the English metropolis functions both figuratively and literally. Figuratively, it identifies problems within the social rather than the natural climate. In the opening paragraph, Dickens notes that the mud and fog has engendered a "general infection of ill temper" (49). It is notably the "most pestilent" Court of Chancery that occupies a position "at the very heart of the fog" (50). John Jarndyce discerns a "subtle poison" in the court that "breed[s] ... diseases" and "communicates some portion of its rottenness to everything" (547–8). This connection is highly ironic because many perceived the nation's legal framework as a bulwark of civilization and indeed a justification for empire. In 1853, Gladstone proclaimed "that if it please Providence to create openings for us in the broad fields of distant continents, we shall ... reproduce the copy of those laws and institutions, those habits and national characteristics, which have made England so famous as she is" (qtd. in Warren 60). In *Bleak House*, English "laws and institutions" are themselves responsible for confusing distinctions between London and the distant Niger delta. According to McWilliam, the miasma of Africa exerts an "insidious influence," secretly laying hold of its victims, mysteriously communicating decomposition and decay from the soil of Africa to the bodies of explorers (80).[9] In Dickens's London, Chancery exerts a similarly insidious influence, infecting and corrupting the whole social body.

Mud, fog, and pestilence also function quite literally, however. *Bleak House* condemns the court of Chancery for exposing the bodies of individual civilians to the wear and tear of natural forces. The houses in Tom-all-Alone's cannot be improved because they are locked up in a Chancery suit. As a result, they routinely collapse, depriving some of life and sending others into the street. Even within the purported "heart of a civilized world," these unfortunate outcasts maintain precarious and barbaric existences. They live in the state of nature in which, as Hobbes (1651) described it, human life is "solitary, poor, nasty, brutish, and short" (84). By failing to protect its subjects from the ravages of nature, the imperial state sacrifices the superiority it holds in relation to sites of savage darkness such as the Niger delta.

In Africa, the "Gate of the Cemetery" marks the entrance to the "fatal Niger." In London, it marks the entrance to a site of uncanny intensity where African forms of fatality arise and disperse within the civilized nation. Dickens identifies the "pestiferous and obscene" graveyard where Captain Hawdon is buried as a particularly unhealthy spot (202). Like the English corpses buried on the banks of the Niger, planted only to rot and breed more disease, Hawdon is "sow[n] ... in corruption, to be raised in corruption" (202). The "poisoned air" that exhales from his grave "deposits its witch-ointment" on the "iron gate" at which both Jo and Lady Deadlock in turn catch the fever that kills them and infects others (203). The narrator appreciates the extent to which the graveyard illustrates the fragility of the distinction between imperial nation and colonial periphery. "Into a beastly scrap of ground which a Turk would reject as a savage abomination, and a Caffre would shudder at," he exclaims, "they bring our dear brother here departed, to receive Christian burial" (202). Although Hawdon is enfolded within the rhetorical embrace of Christian kinship, his corpse receives treatment that even representative heathen would themselves recognize as "a savage abomination." The narrator concludes that the graveyard will provide "a shameful testimony to future ages, how civilization and barbarism walked this boastful island together" (202).[10] The national religion here joins the rank of those civil institutions (the law, philanthropy) already denounced for either actively cultivating or failing to counteract the conditions of barbaric life. Dickens suggests that English civilization will only be able to disentangle itself from barbarism when it discovers how to fulfill the ethical obligations of Christian kinship.

More than any other character, Jo suffers the lot of those who inhabit the intermediary zone between civilization and barbarism. Dickens makes him the subject of several indignant diatribes against those who misdirect compassion to Africa or other tropical locales. At one point, the narrator compares the "genuine foreign-grown savage" to Jo, the "ordinary home-made article," whom he describes as

> dirty, ugly, disagreeable to all the senses, in body a common creature of the common streets, only in soul a heathen. Homely filth begrimes him, homely parasites devour him, homely sores are in him, homely rags are on him: native ignorance, the growth of English soil and climate, sinks his immortal nature lower than the beasts that perish. (696)

In *The Examiner*, Dickens claims that "between the civilized European and the barbarous African, there is a great gulf set" (533). In the novel, however, the example of Jo leads the narrator to wonder about people who "from opposite sides of great gulfs, have, nevertheless, been very curiously brought together" (272). This question applies most directly to the great gulf of class. Both Jo and Lady Deadlock die from a fever that curiously illustrates their common humanity. It also acknowledges an irony much more distasteful to Dickens, that miserable conditions in England bridge the great gulf of race and culture.[11] On his expedition through the slum that has produced Jo, Snagsby confronts "streets and courts so infamous that [he] sickens in body and mind, and feels as if he were going, every moment deeper down, into the infernal gulf" (364). Himself committed to an ideology of clear-cut racial distinctions, Dickens can appreciate the vertiginous sickening induced by the confrontation of conditions that confuse them. Snagsby plummets into a region that is horribly both familiar civilized English home and strange barbaric Africa.

Jo's life and death in London symbolically enact an uneven conflict between the neglected and outcast English subject and pestilential nature of the Niger delta. Working as a voluntary street-sweeper, Jo tries to "keep the mud off the crossing," but his effort to defend the intersection of civilized transport from "slimy and decaying earth" goes unnoticed and unpaid (272). Until it is too late, no one bothers to help Jo clean the "homely filth" that has encroached on his own body. By the end of his life, his clothes have come to look "like bundle of rank leaves of swampy growth, that rotted long ago" (686). The simile recalls the "rotting vegetation" of Africa that Dickens considers with such disgust in *The Examiner*. While the plight of exotic inhabitants of the Niger delta captures the interest and compassion of the African Civilization Society, the "common creature" on the streets at home degenerates into the condition of exotic otherness.

Having been infected by disease at the "pestiferous" graveyard where Hawdon is buried, Jo is forced to wander through African England. The homely savagery of his existence indicates the extent to which metropolitan society has willfully abandoned the religious and ethical principles that presumably distinguish England from Africa. Allen and Thomson describe an excursion in a "pestiferous locality" governed by King Obi on which they are distressed to discover in "a small court-yard" a "boy with a ring round his neck, to which a chain was attached and fastened to the hut" (1: 249). They fear that the boy has been reserved for a human sacrifice; sometimes, they report, such "poor creatures" are "dreadfully mutilated, and left to linger until death terminates their sufferings" (1: 249). Although England boastfully proclaims its fidelity to principles such as Christian charity, individual liberty, and the sanctity of human life, Dickens suggests that outcasts such as Jo suffer a similar fate. Hounded by constables who force him to "move on," Jo is as much oppressed by "freedom" as his African counterpart is by chains (319). Although he lives in a Christian culture, he is nonetheless sacrificed to the strange god of neglect and indifference. Unable to read the signs invested with the presumed superiority of his nation, Jo looks upon the cross on the top of St Paul's Cathedral not as "sacred emblem" but rather as the "crowning confusion of the great, confused city" (326). The fact of his religious illiteracy also demonstrates the confusion of England and Africa within the imperial metropolis.

Many Victorian writers and social critics who sought to challenge the presumed distinctions of imperial rhetoric gesture to the predicament of working-class poverty and the condition of urban public space. Dickens was among the smaller group who additionally discover forms of savagery or barbarism within the private world of middle-class domesticity. If he accuses the institution of overseas philanthropy for neglecting homely savages, he blames middle-class women for making them. The portrait of Mrs Jellyby is based on Mrs Caroline Chisholm, founder of the Family Colonization Loan Society, an organization that sponsored emigration to Australia.[12] Dickens endorses her association in *Household Words* (30 Mar. 1850), but privately he blames her for neglecting her children. "I dream of Mrs Chisholm, and her housekeeping," he confesses in a letter; "[t]he dirty faces of her children are my continual companions" (*Letters* 6: 53). Dickens is haunted, significantly, by the darkened and discolored faces of middle-class English children. His nightmare reflects a pervasive association, already demonstrated by the passage from *Sybil* and descriptions of Jo, between dirt and racial difference, especially the difference of African skin.[13] By switching the site of the middle-class woman's colonial scheme from Australia to Africa, Dickens tightens the ironic connection between neglected domestic duties and racial "confusion" in the imperial metropolis. Homely filth produces "home-made" savages in the middle-class home as well as on the industrial landscape and streets of the slum.

Dickens satirizes Mrs Jellyby with a pattern of metaphors that carefully responds to the location of her misplaced concern. Neglecting her household duties by spending all of her time on the project designed to "cultivate" Africans, Mrs Jellyby ironically transforms her home into wilderness, her family into oppressed savages, reproducing in her English domestic sphere the very conditions she claims to redress in the Niger delta. Esther describes Mr Jellyby as a "mild bald gentleman" who "seemed passively to submit himself to Borrioboola-Gha, but not to be actively interested in that settlement. As he never spoke a word, he might have been a native, but for his complexion" (89). Dickens attributes the appearance of the passive "native" at home to Mrs Jellyby's inversion of normative sexual power relations and refusal to respect gendered spheres of activity. Overwhelmed by his domineering wife, Mr Jellyby, throughout the novel an object of sympathy, can only "passively ... submit himself" to her distant project. The points at which Mrs Jellyby diverges most egregiously from the meek and dutiful housewife become chinks in the barrier between forms of distant savagery and the English domestic sphere.

Caddy Jellyby, forced to labor as a secretary, suffers from her mother's despotism rather than her indifference. She, too, acquires a "complexion" suggestive of racial difference. Esther finds her, after a day of generating Borrioboola-Gha correspondence, attempting to remove the "ink stains on her face" (92).[14] Caddy herself provides a context in which to understand her symbolically discolored skin. "Talk of Africa!" she exclaims, "I couldn't be worse off if I was a what's-his-name – man and a brother" (236). Referring to the abolitionist emblem depicting a shackled African who asks "Am I not a man and a brother?" Caddy suggests that her mother creates slaves at home as well as supplying them to the sinister king of Borrioboola-Gha.[15] Unlike her father, the passive "native," she determines to revolt. Remembering the appropriate name for her oppressed condition, she declares, "I won't be a slave all my life" (238). Caddy rebels against treatment that, according to Dickens, negates the difference between her and the objects of her mother's philanthropic concern. Catherine Gallagher (1985) demonstrates that when Caddy refers to herself as a "slave" she appropriates a trope often used by critics of industrialism to focus attention on the "white" slaves, the disenfranchised workers of England's factories (4). Dickens claims in a letter (20 Dec. 1852) that "Mrs Jellyby gives offense merely because the word 'Africa', is unfortunately associated with her wild Hobby. No kind of reference to slavery is made or intended, in that connexion" (*Letters* VI: 825). In *Bleak House*, it is true, he does not directly satirize the abolitionist agenda of the 1841 Expedition, and in other contexts he passionately opposes the institution of slavery.[16] Caddy's metaphors nevertheless suggest that Dickens is being somewhat disingenuous in his letter. In the novel he adopts the same rhetorical practice used by critics of industrial exploitation, although he documents abuses that transform the middle-class girl, rather than the industrial laborer, into a slave. The domineering woman who claims the authority to establish civilization in distant Africa ironically converts members of her own family into passive and rebellious African "natives."

An analogous pattern of metaphors further indicates that middle-class women who promote overseas philanthropy compromise the distinction between civilization and savagery among their own English children. Mr Jellyby describes his offspring as "Wild Indians" and concludes that "the best thing that could happen to them was, their being all Tomahawked together" (472). When pressed by Esther to interpret this nihilistic despair, Caddy Jellyby translates her father's comment to mean simply that her siblings "are very unfortunate in being Ma's children" (472). While Mrs Jellyby neglects her young in order to devote herself fully to Borrioboola-Gha, Mrs Pardiggle takes the reverse approach, bullying her children to participate in all of her philanthropic schemes. Notably, she achieves the same result as her colleague. As Mrs Pardiggle recites the "contributions" she has exacted from her children, Esther notices that the children grow "absolutely ferocious with discontent. At the mention of the Tockahoopo Indians, I could really have supposed Egbert to be one of the most baleful members of that tribe, he gave me such a savage frown. The face of each child, as the amount of his contribution was mentioned, darkened in a peculiarly vindictive manner" (151). An illustration on the cover of the monthly numbers of *Bleak House* shows a white woman protectively enfolding two African children in her arms. While this illustration does not refer to any episode in the plot, it functions as another jibe against women who promote overseas missions and thus supposedly care more for dark and distant children than for their own fair offspring.[17] Throughout *Bleak House*, Dickens indicates that such women exacerbate the problem of intermingled civilization and barbarism at home by producing savage English children whose faces are "darkened" by dirt and anger.

Gendered missions

The novel's exasperation with forms of "home-made" savagery generates a satiric momentum that carries the attack on overseas philanthropy into a broader ideological arena. In the letter to Christopherson, Dickens discredits overseas philanthropy, but does not explicitly object to other varieties of imperial power – military conquest, political control, or economic domination – wielded by the "great commercial country holding communication with all parts of the world." The note of irony in that grandiose phrase does hint at a buried fault line, however, one which becomes more visible at one striking point in the novel. Surveying Tom-all-Alone's, the narrator suggests that "in truth it might be better for the national glory even that the sun should sometimes set upon the British dominions, than that it should ever rise upon so vile a wonder as Tom" (683). Confronting the extent of "home-made" savagery in London, the narrator questions the measure of England's imperial power that the commissioners of the 1841 expedition uncritically endorsed. Intending to impress African kings with whom they sought to negotiate, they declare that the "Queen of England ... is very powerful; so much so, that the sun never sets upon her dominions" (*Narrative* 1: 299). Although Borrioboola-Gha seems to be an entirely private concern, and thus technically would not strengthen the boast, the narrator nonetheless indicates a conflict between the extent and power of the British empire and the reform of conditions that have produced the most visible and egregious forms of barbarism at home. Lillian Nayder (1992) claims, perhaps responding to the passage quoted above, that "in *Bleak House*, Dickens holds the imperial mission partly accountable for the failure of social reform in England" (691). It is important to note, however, that the relatively restrained tone of the passage, so unlike the scathing invective that characterizes the novel's denunciation of overseas philanthropy, reflects hesitancy. The narrator considers what perhaps "might be better" and submits that the sun should "sometimes set" upon British dominions. Such careful expressions of doubt reveal a lingering commitment to empire that ultimately weathers the rejection of "pretence[s] afar off for leaving evil things at hand alone" (696).

Dickens devises a domestic policy intended to correct the ideological disorder he associates with the 1841 Niger Expedition and its fictional counterpart, Borrioboola-Gha. By redirecting compassionate reform impulses to the imperial nation, he attempts to retrieve London from its slide into the abyss between civilized England and barbaric Africa. By affirming conventional middle-class distinctions between female and male spheres of responsibility, he seeks to rectify the pernicious example set by those "weird old women" who have commandeered male authority and misled the nation. Those two initiatives hold the promise, at least, of recapturing English civilization and justifying imperial sovereignty.

Dickens uses Esther to illustrate the efficacy of his approved model of female reform, a "civilizing mission" in which order, cleanliness, and enlightenment expands incrementally through the agency of a middle-class woman. She gradually and naturally radiates the values and condition of civilization, like the "summer sun" to which her surname refers. Although Esther functions in the novel as a domesticator, one who brings certain of the English savages she encounters within the fold of civilization, Dickens describes her method as natural. Her mode of influence, that is, represents the "natural" one for middle-class women. Deeply involved in the cultural machinery of societies, committee meetings, and ever-circulating documents, Mrs Jellyby adopts an "unnatural" way for a woman to extend her influence, ironically ensuring that the household over which she presides returns steadily to nature.

Esther first proves her ability to reverse the professional woman's disastrous effect in the Jellyby household, in which the distinction between British home and Niger delta is as precarious as on the streets of the slum. "[T]he rooms," as she notes, "had such a marshy smell" (87). Misplaced, misused, and broken objects signify a general disregard for the implements that mark the advances and enable the comforts of civilized domesticity. The drunken "cook" even fails to ensure that food enters the realm of culture. The roast beef would have made "an excellent dinner, if it had had any cooking to speak of, but it was almost raw" (88). Although at first somewhat discomposed by these conditions, Esther soon begins to fight back the primitive darkness by establishing fundamental comforts of civilization, "coaxing a very cross fire that had been lighted, to burn; which at last it did, quite brightly" (90). Recognizing her friend's aptitude, Ada claims that Esther "would make a home out of even this house" (90). Her stay in the Jellyby wilderness is brief, however, and she can only make a temporary impact on the "waste and ruin" she encounters within its walls (476).

Her influence on the Jellyby children demonstrates her talent for bringing the "home-made" savages of the middle-class domestic sphere into the fold of civilization. While Mrs Jellyby sketches plans for the general "cultivation of the coffee berry – *and* the natives" of Borriboola-Gha, Esther reads stories to her children and, significantly, washes Peepy (82). When Esther awakes after her first night in the Jellyby household, she opens her eyes "to encounter those of a dirty-faced little spectre" (94). This fictional embodiment of the Chisholm children, whose dirty faces haunt Dickens, seeks out the woman who washes away the filth that obscures the difference between the "complexion" of the English boy and the child of Borrioboola-Gha. Esther achieves a more lasting accomplishment by transforming Caddy from a sullen and disempowered "slave" into a competent middle-class wife (476). In *The Examiner*, Dickens mocks the Niger Expedition's impossible objectives, among the most naive of which he finds the intention to substitute "free for Slave labour" (532). By focusing her attention on a single middle-class English woman, Esther actually achieves the goal represented by Dickens as insanely ambitious when applied to distant Africa. Caddy suffers, he suggests, not only because she endures oppressive labor, but also because that labor supplants an education in the skills of middle-class domesticity. As Caddy complains to Esther, "I can't do anything hardly, except write" (93). At first, Caddy can only vent her frustration by exclaiming bitterly "I wish Africa was dead!" (92). Esther helps her to overcome this rebellious anger, the response of an embittered "slave." She "soften[s] poor Caroline" over the course of their first meeting and continues, throughout the novel, to perform the modified civilizing mission of facilitating her transition into a position at least approximating that of the middle-class housewife (114).[18] While Mrs Jellyby's treatment of her daughter gives slavery a foothold in the nation, Esther works to "liberate" Caddy into the role of affectionate and dutiful wife and mother.

The forms of savagery that Esther encounters in the Jellyby wilderness provide her with a reform project located within the circle of her concerns as constituted by Dickens. The middle-class woman's proper civilizing mission, he suggests, consists of performing and imparting the duties that sustain the middle-class English domestic sphere and thus preserve distinctions between "home" and Borrioboola-Gha. Although the figure of the gradually expanding circle suggests the potential for incrementally extending "civilization" beyond that sphere, Dickens remains suspicious of projects in which middle-class women attempt to carry the torch too far.

The episode in the brickmaker's house tests the extent of the middle-class woman's civilizing influence. Compelled to accompany Mrs Pardiggle on her philanthropic expedition, Esther and Ada encounter a world even more foreign and violent than the mismanaged Jellyby household. The drunken brickmaker, himself "all stained with clay and mud," proudly owns responsibility for his wife's "black eye" (156).

Filth and bruises discolor the skin of the working-class characters, revealing further types of "darkened" British savages in need of reform. Mrs Pardiggle of course entirely fails to enlighten them, sacrificing what effect she might have by adopting the combative authority of the "inexorable moral policeman" (158). Although Esther continues to feel that she has overstepped the outer limit of her "circle of duty," she and Ada have somewhat better success. When Mrs Pardiggle retreats, they stay behind to ask Jenny, the bruised mother, if her baby is ill. The baby in fact dies at just this moment, but Ada's naive compassion produces a response that Mrs Pardiggle fails to achieve. "Such compassion, such gentleness," reflects Esther, "might have softened any mother's heart" (160). The same verb that conveys Esther's effect on Caddy recurs as Dickens suggests that the middle-class woman's moral influence relies on conventionally female emotions as well as duties. Here, Ada's spontaneous expression of sympathy partly bridges the divide between classes and creates a channel for civilizing enlightenment. While Mrs Pardiggle's Evangelical lesson produces only hostility, Esther and Ada gently whisper to Jenny "what Our Savior said of children" (160). By repudiating Mrs Pardiggle's "businesslike and systematic" philanthropy, they advance civilization a tiny step into the dark places of working-class life (156).[19]

The civilizing influence of the middle-class woman is severely curtailed on this foreign ground. The glimmer of light that Esther and Ada bring to the benighted home only momentarily comforts Jenny and has no lasting effect on the muddy family. Although the brickmaker's family represents a much more legitimate concern than the natives of Borrioboola-Gha, Dickens remains highly skeptical about the viability of missionary forays conducted by middle-class women beyond the "inner circle" of the middle-class domestic sphere. Indeed, Esther articulates the intention to devote herself to "those immediately about [her]," the procedure for reform offered as the sharpest alternative to Mrs Jellyby's "telescopic philanthropy," as an argument against accompanying Mrs Pardiggle to the brickmaker's.

If *Bleak House* represents foreign missions – exemplified most clearly by projects designed to "cultivate" the "natives" of Borrioboola-Gha – as potentially disastrous distractions for the middle-class woman, the novel does not categorically reject all "telescopic" projects. In fact, exceptions to the procedure endorsed by Esther, that "it is right to begin with the obligations of home," quietly emerge throughout the novel. If Mrs Jellyby and Mrs Pardiggle, at their worst, compound the confusion of England and Africa, certain other characters help to repair that distinction, apparently by reapplying the skills they have acquired in imperial outposts to social problems encountered on their return.

Mrs Bagnet marks one important exception to the rule that pits "far-off aims" against the woman's "work at home." Just as her kitchen utensils, which "have done duty in several parts of the world," prove equally useful in London, the traits Mrs Bagnet acquires as wife of a soldier of empire serve her well when attending to the spiritual and physical well-being of her household (442). She says grace "like a military chaplain" and develops "an exact system" for apportioning food with "the kit of the mess" (442). An act of charity she performs also reflects the utility of experience gained in distant dominions. Famous for the ease with which she accomplishes arduous journeys, Mrs Bagnet sets off at a moment's notice to find George's mother. She returns to London with Mrs Rouncewell, herself appearing "quite fresh and collected – as she would be, if her next point, with no new equipage and outfit, were the Cape of Good Hope, the Island of Ascension, Hong Kong, or any other military station" (805). If Esther brings home civilizing compassion, Mrs Bagnet fulfills the "obligations of home" with military efficiency. Because Mrs Bagnet occupies a position on an upper rung of the working class, Dickens can applaud her for adopting a conventionally male "military" bearing that he would likely represent as an unnatural distortion of middle-class femininity. Her exception is further explained by the fact that the distant activities with which she is associated connote force and control rather than philanthropy and vulnerability. By successfully integrating the "telescopic" military duties of empire, Mrs Bagnet begins to reveal Dickens's effort to distinguish between the "foreign mission" and other apparently less objectionable demonstrations of imperial power.

A productive coalition between imperial military service and the work at home emerges with still greater clarity in the depiction of heroic male characters who work to enlighten and alleviate the suffering of "darkened" characters they encounter in "the great wilderness of London" (718). Woodcourt and George Rouncewell both return from imperial adventure and military service equipped to reform savagery at home. Their careers reveal another way in which Dickens seeks imaginative compensation for the tragic deployment of English male heros against the "fatal Niger." In *The Examiner*, he bemoans the fact that the "useful lives of scholars, students, mariners, and officers – more precious than a wilderness of Africans – were thrown away!" (533). He attempts to reverse the formula in *Bleak House*, depicting a scenario in which "useful" men return safely from the colonial periphery and then undertake to aid the natives of the imperial metropolis rather than their relatively worthless counterparts in Africa. As Woodcourt and Rouncewell conduct small-scale civilizing missions in the slum, imperial experience both permeates their charity and reinforces their masculinity. Their compassionate heroism serves to reclaim the legitimacy of imperial dominions that is called into question by the Africanization of London.

The representation of Woodcourt particularly reveals an effort to preserve the variety of English masculine heroism vanquished by the "fatal Niger." Not a terribly compelling character, he acquires a degree more interest and complexity as a fictional descendant of the men on the Niger expedition whom Dickens characterizes as useful and heroic. As a ship surgeon, he shares the profession of doctors McWilliam and Stanger. Allan Woodcourt's name perhaps honors an assistant surgeon who died in Africa, James Woodhouse, as well as Commanders William Allen, co-author of the *Narrative*, and Bird Allen, who also perished on the expedition. Woodcourt establishes his heroism, furthermore, through an episode that aligns him with William Cook, the only civilian commissioner of the 1841 expedition. When Allen and Thomson introduce this figure to their readers, they note that "[t]his gentleman was honourably known to the public for his humane exertions in saving the lives of the crew of the 'Kent' Indiaman, burnt at sea" (1: 37). In the novel, Woodcourt similarly becomes honourably known through his involvement in a "terrible shipwreck over in those East-Indian seas" (555). "Through it all," as Miss Flite describes the adventure to Esther, "my dear physician was a hero. Calm and brave through everything. Saved many lives, never complained in hunger and thirst, wrapped naked people in his spare clothes, took the lead, showed them what to do, governed them, tended the sick, buried the dead, and brought the poor survivors off at last" (556). This list of "humane exertions" echoes the cadence of the tribute to McWilliam and Stanger in *The Examiner*, in which Dickens explains how the "former took charge of [the ship], the latter worked the engines, and, both persevering by day and night – through all the horrors of such a voyage, with their friends raving and dying around them ... brought her in safety to the sea" (533). Dickens patches Woodcourt together from bits and pieces of male heroism gleaned from the *Narrative* of the 1841 Expedition.

In the novel, Dickens attempts to revise the colonial tragedy, in which the Niger extinguishes the useful "gallantry" of men such as Woodhouse. The "gallant deeds" performed by Woodcourt serve to prepare him for more useful and humane service at home (556). As in many Victorian imperial adventure novels for boys, the hero of *Bleak House* discovers his authority, his "intrepidity and humanity," when tested by extreme circumstances in tropical locales (675). In this novel, however, the adventure abroad functions as a preamble to the civilizing mission in the "great wilderness" of London.[20] Immediately after the narrative hesitantly indicates a conflict between empire and social reform, it finds a resolution in the description of Woodcourt walking through the heart of urban darkness:

> A brown sunburnt gentleman, who appears in some inaptitude for sleep to be wandering abroad rather than counting the hours on a restless pillow, strolls hitherward at this quiet time. Attracted by curiosity, he often pauses and looks about him, up and down the miserable by-ways. Nor is he merely curious, for in his bright dark eye there is compassionate interest; and as he looks here and there, he seems to understand such wretchedness, and to have studied it before. (683–4)

Dickens at first identifies Woodcourt only as "a brown sunburnt gentleman." The physical trace of the doctor's recent imperial tour significantly emerges as he makes this philanthropic excursion through the London slum. The reference to the sign of experience gained "afar off" provides an initial indication of the utility of male involvement in empire to the reform of domestic social problems. When Woodcourt "seems half inclined for another voyage," Jarndyce observes that to let him leave England again would be "like casting such a man away" (743). Once his authority is established, further adventures on the imperial periphery would waste a resource needed at the center.[21]

Just as the Jellyby household offers a domestic wilderness for Esther to civilize, the public streets of London supply Woodcourt with a terrain in which to exercise his "intrepidity and humanity" at home. Arguing that Dickens's heros are generally shadowed by the "fear that integrity of self is impossible in ... industrialized, urbanized society," Beth F. Herst (1990) perceives that this fear finds expression in the figure of the metropolitan wilderness. In *Bleak House*, echoes of the Niger expedition help to explain the paradox (6). The Niger delta, the region most hostile to the physical integrity of middle-class English men, corresponds to the urban and industrial society that threatens their social and psychological integrity. Richard Carstone, the alienated legal copier who dies beside his desk, a "wilderness marked with a rain of ink," provides one example of the metropolitan tragedy that Woodcourt strives to surmount with a compassionate heroism that engages him to society and preserves his integrity (188). Braving the "black mud" and "pestillential gas" of the Africanized English slum, he searches for destitute individuals in need of aid.[22] While Mrs Jellyby misdirects scarce resources to the "banks of the African rivers" (82), Woodcourt ministers to those he encounters "on the banks of the stagnant channel of mud which is the main street of Tom-all-Alone's" (684). Applying experience gained abroad, where he has seen wretchedness and "studied it before," he attempts to sooth the miseries he discovers while "wandering abroad" at home. Woodcourt assures Jenny, the brickmaker's wife, as he bandages her head, "I wouldn't hurt you for the world" (684). His cliché expresses a sentiment approved by Dickens, a compassion for the destitute British subject that seems to outweigh an acquisitive interest in "the world." The sentiment, however, obscures the fact that Woodcourt's imperial adventure serves as apprenticeship to the "work at home."

The alliance that Woodcourt and George Rouncewell form to care for Jo further reveals the impress of their imperial careers. The two men form a kind of impromptu military unit as they take responsibility for Jo's welfare. When Woodcourt brings Jo to the shooting gallery, the "trooper" detects the "air" of a sailor in the doctor; he mistakes him for a "regular blue-jacket" and, translating Woodcourt's class position into military authority, defers to him with a respectful "military salute" (693). George suggests, "in a martial sort of confidence, as if he were giving his opinion in a council of war," a plan for washing and clothing Jo (697). Traces of George's military experience, like Woodcourt's adventure, emerge as the narrative depicts a compassionate corrective to the indifference that has produced "savages" like Jo.

Dickens emphasizes that George and Woodcourt address those aspects of the outcast's miserable life that erode distinctions between the "home-made" and "genuine" savage. By washing and clothing Jo, they relieve him of the "homely" filth and "swampy" garments that reduce the English pauper to the condition of African otherness. Woodcourt buys him food and, significantly, coffee, belatedly administering an antidote to fever that is otherwise monopolized by Mrs Jellyby. He also redresses the spiritual neglect that has left Jo "in soul a heathen," teaching him the Lord's Prayer. Although Jo dies midway through the prayer, Dickens intimates that the last-minute missionary work smooths his spiritual progress. After Jo dies, the narrator announces that "light is come upon the dark benighted way" (705). Woodcourt thus follows the policy Dickens articulates in the letter to the Rev. Christopherson, bestowing his "energy on the making of good Christians at home."

The concern for Jo, of course, comes too late to bring him within the pale of civilized life. George's protection of "dirty-faced" Phil Squod represents a somewhat more successful and longer-lasting example of the civilizing work Dickens reserves for humane heroes. Another variety of "home-made" savage, Phil is discolored by a series of industrial accidents that leave him a crippled beggar. George discovers him, "blackened all over," hobbling down the street of a slum, and immediately adopts him as his general subaltern (404). The returned imperial soldier provides Phil with a healing sanctuary from the unfeeling world of industrial labor, which, having eroded distinctions between the native English subject and his African counterpart, abandons him to the streets. Phil expresses his loyalty by referring to George as "Governor" or, significantly, "Commander," a title that corresponds to Miss Flite's nickname for him, "General George" (693). The humble "trooper" never rises to a position of military authority. However, those touched by his kindness in London, recognizing the extent to which military training sustains the authority he does command in charitable matters, award him the commission he could not earn as a soldier of empire.

Imperial military service does not, of course, represent an absolute prerequisite for male altruism. John Jarndyce, to take the most notable exception, does not rely on imperial experience as he extends benevolent aid to those in need.[23] The link that does emerge between imperial military service and the compassionate duties performed by certain men in the public wilderness of London is significant not because it sets an unbroken pattern, but because it clarifies the ideological limits of the gradually expanding circle as it constructs an alternative intersection of empire and gender, one with its own set of contingencies and priorities. As Woodcourt and Rouncewell perform their civilizing duties in the public sphere, having gained experience on the "outer circle first" before returning home to maintain the "inner one," they enact a procedure for reform that simultaneously justifies the possession of distant "dominions" and defines a masculine type of compassionate philanthropy.

The relationship between empire and manliness is mutually constitutive. Just as Esther's intention to devote herself to "those immediately about [her]" reflects and reinforces her modest femininity, their association with the control of distant dominions reflects and reinforces their masculinity. The military vocabulary with which Dickens describes the civilizing care of Jo, for example, reminds readers that the same men who gently attend to him have also proven their courage and fortitude on distant colonial ground. Vestiges of imperial heroism prevent tenderness, that is, from compromising manliness. George's robust physique, like his philanthropic duty, advertises his previous career as a soldier of empire. While Woodcourt remains physically rather indistinct, imperial adventure endows him with a courageous fortitude that translates into sexual desirability. It is only when Esther hears of his valor in "those East-Indian seas" that she confesses her romantic interest in him. Feeling "such glowing exultation in his renown," she "so admired and loved what he had done; that [she] envied the storm-worn people who had fallen at his feet" (556). Esther significantly directs her erotic impulse to Woodcourt's heroic performance, "what he had done" on the periphery of empire, projecting her own passion onto the idolatrous gesture of the grateful survivors. Imperial adventure functions economically in the characterization of the male hero, constructing Woodcourt as a man equipped both to counteract domestic savagery and to fulfill the romantic desires of stay-at-home Esther.

Like Mrs Jellyby, Richard Carstone functions as a negative example within the domestic policy that links national reform to gendered responsibilities. Whereas her interests range too far from home, he fails because an obsession with the Chancery case prevents him from escaping the "inner circle" of the nation. He thus fails to acquire masculine authority by taking part in the control of distant dominions and lacks the "compassionate interest" that represents a crucial component of effective male heroism. Richard pitifully succumbs to the poisonous climate bred by Chancery and feeds the ruinous system with his cash and life.

Before he becomes too infected to imagine an escape from Chancery, Richard flirts with the careers that symbolize manliness and social utility for Dickens. He early professes a desire to go to sea, and expresses a superficial interest in medicine. Early in the novel, he impresses Ada with a reckless disregard for the suit:

> "I can go anywhere – go for a soldier if that's all, and never be missed. I would sell my best chance, if I could, on the shortest notice and the lowest terms."
> "And go abroad?" said Ada.
> "Yes!"
> "To India perhaps?"
> "Why, yes, I think so," returned Richard. (108)

Ada obligingly supplies Richard with an appropriate locale for imperial service, fashioning for him a fantasy of male adventure in an exotic colonial site.[24] He begins to balk, however, as she gives concrete shape to his bravado. The fact that he "return[s]" his hesitant acquiescence suggests the extent to which it is *her* fantasy, not his, and anticipates his inability to make good on his boast. Esther later visits Richard in the port town where he is stationed as an army officer, hoping to persuade him to escape Chancery by serving in Ireland. Richard, who has just resigned his commission, can only ask plaintively, "how could I have gone abroad?" (676). Woodcourt, who becomes a hero in "those East-Indian seas," and George, whose powerful body displays signs of his soldiering career, mark high points of moral and physical masculine development that Dickens associates with imperial military service. Richard, on the other hand, remains oddly "boyish" (675) to the end of his life, his sexual development and heroic potential arrested by the influence which, as Esther soon perceives, blights "all his manly qualities" (378).

Richard cannot himself withstand the moral and social climate of the imperial metropolis, much less save others from its effects. Like Captain Hawdon and Jo, he gradually succumbs to the poisonous fog exhaled by the court of Chancery. The "fatal cause" of Jarndyce and Jarndyce exposes him to an atmosphere as deadly as that which rises from the "fatal Niger" (877). The progress of his moral disease recalls description of the symptoms suffered by fever victims on the 1841 Niger Expedition. The Chancery case, like the sultry delta climate, almost immediately produces an "enervating effect" on Richard, encouraging his inclinations toward "lassitude" and "idleness" and making him thus more vulnerable to disease. According to Allen and Thomson, the onset of the fever produces a range of symptoms. Some experience "prostration of strength and despondency of mind; or high excitement with full pulse, again succeeded by exhaustion"; others become "intractable," responding in a "languid sort of tone, that there was nothing whatever the matter with them; that they were quite well; and wondered why they were obliged to take medicines, or be placed under any restriction" (2: 161). Richard suffers broadly from these symptoms. He intractably declares, "I shall be all right!" and refuses to accept the medicinal advice offered by Esther (584). As the disease advances, he vacillates between the high excitement of "hopefulness" and the depths of suicidal "despondency" (751). In the final stages of his illness, "thin and languid" and increasingly "tired out," he experiences a total prostration of moral and physical strength (878–9). It is in the nature of Chancery, as Jarndyce remarks, to "breed such diseases" as the one that consumes Richard (548).

If the trope of "home-made" savagery generally identifies subjects in need of civilizing compassion, it alternatively functions to blacken the character of exploitative villains. For example, Mr Smallweed, who holds the mortgage on George's shooting gallery, looks up at the towering soldier "like a pigmy" (356). Comparing the imperial soldier to the wizened Smallweeds, the narrator considers "[h]is developed figure, and their stunted forms; his large manner, filling any amount of room, and their little narrow pinched ways; his sounding voice, and their sharp spare tones" (349). The comparison of the large and expansive soldier to the stunted family of pygmies provides an occasion for admiring the imperial growth that, when considered in relation to the urban slum, generates a reappraisal of "national glory." Although exploited financially by the "pigmy" Smallweed, George possesses a moral rectitude, affiliated with his soldiering career, that fortifies his opposition to the usurer. Richard, without such resources, is much more vulnerable to the attack of another villain figured as an African savage. Vholes, the lawyer who tenaciously appropriates Richard's resources, evokes certain aspects of the greedy and deceptive African potentates depicted by Dickens in *The Examiner*. Just as they pretend commitment to end the slave trade only in order to gather presents, Vholes assures Richard that he will advance his suit only in order to absorb his inheritance. Like them, he realizes that the unhealthy climate of Chancery has laid its hold on Richard and gloatingly awaits his death. References to the somber black attire worn by Vholes gradually transmute into suggestions of threatening racial otherness. The lawyer removes his "close black gloves as if he were skinning his hands" and gazes at Richard "as if he were making a lingering meal of him" (607). The narrator compares Vholes and his family to "minor cannibal chiefs" (605). The nightmarish inversion of the civilizing mission, the consumption of the explorer by black-skinned cannibals, is significantly displaced onto the cash of the male character who cannot bring himself to "go abroad."[25]

Out of Africa, out of London

In his representation of the English dark continent at home, Carlyle detects glimmers of "hope." In *Bleak House*, the strange domestic landscape is darker still. By conveying the severity and extent of social problems at home through language used to describe the Niger delta, Dickens ironically thwarts the success of imagined reforms. The rhetoric he appropriates in order to redirect attention from Africa to London succeeds, as it were, too well. The English space figured as tropical Africa becomes as indomitable and deadly as its outlandish counterpart. Impenetrable to reform, it can only be escaped. Those characters who correspond to the surviving members of the Niger Expedition eventually abandon their missions in the public and private wildernesses of the imperial metropolis. Like their predecessors, they muster their forces only to make a tactical retreat from the region of disease, death, and despair.

The failure of the civilizing mission in London is partly disguised by the apparently happy ending, which enacts a final effort to imagine a more ideal and achievable alternative to the African venture organized by Mrs Jellyby. Esther and Woodcourt begin their married life in the strangely duplicated second Bleak House, an offshoot settlement of the home established by John Jarndyce. This "colony," unlike Borrioboola-Gha, extends the circle of a middle-class, domestic civilization within the nation and reinforces rather than subverts traditionally gendered spheres of influence.[26] By respecting the distinctions offended by Mrs Jellyby, it secures the blessing of nature. Dickens replaces signs evocative of his descriptions of a malignant African swamp with references to the "rich and smiling country" that surrounds the second Bleak House, which is propped up by colonnades "garlanded with woodbine, jasmine, and honey-suckle" (912). The second Bleak House exists in harmony with indigenous English plants, emblematic of a nature vastly different from the mud and decay that have invaded London and the Jellyby household.

The missions that Esther and Richard perform in their "colony" of Bleak House continue to reflect the gendered procedures for reform endorsed by Dickens. Having already proven her ability to impart the skills with which the middle-class woman sustains civilization within the domestic sphere, Esther will surely repeat the educational process with her own "two little daughters" (933). While her influence has limited effect in the habitat of the working class, she does preside over the marriage of Charley to a "well to do" country miller and thus completes the rescue of a girl nearly engulfed by the savagery of London (933). This event suggests that the middle-class woman best exerts her benevolent influence over the working class by guiding select individuals through stints of domestic service in the middle-class home. The fact that Charley's sister becomes Esther's new maid indicates that a new cycle has begun. Esther extends the circle of civilization by ensuring that the young women who come under her benign supervision find a secure position within a domestic sphere of a suitable class.

As "medical attendant for the poor," Woodcourt undertakes a duty in the public sphere that provides an outlet for his "compassionate interest" among the destitute natives of Yorkshire (872). Although his service is far removed from the scene of his imperial daring, the affiliation persists between distant male adventure and compassionate service at home. Jarndyce predicts that Woodcourt will secure the position, confiding to Esther that, in the district where the job awaits, her lover's "reputation stands very high; there were people from that part of the country in the shipwreck" (873). The compassionate treatment of British poor is once again enabled by the hero's imperial adventure.

Despite these optimistic touches, it is notable that Dickens locates this happy colony at a farther remove than the first Bleak House from the inadequately civilized "heart of a civilized world" and its varieties of "home-made" savagery. Of course, the conventions of the secularized providential plot encourage a conclusion that allows characters to escape the place of corruption. The "characters who have grace," as Welsh observes, "leave the earthly city behind them" (67). Within a context of the novel's relation to imperial ideology, however, the retreat from the "earthly city" also indicates an inability to solve the problems that have eroded distinctions between the imperial metropolis and the Niger delta. Esther's sketch of the picturesque Yorkshire village excludes feminist philanthropists who neglect their children as well as the grinding poverty of Tom-all-Alone's, but these conditions presumably persist in the sites that have been left behind. Although Jo has died, the myriad other tenants of the slum continue to suffer its brutalizing effects. Mrs Jellyby has forsaken overseas philanthropy only to take up "the rights of women to sit in Parliament" (933). The new mission, no less than the old, will presumably compromise her ability to care for her children and household. That Jo and the Jellyby children metonymically represent vast numbers of home-made savages becomes a particularly disquieting idea in the context of the last chapters. Although a few select individuals are rescued from African London, how many others have been left to accumulate "at compound interest" in its slums and middle-class parlors? Dickens can only imagine the smoothly functioning middle-class civilizing mission by abandoning the dark site that, throughout the narrative, persistently cries out for enlightening care.

In *The Examiner* review, Dickens advocates abandoning Africa to its own excessive savagery, a barbarism too powerfully resistant to the inroads of civilization. Through the rarefied atmosphere of the Yorkshire village, it is possible to glimpse a similar pessimism. Seeking to redirect the civilizing mission to the urban metropolis, Dickens exposes conditions approximating those of the African wilderness within the public and private spheres of London. The conditions that promise to thwart civilizing reforms in Africa are equally indomitable when transplanted to London. The "colony" of Bleak House suggests less an outpost of progress than a tactical retreat to an ideal place in which the social problems the novel foregrounds either do not exist or do so in forms that can be easily controlled. The novel that excoriates Mrs Jellyby for envisioning an idealistic colony rather than solving problems at hand reaches for closure by practicing its own variety of utopian evasion.

5
Mutinous Outbreaks in *The Moonstone*

Wilkie Collins wrote *The Moonstone* (1868) during a period in which few Victorians questioned the legitimacy or necessity of imperial rule in India. It was widely believed that Indians were instinctual, impulsive, and fanatic, that they lacked the mechanisms of self-control that guaranteed sound government at the level of self and society alike.[1] The 1857 rebellion known in England as the Mutiny seemed to confirm the passionate volatility of Indians and their general antipathy to law and order. In the wake of the rebellion, a steady stream of journalistic accounts, full-scale histories, and eye-witness narratives began to appear in England. Although these "Mutiny" texts offer varied perspectives and explanations, most confirm conventional notions about the mutinous nature of Indian subjectivity. In his novel, Collins does not dispute prevailing understandings of "the Indian character," but he does question the extent to which "the English character" differs from its ungovernable colonial counterpart. He does so by appropriating ethnographic commonplaces about Indian subjectivity and society and projecting them onto the English domestic scene. The characters in his novel are overmastered by their own "dark" and irrational obsessions, inordinate desires, unruly aggressions, and fanatical idolatries. This irony subverts accepted oppositions between those who inhabit mutinous India, which Betteredge dismisses as one of the "outlandish places of the earth," and those who inhabit the presumably quiet and reasonable domestic nation (82). Indeed, the mysterious gem, coveted by Indian and English characters alike, exerts a profoundly de-centering power, drawing forth into the light "outlandish" impulses which brood beneath the surface of purportedly civilized English subjectivity. This "first and greatest of English detective novels," as T. S. Eliot called *The Moonstone*, not only reveals the culprit who steals the diamond (377). It also reveals a sustaining illusion at the center of imperial ideology, that passionate excess exists at a comfortable remove, the unique possessions of racially other colonial subjects.

The Moonstone offers a particularly clear view of the uncanny dynamic through which Victorian culture attempts to distinguish the civilized imperial nation from its outlandish colony and how, ironically, the distinctions it draws fall into doubt. The susceptibility of English characters to the influence of the diamond demonstrates the fragility of their own self-command when embattled by "native" passions. The most fearful aspect of the "Oriental strangers" who pursue the diamond, Collins knows, is the secret familiarity of their impulses and behavior (221). The novel satirically dismantles conventional distinctions between Oriental and English, savage colonial other and well-regulated imperial self. Collins constructs what is, as Franklin Blake terms it, a "strange family story," a narrative that uncovers the forgotten and repressed strangeness that inhabits the familiar, the imperfectly repressed savagery that lives on in the family (7). *The Moonstone* shows that the familiar pleasures of the English hearth and home rely upon an imperfectly operating dynamic of repression and projection. They are sustainable only so long as English passions remain hidden in the dark.

Approaching *The Moonstone* as an uncanny text of imperial culture enables a constructive synthesis of two persuasive lines of analysis that have been applied to *The Moonstone*. A long-accepted reading of the novel decodes its symbolic structure as a psychosexual drama in which the theft of Rachel's jewel figuratively enacts a sexual violation. "What is stolen from Rachel," as Albert Hutter (1975) argues, "is both the actual gem and her symbolic virginity" (242).[2] This interpretation helped to establish Collins's fascination with the disruptive force of repressed impulses on codes of propriety meant to restrain them.

Another line of inquiry has emphasized the novel's concern with imperial politics. John Reed (1973), who initiated this perspective, treats the diamond as a reference to "England's imperial depredations," a "symbol of a national rather than a personal crime" (286). The novel, according to Reed, inverts the moral scheme of the civilizing mission by depicting the Hindu priests as "heroic figures, while the representatives of Western culture are plunderers" (283).[3] Ian Duncan (1994) concurs with Reed that the novel exposes the false pretenses of imperial authority, but takes issue with the notion that it simply redistributes moral authority to India. *The Moonstone*, he argues, more disturbingly inverts the distribution of power while continuing to align India with moral depravity. Playing upon the "imperialist panic" generated by the

Mutiny, Collins subjects his readers to the "nightmare of a devilish India," depicting "another world triumphant in its darkness" (305). While Duncan offers a more compelling reading of Collins's representation of India, he, like Reed, emphasizes an opposition that the novel in fact calls into question. Jaya Mehta (1995) similarly claims that *The Moonstone* "counterposes colonial terror to domestic romance," invoking the "nationalist mythology of a quintessentially placid English domesticity as a foil to colonial Indian violence" (612).[4] Arguments that position India as England's other, whether victimized and plundered or nightmarish and vengeful, miss the extent to which the narrative challenges such antithetical constructions.

Sara Suleri (1992) argues that "colonial facts fail to cohere around the master-myth that proclaims static lines of demarcation between imperial power and disempowered culture, between colonizer and colonized" (3). Collins demonstrates that domestic facts similarly throw "lines of demarcation" into disarray and confusion. His novel's representation of English subjectivity and behavior responds skeptically to the post-1857 tendency to draw clear and prejudicial distinctions between English and Indian subjects. It redirects attention from the rebellious colony to mutinous forces that erupt from the dark outlandish terrain of English subjectivity, inhabited by impulses and habits fully as irrational, violent, and passionate as those projected onto India. As Patrick Brantlinger observes, Mutiny narratives propagate a view of colonial insurgents as "wholly irrational, at once childish and diabolic," while aligning British colonial authority with rational order (222). In *The Moonstone*, this racial polarization of subjective faculties, a cornerstone of imperial ideology, falls into disarray. The successful foray of the Hindu priests no doubt enacts, as Lillian Nayder (1997) argues, a "reverse colonization of England" in symbolic retaliation for imperial exploitation (101). But the more striking irony is that irrational and "diabolic" forces need not colonize the imperial nation, because they are already indigenous inhabitants. Collins responds to the depiction of Indian subjects in Mutiny narratives by calling attention to the mutinous instincts and impulses that disrupt the government of the English mind.

Collins's reluctance to endorse sharp distinctions between English and Indian subjectivity reflects the broad cultural influence of universalist theories promoted by nineteenth-century Evangelicalism and evolutionary anthropology. Despite their evident biases, both disciplines maintained a theoretical commitment to the common origin of mankind and thus the existence of a single "human family," as Betteredge terms it (91). This shared belief prepares the ground for uncanny reminders of family ties that emerge in *The Moonstone* and other novels by Collins. By no means a rigorous student of either discipline, he absorbed their broadly disseminated ideas. He was particularly intrigued by the notion that the supposedly civilized modern English self harbored primitive impulses and habits – the trace of unregenerate spiritual corruption or the surviving remnants of a previous cultural stage – antagonistic to the religious and ethical dictates of Victorian culture.

In *The Moonstone*, Collins shows slight sympathy for the Evangelical movement itself, which was by the 1860s a waning cultural force. He satirizes its rhetoric in the person of the self-righteous Miss Clack, who remains ever-conscious of the need to "discipline the fallen nature which we all inherit from Adam" (214). Yet the comic shadow cast on Clack's piety should not obscure the extent to which Collins justifies such vigilance. His novels in general confirm her understanding of the ongoing internalized conflict between the forces of self-command and an intractable natural element. Sir Patrick, a principal character of *Man and Wife* (1870), translates Clack's spiritual struggle into a secular code of ethical development that bears the imprint of contemporary evolutionary assumptions. Articulating one of the chief didactic messages of the novel, he excoriates the national obsession with athleticism for catering to the "inbred reluctance in humanity to submit to the demands" of "moral and mental cultivation" (211). Those who exercise their muscles alone find themselves at the mercy of the "savage instincts latent in humanity – the instincts of self-seeking and cruelty which are at the bottom of all crime" (213). While Clack and Sir Patrick express very different points of view, both understand the modern English self as a precariously balanced governmental structure. The authority in power, aligned with spiritual discipline and ethical/intellectual cultivation, struggles to maintain its rule over rebellious instincts, aligned with an original yet persistent element perceived from the Evangelical perspective as "fallen nature," from the anthropological view as "savage instincts."

Confirming this understanding of subjectivity throughout his work, Collins contests imperial dichotomies by questioning the ability of the modern English self to control the eruption of its primitive instincts and impulses. The notion that civilized subjects share a "fallen nature" and "savage instincts" with colonial others holds subversive potential in relation to the imperial "master-myth." Collins might have contained that potential by applauding the English for disciplining their primitive instincts and impulses more effectively than their colonial counterparts. He might have suggested that only the aberrant criminal few at the center of empire lack the capacity for self-restraint. Yet he emphasizes instead a broad unreliability of self-control. His novels continually demonstrate the persistent presence and disruptive power of "original wildness" and "naked nature."[5] They replay the sudden eruption, or what Collins tends to call the "outbreak," of these subterranean forces into the domestic social field. He cultivates an anxiety about the irrepressibility of English savagery that the criminalization of certain particularly unrestrained individuals does not allay. The conviction that "our ancestor the savage" lurks within all English subjects wears the distinction between civilized and savage in the modern imperial world dangerously thin.[6]

Colonial psychomachia

The 1857 uprising was not the first military rebellion to disrupt colonial India, but in scale and duration it far surpassed preceding ones.[7] English officials and other commentators were particularly incensed by the fact that the rebellion was largely conducted by regiments of sepoys, Indian soldiers presumably loyal to the government that employed them. The rebellion began early in May at the garrison at Meerut when a sepoy regiment refused to use new rifle cartridges. It was widely believed that the cartridges, the paper covering of which had to be bitten off, were greased with cow and pig fat, and thus equally offensive to the religious sensibilities of Hindu and Moslem soldiers. The sepoys who refused orders were put in leg irons and jailed. In the face of this indignity, other regiments rebelled, killing English officers and their families and marching to Delhi. The rebellion then quickly spread to other regiments in Agra, Lucknow, Gwalior, Cawnpore, and other locales throughout northern India. British forces did not reconquer Delhi until mid-September, and did not declare full victory over the rebel soldiers until July 1858.

As English commentators began to debate the underlying causes of this widespread challenge to British rule, all agreed that the uprising had taken the colonial administration by surprise.[8] John Bruce Norton (1857) ruefully considered that technological advancements such as the railroad and telegraph afforded no protection from a rebellion that had "suddenly spr[ung] up among ourselves" (28). The onset is typically described as an "outbreak." As in the pages of Collins's novels, when this term is generally applied to English subjectivity, it conveys in the colonial context the sense of an abrupt and violent eruption of repressed energy. Such remarks reflect a crucial transition in English attitudes toward colonial government in India. In the context of the rebellious "outbreak," the British administration came to be seen less as an effective instrument of social progress and more as a highly precarious structure of control that remained vulnerable to the disruptive attacks of "native" forces.

In an effort to explain the extent to which the "outbreak" took seasoned officers and officials by surprise, many commentators emphasize a tendency in the Indian character toward guile and deceit. According to Charles Ball (1858), the sepoys who initiated the revolt at Meerut "allowed no outward indication of the fires of revenge and hatred that were scorching their hearts" (1: 56). Under the pen name Caubulee, the author of *The Crisis in India* (1857) discovers a religious source of mendacity, observing that the "religion of the Muhummedans [sic] instructs them to break faith with [infidels], and as a general rule they are not to be trusted in times of great temptation" (25). Nana Sahib, a Hindu prince who orchestrated the massacre of an English community at Cawnpore, comes to typify indigenous treachery. "With the usual craft of his tribe," writes Mead, "he was most profuse in his professions of sympathy and friendship at a time when he had made up his mind to earn for himself the reputation of being the most bloodthirsty enemy of our race" (133). The mutinous plot represented an especially heinous example of the general antipathy to truth that English commentators routinely attributed to colonial subjects in India. "The Asiatic," Mead explains, "considers words as mere breath. If a thing is worth having, it is worth lying for" (40).

The events of 1857 seemed to prove the wisdom of acting Governor General Charles Metcalfe, who had earlier sensed an ominous "spirit of disaffection" lying "dormant, but rooted universally among our subjects" (qtd. in Norton 30). The "Mutiny" had awakened this spirit and brought it into the open, exposing the true feelings of Indian colonial subjects that had been disguised by lying professions of loyalty and friendship. According to Mead, "[f]ierce antipathy to our creed, intense loathing of our persons, and never-ceasing dread of English valour and ability, make up the impression which is stamped on the minds of their children in early infancy" (30). In the mind of much of the English public, the mutinous population of India had discarded the mask of thankful consent and shown the true face of its character.

Even those commentators who clearly despise Indians attribute some responsibility for the rebellion to the colonial administration. "[R]ebellion can never break out amongst a people," argues Henry Mead, "unless their rulers are greatly in fault" (70). For the most part, however, texts that consider mistakes and offenses committed by colonial administrators nonetheless deprive colonial discontent of political legitimacy. Indigenous opposition generally appears in the form of extreme emotional and psychological states. Norton, for example, considers in some detail policies that have "destroyed the Native belief in our good faith," faulting the government for having "stirred up the angry passions of the soldiery" (77). By depicting the rebellion as an eruption of "angry passions," English commentators divert attention away from questions about the legitimacy of colonial rule and its distribution of political power. Instead, they represent the rebellion as a psychological conflict inflected by moral and religious dichotomies. According to Mead, the rebels are "children in impulse and tigers at heart," exemplifying irresponsibility and "waywardness" on the one hand and bestial cruelty on the other (143). References to madness are especially frequent. Mead, for example, describes the mutineers as "maddened with excitement and raging for blood" (134). For all the faults attributed to the British administration, it comes to represent rational and humane authority beset by an outbreak of insanity and ferocity. "Mutiny" texts collectively construct a colonial psychomachia in which the forces of reason and madness battle for control of India.

Because religious prohibitions played a significant role in the "outbreak" of rebellion, those English writers who look beyond a "hunger and thirst for blood" for the source of Indian madness find it in the "creeds" practiced by colonial subjects. Ball argues that English desire to avoid interfering with the "idolatrous faith" of Hindu sepoys fostered the growth of insubordination (1: 35). Focusing attention rather on the "Mussulmans of India," Mead describes them as "[b]rutally ignorant and superstitious" and claims that they have "engrafted the idolatry of Asia upon the tenets of the Koran, and look upon all Europeans as being infidels and unclean, whom it is a duty to slay whenever occasion serves" (30). Such comments both convey the general English disregard for predominant Indian faiths and draw a causal link between them and rebellion. English writers often suggest that the idolatries and superstitions of India tended to produce fanaticism. The belief that idolatrous Indian subjects were swept away by irrational religious enthusiasm confirmed the general antithesis between Indian madness and rational colonial governance. According to Julius George Medley (1858), the crisis has shown "not that the natives are incapable of gratitude and attachment, but simply that the madness produced by fanaticism is so strong as to outweigh every other feeling" (201). Such comments contribute to a perception of Indian colonial subjects as fundamentally irresponsible. Reared within religious systems that apparently fostered uncontrollable enthusiasms and antipathies, they could not help but be caught up in a mad rebellion against infidel rulers.

"Mutiny" texts discern an interrelated cause of madness in a congenital fondness for treasure. In another of the ethnographic pronouncements that frequently arise in accounts of 1857, Mead observes that the "[n]atives of India" are "imbued with the most intense love of wealth" (284–5). This passionate attachment helped to explain the many incidents of pillaging and robbery supposedly committed by the sepoys. Soon after the rebellion began, Ball recounts, "detached parties" of the "revolted soldiery ... spread themselves over the country for the sake of "loot" (1: 67). The use of the Hindi-derived word for plunder or spoil quietly reenforces the ethnographic point that such forays enact a characteristic propensity. Caubulee departs somewhat from this explanation by suggesting that a more universal form of resentment stimulates colonial looters. "[D]epend upon it," he declares, "a disregard for the laws, a contempt for Europeans, and a hunger and thirst for blood and plunder have been awakened to an insane pitch by late events in the minds of all natives. ... And this would be the case, under similar circumstances, among the masses in England" (66). Mead, on the other hand, follows most English commentators by drawing a specific connection between the Indian character and the awakened thirst for "blood and plunder." In the quest for "loot" he traces a strand of antipathy for "infidel" Christian rulers. At Mooradabad, the mutineers "made for the treasury," motivated by interlocking "considerations of religion and rupees" (142).

Such descriptions of the outbreak of looting mark a fascinating chapter in the history of England's anxiety-filled attitude toward the wealth of India. In the Victorian period, the memory of eighteenth-century "nabobs" who had amassed vast personal fortunes through unscrupulous trade and "taxation" in India remained very much alive.[9] In *Vanity Fair* (1847), for example, Thackeray satirizes the figure of the nabob in the depiction of Jos Sedley, a corpulent and conceited man who holds the "honorable and lucrative post" of "collector" in India (27). Gobbling revenues in India and curry in London, Jos symbolically registers persistent guilt about England's voracious appetite for colonial territory. English commentary on the 1857 uprising effectively represses this guilt by projecting "disregard for the laws" and thirst for "plunder" onto the Indian population itself. In "Mutiny" texts, it is Indian vandals rather than English colonial traders and collectors who "spread themselves over the country for the sake of 'loot'." The moral transposition effected by such references emerges as well in a parable of Indian deception told by Mead, who observes that "so far did [Nana Sahib] impose upon General Wheeler, that the latter, thinking the treasury somewhat unsafe under the care of Sepoys, applied to him for a guard for its protection" (133). Emphasizing misplaced English trust and Indian villainy, this story does not encourage readers to critically analyze the legitimacy of the process through which the colonial administration itself comes to amass its "treasury" in the first place.

According to many English writers, rebellious madness expressed itself most horrifically in the rape of English women. Caubulee claims that "this particular insult" was perpetrated "systematically wherever the outbreaks have taken place," indicating a "determined and devilish animosity on a scale unprecedented in the annals of Indian insurrections and mutinies" (45). It appears that accounts of systematic attacks on the "honour of Englishwomen," as Ball phrases it, were based on fearful rumor rather than fact (2: 1). (It is true that English women and children were in some instances deliberately killed. In others, Indians protected them at their own risk.) As nightmarish fantasies, rumors of the rape of English women offer crucial insight into fears and fantasies produced by imperial ideology. Jenny Sharpe (1993) offers a persuasive symbolic interpretation in which the "brutalized bodies of defenseless English women serve as a metonym for a government that sees itself as the violated object of rebellion" (7). The imagined rape of English women in India thus helps to translate resistance to British rule into "uncivilized eruption[s] that must be contained" (7).[10] On a more literal but still important level, accounts involving the violation of English women by colonial others reenforce a basic distinction between English and Indian men in relation to the chivalric code on which middle-class Victorian society prided itself. Indian colonial subjects were accused of enacting a "devilish" inversion of deference and protection that was in turn defended by their stalwart opponents. When the "lives and honour of Englishwomen were imperilled," Ball declares, "the brave hearts and strong arms of their indignant countrymen were irresistible, as they sprang forward to save or to avenge them" (2: 1).

As the imagined rape and defense of English women particularly demonstrates, English commentary on the sepoy rebellion of 1857 tended to affirm and sharpen rather than blur what Suleri terms the "lines of demarcation between imperial power and disempowered culture." With few exceptions, "Mutiny" texts uphold rigid distinctions between the character of English and Indian subjects. Whereas Indians are described as deceptive, treacherous, maddened, bloodthirsty, fanatical, and dishonorable, English figures exemplify a set of antithetical virtues. According to Norton, the "sons and daughters" of England have never shown "more devotion to duty, or calmer fortitude" (13). He gestures to "many an act of the noblest courage" and singles out certain figures for their "gallant independence" and "stern determination" (13). It is especially important to note that such praise broadly credits English subjects with the ability to maintain conscious self-control. Their "calm fortitude" distinguishes them from Indians caught up in maniacal fanaticism or given over to base temptation. For Ball, the defense of Lucknow "called forth all the energy and daring which belong to Englishmen in the hour of active conflict" and exhibited throughout "noble and sustained courage" (2: 45) and indeed "transcendent valour" (2: 664). Every form of criminal madness supposedly exemplified by Indian colonial subjects implicitly or explicitly points toward an antithetical form of virtue embodied in English men and women. In the eyes of most English commentators, the battle in India illustrated in stark black and white a set of clearly opposed states of mind and traits of national character.

The polarizing filter of imperial ideology expresses this opposition in terms of race. Although the sepoys who rebelled against British rule represented a range of different religions and ethnic groups, English writers often perceive their opponents as a single uniform mass of undifferentiated racial otherness. Although her response to the uprising is much less sensational than most, Harriet Martineau (1857) proclaims that a "bottomless chasm ... yawns between the interior nature of the Asiatic and the European races" (296). Dismissing the importance of the cartridges that initially sparked the rebellion, Norton insists that "it is not a question of grease which leads to rebellion; but the natural antipathy of race; the sympathy with those of their own creed and country, when the moment comes for making a choice between the ties of allegiance, and those of blood; between the stranger and brother. Fatal to us is the moment of that electric touch of nature which makes them kin" (20). This passage certainly exemplifies some of the complexities that inhabit mid-Victorian definitions of race. In the reference to "ties of ... blood," Norton introduces the biological emphasis that dominates and distorts the understanding of race in our own era, but he also uses the word to denote "creed and country," religious belief and place of origin. Reaching for a sense of clearly opposed sides, Norton elaborates a theory of racial antipathy that necessarily represses the variety of Indian creeds, origins, and bloodlines – the highly visible variety that, ironically, is often accentuated by apologists of colonial rule in order to justify the English colonial administration as a neutral and fair arbitrator. In the wake of the 1857 rebellion, however, English writers preferred to ignore such complexities and perceive themselves as "strangers" to those states of mind and traits of character associated with the "Asiatic" or "Oriental" race.

In some instances, however, glimpses of sympathies that cross the "bottomless chasm" do escape. English writers who associate uncontrollable and fanatical violence with Indian subjectivity, for example, do not always express themselves with the "calm fortitude" that presumably represents a characteristic feature of their race. Considering the supposed rape of English women, Caubulee confesses, "[t]ruly as I write my blood courses like boiling lava through my veins" (46). Such rhetorical flashes of the "angry passions" stirred up by the rebellion were not unusual. In a personal letter (4 Oct. 1857) written during the insurrection, Dickens, a friend and colleague of Collins, fantasizes about possessing the power to enact his rage. Imagining himself as "Commander in Chief in India," he declares, "The first thing I would do to strike that Oriental race with amazement ... should be to proclaim to them, in their language, that I considered my holding that appointment by the leave of God, to mean that I should do my utmost to exterminate the Race upon whom the stain of the late cruelties rested" (*Letters* 8: 459).[11] Although he describes his angry passion as "Demoniacal," Dickens does not seem to appreciate the paradox generated by his fantasy of divinely appointed genocide (*Letters* 8: 459). Desiring to punish Indian colonial subjects for the same variety of murderous hatred he himself expresses, Dickens truly speaks "in [the] language" he attributes to them.[12] Such indications of uncontrollable aggression correspond to the history of the conflict, in which English regiments restored imperial order with a ruthless and arbitrary violence that matched or exceeded atrocities committed by the sepoys. The comments made by Caubulee and Dickens clearly represent unwitting betrayals of sentiments that cut across the distinctions generally upheld and affirmed in "Mutiny" narratives.

Published just a decade after the sepoy rebellion, *The Moonstone* appeared in a period in which England was still reeling from the challenge to its colonial rule and for the most part still inclined to accentuate differences between themselves and Indian colonial subjects. In this context, it is particularly significant that Collins chooses to develop the sort of ironic affinities and sympathies that the writers cited above tend to repress. The Evangelical suspicion with which the pious Miss Clack searches the English soul affords her partial insight, at least, into the novel's skeptical analysis of clear-cut racial oppositions. Attempting to extract an edifying moral from the incident in which the

Hindu priests subject her hero Godfrey Ablewhite to an ignominious search, she exclaims, "How soon may our own evil passions prove to be Oriental noblemen who pounce on us unawares!" (222). The 1857 rebellion, in which "Oriental noblemen" such as Nana Sahib took British colonial authorities "unawares," offers a precedent for the "outrage" committed on Ablewhite in the streets of London, but also for surprise attacks committed by "our own evil passions" against the administrative structures of spiritual self-discipline and rationality. As Miss Clack observes, there is a "dark conspiracy" at work "in the midst of us" (222). Of course, the fact that she describes the "evil passions" as "Oriental noblemen" suggests an attempt to preserve a sense of the foreignness of the desires and rages that disrupt the government of the English subject. Her phrase thus indicates only a step toward the still more distressing knowledge that the novel conveys. For Collins, the "dark" passions are as much "native" to the heart of empire as to the "outlandish places of the earth."

The foreign face of evil passion

The significance of the novel's representation of India and its native subjects emerges in light of this uncanny irony. Collins certainly demonstrates familiarity with conventional depictions of India as the nightmarish antithesis of orderly domestic life in England. Yet the novel also emphasizes the disconcerting irony that the upper-middle-class English home is itself estranged from the ideals of English domesticity. The novel's representation of India and its natives deserves close attention not because it establishes the antithesis of England, but rather because it establishes habits of mind that recur, in muted but detectable ways, in England. The most explicitly "foreign" elements of the plot provide keys to the most familiar.

The history of the Moonstone sketched in the prologue associates India with rapacious violence, fanatical idolatry, deceptive cunning, and congenital "love of wealth." As the texts discussed above demonstrate, these characteristics typified the English mental image of the colony in the years after the uprising. According to the unnamed Herncastle cousin who relates the history of the Moonstone, the gem is for many centuries worshiped as an integral part of a Hindu idol.[13] In the early eighteenth century, however, the Mogul emperor unleashes "havoc and rapine" against his Hindu subjects (3). During this period, a Mohammedan "officer of rank" steals the diamond from a shrine in Benares, where the idol had been transported for protection from Somnauth (3). A succession of three Hindu priests devote themselves to the service of the deity, pursuing the diamond as it passes "from one lawless Mohammedan hand to another" until it becomes the possession of Tippoo, Sultan of Seringapatam (3). Unable to use "open force" against their oppressors, they instead await an opportunity to recapture the gem "in disguise" (3). Before they do so, of course, John Herncastle steals the diamond and removes it to England.

This "wildest" of legends extracted from the "native annals of India" is propelled by a conflict between varieties of unrestrained colonial subjectivity (1). The synechdoche of the "lawless Mohammedan hand" indicates unrestrained desire, a subjectivity abandoned to the pleasures of brutal acquisition. In the Hindu priests, the self-indulgence of the Oriental despot gives place to fanatical self-renunciation. Their pursuit of the Moonstone exemplifies unrestrained devotion, a subjectivity governed by idolatrous superstition. To the Mohammedan, the diamond is treasure, valuable for its beauty and monetary value. To the Hindu priests, the diamond is sacred talisman, valuable because it belongs to the deity before whose will they bow.

If the story of the Moonstone's history offers a stereotypical portrait of unrestrained colonial subjectivity, Collins also shows how such portraits are eagerly received as evidence of the foreignness of the "evil passions." The reception of information supplied by Murthwaite, the traveler recently returned from the "wild places of the East," provides a case in point (73). On the evening when Rachel first wears the diamond, he informs her, "I know a certain city, and a certain temple in that city, where, dressed as you are now, your life would not be worth five minutes' purchase" (73). Without explicitly recalling the events of the 1857 uprising, Collins confirms what was at the time a conventional assumption about the willingness of Indian colonial subjects to treat Englishwomen with violent disregard. Equally notable, however, is the willingness of English men and women to endorse and accept such assumptions. After Murthwaite provides the ethnographic information, the Ablewhite sisters "burst out together vehemently, 'O! How interesting!' " (73). Their reaction reflects the unquestioning attitude that assumes the veracity of the "interesting" picture of violent excess in India. Although Betteredge disdains their enthusiasm, he also relies on Murthwaite's expertise as he constructs the foreignness of India and its subjects. "[C]lever as the Hindoo people are in concealing their feelings." Murthwaite penetrates the disguise of the priests when they appear at the dinner party (79). They turn on him, Betteredge reports, with "tigerish quickness," briefly revealing their murderous impulses before re-assuming their "polite and snaky way" (78). This scene also echoes the assumptions and specific language conventionally applied to Indian colonial subjects in representations of the "Mutiny." If the novel thus reaffirms the ethnographic authority of the figure who can penetrate the deceptive guise of Indian colonial subjects, it also shows how Betteredge accentuates the otherness of those he instinctively suspects with stereotypical metaphors. Like Mead, who sees the "Mutiny" as the undisguised enactment of "tiger instincts," Betteredge similarly dehumanizes the Hindu priests who, with their "tigerish" ferocity and "snaky" indirection, represent dangerous tropical animality that has encroached upon the temperate and familiar regions of English country life.

The ability to construct such clear-cut dichotomies, Collins suggests, relies on a credulous and naive ethnocentrism. In the novel, this attitude is exemplified most clearly by Betteredge, the character most leery of the "outlandish places of the earth." "[H]ere was our quiet English house," he exclaims, "suddenly invaded by a devilish Indian Diamond" (36). The "Indian Diamond" broadly signifies for Betteredge an infernal world in which the antithesis of all that is good, proper, rational, well-ordered, and English prevails. "Who ever heard the like of it," he wonders, "in the nineteenth century, mind; in an age of progress, and in a country which rejoices in the blessings of the British constitution?" (36–7). This devoted servant of the "quiet English house" articulates several striking tributes to the progress and stability of his nation and its subjects. Unlike mutinous Indians (and perhaps as well continental revolutionaries), the English are "an easy people to govern, in the Parliament and in the Kitchen" (65). Just as he guards the circumference of the estate to secure it against the intrusive ploys of the Hindu priests, so too does Betteredge patrol the ideological borders of the imperial nation, defending them against rebellious otherness.

But sometimes, as Freud indicates in "The Uncanny," disturbing secrets are hidden in apparently quiet houses. *The Moonstone* undercuts Betteredge's ethnocentrism by disclosing what appear to be disruptive alien passions within the "quiet English house." Those who inhabit the imperial nation and its domestic spheres fail to offer tractable or well-governed alternatives to volatile colonial subjects. Mutinous English passions may be more deeply repressed and their forms of expression more cleverly hidden, but they become visible over the course of the narrative. As they uncannily erupt within the familiar social realm, they expose the artificiality of the racial oppositions that sustain the imperial project.

In the Shivering Sands, Collins constructs a symbol that both acknowledges and repudiates the tendency to estrange the disruptive passions by projecting them onto racial others. Inspiring intermingled horror and fascination in those who gaze upon it, the Shivering Sands is one of the novel's focal points of uncanny intensity. Its disturbing power emanates from the knowledge it discloses about the structure of human subjectivity in England as well as in India. While the surface of the quicksand appears relatively benign, at certain moments it heaves and ripples, indicating the "spirit of terror" that "live[s] and move[s] and shudder[s] in the fathomless deeps below" (342). Collins describes the surface as the "false brown face," adopting a phrase that certainly recalls the deceptive Hindu priests, whose "polite" demeanor briefly reveals their terrifying intentions. But Collins does not arbitrarily locate the quicksand in Yorkshire, deep in the heart of the imperial nation and notably adjacent to the "quiet English house." This juxtaposition suggests that "quiet English" subjects, no less than their colonial counterparts, conceal volatile passions in their "fathomless deeps."

Collins associates the Shivering Sands most explicitly with Rosanna Spearman, the "silent" maidservant who is "troubled occasionally" by shudders of repressed desire for the unattainable Franklin Blake (23). She reenforces the symbolic import of the Shivering Sands by sinking herself and her confession in its unquiet depths. Her death, however, leads Betteredge to a broadly relevant insight about the nature of the self and its repressed passions. He reflects that "we learn to put our feelings back into ourselves, and to jog on with our duties as patiently as may be" (178). Although he assumes that members of the upper classes can afford to indulge their feelings, the novel does not restrict his insight to a particular class, gender, or race. The comment forges a connection between "quiet English" characters and the Hindu priests, noted for their "patience" and adept at "concealing their feelings" (42). The Shivering Sands bears a sign of racial difference on its "brown face," but only those who read superficially may convince themselves that the knowledge it symbolically conveys applies only to strangers.

Family ties

If the prologue of the novel supplies what would have been a familiar depiction of India, it also emphasizes the forceful appeal of its irrationality and violence to a character invested with imperial authority. John Herncastle, an officer in the imperial army, is easily susceptible to the "evil passions" associated with the colony. As the British force prepares for the assault on Seringapatam, the "fanciful story of the Moonstone" awakens his acquisitive desire and volcanic ire (3). A man of "unlucky temper," Herncastle vows in an "angry outbreak" to capture the jewel for himself (4, 6). Ironically entrusted to "enforce the laws of discipline" after the conquest of the city, Herncastle succumbs to an aggressive "frenzy" in which he seizes the diamond, murdering the Indians who guard it (5). This first English chapter in the story of the Moonstone notably extends a motif established by events that precede the intervention of the purportedly civilized nation. Herncastle is but another "officer of rank" in a conquering force who grasps the diamond in his "lawless hand."

Back in England, the Herncastle family takes decisive action to disavow their unsavory relative. On the strength of testimony given by Herncastle's cousin, the rest of the family repudiates him. "He came back" from India, Blake remembers, "with a character that closed the doors of all his family against him" (33). This version of events suggests that Herncastle has acquired a "character" he did not formerly have, that he has been contaminated in India by essentially alien passions. Yet the effort to ostracize the wayward son, to close the family doors against him, suggests a fearful consciousness of the "electric touch of nature" as much as disapproval. The Herncastles repudiate John because he has extravagantly indulged impulses that they still attempt to hide. If he possesses a more liberal "dash of the savage" than they, he differs from them in degree only (33). His sister Lady Verinder shares his volatile anger, possessing her own "dash … of the family temper" (35). The similar structure of these phrases suggests that "the savage" and "the family temper" might be read synonymously. Rachel exhibits her own "dash" of the family temper when her diamond is stolen, acting "wild and angry" and speaking to Blake "savagely" in an "outbreak of ill-will" (96, 112).

Nor is this dash of savagery limited to blood relatives of Herncastle. Irritated by Rachel's decision to break off her engagement to his son, the senior Mr Ablewhite denounces the Herncastle family, implicitly representing his own line as superior. As he does so, however, he ironically gives vent to savage anger. "[B]ecoming purple" with anger, he looks "backwards and forwards from Rachel to Mr Bruff in such a frenzy of rage with both of them that he didn't know which to attack first" (289). This "outbreak" recalls the "frenzy" which possesses Herncastle, who of course actually attacks and murders multiple opponents in India (4). Collins indicates that even Ablewhite, a "remarkably good-natured man," verges at times on violent fury (285). The "self-registering thermometer" of Ablewhite's complexion grows a "shade deeper" as his rage intensifies, suggesting the emergence of his racially "foreign" self (286). The most distressing "family secret" of the novel is that upper-middle-class

English characters share much in common with members of the "human family" they would like to hold at a distance.[14]

Never less than detestable, Herncastle does perceive the hypocrisy of those who bar their doors against passions already lodging comfortably within. That knowledge provokes his sardonic laugh "*into* himself" when turned away from Rachel's birthday celebration (original italics, 35). By this point on terms of joking familiarity with the family savage who abides within, Herncastle anticipates with cruel pleasure the spectacle of evil passions unleashed by the Moonstone within the "quiet English house."

English superstition

When the diamond arrives in the Herncastle home as a birthday gift to Rachel, the superstitious regard it enjoys begins to indicate how precarious is the distinction between those allotted opposing positions on imperial lines of demarcation. Betteredge, for example, ironically reduplicates the kind of "outlandish" belief system he elsewhere dismisses as "hocus-pocus" (54). His first reaction to the gem suggests that he also becomes enthralled by the "Devilish Indian diamond":

> Lord bless us! it *was* a Diamond! As large, or nearly, as a plover's egg!
> The light that streamed from it was like the light of the harvest moon.
> When you looked down into the stone, you looked into a yellow deep
> that drew your eyes into it so that they saw nothing else. It seemed
> unfathomable; this jewel, that you could hold between your finger
> and thumb, seemed unfathomable as the heavens themselves. ... No
> wonder Miss Rachel was fascinated: no wonder her cousins screamed.
> The Diamond laid such a hold on *me* that I burst out with as large an
> "O" as the Bouncers themselves. (original italics, 68–9)

The Moonstone erodes barriers and distinctions which Betteredge else-where invests with much importance. He finds himself, as he admits, helplessly expressing the giddy enthusiasm of the Ablewhite sisters. His fascination, shared by his young mistress, transects the class divisions which structure the household. Through a symbolic connection, it also links him to Rosanna, the reformed urban criminal whom he admonishes for her morbid obsession with the "yellow deeps" of the Shivering Sands. His hypothetical speculation "that you could hold" the diamond "between your finger and thumb" suggests an awakening of the acquisitive desire that governs John Herncastle.

But most strikingly, Betteredge swoons into a set of mind analogous to those held by the "influence of Oriental religions" and superstitions (42). Murthwaite later asserts that "We have nothing whatever to do with clairvoyance, or with mesmerism, or with anything else that is hard of belief to a practical man" (317). Yet the novel indicates that "practical" English subjects are as prone to fanatic obsessions and irrational superstitions as "Oriental strangers." The ethnocentric steward, another apostle of English common sense, quickly succumbs to the mesmeric grip of the Oriental talisman. As he confesses, it lays "such a hold" on him, drawing his "eyes into it so that they saw nothing else." In the spirit of exposing a hypocrisy (rather than admonishing a sin), Collins appropriates the Evangelical habit of unveiling forms of idolatry that have crept into Christian culture. In *Practical Christianity* (1797), Wilberforce defines "idol" broadly as whatever "draws off the heart from [God], engrosses our prime regard, and holds the chief place in our esteem and affections" (86). In this sense, Clack justifiably refers to Betteredge as a "heathen old man" (216). His "prime regard" is easily engrossed by the Moonstone and, of course, by Defoe's sacred text.

Collins is particularly concerned to indicate that habits of mind triggered by the foreign diamond precede its arrival. The appearance of the Moonstone only provides a new occasion for the exhibition of familiar impulses and habits of mind. Early in his account, Betteredge memorably asserts, "I am not superstitious," only then to confess his superstitious regard for *Robinson Crusoe*, the text from which he draws clairvoyant readings of the future (9). After describing a search for guidance within its pages he remarks with relief, "I saw my way clear" (13). Long before the devilish Oriental diamond appears, Betteredge practices his own heathen cult, worshiping as his divine oracle, no less, a story that narrates the civilizing genius of the English hero.[15] As he holds the novel in his hands, searching the pages for esoteric wisdom, he represents merely an older version of the "sensitive" English boy who, employed as medium by the Hindus, reads the future in "the ink in the hollow of his hand" (19). The distinction between Betteredge's homely reading and their outlandish ritual is, as it were, paper thin (54).

The English "fascination" for the Moonstone does not therefore mark a reverse colonization of the imperial nation by Oriental superstition. Rather, it reveals purportedly "foreign" modes of idolatry already in place, although unacknowledged, in England. The displacement of the diamond from Indian to English culture exposes the artificiality of racial distinctions sustained by imperial rhetoric.[16] The effort to estrange the variety of mind subject to the "influence" of the mysterious and valuable jewel, already problematic after John Herncastle's violent "frenzy," becomes increasingly untenable as more English characters fall under its spell.

Religion and rupees

The Moonstone's experience in England uncannily repeats its history in India, specifically because presumably alien habits of mind secretly inhabit revered ideas and institutions as well as despicable tendencies that find their home in Victorian culture.[17] Recall that, long before the intervention of the British empire, the diamond graces the figure of a Hindu idol regarded as "the inviolate deity" by its worshipers (2). The deity is then violated by a Mohammedan officer who steals the diamond, revering it for its material rather than its sacred value. In revenge for the hypocrisy of his family, Herncastle sets in motion a process that reveals the full extent to which the English domestic sphere harbors the same instincts and impulses that determine the diamond's stormy history in India. Specific forms of idolatrous worship and lawless acquisition change to reflect their unique shape in Victorian culture. The Hindu cult of the Moon god gives way to the English cult of domesticity. Mohammedan despot transmutes into materialistic scoundrel. Yet these parallels expose the persistent presence of heathen idolatry and savage self-seeking at home.

Critics have argued that the theft of the jewel from Rachel exposes a correspondence between patriarchal authority in the middle-class domestic sphere and British imperial authority in India. Nayder observes that in "his dual role of protector and thief, Blake illuminates the paradox of Victorian guardianship, in both its patriarchal and its imperial guises" (122).[18] While the novel does align the heroine with colonial savagery and perhaps implicitly positions Blake as her colonial governor, it gives even more reason to perceive within the heterosexual relationships centered on Rachel uncanny echoes of the ways that Oriental strangers variously revere and despoil the idol. This correspondence largely confirms Nayder's point about the paradox of male guardianship, however, since even those who bow before the deity and its talisman insist upon possessing the objects they worship.

On the verge of marriage, Rachel has attained the status of a deity in the Victorian cult of domesticity. Both before and after the theft of the diamond, men in her circle approximate the idolatrous service exemplified by Indian devotees. Blake first expresses his "devotion" by renouncing cigars when she mentions her dislike of the smell (61). Her word is also law for Bruff, who affirms the innocence of Ablewhite on the strength of her unsupported testimony. The practical lawyer abandons rules of evidence when the English deity speaks. Betteredge, who confesses himself "an average good Christian" only when "you don't push [his] Christianity too far," exhibits the fierce loyalty of those in thrall to "Oriental religions" (185). Aggravated by Cuff's effort to implicate Rachel in the theft, his fanaticism "break[s] out," provoking him to grab the Sergeant by the throat and pin him against the wall (149). Holding "on like death to [his] belief in Miss Rachel," Betteredge reveals a liberal "dash" of the ferocity that drives the Hindu priests to smother Ablewhite (170). Collins suggests that those Victorians who perceive their culture untainted by the fanaticism of heathen religions may find evidence to the contrary in the chivalric code that structures sexual relations in the middle-class cult of domesticity. This suggestion is especially ironic in light of the "Mutiny" narratives that consistently oppose chivalrous England to India.

Ablewhite, who secretly despises this sacred cult, violates the deity in the manner of his Mohammedan predecessors. In his culture, of course, the cult has power and legitimacy, and this forces him to practice deception and subterfuge like the Hindu priests. Ablewhite plays the role of mild philanthropist and seems to adhere with special devotion to Victorian chivalric codes. He is the gracious assistant to multiple "Ladies' Charities" and pays homage to Rachel in affectionate birthday verses (61). This sensitive facade conceals the varieties of acquisitive desire conventionally associated with Mohammedan despotism. In a secret villa, Ablewhite indulges the opulent lifestyle of an Oriental potentate, supporting his sensual gratifications with appropriated wealth. The gentle consideration he shows for women masks the sexual appetite of the stereotypical Sultan. Although Ablewhite keeps only a single mistress, his villa includes "a conservatory of the rarest flowers" and "jewels which are worthy to take rank with the flowers" (503). Given the associations of female sexuality with flowers and jewels (a particularly resonant metaphor in this novel), the villa takes on the symbolic character of an English harem. In light of Collins's sensitivity to post-1857 representations of India, it is not too much of a stretch to see glimpses of the hated pretender Nana Sahib in the characterization of Ablewhite. If Ablewhite does not descend to murder, he does deceptively acquire the trust of ladies and dupes men into thinking him a trustworthy guardian of treasure.

At any rate, Ablewhite certainly regards both Rachel and her diamond as loot to plunder from the temple of domesticity. He views the diamond as a financial resource with which to sustain his sensual life, and sees Rachel herself as yet another flower for his conservatory. His desire is not as apparent as his financial chicanery, but Betteredge does at one point catch him "ogling" the heiress (69). In her analysis of nineteenth-century imperial discourse, Inderpal Grewal (1996) observes that the image of the "woman 'caged' in the harem, in purdah, becomes the necessary Other for the construction of the Englishwoman presumably free and happy in the home" (54). Skeptical of such oppositions, Collins intimates that an Englishwoman may well find herself caged within a marriage that replicates the power structure of the harem.

Collins indicates that the English cult of domesticity, like the harem, limits the freedom and independence of women. Language that links Rachel to the diamond itself clarifies both the sources of her authority over her idolaters and, as well, the restrictions placed upon it by them. She becomes the "centre-point towards which everybody's eyes were directed" because she, like the diamond, has great worth and great beauty (72). Her vast wealth and multifaceted beauty help to explain the mysterious influence she wields over those men who succumb to her "charming" and "irresistible" power (53, 304). The sad case of Rosanna, who lacks her mistress's "handsome income" as well as her physical advantages, highlights the point that only beautiful women of a certain socio-economic position might expect to win the idolatrous regard of men in Victorian England (301). Yet Rachel pays a significant price for the power she wields. She embodies the symbolic instability of the diamond, which is always, even within the framework of the sacred cult, both sacred talisman and desirable possession. The patriarchal cult in England, like its colonial counterpart, must own the object of its adoration. It is a sanctified variety of acquisitive desire that Blake expresses in his desire to see and to possess, to have and to hold, the idol he serves. It is particularly ironic that Collins discloses the operation of primitive possessive impulses within the cult of domesticity, for many Victorians believed that the status afforded middle-class women marked one of the essential distinctions between their culture and savagery. It is this popular assumption that John Stuart Mill rebukes in *The Subjection of Women* (1869). To his eye, as to Collins's, relations between the sexes in supposedly civilized England carries the "taint of brutal origins" (476).

The theft of the diamond, the crime committed at dead of night in the "quiet English house," thus represents a twofold outbreak of primitive possessiveness, implicating both Blake, the idolatrous servant, and Ablewhite, the lawless thief. Collins introduces the tantalizing possibility that Rachel will reject both forms of outlandish subordination that her cousins represent. The Moonstone's mysterious flaw corresponds to what Betteredge calls the single "defect" in the character of "this charming woman," her "independence" or "self-will" (58). The history of the diamond suggests that it possesses a maddening "independence" as well, tending as it does to wander away from those who desire to possess it (41). Rachel exerts her independence after witnessing the symbolic assertion of ownership by her chief devotee. She resigns her post as deity, abandoning the temple and retreating into inscrutable silence. Just as the Hindu cult recaptures its talisman, however, the English cult of domesticity eventually reclaims Rachel. Victorian England clings to its forms of heathen worship as tenaciously as India.

Face to face with strangers

As the romantic and criminal story lines draw to a close, Collins offers no sense of a triumphant transcendence of imperial dichotomies. Both plots continue to emphasize the strength of Victorian cultural investment in the otherness of heathen idolatry and savage self-seeking. Yet both plots also ensure that the complicity of English characters in outlandish modes of thought and behavior at least comes to light. And both plots continue to erode, through very different mechanisms, lines of demarcation between colonizer and colonized.

The happy ending of the romantic plot reflects the result of a sympathetic relationship that bridges the social divide between the English lovers and Ezra Jennings. In the context of England's self-proclaimed mission to enlighten the dark places of the earth, it is deeply ironic that the solution of the mystery in England, the "toilsome journey from the darkness to the light," depends on this racially hybrid colonial subject (369). Jennings has been treated recently with a degree of asperity for placing himself in the role of colonial servant and for thus seeming to countenance British imperial rule.[19] Yet he himself does hold a position of authority; throughout the final section, Blake agrees to be "guided implicitly by [his] advice" (431). Indeed, Jennings usurps the presumed role of British civilizing authority in India and reverses the path of reform by correcting injustice and diffusing refined sentiment in outlandish England. While English characters inflict passionate violence on India in the "storming" of Seringapatam, Jennings "enter[s] to us," as Blake phrases it, "quietly" (1, 358). The peaceful intervention of the racial hybrid counteracts the conventional association of brutal violence with colonial subjects.

The fact that Jennings is a physician suggests that he offers a healing curative for a culture sickened by racial dichotomies. The remedy he offers, the capacity to perceive arbitrarily drawn "lines of demarcation" and to tolerate their dissolution, is inscribed in and on his body. As the child of an English man and a woman indigenous to "one of our colonies," Jennings subverts in his biological heritage the barrier dividing colonizer and colonized (411).[20] The symbolic code of his weird appearance further calls that barrier into doubt. His most notable feature, his "piebald" hair, opposes black and white "without the slightest gradation of grey" (358). Collins emphasizes the abnormality of this stark division, referring to it as an "extraordinary contrast" that has occurred only through "some freak of nature" (358–9). The ideological separation of racial identities is, he suggests, as fully "capricious" as the principle that has divided the colors of Jennings's hair (358). It is further remarkable that the dividing "line between the two colors," preserves "no sort of regularity. At one place, the white hair ran up into the black; at another, the black hair ran down into the white" (359). Those who gaze upon Ezra Jennings confront a symbolic text that graphically illustrates the construction and inevitable confusion of antithetical racial categories.

Because he unsettles imperial dichotomies, however, Jennings calls forth the intense dread of the uncanny. A servant at the Verinder estate experiences "downright terror" in his presence (460). Mrs Merridew, Rachel's chaperone, "utter[s] a faint little scream at the first sight of [his] gipsy complexion and [his] piebald hair" (462). Jennings inspires, as he ruefully observes, near universal "dislike and distrust" (441). His ostracization is tragic because, unlike the novel's other uncanny symbols, he demonstrates the universality of human nature by exemplifying certain of its most admirable qualities. While the Moonstone awakens and intensifies acquisitive desire and idolatrous obsession, the colonial hybrid kindles sympathy and compassion. Revealing the precious associations he holds for "little hedgeside flowers," Jennings speaks in the voice of a Wordsworthian persona who taps into the great fund of human sympathy and compassion by projecting significance onto the "meanest flower that blows" (411).[21] Both Blake and Rachel find it possible to look beyond his deceptively foreign appearance to appreciate such familiar sentiments. Although Rachel is at first taken aback by his aspect, she refuses to treat him "like a stranger" (460). As Blake repeatedly comes "face to face with Ezra Jennings," he begins to sense the "inscrutable appeal to [his] sympathies" emanating from the "strange man" (408, 410). Collins rewards them for overcoming the "terror" inspired by hybridity by reuniting them within the fold of tenderness over which Jennings presides. Notably, both first express their love for each other to Jennings.

If Jennings shows that strangers possess familiar sentiments, his detective work correspondingly discloses the unfamiliar terrain of the English self. He counteracts the projection of criminal instincts and savage impulses onto racial others by guiding Blake toward a degree, at least, of self-knowledge. On the morning following the theft of the diamond, Blake confidently asserts that the "Indians have certainly stolen the Diamond" (89). Even after he discovers evidence that implicates himself, he remains at a loss to explain his motivations. Jennings surmises that opium, secretly administered by Dr Candy, impels Blake "to possess [him]self of the Diamond, with the purpose of securing its safety" (437). The experiment he devises to prove this supposition repeats and exposes the process of projecting possessive idolatry onto colonial otherness. As Blake drops into an opium-induced trance, Jennings recalls to his mind the "unexpected appearance of the Indians at the house" (470). It is, ironically, fear of the Hindu priests that provokes Blake to mimic their effort to possess themselves of the jewel. As they prowl outside the house, intending to secure the safety of their deity's jewel, he unconsciously performs a parallel act of idolatrous service within. Although Blake owns his actions, he never self-consciously perceives the extent to which he is as fanatical and irrational an idolater as those he scapegoats. Such self-consciousness might in turn have triggered the recognition that, after all, the Moonstone belongs to their deity, not to his. The experiment is, as Jennings admits, only "partially successful" (476).

The conclusion of the criminal plot forcefully demonstrates the inevitable return to the English self of impulses projected onto the racial other. The "noticeably dark complexion" Ablewhite assumes to avoid detection while spiriting the diamond away yet again throws criminal suspicion onto colonial subjects (482). From one perspective, the disguise indicates the extent to which Ablewhite has fallen into line with the lawless Mohammedan hands that have preceded him. At the same time, it deprives Victorian culture of the consoling affiliation of self-seeking and cruelty with racial otherness. The "swarthy complexion" is a disguise, but then so too is the white face of benevolent philanthropy (498). Surface colors, like the "false brown face" of the Shivering Sands, are ultimately less accurate guides to the nature of character than the variety of passions that seethe beneath the surface.

The unmasking of Ablewhite dramatizes the terror provoked by the realization that the familiar English philanthropist has all along concealed lawless acquisitive desire. Significantly, Blake is able to gaze with grim distaste upon the body of a dark criminal. His nerves, however, are simply "not strong enough to bear it" when Cuff reveals the "livid white" skin beneath the "swarthy complexion" (498). Cuff is more stoic, but the task of stripping away the swarthy disguise etches "horror in his face" (498). The intensity of these reactions indicates the extent to which Victorian culture is repelled by the knowledge that the "savage instincts" of "self-seeking and cruelty" do not remain "latent," even in the most apparently able and white of English subjects.[22]

The scene of Ablewhite's unmasking emblematically captures the larger symbolic and thematic structure of *The Moonstone*, which strips the foreign disguise from the face of familiar English passions. The uncanny logic of the novel repeatedly subverts prevailing assumptions about differences between familiar English selves and outlandish Indian others. The irrational superstitions, idolatrous obsessions, and acquisitive desires that Victorians associate with the volatile colony come spilling back across the lines of demarcation, ironically arising within the "quiet English house" itself.

6

Portions Wholly Savage: Ongoing Reforms at Home and Abroad

> We shall probably understand how to deal wisely with the negro race by and by. At present, what with contempt at one time and sentimentalism at another, we contrive to treat them first as animals, and next and immediately after as intellectual beings, as if the act of emancipation made them civilized and responsible creatures. It is very probable that the insurrection in Jamaica, while teaching us the error we have fallen into, will warn the Americans of what may be theirs. Our peculiar error has been that when we had once accomplished the plain duty of granting the negroes freedom, we thought that we had done everything.
>
> George Meredith[1]

In *Lord Ormont and His Aminta* (1894), George Meredith depicts a heroine who rebels against her overbearing husband. After Lord Ormont returns to England from India, having lost his commission in the Indian army for using excessive force, Aminta abandons him to live with her lover, Matthew Weyburn, a scholar who promotes internationalism and sexual equality. In this broad outline, the novel seems, like other New Woman novels of the period, to endorse a woman's bid for freedom within oppressive patriarchal culture. Yet Meredith specifically withholds self-governing sovereignty from Aminta, restricting her agency through a pattern of figures comparing her to India. He seeks to amend the oppressive treatment of the "dark brown-red" heroine not by granting her independence, but rather by reforming the colonial authority to which she is subject (123). The sequence of romantic relationships in the novel corresponds to an idealized historical narrative of colonial relations between England and India. Meredith characterizes Lord Ormont as a military force that first conquers and subjugates Aminta, Matthew as a colonial government concerned to cultivate her intellectual and moral progress. Thus conferring authority upon a newly installed administration committed to "civilizing" the heroine, the novel strategically defers her own independence.

Domestic autoethnography assists the ideological maneuvers of the plot in two distinct ways. Drawing on long-standing associations of despotic rule with the East, Meredith satirizes Lord Ormont and his sexual politics by depicting him as an Oriental potentate. Meredith also draws on contemporary sources that respond to the emerging independence movement in India. In essays by William Scawen Blunt and other advocates of liberal imperialism, Meredith discovered a narrative of the colonial relationship that appealed to his vision of political progress initiated and controlled by patriarchal government. From this narrative Meredith appropriates an ethnographic portrait of India as a hybrid colony, partly reformed into a likeness of civilized England and partly still savage. By projecting this representation of India onto the heroine, Meredith effectively undermines her quest for independence, diverting the reform energy generated by the satire on oppressive patriarchal authority into the endorsement of a liberal male alternative.

Deferring autonomy on two fronts

The metaphoric connection at the heart of the novel reflects Meredith's perception of a link between two contemporary political causes: the feminist movement in England and the independence movement in India.[2] In the middle decades of the century, the feminist campaign had gathered momentum as women began to participate in public associations devoted to broadening educational, social, and political rights and opportunities. Different groups, of course, pursued different agendas, and a wide array of political, religious, and social principles differentiated the many organizations that comprised the emerging feminist movement.[3] The campaign to extend the franchise and open political office to women certainly represented a broadly shared goal, however. In the late 1860s, women in London, Manchester, and other metropolitan centers began to form societies to promote women's suffrage. In 1867, John Stuart Mill used his recently acquired seat in Parliament to submit a petition to extend the vote to women. In the early 1870s, The *Women's Suffrage Journal* began publication and women gained the right to serve on local school boards. In 1894, the year that *Lord Ormont* was published, the National Union of Women's Suffrage Societies was formed.

Meredith died several years before the suffrage movement began to achieve its central objective, but in the last decades of his life he witnessed its growth and consolidation.

In the same period, Meredith witnessed the first steps toward self-rule in India. Earlier in the century, liberal architects of imperial policy had justified colonial governance as an instrument that would eventually allow India to govern itself. In his "Government of India" speech, for example, Thomas Babington Macaulay (1833) reflected "that the public mind of India may expand under our system till it has outgrown that system; that by good government we may educate our subjects into a capacity for better government; that, having become instructed in European knowledge, they may, in some future age, demand European institutions" (718). Fifty years later, some western-educated Indians believed that the time had come. In 1885, without support or encouragement of colonial administration, they formed the Indian National Congress. In its first years, Congress advocated distinctly moderate political reforms. Nonetheless, the organization of a "national" legislative body by indigenous politicians presented a challenge to British colonial authority. Since Congress was clearly modeled on "European institutions," its founding could not be dismissed as an eruption of devilish fanaticism, as the 1857 "Mutiny" had been.

Efforts undertaken by women and colonial subjects to gain self-governing responsibility received a highly ambivalent response from the liberal establishment. "For the most part," as Barbara Caine argues, "liberalism accepted as natural the existing sexual division of labour, and thus regarded the hierarchical relations of marriage and the confinement of women to the domestic realm as unproblematic" (103–4). For many liberals, furthermore, the hierarchical relations of colonialism were not only unproblematic, but worth preserving and defending. When Gladstone introduced the Irish Home Rule bill in 1886, a significant number of his colleagues sided with Conservatives to defeat it, forming a faction known as the Liberal Unionists. (A bill promoting *Indian* Home Rule would have been inconceivable at the time.) Meredith supported Gladstone's bill, but he also made clear his belief that the colonial relationship should not be abandoned. In his essay "Concession to the Celt" (1886), he reassuringly projects this belief onto the Irish themselves, asserting that the "vital necessity of the Union for both countries, obviously for the weaker of the two, is known to them" (450). Despite his support of Irish Home Rule, Meredith represents the colonial relationship as a marriage worth preserving for the sake of the "weaker" vessel. "Ireland is a nation," he equivocally observes, "naturally dependent though she must be" (451). Social movements that challenged presumably natural hierarchies of colonial and sexual relationships clearly tested the extent to which English male liberals were able to perceive arbitrarily imposed limits on individual liberty and were willing to contest them.[4]

In order to justify their support for policies that severely restricted the political liberty of colonial subjects, Victorian liberals relied upon a rhetoric of deferral. Like Macaulay, they gesture toward "some future age" when good colonial government will have fulfilled its educational mandate, strategically postponing the time when colonial subjects might safely be granted political equality. In his often-cited "Minute on Indian Education" (1835), Macaulay had advocated an educational system for India that he expected would create a "class of persons, Indian in blood and colour, but English in taste, in opinions, in morals, and in intellect" (729). His late-Victorian political heirs celebrate the ameliorative power of a colonial authority that had partly fulfilled this mission. Yet they also express misgivings about the "class of persons" who had remained entirely untouched by the transformative power of English education. Ethnographic reports of pockets of unreformed savagery confirmed the suspicion that India had not yet been thoroughly reshaped in the image of Englishness, that more work remained. In response to the emerging independence movement in India, late-century liberal imperialists thus repeat Macaulay's gesture of deferral, projecting onto some yet more distant future age the bestowal of political independence.

The device of deferral requires the exhibition of a partially reformed colonial subject. According to Homi Bhabha (1994), imperial reform discourse expresses its ambivalence by constructing a colonial subject characterized by "mimicry," a figure suspended between identification with reforming authority and otherness, *"almost the same, but not quite"* (his italics, 86). Those who debated the question of Indian self-government often represented the colony as a partially reformed other. In *Lord Ormont*, Aminta is likewise characterized as incompletely reformed. Despite her remarkable advances, the narrative continues to disclose traces of primitive savagery, marks of essential difference and inferiority. Her unstable development reveals a strong conservative counter-drift within Meredith's vision of social progress for women and colonial subjects alike. A liberal opponent of oppressive power, Meredith nonetheless questions the reliability of those who have been subject to it. Their imperfect mimicry of civilizing authority reflects his reluctance to trust them with self-government.

The concept of mimicry provides an extremely useful tool for exposing such reluctance, but Bhabha's representation of its subversive power requires qualification. "The *menace* of mimicry," Bhabha claims, "is its *double* vision which in disclosing the ambivalence of colonial discourse also disrupts its authority" (original italics, 88). While those who seek to expose the false promise of the civilizing mission can appreciate such disruptive effects, it is crucial to note that civilizing authority uses the figure to justify ongoing supervision. Narratives of imperial progress seek to strengthen the position of civilizing authority by strategically displaying subjects who have been partly assimilated, gesturing at once to the work that has been accomplished and that which evidently remains to be done. "The slippage between difference and identity," as Anne McClintock observes, "is rendered non-contradictory by being projected onto the axis of *time*" (her italics, 66). The figure of mimicry that Meredith extracts from late-century liberal discourse on India functions to postpone the independence of English heroine and Asian colony alike, extending indefinitely the tenure of the liberal administration that has supposedly been installed in order to lead the colonial subject toward independence.

As Meredith re-tailors the figure of mimicry for use within his romantic plot, he unwittingly exposes the false promise on which liberal colonial authority rests. The duplicity of rhetoric designed to justify an unequal distribution of power becomes particularly clear in relation to the susceptibility of English men to savage instincts. Like Collins, Meredith perceives the distinction between English and colonial subjects to be highly precarious in part because English men are prone to "outbreaks" of uncivilized instincts and impulses. In *The Egoist*, the depiction of Willoughby Patterne develops this irony at length. The representation of Lord Ormont again emphasizes that the English gentleman, a figure assumed to embody the values of metropolitan civilization, is controlled by primitive instincts in romantic and colonial affairs alike. Significantly, Matthew Weyburn is himself prone to the "outbreak" of the primitive male desire to conquer and subdue. The novel suggests that the legitimacy of his claim to civilized authority rests on a superior ability to control the instinct of brutal acquisition. Its conclusion, however, ironically suggests an effort to accommodate rather than to restrain this instinct.

Contingent emancipations

Appreciations of Meredith have tended to slight the importance of imperial discourse to his work.[5] Critics who relegate empire to the margins of his thought overlook a contradictory site of conservative, even authoritarian, political arrangements within his liberal agenda. Consider, for example, his response to Governor Eyre's violent repression of a

Jamaican uprising in 1865 (see epigraph).[6] In his analysis of the affair, Meredith foregrounds not the enforced racial and socio-economic inequalities of Jamaican society nor the retributive violence authorized by Eyre, but rather what he perceives to be the root cause of the revolt: the extension of unregulated liberty to the Jamaicans. He admits the "plain duty of granting the negroes freedom" from slavery, but mocks the assumption that freedom itself transforms slaves into "civilized and responsible creatures." Destructive "insurrection" occurs, Meredith suggests, when "emancipation" takes the form of an abrupt and isolated "act." It is a "peculiar error," he indicates, to liberate slaves without proceeding to cultivate their intellects and to teach them how to conduct themselves with self-restraint. Meredith evidently perceives "emancipation" as only an initial step in an extended process of civilizing reform, adopting the conventional sense of the word within civilizing discourses. His contemporary Henry H. M. Herbert, the Earl of Carnarvon (1878), for example, represents "emancipation from servitude" as "but the foretaste of the far higher law of liberty and progress" which colonial subjects under the "beneficent rule of Great Britain" will, in time, attain (764).

The suggestion that an "act of emancipation" ideally only initiates an extended process of subordinate reform certainly casts Meredith's support for "Emancipation of Woman" in new light.[7] While certain critics have begun to reassess Meredith as a feminist, the perspective which his use of civilizing rhetoric affords on contradictions within his vision of progress for women has yet to be fully examined.[8] As his response to the Jamaican uprising suggests, he relies on unequal power structures to propel the progressive evolution of human society or, as he terms it, the "constant advancement of the race."[9] The imperial model of "emancipation" certainly informs the analogies he draws between women and colonial subjects. Indeed, Meredith indicates that women whose development has been stunted by patriarchal despotism are no more prepared for the rigors of civilized self-rule than rebellious "negroes" in Jamaica. Seeking to fulfill the "plain duty" of freeing women from slavery while guarding against passionate "insurrection," he develops a model of a colonial male authority that "emancipates" them from oppressive authority, but also subordinates them to "beneficent" male rule.

It is crucial to perceive both sides of this equation when assessing Meredith's contribution to what Suvendrini Perera describes as the "interplay between the continually evolving discourses that constituted and managed both gender and empire" (65). Meredith partially shares the impulse of Victorian women writers who, as Susan Meyer (1996) argues, challenge the patriarchal tradition of comparing European women to colonial subjects in a self-serving effort to reenforce the essential inferiority of both groups. In *The Egoist* (1879), for instance, Meredith exposes and satirizes the language with which Dr Middleton imagines the control of Clara, who resists his authority by refusing to marry Willoughby Patterne. Dr Middleton smugly predicts that his daughter will capitulate, just "as the aboriginals of a land newly discovered by a crew of adventurous colonists do battle with the garments imposed on them by our considerate civilization; – ultimately to rejoice with excessive dignity in the wearing of a battered cocked-hat and trousers not extending to the shanks" (498). In this instance, the clash of connotations discredits the patriarchal alliance formed to bully Clara into a marriage she abhors. The presumed benevolence of "our considerate civilization" is called into question by the description of its emissaries as a "crew of adventurous colonists," an expression suggesting those responsible for bold forays and aggressive conquests. The condescending humor of the passage, based on a blatant use of the figure of mimicry, further undermines a sense of legitimate concern. Dr Middleton predicts that Clara will exhibit compliance in the comically inept mode of "aboriginals" who ape civilized habits the world over. Thus gloating over the effect of "imposed" reforms, he reveals a despotic impulse that Meredith seems to condemn.

Crucially, however, Meredith denounces colonial authority only when the governmental figure manifests no desire to foster the development of the disempowered other. Meyer argues that Victorian women writers, in response to the patriarchal discourse exemplified by Dr Middleton, themselves compare European women to colonial subjects in order to indicate a "shared experience of frustration, limitation, and subordination" (7). Occasionally, as in the case of *Wuthering Heights*, such comparisons "unleash energies of rebellion against the British empire that are also linked with rebellion against the social position of white women" (26). As his comment on the Jamaican uprising indicates, Meredith anxiously strives to contain such rebellious energy.[10] His response to the discourse exemplified by Dr Middleton is characterized by the effort to reclaim the metaphoric connection between colonial and gender hierarchies for the construction of legitimate male authority. In *Diana of the Crossways* (1885), he begins to develop a model of *truly* "considerate" colonial authority. Diana Merion, an intelligent and high-spirited Irish woman, defines such authority through a critique of colonial policy in Ireland. She encourages English officials to put more effort into "study[ing] the Irish" and endorses a comparison of governing them "to the management of a horse: the rider should not grow restive when the horse begins to kick: calmer; firm, calm, persuasive" (243). Redworth, the level-headed English politician who first uses this figure, applies his subtle "management" strategies to the Irish heroine as well. Devotedly studying Diana through a sequence of tumultuous affairs, he eventually persuades her to "run into [the] harness of a marriage that fully integrates colonial and gender power relations" (466). Finally celebrating the "Irishwoman's bestowal of her hand on the open-minded Englishman she had learned to trust," the novel works to replace the destructive dynamic of oppression and rebellion with a colonial relationship characterized by the concern of the government and the consent of the governed (488).

It is in *Lord Ormont*, however, that Meredith most fully develops a model of colonial male authority that acquires legitimacy by effecting the moral and intellectual progress of its subjects through sympathetic understanding and "persuasive" direction. While generally dismissed as uncharacteristically sentimental, the novel repays close attention for elaborating this ideological supplement to Meredith's vision of female "emancipation."[11] Graham McMaster (1991) provides a welcome exception to arguments that slight Meredith's imaginative investment in imperialism, but his claim that *Lord Ormont* "has as its purpose a liberal-radical undermining of the legitimacy of Victorian England" and its "patriarchal, masculine and imperial institutions" distorts the novel's project, which is to strengthen these institutions through reform (39). Meredith certainly despises conquest, imperial and romantic alike, driven by the male will to subjugate. He pejoratively describes Cecil Rhodes, for example, as a "trickster" who "plunge[s] the English upon Imperialism" in Africa; he also observes with a note of concern that the aggressive imperialist "subjugates many, my fair friend Flora Shaw among them" (*Letters* 3: 1356). In a telling qualification, however, Meredith notes that Rhodes's seductive "cry of Cape to Cairo" would not "be bad if he had roused [the English] to anticipate their new duties in consequence" (*Letters* 3: 1356). *Lord Ormont* extends this qualification to cover the case of ruling the fair at home as well as the dark abroad. Seeking to redeem colonial male authority as a vehicle for liberal reform, Meredith suggests that those who accept the "duties" of empire legitimize the power they hold.

Colonial progress in India

In *Lord Ormont*, Meredith imagines an alternative to imperial subjugation through figures drawn from the late-Victorian liberal discourse on India.

The *actual* treatment of the colony during this period did not strike him as ideal. In fact, he repudiates "these English," in language anticipating the novel's link between colonial and sexual relationships, for the "present hugging of their India, which they are ruining for the sake of giving a lucrative post to younger sons of their middle class" (*Letters* 2: 564). In the liberal program for the reform of exploitative "hugging," however, Meredith discovers a model of constructive civilizing authority. This program is exemplified by Viceroy Ripon's Resolution on Local Self-Government (1882), which granted Indians the right to sit on local administrative councils. Liberal proponents of this measure, however, provide remarkable instances of civilizing ambivalence. Primarily invested in the consolidation of liberal colonial government, they call into question their own vision of progress by expressing grave misgivings about the capacity of India to handle the weighty responsibilities of civilized self-rule. An essay advocating Ripon's policy by Wilfrid Scawen Blunt (1885) will illuminate figures that resurface in the novel to justify the highly contingent "emancipation" of the woman-as-India.[12] Although I have no positive evidence to confirm that Meredith read this work, it is far from unlikely. The essay culminated a series by Blunt which ran in the *Fortnightly Review* concurrently with *Diana of the Crossways*. Meredith was personally acquainted with Blunt and trusted his opinion on imperial affairs. After reading his book on Egypt, Meredith observed that Blunt "speaks with knowledge."[13]

Blunt represents Ripon's policy as a necessary departure from a disgraceful history of exploitation stretching seamlessly forward from the reign of the East India Company, which managed the colony "without scruple" in its search for private profit (389). Like the Company from which it gradually gained administrative control, the crown continues to advance the "interests of English trade and English adventure" with slight regard for the "advantage of the natives" (389). Blunt admits that "English rule, with all its defects" has incidentally sparked an "immense revival of intellectual and moral energy" by supplanting the despotic princes who "held India in mental chains" (387). Yet he faults the colonial administration for failing to cultivate the progress it has awakened, for remaining "too conservative, too selfish, too alien to the thoughts and needs of India" (389–90). Claiming to possess the sympathetic understanding the government lacks, he explains that "[w]hat India really asks for" and, in the name of justice and progress, should receive, is "self-government" (393).

This essay's foremost priority, however, is to strengthen the position of the liberal colonial administration that will grant and regulate steps toward self-government. Blunt objects to insensitive and oppressive rule because it obstructs progress, but more fundamentally because it jeopardizes the authority of the government that to his mind represents the only hope for progress. Blunt lends urgency to the reforms he advocates by reminding readers, implicitly recalling the "Mutiny" of 1857, that the "consent of the people has always underlain the exercise of our power" (388). Particularly anxious about another rebellion, Blunt senses a "daily increasing danger" that colonial consent will be "overpowered by a passionate sentiment evoked by some chance outbreak" (388). Venting an often-expressed Victorian concern, he predicts that Russia will, if given the opportunity, seek to intensify the "disaffection of our Indian fellow-subjects ... and will encourage them to resistence" (388). While the colony is, on the one hand, prepared to accept the mantle of self-governing responsibility, it is also disturbingly prone to passionate outbreaks of violence and highly vulnerable to seductive attention of predatory rivals. The paradoxical emphasis begins to demonstrate Blunt's ambivalent attitude to the colony.

Indeed, Blunt is just as much concerned to restrict as to advocate self-government. He repeatedly emphasizes the inability of colonial subjects to conduct civilized government on a scale broad enough to supplant the necessity of British colonial rule. "The Indians," he notes, "are no single race; they profess no one creed, they speak no one language" (387). While "Mutiny" texts emphasize the racial uniformity of India, the late-century liberal discourse emphasizes the subcontinent's heterogeneity, in part to deny the possibility that colonial subjects can transcend sectarian interests rooted in racial, religious, and cultural identity. As another liberal commentator observes, the "British position in India is chiefly strong in its umpire-like character between sections of the population extremely ill-disposed towards each other."[14] Such comments position the colonial government as the sole arbiter of impartial justice, the sole possessor of the disinterested perspective required for civil government. The figure of combative heterogeneity works hand in hand with the figure of mimicry. As "highly civilised as portions" of India have become, Blunt observes that the colony "contains within its borders portions wholly savage. There are tribes in all the hills still armed with spear and shield" (387). Mimicking its colonial government, India reflects English civility on its surface, but remains recalcitrantly savage deep "within its borders" (387). Blunt uses references to the colony's heterogeneity and pockets of savagery to account for the moderate restraint of the proposed "self-government" measures.

Civilizing authority contains its apparently contradictory emphases, as McClintock argues, by projecting ongoing reforms. While local government may be ceded to colonial subjects, supervisory "Imperial power should," in the "present age" at least, most certainly "remain in the hands" of the British viceroy (394). Echoing Macaulay's gesture of deferral, Blunt glimpses the possibility of full self-government for India in the "dim future" (394). The "work of education," he recognizes, is simply "not yet complete" (387).

Colonial government gone native

Lord Ormont traces a parallel path in its effort to negotiate a transition from "selfish" colonial rule to legitimate civilizing authority. No more than in Blunt's essay does this path lead, in the foreseeable future, to full self-governing authority for the woman figured as colony. Providing ample evidence to prove the necessity of ongoing reforms, Meredith confers authority instead on the governor who desires to "hug" Aminta, to maintain the colonial tie and preserve the power relations that characterize it, in order to facilitate her development.

If *Lord Ormont* adopts the objectives and ideological maneuvers of the late-Victorian liberal discourse on India, it reconstructs an earlier era in an effort to convey a sense of definitive change and progress. Like Blunt, Meredith perceives in the enduring legacy of "selfish" colonial adminis-tration a disturbing sense of continuity. When the civilizing mission gained ascendence in the early nineteenth century, it promised a new ethical orientation for colonial rule.[15] Yet the late-century government of India continues to be characterized by exploitative "hugging." Meredith fashions the novel as an idealized corrective to a history in which the positive and negative effects of colonial rule are inextricably tangled. Set in the early nineteenth century, it depicts a clearly articulated shift from oppressive to liberating government produced by the emergence and consolidation of a liberal administration.

Meredith first announces this shift through a public debate sparked by Lord Ormont's military career in India, where he peremptorily attacks an "influential Indian Prince" supposedly plotting rebellion (21). Those supporting Ormont promote the aggressive military perspective Meredith associates with the first phase of colonialism. They admire the impulsive general for drawing the "sword … out smartly at the hint of a warning to protect the sword's conquests" and applaud his use of "decisive Oriental" methods suited to "native tastes" (21–2). Those opposing Ormont convey the emergent perspective of civilizing assimilation, arguing that colonial government should, rather than conforming to the despotic model supposedly inherent to India, aim to use its power to reform the benighted other. Perceiving Ormont as "drunk of the East," they repudiate his cultural transgression in the style of those who faulted eighteenth-century Company agents for adopting the "military and despotical" mode of "Oriental" authority (22).[16] Colonial authority, they argue, should uplift Indians by relying on the disciplinary effects of impartial justice exemplified by "modern English magisterial methods" (21). The "Book of the Law" should be "conciliatingly addressed to their sentiments by a benign civilizing Power" (21–2). In the dismissal of Lord Ormont, Meredith indicates the eclipse of aggressive militarism by this civilizing theory of colonial government in India.

This shift corresponds, within the romantic plot, to the sequence of Aminta's relationships in England. The phrase with which Lord Ormont asserts possession of his wife – "I have a jewel" (123), he claims – reveals an ominous disinclination to relinquish the variety of absolute authority he claims in India, conventionally figured in the novel as "that splendid jewel" (20) in England's imperial crown. "[H]ugging" Aminta to himself without regard for her advantage, Ormont refuses to avow his marriage, thwarting propriety by seeming to keep a mistress in an obscure effort to show disdain for the society that has deprived him of his post. Aminta's efforts to win public acknowledgment as Lady Ormont only provide him with a field in which to redeploy his aggressive military impulses; he constructs his wife as a "Fair Enemy" whose maneuvers he opposes in "direct engagements" (125). Ormont savors the conquest and possession of Aminta while refusing to accept the "duties" of empire, exemplifying the will to subjugate and exploit that Meredith associates with Oriental despotism.

Meredith repudiates the "conservative" and "selfish" patriarchal authority by aligning him with Oriental despotism in private as well as public affairs. Casting an "old-world eye upon women" (272), Ormont arrogantly asserts that they are "happier enslaved" (278). Although Aminta eventually understands that her husband, whom she learns to compare to an "Ottoman Turk on his divan," intends to keep her "enslaved," social and legal restrictions block her escape (201). Meredith thus additionally associates English marriage conventions with the outdated Oriental world. He justifies the novel's most radical proposition, that Aminta justifiably abandons her husband, by representing the "enthronement" of marriage law in social opinion as the "rule of the savage's old deity, sniffing blood sacrifice" (286). The "immolation" of women to this primitive deity "arrests the general expansion to which we step" and "decivilizes" society (286). Through a figurative reference to sati, the Hindu custom of widow "immolation" (outlawed by

Governor Bentinck in 1829), Meredith criticizes the "sacrifice" of Aminta to the will of her living husband.[17] Again connecting Lord Ormont's domestic regime to the period prior to "civilizing" interventions in India, the sati image implicitly anticipates the installation of a reform-minded administration.

Meredith objects to despotic government for precluding the progress of colonial subjects, a fact demonstrated in the kind of rebellion it provokes. Before Matthew appears on the scene, Aminta begins to subvert her husband's rule by encouraging the advances of Adolphus Morsfield, a superficially gallant admirer whose courtly manners mask regressive predatory desire. Her rebellious flirtation recalls Blunt's warning that insensitive colonial rule triggers such outbreaks of "passionate sentiment" as the deluded belief among Indians "that the exchange from English to another foreign rule would improve their condition" (388). According to Meredith, patriarchal autocracy, like its colonial counterpart, predetermines "passionate" rebellions by confining women "to the vast realm of feeling" (93). When provoked by "Injustice," the "unsatisfied heart of woman" wanders into the "vast realm of thinking. Once there, and but a single step on the road, she is a rebel against man's law for her sex" (93). While she may continue to "think submissively," her heart leads a subconscious "revolt" (93). In Blunt's political romance, Russia insidiously presents itself as the "friend to India," attempting to woo the colony from its current ruler (388). In *Lord Ormont*, Morsfield plays the role of opportunistic and deceptive "friend" who exploits the passionate disgruntlement provoked by unjust authority. Although Meredith justifies Aminta's discontent, her passionate "revolt" begins to suggest that she, like Indians duped by Russian flattery, remains unprepared for the intellectual and moral rigors of self-governing independence.

The reform of colonial male government

Meredith thus takes steps to avoid the "peculiar error" of extending unlimited freedom to the rebellious woman whose "dusky" complexion, praised for its "Oriental luster," symbolizes not only her oppression, but also her uncivilized and irresponsible nature (69, 181).[18] While Meredith releases the woman-as-India from despotic colonial rule, readings of the novel that discover in the repudiation of Lord Ormont a stable commitment to the independence and equality of women or, for that matter, of colonial subjects, fail to appreciate the degree to which he subscribes to the logic of the civilizing mission. Rather than rejecting, as McMaster would have it, the "material and ideological structures through which domestic and colonial power were maintained," Meredith seeks to strengthen those structures by reforming them, making them more likely to secure the "consent" of colonial subjects and thus achieve administrative efficiency (45). Ormont's loss of command in India foreshadows the loss of "his" Aminta, but her "emancipation" is granted on condition that she accept subordination to a more liberal and progressive administration. The novel depicts not the rejection, but the increasing sophistication of colonial "management" strategies in its movement from military subjugation to "persuasive" control.

Meredith, like Blunt, locates the only potential for colonial development in this progressive evolution of patriarchal government. In the novel, Matthew enacts the full evolution Blunt can only hopefully imagine, steadily maturing from a youth who reveres Lord Ormont's military rule into a "benign civilizing Power" fully attuned to the "thoughts and needs" of the woman-as-India. When Matthew becomes Ormont's secretary and is thereby reacquainted with his adolescent sweetheart, he must strive to overcome the imperial will to possess and dominate. As Ormont discourses "with racy eloquence of our hold on India," Matthew is held by Aminta's "large dark eyes," evocative to him of "southern night. They sped no shot; they rolled forth an envelopment" (62). Her gaze displays a "realm in a look" and, unable to stop thinking of her, he feels that "she was round him, like the hills of a valley" (65–6). Figuring Aminta's body as colonial terrain, these images of sexual fear and desire recall the defining moment in Lord Ormont's career, when he rides "across a stretch of country including hill and forest" to defeat the rebels "who might," had they known the odds in their favor, "have enveloped" the British force (22). In a highly relevant analysis of the imperial trope of "feminizing the land," McClintock observes that the "erotics of imperial conquest were also an erotics of engulfment ... accompanied, all too often, by an excess of military violence" (24).

Testing Matthew with the temptation to which Lord Ormont succumbs, Meredith works to construct a self-restrained authority figure who can transcend this dynamic, replacing the "racy" thrill of conquering and subjugating foreign ground with the dutiful cultivation of it. When Matthew first sees Aminta as a grown woman, he too succumbs to "his man's nature – the bad in us, when beauty of woman is viewed; or say, the old original revolutionary, best kept untouched; for a touch or a meditative pause above him, fetches him up to roam the civilized world devouringly and lawlessly" (64). In language that blends Evangelical suspicion of "bad in us" with the anthropological conviction that "old original" impulses remain dormant in the mind, Meredith represents male sexual desire as a primal force antagonistic to civilization. A masturbatory "touch" or "meditative pause" empowers predatory male desire, releasing it into "the civilized world," where it hunts for sexual prey. While under the spell of Ormont's martial theme, Matthew briefly abandons himself to his desire. Imaginatively transported to the landscape of the feminine, a "measureless realm" like India, he gives himself over to the erotics of engulfment, "march[ing] ... to the music of sonorous brass for some drunken minutes" (64). Then, however, Matthew demonstrates the extent to which he has surpassed his hero by repressing his desire.

As the representation of Lord Ormont's cultural transgression suggests, imperial discourse manages the disturbing appeal of the erotics of engulfment by attributing it to the contaminating influence of primitive otherness. Those who support Ormont excuse him for succumbing to the "native taste" for despotism. In romance, too, his many affairs testify to a nature "notoriously susceptible" to female charms (181). Meredith suggests that Lord Ormont, like the "military and despotical" officials of the East India Company, "goes native"; his conquests reveal, ironically, that the varieties of alterity over which he assumes command have actually captured him. Because Matthew responds with self-restraint to the seductive force located in the "southern night" of Aminta's gaze, he proves himself more able to withstand the allure of primitive terrain and thus qualified to facilitate its reform.

The premium the novel thus places on male self-control as the engine of progress in turn carries significant implications for the agency of the English woman and the colony to which she is compared. Meredith suggests that Aminta emanates a seductive and enveloping aura that calls forth the imperial male will to subjugate with despotic force.[19] Her aunt notably describes her as "born to create violent attachments" (100). Clearly sharing responsibility for the oppressive treatment from which she suffers, Aminta must await a man who can help her transcend the destructive power relation sadly adapted to her own "native taste."

Through the professional development of the hero, Meredith charts the gradual ascendance of a liberal male colonial authority equipped to undertake this mission. While Matthew reveres Ormont's military prowess as an adolescent, he himself acquires authority as a writer and teacher. Hired to edit the colonial campaigner's memoirs, he significantly distinguishes himself through critical refinement of the "work," in a broad sense, that his hero has accomplished. When Ormont petulantly burns an essay, Matthew observes that Aminta is also a "priceless manuscript cast to the flames" (119). Regarded by her husband as an inert trophy of conquest, a "jewel" in the imperial male crown, Aminta is refigured by Matthew as a text worthy of editorial development, undervalued by the soldier who would rather destroy that which he cannot improve. His astute literary judgment demonstrates the sympathetic understanding that, according to Blunt, British government tragically lacks. When Aminta wonders how her lover has learned "to read at any moment right to the soul of a woman." she credits him with the ability to discern the "thoughts and needs" of colonial subjects (285). The pen of the sensitive editor proves to be a much more effective instrument of improvement than the sword of the vindictive commander.

Matthew leaves the employ of Ormont to found a "modern" academy. Declaring that the "schoolmaster ploughs to make a richer world," he articulates the liberal progressive values that transform the woman-as-India from field of conquest into site of cultivating education (154). Concerned to differentiate this administration from Ormont's regime, Meredith disguises its affiliation to power. Aminta compares Matthew's appearance to an "intervention distinctly designed to waken the best in her" (134). Under his almost invisible influence, she experiences the "sprouting of a mind repressed" (290). While civilizing guidance operates discretely, the novel clearly indicates the moral and intellectual assimilation of Aminta, who gradually gives "her mind to [Matthew's] voice" (285). This willing submission expresses a point made by Frantz Fanon (1963) among others, that colonial authority achieves hegemony when the colonial subject "admits loudly and intelligibly the supremacy of the white man's values" (44). Aminta admits the supremacy of Matthew's values by absorbing his disdain for class distinctions, renouncing the "ambition to be a fine lady" that partly motivates her marriage to Ormont (202). While she at first despises Matthew for becoming a schoolmaster rather than soldier, she also becomes increasingly persuaded by his idealistic coeducational scheme, fantasizing about taking an active role in his academy as teacher of the female students. Her dream of professional agency holds out the hope that the civilizing mission will indeed fulfill its promise to lead the subject woman forth into the enlightened world of sexual equality.

Meredith, however, firmly restricts the agency to which the heroine has access. Blunt constructs a model of local self-government balanced and restrained by imperial supervision, certain that a reformed British administration represents the only hope for the continued progress of the partially civilized colony. Meredith, similarly, grants his heroine a form of local self-government, which she uses to legislate an end to her marriage. He remains nonetheless committed to preserving the woman's submission to the "Imperial power" of male authority in its reformed shape. Freeing herself from the oppressive military regime, Aminta significantly re-enlists her loyalty in Matthew, whom she identifies as her true "companion *and leader*" (193, my italics). The liberal colonial government thus wins the enthusiastic "consent" of the heroine.

Once the romantic plot has secured the consent of Aminta to her new male leader, it loses interest in the effort to imagine her social progress. Curiously, the school described in the final chapter, the supposed fulfillment of Matthew's progressive ideals, apparently has enrolled no female students for Aminta to teach. Matthew's commitment to coeducation evaporates without explanation. The fact that Aminta's vision of professional fulfillment remains only a dream reveals a bait-and-switch duplicity within the variety of female "emancipation" that the novel illustrates. In his defense of local self-rule in India, Viceroy Ripon's finance minister frankly expressed a similar perspective. "We shall not subvert the British Empire," he proclaims, "by allowing the Bengali Baboo to discuss his own schools and drains. Rather shall we afford him a safety-valve if we can turn his attention to such innocuous subjects" (qtd. in Brown 1985: 127). Granting Aminta the right to dissolve her marriage similarly functions as a "safety-valve," giving the disgruntled woman enough control over her life to dampen her rebellious spirit. Meredith ultimately perceives limited forms of self-government as astute conciliations intended to preserve the "colonial" union.

Mimicry and colonial subjection

Lord Ormont adopts the rhetorical strategies of the contemporary liberal discourse on India to justify its continuation of the colonial relationship, particularly relying on the representation of the colony as only partially civilized, an unstable parody of its colonial government. When wondering if she could provide Matthew with a suitable match in qualities such as intellect, moral strength, and "self-command," Aminta concludes that "[t]o imitate was a woman's utmost" (283). Although the novel applauds her effort to imitate the "benign civilizing Power," it unveils within her subjectivity an essential wildness that botches the performance. Alternately revealing signs of progress and of unreformable difference, Aminta remains trapped within the state of mimicry. She is partially reformed into a likeness of Matthew, his female equal, and partially unalterably other, his female subordinate. Her faltering imitation exposes the strategy through which the narrative justifies the ongoing supervision of progressive male authority.

In his analysis of the mistakes committed in Jamaica, Meredith characterizes the treatment of the "negro race" as swinging from one to another erroneous extreme. "[W]e contrive to treat them first as animals," he laments, "and next and immediately after as intellectual beings." *Lord Ormont* attempts to avoid unreasonable extremes by foregrounding the process of intellectual development, but the novel ironically continues to treat Aminta as an animal even as it lauds her "sprouting" mind. Matthew, for example, thinks of her late in the novel as a fragile and helpless "gazelle in the streets of London city" (315). The character responsible for narrowing the gap between the colonial subject's undeveloped mind and the civilized intellect here heightens the contrast, representing Aminta as an animal removed from its proper colonial habitat to the imperial metropolis, vulnerably placed on an epistemological grid it can never comprehend. In another instance, the narrator forgives an irrational action on Aminta's part by observing that woman "is a creature of the apparent moods and shifts and tempers only because she is kept in narrow confines, resembling, if you like, a wild cat caged" (195). Attributing female irrationality to the cage of patriarchal oppression, the figure relies on the conception of woman as "wild cat," more predictable, perhaps, when released from "narrow confines," but "wild" still. For all that the novel approves of her intellectual development, it ascribes to Aminta an essential animal wildness that calls into doubt the degree to which she can ever hope to attain civilized responsibility.

Perceiving the subjective civilizing process as one in which the intellect increasingly gains control of impulses and emotions, Meredith represents female passion as a constant disruptive threat. Historically confined to the "realm of feeling," women must paradoxically rely on faculties antithetical to civilized "self-command" to drive their development. It is through her love for Matthew that Aminta learns to disdain the "savage passions" that govern sexual relations in Lord Ormont's aristocratic world (165). Yet her love, itself a passionate force, also accentuates her own affiliation to the savage. She reveals her desire for Matthew in a blush that "kindle[s] the deeper of her dark hue" (241). The physical sign of her status as an irresponsible colonial subject ominously intensifies along with her affection.

Despite the intellectual and moral advances Aminta achieves, she remains as volatile as the partially civilized India, containing "within [her] borders portions wholly savage." When Lord Ormont sends her a note vaguely referring to an "accident" at the fencing rooms (actually a report of Morsfield's death), Aminta impulsively fears that he has killed Matthew. Assessing her husband's character to determine his guilt, she "most unjustly" views him as a thoroughly "repulsive figure" (298). The narrator explains this act of injustice by noting that the

> heart of a woman is instantly planted in jungle when the spirits of the two men closest to her are made to stand opposed by a sudden excitement of her fears for the beloved one. She cannot see widely, and is one of the wild while the fit lasts; and, after it, that savage narrow vision she had of the unbeloved retains its vivid print in permanence. (297–8)

Possessing the "heart of a woman," Aminta cannot transcend the selfish fears and desires that Meredith associates with torrid colonial subjectivity. The narrator first represents her sudden displacement from temperate regions of civilized judgment as an abrupt response to certain circumstances, an instance of reverting to "one of the wild," of returning to the "jungle," always potentially possible but yet contained within "the fit" of passion. As the passage continues, however, it calls into question the temporal borders it first establishes. The "savage narrow vision," while perhaps in full command only briefly, nevertheless "retains its vivid print," extending beyond the interval of passionate intensity to corrupt disinterested judgment "in permanence." It becomes clear that women never really leave the "jungle"; savagery is not a condition to which they revert, but rather from which they cannot fully escape.

Passionate female volatility functions in the novel, as in Blunt's representation of India (and Meredith's representation of Ireland), to discredit the colonial subject as a governing authority in her own right. The novel alienates her from the principle that it identifies as the engine of progress. Articulating the broad-minded perspective of the "liberal mind," Matthew declares that "[u]nless we have justice abroad like a common air, there's no peace, and no steady advance" (210). Her vision obstructed by the jungle growth of passions, Aminta herself cannot be trusted to "see widely" in this way, although she does learn to appreciate that her lover possesses "the larger view" (201). In fact, she eventually decides that he personifies the very principle that she offends, concluding that Matthew "is just – he is Justice" (285). In light of her inevitably unjust woman's heart, the ability to perceive his superiority marks the *limit* of her own reform. Although Matthew exerts an influence over the coastline of Aminta's subjectivity, the passionate "darker" self holds sway "in the hills," contesting his authority in sudden rampages that disrupt her civilizing progress. The "work of education" remaining clearly incomplete, the prospect of self-governing authority for Aminta fades into the "dim future"; the liberal colonial government, meanwhile, acquires supervisory legitimacy.

Unregenerate imperial desire

Meredith displays the moral and intellectual advances achieved by Aminta in order to prove the superiority of "benign civilizing" methods over military despotism rather than to expand her agency and authority. Like Blunt, he is primarily concerned to secure the "consent" of the woman-as-India to the governance of liberal colonial authority. While the possessive pronoun in the title gathers ironic significance as it becomes increasingly clear that Aminta will not for long consent to be owned by Lord Ormont, the greater irony is that the novel ultimately accommodates the male desire to conquer and possess the colonial terrain of woman. It discredits, certainly, Ormont's imperial will to subjugate, which it associates with Oriental despotism. Matthew's triumph, on the other hand, shows that Meredith sanctions the possession of women when attended by the promise of fair and progressive government. Before Aminta leaves her husband, Matthew's "hot blood" urges him "to take his own, to snatch her from a possessor who forfeited by undervaluing her. This was the truth in a better-ordered world: she belonged to the man who could help her to grow" (289–90). Matthew restrains his primitive instinct; his self-command prevents him from following the impulse to "snatch" the woman he desires. The novel, however, effectively grants him his vision of a "better-ordered world." Observing that "[h]er faith in [Matthew's] guidance was equal to her dependence," the narrator announces Aminta's willing subordination to the colonial government that helps her "to grow" (282). Despite his professed interest in the "Emancipation of Woman," Meredith offers a merely more tolerable form of subjection to a progressive colonial administration that, governing with "Justice," justifies its ownership.

In *Lord Ormont and His Aminta*, the narrative structure of the civilizing mission subverts the potential for a social progress that leads to the heroine's self-governing independence. Divesting Aminta of responsibility for her own development, Meredith instead institutionalizes a liberal administration to lead her forth from the degradations of her oppressive marriage and benighted patriarchal culture. Ultimately unwilling to deprive this "benign civilizing Power" of its justification for ruling, he suggests that Aminta indefinitely requires an ideally just authority who "understand[s] how to deal wisely" with her partially civilized nature and perceives the hazards of granting freedoms without imposing controls.

Notes

1 Crossing the Divide

1. Let me take the opportunity to clarify my use of important terms. First, I use the word "colonial" as an umbrella term that reflects the English perspective toward Asia, Africa, and the Americas and other non-European sites inhabited by people deemed to be racially different and inferior. In the Victorian period, this perspective encompassed places (like India) that were already officially subordinated to colonial rule, but also those (like tropical Africa in the middle of the century) that were not. Although I recognize the historical inaccuracy in the latter case, I have nonetheless chosen to use the term throughout this book both for the mere sake of consistency and, more important, because it emphasizes the extent to which imperial power, the presumed ability and right to incorporate distant peoples and territories into British dominions, represented an essential strand of English identity in the Victorian period. From the metropolitan perspective, all those perceived as racially and culturally distinct and inferior were colonial others, regardless of their actual political status in relation to the British empire. Second, I use the terms "English" and "Englishness" to designate the national identity formulated in part through opposition to colonial otherness. The empire, the political forum of this dynamic, was of course in name British, but, as Linda Colley reminds us, England formed the British state through an early exertion of imperial power over adjacent states. The terms are often used synonymously by Victorian writers, but the extent to which Britishness was an Anglocentric construction is reflected in the fact that nineteenth-century writers frequently represent imperial influence as the assimilation of colonial subjects to Englishness rather than Britishness. In his well-known "Minute on Indian Education," Thomas Babington Macaulay imagines formulating a "class of persons, Indian in blood and colour, but English in taste, in opinions, in morals, and in intellect" (729).
2. In *The Lords of Human Kind* (1986), V. G. Kiernan catalogs a vast array of Victorian expressions of superiority and difference.
3. Other critics have confirmed Said's general point. Abdul R. JanMohamed (1985) extended the antithetical structure of Orientalism to all colonialist discourse, which collectively narrates a "manichean allegory" by propagating "oppositions between white and black, good and evil, superiority and inferiority, civilization and savagery, intelligence and emotion, rationality and sensuality, self and Other, subject and object." In her illuminating history of the emergence of Britain as political and imaginative entity, Linda Colley (1992) argues that Britons "came to define themselves as a single people not because of any political or cultural consensus at home, but rather in reaction to the Other beyond their shores" (6). She emphasizes the function of religious differences in this process, observing that Britons repressed internal divisions by defining "themselves as Protestants struggling for survival against [France,] the world's foremost Catholic power. ... And, increasingly, as the wars went on, they

defined themselves in contrast to the colonial peoples they conquered, peoples who were manifestly alien in terms of culture, religion and colour" (5).

4. By attending to the suspicion that an *abhorred* colonial "otherness" dwelt within the English state and subject, I attempt to capture an irony that complements the one pursued by Robert J. C. Young (1995). The "fixity of identity for which Englishness developed such a reputation arose," he argues, "because it was in fact continually being contested, and was rather designed to mask its uncertainty, its sense of being estranged from itself, sick with desire for the other" (2). While Young demonstrates that English identity hides a secret desire, I aim to show that it hides an equally powerful repulsion, not directed toward the colonial other (the repudiation of whom helps to form the mask of Englishness), but rather toward aspects of itself that horribly mirror colonial otherness.

5. Some readers have thus assumed that this passage represents a strange contradiction in *Orientalism*. In his polemical response to the book, for example, John M. MacKenzie (1995) refers to this quotation as "one of the most enigmatic and least developed passages in Orientalism" (10). In defense of Said, Rajan argues that his "language is more qualified than the reports of it that are offered" by detractors such as MacKenzie (216).

6. In addition to Bhabha, whose essays have been especially influential, Sara Suleri (1992) has helped to expand appreciation of the ambivalence of colonial discourse. Her *Rhetoric of English India* is grounded on the notion that the "story of colonial encounter is in itself a radically decentering narrative that is impelled to realign with violence any static binarism between colonizer and colonized" (2). The violence with which binarisms are enforced indicates the presence of a "terror" that in turn "suggests the precarious vulnerability of cultural boundaries in the context of cultural exchange" (2).

7. In *Imperial Leather* (1995), Anne McClintock offers interesting readings of Victorian advertisements that reflect these assumptions. See her chapter "Soft-Soaping Empire: Commodity Racism and Imperial Advertising" (207–31). It would be inaccurate to assume that imperial trade simply reaffirmed notions of English imperial supremacy. As Barry Milligan (1995) observes in his fascinating study of opium in nineteenth-century English culture, the consumption of colonial products ironically tapped into a fear that "foreign" products might destabilize or transform English identity. Milligan argues that the "threat of Oriental commodities is significant enough when they are figuratively ingested into 'British' culture, as in the case of Persian rugs, Chinese porcelain, and Japan-lacquered objets d'art. But when the foreign commodities in question are literally swallowed by individual British bodies, the figurative aspect of the threat is literalized ... opium is perhaps the most broadly representative case, for not only was it literally ingested by British bodies (as were tea, spices, and so forth) but it also had a reputation for altering the consciousness of its user" (29–30). Also see Leask, who offers a complementary reading of Thomas De Quincey. "To be an *English* opium-eater." Leask suggests, "was to consume (although maybe ... to be consumed by) the East" (original italics, 208).

8. Although I reach different conclusions than Perera, I am indebted to her methodology. By focusing on a different set of figures of colonial alterity that emerge within the representation of English life and subjectivity, I seek to extend as well as challenge her analysis of the "interlocking vocabularies"

through which Victorian novelists engaged debates about gender and empire (8).

9. Deirdre David (1995), who, like Perera, focuses on the interrelation of gender and imperial ideologies, foregrounds texts in which English women function as "resonant symbols of sacrifice for civilizing the 'native' and ... as emblems of correct colonial governance" (5). In what she calls a "sustained quarrel with the project of imperialism, the cult of domesticity and the invention of industrial progress," Anne McClintock (1995) productively complicates this field of study by emphasizing that Victorian texts in which empire and gender converge also simultaneously participate in the construction of class differences. Firdous Azim (1993) makes the broadest and least convincing claim, arguing that the novel is an inherently imperial genre. The "central subject who weaves the narrative" of the novel, she claims, "is also based on the forceful negation of other elements, deliberately ignoring other subject positions. This purpose is served by an invocation of the Other and its subsequent dismissal. Thus the novel is an imperialist project, based on the forceful eradication and obliteration of the Other" (37). In Azim's formulation, any domestic novel, by virtue of being a novel, reinforces the imperial project.

10. Perera, David, and others have complicated the generic division that Martin Green (1979) formulates between novels of the Great Tradition, which "invite explanation in terms of the class system and the Industrial Revolution" as they narrate the "stories of the sisters and their courtship," and novels that invite explanation in terms of empire as they narrate the stories of the brothers and their adventures in distant realms (xiv–xv).

11. There are of course some notable exceptions. Cannon Schmitt (1997), who discusses eighteenth- and nineteenth-century gothic novels, argues that "if Continental Europe, the East, or South America provides an antithesis against which Englishness might be elaborated, their menacing and alluring alterity eventually makes good on its threat. The English are displaced, figuratively if not physically: their Englishness admits of Otherness, and England itself becomes an alien nation" (3). Focusing on figures that link British women to racial others in works by Victorian women writers, Susan Meyer (1996) questions the extent to which the texts she studies endorse empire. While she admits that the trope of race primarily directs attention to the "frustration, limitation, and subordination" suffered by rebellious British women, she further argues that it allows attentive readers to reconstruct and critique a repressed history of imperial oppression suffered by racially other colonial subjects. The "complicated interplay between the ideologies of race and gender allows ... nineteenth-century women writers to make at times a surprisingly forceful critique of empire" (28). Reconstructing what he refers to as a " 'debate' occurring within the context of a culture-wide imperialist mentality which is pervasive but also challenged," Daniel Bivona (1990) argues that domestic narratives such as *Sybil*, *Alice's Adventures in Wonderland*, and *Jude the Obscure* undermine imperial authority (viii). Although he offers interesting and often persuasive readings, he positions texts within the "debate" over empire according to their treatment of the broad epistemological "question of how and under what conditions the alien may be appropriated" (viii). This approach allows

readings of any narrative in which this question arises to be read as an implicit commentary on empire. Thus he unconvincingly presents Alice's inability to master the rules of Wonderland as a "profound challenge to English ethnocentric complacency" (51).

12. Although ethnography is often associated with the particular academic discipline of anthropology, it actually represents a large family of discourses. As Pels and Salemink emphasize, anthropology belongs to a "much broader field of ethnographic practice" (7). Missionaries, imperial administrators, and travelers all contributed to the field of nineteenth-century Western ethnography as they sought for a range of different reasons to describe the manners and customs of colonial others.

13. William Pietz offers a fascinating discussion of European Enlightenment attitudes toward African religious practices in his series of articles entitled "The Problem of the Fetish" (1985, 1987, 1988). Dickens has clearly inherited the eighteenth-century conception of fetishism as "institutionalized religious delusion" featuring the "worship of haphazardly chosen material objects" (1988: 106).

14. Tim Fulford (2003) analyzes a parallel example drawn from the late eighteenth-century, when profits reaped by the "nabobs" of the East India Company fueled a "culture of consumption and excess" in London that threatened to transform the national identity; "[l]ike despotic Oriental rulers, Britons were learning in the East to consume others in their greed for power and pleasure" (11–12). Satirists and caricaturists objected to the trend by depicting English aristocrats and politicians as besotted Eastern despots. "Oriental imagery was a staple of the new satire," Fulford contends, "a graphic illustration of the conspicuous consumption engendered by empire" (24).

15. Freud attributes this quotation to Kuno Fischer, *Über den Witz* (1889).

16. In another of the traditional books on satire that appeared in the 1960s, Leonard Feinberg (1967) suggests that satire brings to light "truths [that] are simply too uncomfortable to admit" (266). He particularly attends to the device used by Thackeray and Dickens, "disparaging comparison[s]" that serve to disclose "unobserved similarities" (130).

17. In *The Ego and the Id*, Freud considers certain neurotic "maladies" produced by the "critical agency" when it "displays particular severity and … rages against the ego in a cruel fashion" (19: 51).

18. Gary Dyer (1997) explains the disappearance of formal verse satire in the 1820s and 1830s on a combination of market forces and the ascendance of middle-class Evangelicalism and related social mores that "restrained verbal attack and, along with it, satire" (139). Dyer builds an impressive case to support this point, although his argument seems most persuasive in relation to satire directed against personal targets. The passage from Booth, and indeed much of the material considered in this book, documents an interesting collaboration between the Evangelical reform impulse and satire.

19. In *Writing the Urban Jungle* (2000), Joseph McLaughlin offers a compelling extended reading of Booth's text (79–103).

20. The historical, ideological, and geographical transmutations of the English colonial civilizing mission represent a vast topic. In relation to India, Eric Stokes (1959) offers what remains an excellent review of the liberal reform agenda. Also see Gauri Viswanathan (1989) and Thomas R. Metcalf (1995).

For analysis of the English civilizing mission in Africa, see Comaroff and Comaroff (1991), particularly their chapter "Africa Observed: Discourses of the Imperial Imagination" (86–125) and Philip Curtin (1964), particularly his chapter "Techniques for Cultural Change" (259–86). Stiv Jakobsson (1972) provides particularly thorough coverage of abolitionist activities in relation to West Africa and the West Indies. Also see Ronald Robinson and John Gallagher (1961), and T. O. Beidelman (1982).

21. See the first two chapters of T. O. Lloyd's *The British Empire 1558–1983* (1984) for a more detailed overview of early colonial ventures.

22. Although politically naive and somewhat adulatory, Ernest Marshall Howse (1952) details the Clapham Sect's influence on imperial policy. Eric Stokes explains the intellectual shared ground between the Clapham Sect and the Utilitarian liberals who controlled colonial policy in India. See his first chapter, "The Doctrine and Its Setting" (1–80).

23. Due to the political influence of its members, the Clapham Sect had a particularly direct impact on imperial policy. The missionary projects it sponsored, however, represented only a fraction of the many similar initiatives undertaken in the late-eighteenth and nineteenth centuries. Their vehicle, the Church Missionary Society, was joined in the field by societies affiliated with other churches and denominations. Indeed, William Carey, a representative of the Baptist Society for Propagating the Gospel Among the Heathen, had founded a mission in Bengal as early as 1793. The Congregationalists established the London Missionary Society to conduct their colonial projects in 1795. The Methodists founded the Wesleyan Missionary Society in 1813. The Society for the Propagation of the Gospel in Foreign Parts, originally established in 1701 to minister to British citizens abroad, gradually transformed in the early nineteenth century into the High Church Anglican organization for converting distant heathen. Susan Thorne (1999) provides a particularly useful historical source. Although she focuses particularly on Congregational missions, her findings are broadly applicable. For further historical commentary on religious missionary activity, see Jeffrey Cox (1995), Sue Zemka (1991), Brian Stanley (1990), and Stiv Jakobsson (1972).

2   Strange Relations: The Evangelical and Anthropological Roots of Imperial Anxiety

1. Benedict Anderson (1991: 7). This idea has proven particularly useful to Linda Colley and many other critics who seek to analyze ideological strategies of differentiation.

2. For further discussion of the urban jungle trope, see Judith Walkowitz (1992).

3. Christine Bolt's *Victorian Attitudes to Race* (1971) remains an essential guide to the intricacies of the notion of race in the nineteenth century. Mr Earnshaw's description of Heathcliff as "dark almost as if it came from the devil" begins to show how a pejorative rhetoric of racial difference casually associated biological features such as skin color with moral character. As Bolt points out, Victorian culture entirely confused biological and cultural attributes in the concept of race, which "came to be seen as the prime determinant of all the important traits of body and soul, character and personality, of human beings

and nations. In other words, race became far more than a biological concept: race and culture were dangerously linked" (9).

4. From this perspective, *Wuthering Heights* represents a forerunner of a group of late-Victorian "invasion-scare" narratives. Patrick Brantlinger (1988) suggests that the recurrence of the "invasion-scare" plot, in which "the outward movement of imperialist adventure is reversed" and the metropolitan center is invaded by threatening peripheral forces, reveals a pervasive anxiety about "the weakening of Britain's imperial hegemony" (229). See Susan Meyer (1996) for a fine reading of the novel as an enactment of "the worst nightmare of the imperialist power: reverse colonization" (112).

5. Marianne Thormählen (1999) provides the most thorough and subtle analysis of the religious context of fictional works by the Brontë sisters. Her first chapter provides a fine overview of Evangelicalism, the creed that "was of such fundamental importance in Patrick Brontë's home" (14). Also see Felicia Gordon (1989: 73–85) and Tom Winnifrith, *The Brontës and Their Background: Romance and Reality* (1973: 28–75).

6. Nancy Armstrong (1992) compares the novel's depiction of remote Yorkshire and its indigenous inhabitants to the work of mid-century folklorists and photographers, arguing that all these forms of representation participate in a process of "internal colonization." The "inscription of unfamiliar landscapes and bodies provides not only a record of the passing of regional cultures," she contends, "but also the technology for converting them into an ethnic periphery" (447).

7. Evangelicalism comprehended a diverse range of beliefs and practices within the Anglican Church and dissenting sects of Protestantism. As religious historians attempt to assess its doctrines and effects, they frequently point out that it was a "fragmented rather than a unitary movement," as David Englander (1988) observes. In *The Religion of the Heart: Anglican Evangelicalism and the Nineteenth-Century Novel* (1979), Elisabeth Jay offers an effective overview of the movement in her chapter on "Evangelical Doctrine" (53–105). Also see Ian Bradley (1976) and Michael Hennell (1979), the latter of whom approaches the movement through biographical sketches of principal figures. Although dated, the account of the movement in Overton and Relton (1906) remains useful as a guide to major figures and publications. See their chapter on "The Later Evangelicals" (230–50).

8. Susan Thorne (1999) carefully recovers the disputes and tensions that often marked the relationship between religious missionaries and other imperial factions, but she points out that, nonetheless, "Christian missions figured in official as well as missionary rationales as the ultimate gift exchanged in the colonial encounter, one that bestowed upon violent, superstitious, and perishing peoples the benefit of eternal salvation" (39).

9. George W. Stocking provides a lucid review of the different intellectual strands of Victorian anthropology. In the discussion which follows, I rely heavily on his analysis of pre- and post-Darwinian views and the impact of anthropological inquiry on the understanding of the relationship between civilization and savagery. Particularly see his chapter "The Darwinian Revolution and the Evolution of Human Culture" in *Victorian Anthropology* (New York: Free Press, 1987), 144–85. I should clarify that my use of the term "anthropology" smooths over a crucial Victorian debate between those who subscribed to the single

origin thesis and embraced the evolutionary paradigm, who generally belonged to the Ethnological Society of London (founded 1843), and those who believed that the different races were actually different species. In the early 1860s, the latter split off to form the Anthropological Society of London. In 1871, the two factions re-joined in the Anthropological Institute. See Stocking, 248–54.

10. Evolutionary theory could also provide theoretical support for the survival of the "fittest" races. In a chilling passage of *The Origin of Civilization*, Lubbock contemplates the "almost invariable rule that [the lower] races are dying out, while those which are stationary in condition, are stationary in numbers also; on the other hand, improving nations increase in numbers, so that they always encroach on less progressive races" (322).

11. Talal Asad (1991) casts doubt on the extent to which anthropological knowledge ever really helped to maintain "structures of imperial domination." Anthropological data was "often too esoteric for government use, and even when it was usable it was marginal in comparison to the vast body of information routinely accumulated by merchants, missionaries, and administrators" (315).

12. According to Stocking (1973), the ethnologist James Cowles Prichard exemplifies the pre-Darwinian effort to advance anthropological inquiry within the framework of the Christian narrative. Influenced as a student at Cambridge by the Evangelical revival, Prichard developed anthropological ideas that remained "rooted in the age-old tradition of Christian chronological writing" (xlix). Throughout his career, he relied on theories that "attempted, on the basis of linguistic and cultural similarities, to trace all mankind back to a single family which had been dispersed over the face of the earth after the Flood" (xlix).

13. Johannes Fabian (1983) contends that the "denial of coevalness," by which he means the "persistent and systematic tendency to place the referent(s) of anthropology in a Time other than the present," as one of the central "distancing devices" used by evolutionary anthropologists (31).

14. The depiction of the missionary as father to child-like natives confirms Anne McClintock's analysis of the colonial mission station as an "institution for transforming domesticity rooted in European gender and class roles into domesticity as controlling a colonized people. Through the rituals," and, it follows, the language of domesticity, "colonized peoples were wrested from their putatively 'natural' yet, ironically, 'unreasonable' state of 'savagery' and inducted through the domestic progress narrative into a hierarchical relation to white men" (34).

15. A passage from the *London Christian Instructor* similarly challenges religious ethnocentrism with a hypothetical scenario. The anonymous author of "On the Worship of Idols" (1818) concludes "that a child born in England, had it been his lot to be born in an idolatrous country, would have been an idolater" (25).

16. The evidence I have collected leads me to dispute a historical trend asserted by Susan Thorne (1999), who argues that eighteenth-century Evangelicals held the belief that "heathenism was ever present and that Satan must first be rooted out from within our midst, which extended right down to the individual Evangelical. Victorian missionary practice, by contrast, was predicated on the assumption that heathenism resided outside the individual, that it was a characteristic feature of entire communities" (33). In light of sermons written by Robinson (1833), Grant (1844), Wright (1890), and other

Victorian ministers, I see strong evidence of the notion that heathenism exists within the English Christian subject.

17. In Exodus, Moses delivers the injunctions against idolatry, telling the people that God has said, "Thou shalt have no other gods before me. Thou shalt not make unto thee any graven image, or any likeness of any thing that is in heaven above, or that is in the earth beneath, or that is in the water under the earth. Thou shalt not bow down thyself to them, nor serve them; for I the Lord thy God am a jealous God" (*King James Bible*, Exodus 20.3–5).

18. Noel Annan (1952) rightly insists that the thought of this "militant agnostic" (123) was "hewn in Evangelical rock" (118). Annan does not specifically discuss the iconoclastic impulse, but he does observe that children reared in Evangelical homes like Stephen's were taught to "distinguish between right and wrong, the good and the wicked, the precious and the worthless" (112). For Stephen, idolatry clearly results from a failure to distinguish accurately between the precious and the worthless.

19. Stephen mis-spells the name of the idol, "Cham Chi-Thaungu." The episode to whch he alludes occurs in *The Farther Adventures of Robinson Crusoe* (1819).

20. Victorian anthropologists generally distinguish between an idol, a constructed image that represented a god, and a fetish, a material object that actually was a god. As Peter Melville Logan (2002) demonstrates, George Eliot was particularly intrigued by the notion of fetishism, which she studied in the writings of Comte and Feuerbach, continental philosophers who anticipated the work of British anthropologists by perceiving traces of primitive fetishism at work in modern European Christian cultures. As Logan explains, "the structure of fetishism," which was "thought of as a failure of objective or rational perception," made it "useful in the domestic context as a mode of social critique" (28). In a section of his essay that parallels my argument, he detects in the work of Eliot a "transposition of ethnological themes onto contemporary life," a process he terms "domestic primitivism" (28). He observes that Eliot "uses domestic primitivism to represent Victorian life as a reversion to an earlier stage of social development" (28). Logan's argument pursues the irony that Eliot's realist aesthetic reduplicates fetishistic modes of thought that she exposes in her characters. For further discussion of the distinction between idolatry and fetishism, see Pietz (1987).

21. See Radford for a fine reading of *The Return of the Native* and Hardy's other works in the context of evolutionary anthropology.

22. *Lord Ormont and His Aminta* (1894: 64).

23. The representation of the subjection of women as a lingering taint of the brutal past echoes the work of evolutionary anthropologists such as Tylor. However, Mill arrived at his evolutionary approach before they began to publish their central works through his study of Comte and other continental philosophers. See Stocking, *Victorian Anthropology* (38–41).

3 The Juggernaut Roles in England: The Idol of Patriarchal Authority in *Jane Eyre* and *The Egoist*

1. English spellings of the word "juggernaut" varied in the nineteenth century, as the quotations throughout this chapter demonstrate. I adopt the modern spelling, capitalizing the initial letter when referring to the idol in Puri.

2. I am grateful to Jeffrey Spear for calling my attention to the Punch cartoon. It is reprinted by Richard D. Altick (1973: 157).

3. Also see W. J. Macpherson (1955–56) for an extended discussion of the practical and ideological motivations for building railroads in India.

4. The "hybrid construction" is for Bakhtin an especially concentrated form of "heteroglossia," the term he uses to describe the process by which the novel (especially the English comic novel) "parodically reproduces ... generic, professional and other strata of language" (301). Bakhtin's analysis of novelistic discourse is grounded on the principle that "[e]ach word tastes of the context and contexts in which it has lived its socially charged life" (293). Hybrid constructions such as "juggernaut" provide a forum for the dialogic interaction of perspectives emerging from the different contexts that have shaped the word's social history.

5. See the *Asiatic Journal* for transcripts of Company debates over the pilgrim tax (1827: 689–735; 1830: 87–118). Judith M. Brown (1985) discusses the Company's effort to supplement trade profit with other income sources such as land revenue, which rapidly became "the single most significant source of government revenue" (64) and the less significant, but still profitable, pilgrim tax (74). Also see Thomas R. Metcalf (1995: 36–7).

6. Johnston observes that the "relationship between missionaries and the colonial state was one fraught with complications, ambiguity, and extreme provisionality" (72). The controversy over the pilgrim tax amply demonstrates the potential for hostility and antagonism within this relationship.

7. For accounts of Evangelicalism in the broader context of the many distinct theories and interest groups influencing colonial policy in the eighteenth and nineteenth centuries, see Eric Stokes (1959: 27–47) and Brown (1985: 68–81).

8. This intervention is in some sense divine, in that it rescues Goonah Purist from idolatrous suicide and enables him to continue on the path of Christian enlightenment. The agent is human and fallible, however, a Mohammedan subject who attempts to convert him to another false religion, albeit a monotheistic one.

9. F. Mansbach informs readers that the "excess of fanaticism, which is stated erroneously in several missionary accounts to prompt pilgrims to court death by throwing themselves in crowds under the wheels of the car of, has either never existed, or has long ceased to actuate the present worshippers of that idol" (256). In the *Hobson-Jobson* entry for the word, Henry Yule and A. C. Burnell (1886) also make a point of noting that the "popular impression in regard to the continued frequency of immolations ... was greatly exaggerated" (466).

10. This conservative and pessimistic attitude toward India represented an abiding force in British colonial policy, counteracting secular reform initiatives proposed by Utilitarian theorists like James Mill as well as the spiritual enlightenment of the colony envisioned by Evangelicals. In 1813, for example, Charles Buller dispatched a letter to the Court of Directors of the East India Company in which he asserts that "whoever knows any thing of the Hindoos, must be aware that their veneration for antiquity will not allow them to depart from any thing which has once formed a part of their ceremonies" (599).

11. Mill observes in his *History of British India* that "[i]t is only in rude and ignorant times that men are so overwhelmed with the power of superstition as to pay unbounded veneration and obedience to those who artfully clothe themselves with the terrors of religion. The Brahmins among the Hindus have acquired and maintained an authority, more exalted, more commanding, and extensive, than the priests have been able to engross among any other portion of mankind" (45).

12. Winifred Gérin (1967) notes that William Wilberforce, a principal architect of the Evangelical colonial mission, was a patron of the school run by William Carus Wilson, prototype of Brocklehurst in *Jane Eyre* (2). Marianne Thormählen (2000) discusses the "clear and numerous" parallels between St John Rivers and Henry Martyn, a close college friend of Patrick Brontë who, as Chaplain to the East India Company and translator of Christian texts into Hindustani and Urdu, devoted his life to the Evangelical project in India (215). Also see Mary Ellis Gibson (1999). In addition to such family connections, newspapers, periodicals, and sermons in the 1830s and 1840s make frequent reference to the Evangelical mission abroad. The *Methodist Magazine*, received by Aunt Branwell (who kept house for her brother-in-law after the death of his wife) included a section of "Missionary Notices" in each number. The slighting reference to "mad Methodist Magazines" in *Shirley* suggests that Brontë did not think highly of this periodical, but she likely would have read it on a regular basis (389). The topic of Juggernaut arises with some frequency in the "Missionary Notices." In the 1840 volume, for example, Rev. C. Lacey published a short description of his visit to the temple, taking the opportunity to express frustration with the ongoing "British connexion with Juggernaut" (3rd ser. 19: 608–9).

13. In extracting this generally agreed upon point, I am of course neglecting many subtle distinctions and points of debate among postcolonial treatments of *Jane Eyre*. Also see Gayatri Spivak (1985), Mary Ellis Gibson (1987), Cynthia Carlton-Ford (1988), Suvendrini Perera (1991), Firdous Azim (1993), Joyce Zonana (1993), Deirdre David (1995), and Susan L. Meyer (1996).

14. Both Sharpe and David emphasize association between Hindu women and sati, but Juggernaut worship represents another case of what was perceived as barbaric superstition.

15. I have not found evidence proving that Brontë read *The Curse of Kehama*, but it seems likely given the popularity of the poem and her esteem for Southey. In a letter to Ellen Nussey (4 July 1834), she numbers him among a list of "first rate" poets (*Letters* 1:130) and indeed in 1837 exchanged letters with him when she sought his advice on her own abilities as a poet. His discouraging reply evidently did not erode her respect for him. (See her grateful response to Southey, 16 March 1837.) Margaret Smith notes that "Southey's long 'oriental' poems," including *Kehama*, would have particularly appealed to Brontë, "whose juvenile tales were similarly exotic" (*Letters*, 168n).

16. Nancy L. Paxton (1999) discusses the poem's rape motif in the context of other Oriental rape scenes in the poetry of Byron and Shelley (45–52).

17. Lucy excoriates other characters for idolizing love interests, but she secretly indulges the same inclination throughout the novel. Like Jane, she experiences an ongoing struggle between reason and the "heathen" passions. When indulging a fantasy about expressing her love for the unattainable

Graham, for example, she describes herself as receiving "a spirit, softer and better than Human Reason" (308). This "spirit," associated with the desiring imagination, defies the government of Reason and its policy of self-restraint by allowing Lucy to indulge her fantasies, despite the likelihood that they will only generate eventual disappointment. Lucy so appreciates the visitation that she exclaims to the spirit, "[w]hen I bend the knee to other than God, it shall be at thy white and winged feet, beautiful on mountain or on plain. Temples have been reared to the sun – altars dedicated to the Moon. Oh, greater glory! To thee neither hands build, nor lips consecrate; but hearts, through ages, are faithful to thy worship" (308). The colonial administration of reason maintains superficial order during the day, but cannot apparently prevent the worship of strange gods by the yearning heart at night.

18. Charles J. Hill (1954) notes that "the conception of egoism as a survival of primitive brutishness becomes ... the informing idea" of the novel (520). Patricia O'Hara (1992) argues that Meredith's sense of the "degraded status of civilized women" leads him in *The Egoist* to present "an alternative reading of social evolution and the moral progress of civilization" (2). My approach to the novel confirms O'Hara's point that Meredith punctures Victorian "pretensions to moral and intellectual superiority over the savage 'other' " by depicting a society which, although supposedly civilized, harbors "primitive" forms of male egoism and female degradation (2).

19. George W. Stocking (1987) explains the doctrine of survivals and its principle expositors (162–3).

20. Like many other Victorian writers, Meredith particularly associates primitive patriarchal despotism with the Orient. In *The Egoist*, he intertwines references to Juggernaut with figurative patterns based on the harem and sati. Sophie Gilmartin (1997) discusses the function of sati images in *The Egoist*.

21. Perera considers a passage in which Dr Middleton compares his daughter Clara to "the aboriginals of a land newly discovered" by the "considerate" civilizing force of Willoughby (349). The analogy, she plausibly argues, shows that "the inscription of empire" in the English domestic novel is often "coded as an inscription of gender" (9). It is important to note the ironies that in this case undercut the patriarchal double "inscription." Dr Middleton exposes his own corrupt motives through his clumsy use of civilizing rhetoric. See Chapter 6 for an extended discussion of the ironies, intentional and unwitting, that beset this ideological connection in the work of Meredith.

22. See Carolyn Williams (1983) for a fine discussion of the language and idea of evolution in *The Egoist*.

4 Failed colonies in Africa and England: Civilizing Despair in *Bleak House*

1. In *Dickens at Work* (1958), Butt and Tillotson note that Dickens uses the satire on Mrs Jellyby to disparage both "female emancipation" and the type of "misguided philanthropy" that ignores domestic duties in favor of distant projects (194). Also see A. Abott Ikeler (1981) and Brahma Chaudhuri (1988). Norris Pope (1978) considers a broad range of public and private comments in which Dickens represents the foreign missionary effort as occupied

"with useless and vexatious projects, while ignoring urgent social problems at home" (127). R. Bland Lawson (1991) traces the influence of Carlyle in Dickens's general contempt for overseas missions, arguing that both *Bleak House* and *Past and Present* (1843) ridicule the practice of "devoting time and money to causes that are continents away rather than taking care of the distressed and impoverished at home" (25).

2. Robbins suggests that Dickens undercuts the "politics of presence" by representing egregious problems that cannot be solved by individual measures, implicitly endorsing supposedly disparaged forms of institutional responsibility. The spiritual and educational neglect of Jo, for example, indicates a social problem that cannot be solved by any single person.

3. Both David and Perera, particularly the latter, make interesting comments about *Bleak House*, but both focus primarily on *Dombey and Son* in their analyses of Dickens.

4. Temperley (1991) provides a thorough account of the 1841 Niger Expedition. In *The Image of Africa: British Ideas and Action, 1780–1850*, Philip D. Curtin (1964) considers expedition in the context of a broader historical perspective (289–317). Also see Pope (99–108).

5. Despite the fact that the chief organizers of the Niger expedition were men, Dickens is clearly reacting to a broad social dynamic in which Victorian women discovered a form of agency through overseas philanthropy. In her historical account of this dynamic, Susan Thorne argues that "foreign missions were being feminized in fact as well as in fiction during the second half of the nineteenth century. From the 1840s and 1850s on, women began to play an ever larger role in the propaganda and the practice of the LMS [London Missionary Society] as objects and agents of missionary outreach in the foreign mission field" (91).

6. The etymologies of the two words are distinct. See the *OED* entry on *weird*.

7. Pope describes Exeter Hall, the meeting place of many Evangelical philanthropic societies, as "the accepted monument to the missionary and charitable zeal of English Protestantism" (1). He provides a thorough account of Dickens' animosity for the organizations that used the building as their forum. Perera uses Dickens' review of the *Narrative* primarily to support her analysis of the link between gender and imperial trade in *Dombey and Son*, but also briefly considers it in relation to *Bleak House*, arguing that the "usurpation of the masculine platforms of economy and colonial policy by 'weird old women' (both politicized women and men feminized by humanitarianism) simultaneously perverts the ideology of gendered spheres of influence at home and guarantees disaster abroad" (61).

8. In his interesting discussion of General Booth's *In Darkest England*, Joseph McLaughlin (2000) admits that mid-century writers such as Dickens, Engels, and Mayhew "prefigure Booth's figuration of the East End as an imperial space," but argues that "none of them use an imperial metaphorics as a guiding trope" (80). In *Bleak House*, however, the civilizing mission to the Niger certainly functions as a "guiding trope," predating Booth's text by nearly 40 years.

9. In *The Examiner*, Dickens particularly attends to the insidious nature of the fever. "[L]ittle can be positively stated" regarding its cause, he observes, for the "the most delicate chemical tests failed to detect, in the air or water, the presence of those deleterious gases which were very confidently supposed to exist" (533). This quotation closely follows a passage in Allen and Thomson's *Narrative* (2: 165).

10. An early issue of *Household Words* (6 April 1850) includes an essay entitled "Heathen and Christian Burial" which perhaps influenced Dickens in his treatment of Hawdon's burial. "If from the heights of our boasted civilisation," the article begins, "we take a retrospect of past history, or a survey of other nations – savage nations included, – we shall, with humiliation, be forced to acknowledge that in no age and in no country have the dead been disposed of so prejudicially to the living as in Great Britain" (1: 43). This writer also finds in the condition of metropolitan burial grounds an indication that England cannot fulfill the "boast" of imperial civilization by demonstrating its superiority to "savage nations."

11. In a letter to John Forster (7 Oct. 1849), Dickens considers possible subjects for articles in *Household Words*. Among other projects, he imagines writing "a history of Savages, showing the singular respects in which all savages are like each other; and those in which civilised men, under circumstances of difficulty, soonest become like savages" (*Letters* 5: 622). He perhaps fulfills the second part of this project in the portrait of Jo, "under circumstances of difficulty" in a society more concerned with the "foreign-grown savage" than with its own variety.

12. See Harry Stone (1968), for a description of the collaboration between Dickens and Mrs Chisholm. In "A Bundle of Emigrants' Letters" (1850), Dickens observes that "there are strong reasons in favor" of emigration to Australia, particularly for those who are "ready and willing to labour," but cannot find work at home (1: 88). The fictional counterpart of this statement is found in *David Copperfield* (1850), in which Australia provides an ideal destination for the disgraced Peggotty family and the restless Micawbers. For Dickens, Australia actually holds the potential for fulfilling the colonial dream that Africa thwarts.

13. If dirt transformed English subjects into "children of the tropics," soap and water had the corresponding effect on Africans. In a letter to the editor of *John Bull* (8 June 1823), the writer rejects the civilizing mission in Africa as an expensive attempt to "wash the Blackamoor white" (qtd. in Curtin 261). See McClintock for an analysis of Victorian soap advertisements that graphically portray the same connection (212–17).

14. Jeffrey Spear aided my argument with this observation. Dickens later suggests that Caddy's baby inherits the "stain" of her enforced labor. He describes the child as having "curious little dark veins in its face, and curious little dark marks under its eyes, like faint remembrances of poor Caddy's inky days" (736). Captain Hawdon's experience renews the association of secretarial work with Africa. Although he does not himself undergo a metaphoric racial transformation, his desk, "a wilderness marked with a rain of ink," suggests another intrusion of the tropical desolation Dickens associates with the Niger delta (188).

15. Joel J. Gold (1983) argues that Dickens covertly associates Mrs Jellyby herself with African slave dealers. He suggests that Dickens read a passage from a travel narrative entitled *Egypt and Nubia*, published six years before *Bleak House*, in which the author describes seeing "a caravan of Jelabi, or slave pedlars, who are in the habit of trafficking between Darfour and Cairo" (37).

16. In *American Notes* (1842), for example, Dickens describes slavery as "that most hideous blot and foul disgrace" (26). In his description of a visit to

Washington DC, he accentuates an ironic contrast between slavery and the principles affirmed by statesmen within the halls of Congress and in copies of the Declaration of Independence proudly exhibited on its walls. The ideals of "Liberty and Freedom" are "blot[ted]" out by "that traffic, which has for its accursed merchandise men and women, and their unborn children" (119).

17. In Elizabeth Barrett Browning's poem "Aurora Leigh" (1857), Aurora partly justifies her rejection of Romney to herself by imagining that he could force her to make a similar transaction. His commitment to social justice, she fears, would lead him to rupture the "natural" bond of maternal affection by "chang[ing] my sons ... for black babes / Or piteous foundlings" (61).

18. Caddy takes a step down on the class ladder in her marriage to Prince Turveydrop, in whose dancing school she takes a leading role. Dickens significantly approves of the mother who works outside the domestic sphere in response to economic necessity, as long as she expends her compassion on her family. Esther describes, in her final comments on Caddy, how the circle of domestic civilization expands through maternal affection. Having herself "softened" the bitter girl, she notes approvingly that "there never was a better mother then Caddy, who learns, in her scanty intervals of leisure, innumerable deaf and dumb arts, to soften the affliction of her child" (933).

19. In the representation of Esther's civilizing mission, Dickens subtly questions absolute distinctions between public and private roles for the middle-class woman, although not to the extent that Ruskin does when, in an often quoted passage from "Of Queen's Gardens" (1864), he observes that "[a] woman has a personal work or duty, relating to her own home, and a public work or duty, which is also the extension of that. ... what the woman is to be within her gates, as the center of order, the balm of distress, and the mirror of beauty; that she is also to be without her gates, where order is more difficult, distress more imminent, lovliness more rare" (136–7). Esther does work "without her gates" in the Jellyby household and the brickmaker's hovel, but it is equally important to notice that this work takes place within the private sphere. Dickens indicates that the middle-class woman might in some instances perform charitable work outside her own home, but *the* home remains her proper sphere of influence.

20. Patrick A. Dunae (1980), in his analysis of late-Victorian imperialist boy's literature, notes the popularity of the theme in which young heroes "became authorities in their own right and vented their energies by expanding the Queen's realms or by defending her possessions overseas" (108). Woodcourt's adventure marks an early instance of the Victorian hero who finds his authority on the periphery of empire, but Dickens significantly shows Woodcourt using that authority and venting his energies by reforming the Queen's inadequately civilized territories in London.

21. Dickens also remains wary of too much experience on the imperial periphery. Woodcourt becomes a hero on a specifically imperial tour, but one that apparently involves no direct contact with the continent itself or its indigenous people. While "those East-Indian seas" provide a theater on which to stage the development of compassionate heroism in *Bleak House*, Dickens reveals in other contexts reservations about the effect of imperial power on British men. His reservations surface, for example, in *Dombey and Son* (1846–48), in which he represents Colonel Bagstock as a sadist who perpetually abuses a "dark

servant" (451). In *The Mystery of Edwin Drood* (1870), the hot-tempered Neville attributes his haughtiness to contact with "abject and servile dependents, of inferior race" (90). Both of these characters, Dickens suggests, have been contaminated by the imperial hierarchy of power.

22. Judith Walkowitz (1992) observes that Dickens and Henry Mayhew "adapted the language of imperialism to evoke features of their own cities. Imperialist rhetoric transformed the unexplored territory of the London poor into an alien place, both exciting and dangerous" (18). Her description of Dickens himself as one of the "engaged urban investigators of the mid- and late-Victorian era" who patrolled the back-streets of the metropolis with the "earnest (if still voyeuristic) intent to explain and resolve social problems" might also be applied to Woodcourt (18).

23. Dickens offers Jarndyce as a responsible father figure in relation to Skimpole in the same way that he opposes Esther to Mrs Jellyby. Significantly, Skimpole demonstrates his irresponsibility partly by revealing aesthetic interests in matters far afield. Considering the "Slaves on American plantations," he light-heartedly declares, "they people the landscape for me, they give it a poetry for me" (307). On the one hand, this revery reveals the questionable morality of Skimpole's aesthetic detachment. Esther's reaction to it, however, enforces the novel's effort to generate sympathy for the neglected and exploited "at home" before considering injustices abroad. Rather than criticizing Skimpole for drawing pleasure from the plight of exploited Africans, she substitutes the more immediate objects of concern, wondering whether he "ever thought of Mrs Skimpole and the children, and in what point of view they presented themselves to his cosmopolitan mind" (307–8). The irresponsible dilettante, like the impractical philanthropist, meets with censure from the character who remains always mindful of the "obligations of home."

24. Dickens' attitude toward India becomes much darker after the 1857 sepoy rebellion (See 127), but in *Bleak House* it provides him with a colonial locale that signifies exotic adventure without the threat of disease and death that Africa holds.

25. In *The Night Side of Dickens* (1994), Harry Stone establishes the centrality of the cannibal metaphor in the work of Dickens. Stone documents how Dickens associates cannibalism both with foreign or peripheral savagery, as in the case of Vholes – whose black gloves, indistinguishable from his skin, signify racial otherness – and with an indigenous variety, in the tradition of Hogarth and fairy tales. Arguing that cannibalism in one of its manifestations taints most of the evil characters in *Bleak House*, he proposes that the novel's lesson is that "all obey society's golden rule: eat or be eaten – or, more exactly, eat *and* be eaten. We consume our neighbors, we even batten on our progeny and our progenitors, Dickens is saying, instead of loving them. Mr. Vholes' cannibalism is only the most unadorned representation of this grim truth and of society's law" (150).

26. The second Bleak House recalls Dickens' idealized description of Australian colonies in the *Household Words* article in which he endorses Mrs Chisholm's Family Loan Colonization Society. Dickens imagines that "from little communities thus established other and larger communities will rise in time, bound together in a love of the old country still fondly spoken of as Home" (1: 88). Esther manifests the emigrant's nostalgia when she reports that, after

Jarndyce has given the second Bleak House to herself and Woodcourt, "all three went home" to the first Bleak House.

5 Mutinous Outbreaks in *The Moonstone*

1. This basic assumption surfaces in justifications of British rule in India in many distinct imperial discourses throughout the nineteenth century. Charles Grant, a missionary who wrote an influential treatise on the character of the "people of Hindustan," described them in 1797 as "a race of men lamentably degenerate and base ... governed by malevolent and licentious passions" (qtd. in Stokes 1959: 31). In 1833, Thomas Babington Macaulay represents the administration of the East India Company, despite its serious flaws, as the advent of the government of reason. "I see that we have established order," he definitively states, "where we found confusion" (704). In 1888, John Strachey, a member of the Viceroy's council, anticipates a return to "confusion" should the British leave India. "We cannot foresee the time in which the cessation of our rule would not be the signal for universal anarchy and ruin, and it is clear that the only hope for India is the long continuance of the benevolent but strong government of Englishmen" (qtd. in Stokes 1959: 284). The "Mutiny" texts discussed below represent a development of a long-standing discursive tradition.
2. Two additional psychosexual readings of the novel: Lewis A. Lawson, "Wilkie Collins and *The Moonstone*" (1963) and Charles Rycroft, "Detective Story: Psychoanalytic Observations," *The Psychoanalytic Quarterly* (1957). Feminist accounts which interpret Blake's sexual "conquest" as broadly indicative of Rachel's subordination to patriarchal power have developed the standard psychosexual interpretation. Tamar Heller (1992) argues, for example, that the diamond "signifies not merely [Rachel's] virginity but what Bruff calls her 'self-dependence' as well" (146).
3. For a more recent account which compellingly reads the novel as a critique of British imperial practices, see Lillian Nayder (1997: 115–25). This line of argument is contested by Ashish Roy (1993), who claims that the novel is a "prototypical imperialist text exhibiting imperialist rule and a justification of that rule within a single narrative strategy" (657).
4. Although I disagree with this thesis, Mehta's account is historically informative, sophisticated in its close readings, and often persuasive in its claims. The thesis is balanced by the observation that Collins "draws attention to the crosscutting of race and class ... and the arbitrariness of racial identity" (623).
5. Wilkie Collins, *No Name* (1862: 641); *The Evil Genius* (1886: 264).
6. *The Evil Genius* (264).
7. Andrew Ward (1996) provides a very thorough account of the uprising and the British retribution. Also see Eric Stokes (1986) and Christopher Hibbert (1978). In *They Fight Like Devils* (2001), D. A. Kinsley generates sympathy for the British imperial project by adopting the perspective of the besieged British communities and by casting the British campaign to regain control of the subcontinent as an epic battle devoid of ideological significance.
8. For a survey of literary responses to the Mutiny, see Patrick Brantlinger (199–224).

9. Balachandra Rajan (1999) offers a compelling discussion of an earlier phase of English anxiety about Indian wealth in his chapter on *Paradise Lost*. The poem, he argues, offers two conflicting images of India. In the first, which serves to justify the exploitation of the colony, India appears as the site of corrupt opulence. Yet Milton also compares the "flying fiend" to the trading vessels of Western merchants (qtd. in Rajan 53). Rajan argues that the poem thus "inscribe[s] the Satanic voyage within subsequent voyages of exploration and conquest" and associates Western hunger for Eastern luxuries with self-indulgent desire and original sin (55). Also see Sara Suleri's chapter on the trial of Warren Hastings (49–74).

10. Nancy L. Paxton (1999) builds upon Sharpe's work by developing the argument that the "Mutiny" rape represented only one of a number of different rape scenarios associated with the colony.

11. Dickens's dark fantasy provides an especially violent example of a point made by Leask, who observes that while the anxieties of imperial culture "sometimes block or disable the positivities of power ... they are just as often productive in furthering the imperial will" (3).

12. An earlier instance of this irony occurs in "The Noble Savage," in which Dickens bashes the romantic ideal to which the title refers, notoriously giving vent to a genocidal hatred for the collective "savage." Throughout the essay he emphasizes the extent to which "the savage" demonstrates a careless disregard for human life, calling him "murderous" and "bloodthirsty" and noting that he wages continual "wars of extermination" (467, 469). Although Dickens confesses that he has "no reserve on this subject," he does not seem to appreciate the extent to which his abhorrence for "the savage" leads him to implicate himself in his own definition of savagery. He imaginatively wages a war of extermination, representing his foe as "something highly desirable to be civilised off the face of the earth," and reveals more than a touch of "bloodthirsty" passion, arguing that it would be "justifiable homicide to slay" the African Bushmen who irritate him at a London exhibit (467, 469). In this essay, furthermore, Dickens observes of "the savage" that "his 'mission' may be summed up as simply diabolical" (470). This comment compounds the later irony of the "demoniacal" mission that he imagines undertaking in India.

13. Collins does not name the Hindu idol and critics have advanced readings of the novel based on different assumptions about its identity. William M. Burgan (1995), who provides a detailed source study of texts Collins relied upon for information about Hindu mythology, identifies the deity as Siva, god of destruction and generation. Mark M. Hennelly (1984) alternatively identifies the deity as Vishnu. Both interpretations argue that the novel's symbolic and thematic structure reflects the duality of these mythological figures.

14. Elisabeth Rose Gruner (1993) also argues that *The Moonstone* undermines the conventional Victorian ideal of the upper-middle-class family as a safe and secure "sphere" which excludes disreputable elements, although she emphasizes its connection to sordid crime rather than to colonial savagery. "For Collins," she argues, "the Victorian family, far from protecting one from the increasingly complex and dangerous public world, is itself the source of many of its own complexities and dangers" (128).

15. Arguing that *The Moonstone* "takes large comfort" from *Robinson Crusoe*, the "workmanlike myth of colonial enterprise" (657), Roy conflates the novel with Betteredge and misses the irony of his clairvoyant readings.

16. The enforced removal from India of the famous Koh-i-noor diamond, one of the Moonstone's several historical precedents, complements this point. After annexing the Punjab in 1849, Governor-General Dalhousie demanded that Maharaja Dalip Singh cede the Koh-i-noor to Queen Victoria, who added it to the stock of crown jewels. In an interesting analysis of this transaction, Mehta observes that the "incorporation of loot from the conquered into imperial regalia has ancient and primitive antecedents; at once magical and metaphorical, it performs a kind of visual cannibalism" (616). If the acquisition of the Koh-i-noor demonstrated imperial power, it also ironically reveals the survival of primitive impulses and rituals within Victorian culture.

17. Hennelly argues that the diamond's "travels in both India and England apparently serve to locate thematic values in either one or the other culture. But the actual point is the reverse, namely, that such an identification of national characteristics is too reductive and narrow-minded and that the insular Victorians, especially, must integrate what they see as Indian (or lunar) values into their own petrified culture" (42). While the novel confirms his point about the dangers of reductive national identities, it does so not by *advocating* the integration of "foreign" values, but rather by documenting the extent to which they are already integrated.

18. Also see Heller (144).

19. See Nayder (122–3).

20. In *The Races of Men* (1862), an anthropological study that provided theoretical support for apologists of empire by disputing the assumption of common origins, Robert Knox represents the racial hybrid as a "degradation of humanity ... rejected by nature" (qtd. in Young 1995: 15). Collins emphasizes the fact that Jennings is rejected by human communities rather than by nature. In the symbolic text of the hybrid's hair, analyzed below, it is the "capricious" division of black and white which is described as a "freak of nature."

21. William Wordsworth (1965: 191).

22. In a letter (4 July 1860) written in Ireland, Charles Kingsley provides another vivid example of the disturbing force of experiences that disrupt the color-coded antitheses of empire. For Kingsley, it is the Irish peasant rather than the English criminal who causes an uncanny return of colonial otherness. After a passage in which he enthusiastically reports on the salmon fishing, he abruptly shifts tone:

> But I am haunted by the human chimpanzees I saw along that hundred miles of horrible country. I don't believe they are our fault. I believe there are not only many more of them than of old, but that they are happier, better, more comfortably fed and lodged under our rule than they ever were. But to see white chimpanzees is dreadful; if they were black, one would not feel it so much, but their skins, expect where tanned by exposure, are as white as ours (2: 125).

Neither a story of benevolent imperial progress nor the distancing effect of bestial metaphor can erase this "dreadful" confrontation. Kingsley remains "haunted" by the sight of colonial others whose "skins ... are as white as ours."

6   Portions Wholly Savage: Ongoing Reforms at Home and Abroad

1. The epigraph appeared in Meredith's column "The Week" in the *Ipswitch Journal* (18 Nov. 1865). The column is reprinted in full by Richard L. Newby (1988: 325). Anne L. Ardis (1990) argues that the " 'natural' inevitability of the marriage plot is challenged as New Woman novelists replace 'the pure woman', the Victorian angel in the house, with a heroine who is either sexually active outside of marriage or abstains from sex for political rather than moral reasons" (3). Also see Gerd Bjørhovde (1987).

2. As I discuss below, Meredith persistently associates sexual and colonial politics. Recent postcolonial historical work has shown the danger of drawing easy parallels between English feminism and colonial independence movements, for English middle-class women sometimes acquired rights and responsibilities at the expense of colonial subjects. Mary Procida (2002), whose work focuses on the wives of imperial officials in India, argues that Anglo-Indian women found a "broader scope for public activity in the empire" (6). The extent to which they discovered in India opportunities to wield typically male forms of power indicates that the "binary categories of public and private, masculine and feminine, the worls and the home, must be rethought in the context of the Raj" (7). Also see Antoinette Burton (1994).

3. This chapter cannot provide more than a highly schematic review of a movement noted for its ideological complexity. Barbara Caine (1997) and Philippa Levine (1987) provide excellent historical accounts of the Victorian feminist movement. Kathryn Gleadle (2001) offers useful chapters on protests led by working-class women (111–21) and middle- and upper-class women (154–71). For an approach that attends to the colonial context of the British feminist movement, see Antoinette Burton (1994).

4. The contradiction is particularly apparent in the career of John Stuart Mill, who wrote some of the most famous theoretical discussions of liberalism while working as an official of the East India Company. In "On Liberty" (1859), Mill notably exempts from his assertion that "[o]ver himself, over his own body and mind, the individual is sovereign" those subjects from "backward states of society in which the race itself may be considered in its nonage" (14). "Despotism," he further explains, "is a legitimate mode of government in dealing with barbarians, provided the end be their improvement" (14–15).

5. See discussion of Meredith criticism in Chapter 3.

6. For an informative account of this affair, see Bernard Semmel, *Jamaican Blood and Victorian Conscience: The Governor Eyre Controversy* (Boston: Houghton Mifflin, 1963).

7. In his early article, Foster Watson (1910) refers to a conversation in which Meredith cited "Education and the Emancipation of Woman" as the "two aims which especially stirred and held him" (305). The remark is also noted by C. L. Cline (1966: 338). More recent critics extend the association between Meredith and feminist objectives. Merryn Williams (1984) describes him as

the "most committed feminist" of the major novelists who "looked sympathetically at the problems of the late-nineteenth-century woman" (170). Michael Wheeler (1985) discovers in Meredith's style an effort to "subvert the received ideas of a male-dominated, bourgeois, Christian culture" (160). Proclaiming Meredith the "one unqualified hero of the feminists of his time," Lloyd Fernando (1977) emphasizes Meredith's "sympathy for women who attempted to make independent decisions" (74) and his corresponding antipathy for "male attitudes that contribute to the subjection of women" (65). Jenni Calder (1976) argues that Meredith's heroines "strike out for themselves against immense pressures to conform and submit, and carve out independent lives," (126) although she also observes that the sexual unions Meredith arranges for these women "seem anti-climactic, even a betrayal of [their] creative independence" (202).

8. Two critics have recently argued that Meredith's novels undermine his professed commitment to sexual equality by refurbishing the very narrative structures he associates with patriarchal oppression. Carolyn Williams (1985) finds that "an inherent ambivalence lies at the heart of Meredith's attempted integration of progressive, feminist goals with comedy as a genre" (48). Laurie Langbauer discovers a similar irony within *Diana of the Crossways*, which, she argues, ultimately confirms the gendered distribution of power of sentimental romance (52).

9. Qtd in Lionel Stevenson (1953: 342).

10. His response to the Irish Home Rule bill suggests another effort to contain the eruption of colonial violence. He represents Home Rule as a "concession" made to tame the "wild fellow the Celt," who, when provoked by rigid authority, becomes "unrestrained in his cries and his deeds" (450).

11. Lionel Stevenson argues that the novel's "unwonted mellowness is responsible for a pervasive weakness" (313). In a reading more sensitive to political concerns, Barbara Hardy (1971) observes that Meredith "can become as ludicrously ecstatic, soft and blurred on the subjects of feminism, England and co-education as Dickens could on the subject of womanly virtue, religion and child-death" (297). It is important to note, however, that the novel's sentimental treatment of the relationship between Aminta and Matthew endorses an unequal distribution of power which actually undermines feminism and coeducation.

12. Wilfrid Scawen Blunt, "The Future of Self-Government," *Fortnightly Review* 37 (1885): 386–98. This essay culminates a series of five articles (jointly titled *Ideas About India*) in which Blunt elaborates the liberal perspective on self-government in India. For other contemporary examples, see the following articles. Andrew H. L. Fraser, "Local Self-Government in the Central Provinces of India, *Fortnightly Review* 39 (1886): 238–47. Henry M. Hyndman, "Bleeding to Death," *Nineteenth Century* 8 (1880): 157–76. Henry George Keene, "Some Aspects of Lord Ripon's Policy," *Fortnightly Review* 33 (1883): 901–10 and "Home Rule for India," *National Review* 15 (1890): 261–76.

13. George Meredith, vol. 29 of *The Works of George Meredith*, 585.

14. Keene (910).

15. For historical sources on the theory and practice of "civilizing" rule in India, see Chapter 1, note 20.

16. Adam Smith (1993: 369). Wealthy traders were known in England as "nabobs" (an anglicization of the Hindi word for governor), a title reflecting

the sense that East India Company officials brought their despotic habits formed abroad back home with them. "The riches of Asia have been poured in upon us," William Pitt writes in 1770, "and have brought with them not only Asiatic luxury, but, I fear, Asiatic principles of government" (qtd. in Sutherland 571).

17. Victorian writers who rely on representations of the "Orient" as a symbol for misogynist culture often use sati as a figure for circumstances in which a woman's subjectivity is metaphorically sacrificed for a man. In *The Egoist*, for example, Willoughby Patterne comforts himself with the thought that "[h]e had inspired one woman with the mysterious, man-desired passion of self-abandonment, self-immolation!" (383).

18. Although Aminta is figuratively associated with India, her actual heritage is uncertain. In the first chapter, she is enrolled in an English girl's school, where her complexion is "dark enough to get herself named Browny" (3). Her surname, Farrell, is Irish, and "Rumour called her a Spaniard" (37). Although her racial, ethnic, and geographical origins remain ambiguous, it is clear that she identifies with English culture.

19. This representation of Aminta draws from a long ethnographic tradition of depicting India and its inhabitants as passive and feminine, awaiting the rape of aggressive male conquerors. In his *Memoir of a Map of Hindoostan* (1783), James Rennell, the first Surveyor General of Bengal claims that the "softness and effeminacy" of the Indian character emanates from the very land itself; it is "induced by the climate, and the yielding nature of the soil, which pro-duces almost spontaneously" (xxi). Such language serves to naturalize and eroticize the conquest of India by "foreign invader[s]," whose attacks are "invited" by the feminine character of the land and her people (xxi).

Works Cited

Allen, William and T. R. H. Thomson. *A Narrative of the Expedition Sent by Her Majesty's Government to The River Niger in 1841 under the Command of H. D. Trotter.* 2 vols. 1848. London: Frank Cass, 1968.

Altick, Richard D. *Victorian People and Ideas.* New York: Norton, 1973.

Anderson, Benedict. *Imagined Communities: Reflections on the Origin and Spread of Nationalism.* London: Verso and New Left Books, 1983.

Annan, Noel. *Leslie Stephen: His Thought and Character in Relation to his Time.* Cambridge: Harvard UP, 1952.

Ardis, Anne L. *New Women, New Novels: Feminism and Early Modernism.* New Brunswick: Rutgers UP, 1990.

Armstrong, Nancy. "Imperialist Nostalgia and *Wuthering Heights.*" *Wuthering Heights.* Ed. Linda H. Peterson. Case Studies in Contemporary Criticism Ser. Boston: Bedford, 1992. 428–49.

Asad, Talal. "Afterword: From the History of Colonial Anthropology to the Anthropology of Western Hegemony." *Colonial Situations: Essays on the Contextualization of Ethnographic Knowledge.* Ed. George W. Stocking. Madison: U of Wisconsin P, 1991. 314–24.

Austen, Jane. *Mansfield Park.* 1814. New York: Oxford UP, 1998.

Azim, Firdous. *The Colonial Rise of the Novel.* New York: Routledge, 1993.

Bakhtin, Mikhail. *The Dialogic Imagination.* Austin: U of Texas P, 1981.

Ball, Charles. *The History of the Indian Mutiny.* 2 vols. New York: S.D. Brain, 1858.

"The Barbarisms of Civilisation." *Blackwood's Edinburgh Magazine* 90 (July 1861): 87–100.

Baucom, Ian. *Out of Place: Englishness, Empire, and the Locations of Identity.* Princeton: Princeton UP, 1999.

Beidelman, T. O. *Colonial Evangelism: A Socio-Historical Study of an African Mission at the Grassroots.* Bloomington: Indiana UP, 1982.

Bhabha, Homi K. "Introduction." *Nation and Narration.* Ed. Homi K. Bhabha. New York: Routledge, 1990.

——. "Of Mimicry and Man: the Ambivalence of Colonial Discourse." *The Location of Culture.* New York: Routledge, 1994. 85–92.

Bivona, Daniel. *Desire and Contradiction: Imperial Visions and Domestic Debates in Victorian Literature.* New York: Manchester UP, 1990.

Bjrhovde, Gerd. *Rebellious Structures: Women Writers and the Crisis of the Novel 1880–1900.* Oslo: Norwegian UP, 1987.

Blunt, Wilfrid Scawen. "The Future of Self-Government." *Fortnightly Review* 37 (1885): 386–98.

Bolt, Christine. "Race and the Victorians." *British Imperialism in the Nineteenth Century.* Ed. C. C. Eldridge. New York: St. Martin's Press, 1984. 126–47.

Booth, William. *In Darkest England and the Way Out.* New York: Funk and Wagnalls, 1890.

Bradley, Ian C. *The Call to Seriousness: The Evangelical Impact on the Victorians.* New York: MacMillan, 1976.

Brantlinger, Patrick. *Rule of Darkness: British Literature and Imperialism, 1830–1914.* Ithaca: Cornell UP, 1988.

Brontë, Charlotte. *Shirley.* 1849. New York: Oxford UP, 1979.

——. *Villette.* 1853. New York: Penguin, 1979.

——. *Jane Eyre.* 1847. New York: Oxford UP, 1980.

——. "Editor's Preface to the New Edition of *Wuthering Heights.*" *Wuthering Heights.* Ed. Ian Jack. New York: Oxford UP, 1995. 367–71.

——. *The Letters of Charlotte Brontë.* Ed. Margaret Smith. 2 vols. to date. Oxford: Clarendon, 1995–2000.

Brontë, Emily. *Wuthering Heights.* 1847. New York: Oxford UP, 1995.

Brown, Judith M. *Modern India: The Origins of an Asian Democracy.* New York: Oxford UP, 1985.

Brown, William. *The History of Missions; Or, of the Propagation of Christianity among the Heathen, Since the Reformation.* 2 vols. Philadelphia: B. Coles, 1816.

Browning, Elizabeth Barrett. *Aurora Leigh.* 1856. New York: Oxford UP, 1993.

Buchanan, Claudius. *Christian Researches in Asia.* Wilmington: R. Porter and G. Metz, 1813.

——. *An Apology for Promoting Christianity in India.* Pittsburgh: Robert Ferguson, 1815.

Buller, Charles. "Copy of a Letter from Charles Buller, Esquire, to the Court of Directors of the East India Company; dated the 19th May 1813: – Detailing the Conduct of the Bengal Government, with reference to Temple of Jaggernaut." *British Parliamentary Papers Relating to India 1662–1947.* Vol. 8 (1812–13). Delhi: B. R. Publishing, 1992. 597–9.

Burgan William M. "Masonic Symbolism in *The Moonstone* and *The Mystery of Edwin Drood.*" *Wilkie Collins to the Forefront.* New York: AMS Press, 1995. 101–48.

Burton, Antoinette. *Burdens of History: British Feminists, Indian Women and Imperial Culture, 1865–1915.* Chapel Hill: U of North Carolina P, 1994.

Butler, Judith. "Gender as Performance: An Interview with Judith Butler." By Peter Osborne and Lynne Segal. *Radical Philosophy* 67 (1994): 32–9.

Butt, John and Kathleen Tillotson. *Dickens at Work.* Fair Lawn, NJ: Essential Books, 1958.

Buxton, Thomas Fowell. *The African Slave Trade and Its Remedy.* London, 1839.

Caine, Barbara. *English Feminism 1780–1980.* Oxford: Oxford UP, 1997.

Calder, Jenni. *Women and Marriage in Victorian Fiction.* New York: Oxford UP, 1976.

Carlton-Ford, Cynthia. "Intimacy without Immolation: Fire in *Jane Eyre.*" *Women's Studies* 15 (1988): 375–86.

Carlyle, Thomas. *Chartism.* 1839. *Selected Writings.* Ed. Alan Shelston. New York: Penguin, 1971. 151–232.

Carey, William. *An Enquiry into the Obligations of Christians to Use Means for the Conversion of the Heathens.* Leicester: Ann Ireland, 1792.

Caubulee. *The Crisis in India : Its Causes and Proposed Remedies.* London : Richard Bentley, 1857.

Chaudhuri, Brahma. "Dickens and the Women of England at Strafford House." *English Language Notes* 25 (June 1988): 54–60.

Clapperton, Hugh. *Journal of a Second Expedition into the Interior of Africa.* London: John Murray, 1829.

Claydon, Tony and Ian McBride. "The Trials of the Chosen Peoples: Recent Interpretations of Protestantism and National Identity in Britain and Ireland." *Protestantism and National Identity*. Eds, Tony Claydon and Ian McBride. Cambridge: Cambridge UP, 1998.

Cline, C. L. "George Meredith." *Victorian Fiction: A Guide to Research*. Ed. Lionel Stevenson. Cambridge: Harvard UP, 1966.

Colley, Linda. *Britons: Forging the Nation 1707–1837*. New Haven: Yale UP, 1992.

Collins, Wilkie. *The Evil Genius: A Domestic Story*. 1886. Peterborough, Ontario: Broadview Press, 1994.

——. *Man and Wife*. 1870. New York: Oxford UP, 1995.

——. *The Moonstone*. 1868. New York: Oxford UP, 1998.

——. *No Name*. 1862–63. New York: Oxford UP, 1998.

Comaroff, Jean and John Comaroff. *Of Revelation and Revolution: Christianity, Colonialism, and Consciousness in South Africa*. Chicago: U of Chicago P, 1991.

Cox, Jeffrey. "The Missionary Movement." *Nineteenth-Century English Religious Traditions: Retrospect and Prospect*. Ed. D. G. Paz. Westport, CT: Greenwood Press, 1995. 197–220.

Curtin, Philip D. *The Image of Africa: British Ideas and Action, 1780–1850*. Madison: U of Wisconsin P, 1964.

David, Deirdre. *Rule Britannia: Women, Empire, and Victorian Writing*. Ithaca: Cornell UP, 1995.

"Debate at the East-India House." *The Asiatic Journal and Monthly Register for British and Foreign India, China, and Australia* 23 (Jan.–June 1827): 689–735.

——. *The Asiatic Journal and Monthly Register for British and Foreign India, China, and Australia* 3 n.s. (Sept.–Dec. 1830): 87–118.

Dickens, Charles. "A Bundle of Emigrants' Letters." *Household Words* 1 (Mar. 1850): 19–24. Rpt. in *Charles Dickens's Uncollected Writings from* Household Words *1850–1859*. Vol. 1. Ed. Harry Stone. Bloomington: Indiana UP, 1968. 2 vols. 85–96.

——. *American Notes*. 1842. American Notes *and* Pictures from Italy. New York: Oxford UP, 1989. 1–254.

——. *Bleak House*. 1852–53. New York: Penguin Books, 1971.

——. *David Copperfield*. 1849–50. New York: Penguin Books, 1966.

——. *Dombey and Son*. 1846–48. New York: Penguin Books, 1970.

——. *Little Dorrit*. 1855–57. New York: Penguin, 1985.

——. *The Mystery of Edwin Drood*. 1870. New York: Penguin Books, 1974.

——. "The Noble Savage." *Household Words* 7 (June 1853): 337–9. Rpt. in The Uncommercial Traveller *and* Reprinted Pieces. Oxford: Oxford UP, 1989. 467–73.

——. *The Pilgrim Edition of the Letters of Charles Dickens*. Ed. Madeline House, Graham Storey, and Kathleen Tillotson. 12 vols. Oxford: Clarendon Press, 1965–2002.

——. "Review of the *Narrative of the Expedition sent by Her Majesty's Government to the River Niger in 1841*." *The Examiner*. 19 August 1848: 531–3.

Disraeli. *Sybil; Or The Two Nations*. 1845. New York: Penguin, 1985.

Dunae, Patrick A. "Boy's Literature and the Idea of Empire, 1870–1914." *Victorian Studies* 24.1 (1980): 105–22.

Duncan, Ian. "The Moonstone, the Victorian Novel, and Imperialist Panic." *Modern Language Quarterly* 55.3 (1994): 297–319.

Dyer, Gary. *British Satire and the Politics of Style 1789–1832*. Cambridge: Cambridge UP, 1997.

Eldridge, C. C. *England's Mission: The Imperial Idea in the Age of Gladstone and Disraeli, 1868–1880*. Chapel Hill: U of North Carolina P, 1974.

Eldridge, C. C. *Victorian Imperialism*. Atlantic Highlands, NJ: Humanities Press, 1978.

——. "Sinews of Empire: Changing Perspectives." *British Imperialism in the Nineteenth Century*. Ed. C. C. Eldridge. New York: St. Martin's Press, 1984. 168–89.

Eliot, George. *The Mill on the Floss*. 1860. New York: Penguin, 1985.

Eliot, T. S. "Wilkie Collins and Dickens." *Selected Essays, 1917–1932*. New York: Harcourt, 1932. 373–82.

Englander, David. "The Word and the World: Evangelicalism in the Victorian City." *Religion in Victorian Britain*. 5 vols. Ed. Gerald Parsons. Vol. 2. Manchester: Manchester UP, 1988. 14–38.

Fabian, Johannes. *Time and the Other: How Anthropology Makes Its Object*. New York: Columbia UP, 1983.

Fanon, Frantz. *The Wretched of the Earth*. New York: Grove Press, 1963.

Farrar, F. W. "Modern Idolatry." *Sunday Magazine* 20 (1884): 770–4.

Fay, Eliza. *Original Letters from India, 1779–1815*. London: Hogarth Press, 1986.

Feinberg, Leonard. *Introduction to Satire*. Ames: Iowa State UP, 1967.

Fernando, Lloyd. *"New Women" in the Late Victorian Novel*. University Park: Penn State UP, 1977.

Forster, E. M. *A Passage to India*. 1924. New York: Harcourt, 1984.

Freud, Sigmund. *The Standard Edition of the Complete Psychological Works of Sigmund Freud*. Ed. James Strachey. 24 vols. London: The Hogarth Press, 1953–74.

Fulford, Tim. " 'Getting and Spending': The Orientalization of Satire in Romantic London." *The Satiric Eye: Forms of Satire in the Romantic Period*. Ed. Steven E. Jones. New York: Palgrave Macmillan, 2003.

Gallagher, Catherine. *The Industrial Reformation of English Fiction: Social Discourse and Narrative Form*. Chicago: U of Chicago P, 1985.

Gatrell, Simon. "England, Europe, and Empire: Hardy, Meredith, and Gissing," *The Ends of the Earth: 1876–1918*. London: Ashfield, 1992. 67–82.

Gérin, Winifred. *Charlotte Brontë: The Evolution of Genius*. Oxford: Clarendon, 1967.

Gibson, Mary Ellis. "The Seraglio or Suttee: Brontë's *Jane Eyre*." *Postscript: Publication of the Philological Association of the Carolinas* 4 (1987): 1–8.

——. "Henry Martyn and England's Christian Empire: Rereading *Jane Eyre* through Missionary Biography." *Victorian Literature and Culture* 27.2 (1999): 419–42.

Gikandi, Simon. *Maps of Englishness: Writing Identity in the Culture of Colonialism*. New York: Columbia UP, 1996.

Gilmartin, Sophie. "The Sati, The Bride, and the Widow: Sacrificial Woman in the Nineteenth Century." *Victorian Literature and Culture* 25.1 (1997): 141–58.

Gleadle, Kathryn. *British Women in the Nineteenth Century*. Basingstoke: Palgrave, 2001.

Gold, Joel J. "Mrs Jellyby: Dickens's Inside Joke." *Dickensian* 79 (1983): 35–8.

Gordon, Felicia. *A Preface to the Brontës*. New York: Longman, 1989.

Grant, Anthony. *The Past and Prospective Extension of the Gospel by Mission to the Heathen*. London: Rivington, 1844.

Grant, Charles. *Observations on the State of Society among the Asiatic Subjects of Great Britain, Particularly with Respect to Morals; and on the Means of Improving it. British Parliamentary Papers Relating to India 1662–1947*. Vol. 10 (1812–13). Delhi: B. R. Publishing, 1992. 31–142.

Graham, John. *Practical Sermons, on the Ten Commandments*. York: A. Barklay, 1826.

Green, Martin. *Dreams of Adventure, Deeds of Empire*. New York: Basic Books, 1979.

Green, William. Frontispiece. *The Indian Pilgrim; or, the Progress of the Pilgrim Nazareenee, (Formerly Called Goonah Purist, or the Slave of Sin,) From the City of the Wrath of God to the City of Mount Zion. Delivered under the Similitude of a Dream*. By Mary Martha Sherwood. 7th Edn. London: Houlston and Son, 1832.

Grewal, Inderpal. *Home and Harem: Nation, Gender, Empire, and the Cultures of Travel*. Durham, NC: Duke UP, 1996.

Griffin, Dustin. *Satire: A Critical Reintroduction*. Lexington: U of Kentucky P, 1994.

Gruner, Elisabeth Rose. "Family Secrets and the Mysteries of *The Moonstone*." *Victorian Literature and Culture* 21 (1993): 127–45.

"Gypsies." *Blackwood's Edinburgh Magazine* 99 (May 1866): 565–80.

Hardy, Barbara. "*Lord Ormont and His Aminta* and *The Amazing Marriage*." *Meredith Now: Some Critical Essays*. Ed. Ian Fletcher. New York: Barnes and Noble, 1971.

Hardy, Thomas. *The Return of the Native*. 1878. New York: Penguin, 1985.

Headrick, Daniel R. *The Tools of Empire: Technology and European Imperialism in the Nineteenth Century*. New York: Oxford UP, 1981.

"Heathen and Christian Burial." *Household Words* 1, 2 (1850): 43–8.

Heber, Reginald. "From Greenland's Icy Mountains." 1819. *Heber's Hymns*. London: Sampson Low, Son, and Marston, 1870.

Heller, Tamar. *Dead Secrets: Wilkie Collins and the Female Gothic*. New Haven: Yale UP, 1992.

Hennell, Michael. *Sons of the Prophets: Evangelical Leaders of the Victorian Church*. London: SPCK, 1979.

Hennelly, Mark M. "Detecting Collins' Diamond: From Serpentstone to Moonstone." *Nineteenth-Century Fiction* 39 (1984): 25–47.

Herbert, Henry H. M. (Earl of Carnarvon). "Imperial Administration." *Fortnightly Review* 29 (1878): 751–64.

Herst, Beth F. *The Dickens Hero: Selfhood and Alienation in the Dickens World*. New York: St. Martin's, 1990.

Hibbert, Christopher. *The Great Mutiny: India, 1857*. New York: Viking, 1978.

Highet, Gilbert. *The Anatomy of Satire*. Princeton: Princeton UP, 1962.

Hill, Charles J. "Theme and Image in *The Egoist*." *The University of Kansas City Review* 20 (1954): 281–5. Rpt. in *The Egoist*. Ed. Robert M. Adams. New York: W.W. Norton, 1979. 518–24.

Hill, G. D. *Practical Sermons on the Ten Commandments*. London: Francis and John Rivington, 1845.

Hobbes, Thomas. *Leviathan*. 1651. Ed. J. C. A. Gaskin. New York: Oxford UP, 1996.

Hodson, Thomas. "Sketches of Hindooism." *The Wesleyan-Methodist Magazine*. 4th ser. 7.1 (Jan. 1851): 58–65.

Howse, Ernest Marshall. *Saints in Politics: The "Clapham Sect" and the Growth of Freedom*. Toronto: U of Toronto P, 1952.

Hutter, Albert D. "Dreams, Transformations, and Literature: The Implications of Detective Fiction." *Victorian Studies* 19.2 (1975): 181–209.

Ikeler, A. Abbot. "The Philanthropic Sham: Dickens' Corrective Method in *Bleak House*." *College Language Association Journal* 24 (1981): 497–512.

Jakobsson, Stiv. *Am I Not a Man and a Brother? British Missions and the Abolition of the Slave Trade and Slavery in West Africa and the West Indies 1786–1838*. Uppsala: Gleerup, 1972.

Jay, Elisabeth. *The Religion of the Heart: Anglican Evangelicalism and the Nineteenth-Century Novel.* Oxford: Clarendon, 1979.

JanMohamed, Abdul R. "The Economy of Manichean Allegory: The Function of Racial Difference in Colonialist Literature." *Critical Inquiry* 12.1 (1985 Autumn): 59–87.

Johnston, Anna. *Missionary Writing and Empire, 1800–1860.* Cambridge: Cambridge UP, 2003.

Kaye, John William. *Christianity in India: An Historical Narrative.* London: Smith, Elder, 1859.

Kelvin, Norman. *A Troubled Eden: Nature and Society in the Works of George Meredith.* Stanford, CA: Stanford UP, 1961.

Kiernan, V. G. *The Lords of Human Kind: Black Man, Yellow Man, and White Man in an Age of Empire.* New York: Columbia UP, 1986.

Kingsley, Charles. *The Novels, Poems, and Memories of Charles Kingsley.* 14 vols. New York: J. F. Taylor, 1899.

Kinsley, D. A. *They Fight like Devils: Stories from Lucknow during the Great Indian Mutiny, 1857–58.* New York: Sarpedon, 2001.

Lacey, C. "British Connexion with Juggernaut." *The Wesleyan-Methodist Magazine. Being a Continuation of the Arminian or Methodist Magazine* 3rd ser. 19 (1840): 608–9.

Laird, MacGregor and R. A. K. Oldfield. *Narrative of an Expedition into the Interior of Africa, by the River Niger.* London: Richard Bentley, 1837.

Lander, Richard and John. *Journal of an Expedition to Explore the Course and Termination of the Niger.* London: John Murray, 1832.

Langbauer, Laurie. *Women and Romance: The Consolations of Gender in the English Novel.* Ithaca: Cornell UP, 1990.

Lawson, Lewis A. "Wilkie Collins and *The Moonstone.*" *American Imago* 20, 1 (1963): 61–79.

Lawson, R. Bland. "The 'Condition of England Question': *Past and Present* and *Bleak House.*" *The Victorian Newsletter* 79 (1991): 24–7.

Leask, Nigel. *British Romantic Writers and the East: Anxieties of Empire.* Cambridge: Cambridge UP, 1992.

Levine, Philippa. *Victorian Feminism, 1850–1900.* Tallahassee: Florida State UP, 1987.

Lloyd, T. O. *The British Empire 1558–1983.* New York: Oxford UP, 1984.

Logan, Peter Melville. *Studies in the Literary Imagination* 35.2 (Fall 2002): 27–51.

Lonoff, Sue. *Wilkie Collins and His Victorian Readers: A Study in the Rhetoric of Authorship.* New York: AMS Press, 1982.

Lubbock, John. *The Origin of Civilisation and the Primitive Condition of Man. 1870.* Ed. Peter Rivière. Chicago: U of Chicago P, 1978.

Macaulay, Thomas Babington. "Government of India." *Macaulay Prose and Poetry.* Ed. G. M. Young. Cambridge: Harvard UP, 1970. 688–718.

——. "Minute on Indian Education." *Macaulay Prose and Poetry.* Ed. G. M. Young. Cambridge, MA: Harvard UP, 1970. 719–30.

MacKenzie, John M. *Orientalism: History, Theory, and the Arts.* New York: Manchester UP, 1995.

Macpherson, W. J. "Investment in Indian Railways, 1845–1875." *The Economic History Review* 8 (1955–56): 177–86.

Mansbach, F. "A Description of the Temple of Jagannát'ha and of the Rat'h-Játrá, or Car Festival." *Transactions of the Royal Asiatic Society of Great Britain and Ireland* 3 (1833): 253–60.

Martineau, Harriet. *British Rule in India: A Historical Sketch.* London: Smith, Elder, 1857.

McClintock, Anne. *Imperial Leather: Race, Gender, and Sexuality in the Colonial Contest.* New York: Routledge, 1995.

McLaughlin, Joseph. *Writing the Urban Jungle: Reading Empire in London from Doyle to Eliot.* Charlottesville: UP of Virginia, 2000.

McLennan, John F. *Primitive Marriage: An Inquiry into the Origin of the Form of Capture in Marriage Ceremonies.* 1865. Ed. Peter Rivière. Chicago: U of Chicago P, 1970.

McMaster, Graham. "All for Love: The Imperial Moment in *Lord Ormont and His Aminta,*" *Shiron* 30 (1991): 35–55.

McWilliam, James Ormiston. *Medical History of the Expedition to the Niger During the Years 1841–1842, Comprising an Account of the Fever which Led to Its Abrupt Termination.* London: John Churchill, 1848.

Mead, Henry. *The Sepoy Revolt: Its Causes and Consequences.* London: G. Routledge, 1858.

Medley, Julius George. *A Year's Campaigning in India, from March, 1857, to March, 1858.* London: W. Thacker, 1858.

Mehta, Jaya. "English Romance; Indian Violence." *The Centennial Review* 34 (1995): 611–57.

Meredith, George. "Concession to the Celt." *Fortnightly Review* 11 n.s. (October 1886): 448–51.

——. *Diana of the Crossways.* 1885. Vol. 16. *The Works of George Meredith.* 29 vols. New York: Russell and Russell, 1968. Rpt. of *The Memorial Edition.* London: Constable, 1909–12.

——. *Lord Ormont and His Aminta.* 1894. Vol. 18. *The Works of George Meredith.* 29 vols. New York: Russell and Russell, 1968. Rpt. of *The Memorial Edition.* London: Constable, 1909–12.

——. *The Letters of George Meredith.* Ed. C. L. Cline. 3 vols. London: Oxford UP, 1970.

——. *The Egoist.* 1879. Ed. Robert M. Adams. New York: Norton, 1979.

Metcalf, Thomas R. *Ideologies of the Raj.* The New Cambridge History of India Ser. Cambridge: Cambridge UP, 1995.

Meyer, Susan. *Imperialism at Home: Race and Victorian Women's Fiction.* Ithaca: Cornell UP, 1996.

Mill, James. *History of British India.* Ed. William Thomas. Chicago: U of Chicago P, 1975.

Mill, John Stuart. *On Liberty.* On Liberty *and Other Essays.* Ed. John Gray. New York: Oxford UP, 1991. 1–128.

——. *The Subjection of Women.* On Liberty *and Other Essays.* Ed. John Gray. New York: Oxford UP, 1991. 469–582.

Milligan, Barry. *Pleasures and Pains: Opium and the Orient in Nineteenth-Century British Culture.* Charlottesville: U of Virginia P, 1995.

Mitchell, Arthur. *The Past in the Present: What is Civilization?* New York: Harper, 1881.

Moll, Marie. "George Meredith and the Marriage Problem." *George Meredith and His German Critics.* Ed. Guy B. Petter. London: H. F. and G. Witherby, Ltd, 1939. 178–81.

Moore, R. J. "India and the British Empire." *British Imperialism in the Nineteenth Century.* Ed. C. C. Eldridge. New York: St. Martin's Press, 1984. 64–84.

Mullens, Joseph. *London and Calcutta, Compared in Their Heathenism, Their Privileges, and Their Prospects: Showing the Great Claims of Foreign Missions upon the Christian Church.* London: James Nisbet, 1868.

Mundy, Godfrey Charles. *Pen and Pencil Sketches, Being the Journal of a Tour in India.* 2 vols. Vol. 2. London: John Murray, 1832.

Nayder, Lillian. "Class Consciousness and the Indian Mutiny in Dickens's 'The Perils of Certain English Prisoners.'" *Studies in English Literature 1500–1900* 32 (1992): 689–705.

——. *Wilkie Collins.* New York: Twayne, 1997.

Newby, Richard L. "George Meredith and the Governor Eyre Case Again." *Notes and Queries* 35 (1988): 325.

Norton, John Bruce. *The Rebellion in India: How to Prevent Another.* London: Richardson, 1857.

O'Hara, Patricia. "Primitive Marriage, Civilized Marriage: Anthropology, Mythology, and *The Egoist.*" *Victorian Literature and Culture* 20 (1992): 1–24.

"On the Worship of Idols." *London Christian Instructor* 1 (1818): 22–9.

"Our Rural Population and the War." *Blackwood's Edinburgh Magazine* 78 (Dec. 1855): 734–56.

Overton, John H. and Frederic Relton. *The English Church from the Accession of George I to the End of the Eighteenth Century (1714–1800).* 1906. New York: AMS Press, 1973.

Park, Mungo. *Travels in the Interior Districts of Africa: Performed under the Direction and Patronage of the African Association, in the years 1795, 1796, and 1797.* London: W. Bulmer, 1799.

Parks, Fanny. *Wanderings of a Pilgrim in Search of the Picturesque.* 2 vols. 1850. Vol. 2. New York: Oxford UP, 1975.

Paxton, Nancy L. *Writing under the Raj: Gender, Race, and Rape in the British Colonial Imagination, 1830–1947.* New Brunswick, NJ: Rutgers UP, 1999.

Pels, Peter and Oscar Salemink. "Introduction: Locating the Colonial Subjects of Anthropology." *Colonial Subjects: Essays on the Practical History of Anthropology.* Ed. Peter Pels and Oscar Salemink. Ann Arbor: U of Michigan P, 1999.

Perera, Suvendrini. *Reaches of Empire: The English Novel from Edgeworth to Dickens.* New York: Columbia UP, 1991.

Pietz, William. "The Problem of the Fetish, I" *Res* 9 (1985): 1–21.

——. "The Problem of the Fetish, II: The Origin of the Fetish." *Res* 13 (1987): 23–45.

——. "The Problem of the Fetish, IIIa: Bosman's Guinea and the Enlightenment Theory of Fetishism." *Res* 16 (1988): 105–23.

Pope, Norris. *Dickens and Charity.* New York: Columbia UP, 1978.

Poynder, John. "Debate at the East-India House." *Asiatic Journal* 23 (1827): 689–735.

Pratt, Mary Louise. *Imperial Eyes: Travel Writing and Transculturation.* New York: Routledge, 1992.

Prichard, James Cowles. *Researches into the Physical History of Man.* 1813. Ed. George W. Stocking. Chicago: U of Chicago P, 1973.

Procida, Mary. *Married to the Empire: Gender, Politics and Imperialism in India, 1883–1947.* Manchester: Manchester UP, 2002.

Radford, Andrew. *Thomas Hardy and the Survivals of Time.* Aldershot: Ashgate, 2003.

Railton, George Scott. *Heathen England and What to Do for It: A Description of the Utterly Godless Condition of the Vast Majority of the English Nation.* London: Partridge, 1891.

"The Railway Juggernaut of 1845." Cartoon. *Punch* 19 (July–Dec. 1845): 47.

Rajan, Balachandra. *Under Western Eyes: India from Milton to Macaulay.* Durham: Duke UP, 1999.

Reed, John R. "English Imperialism and the Unacknowledged Crime of the Moonstone." *Clio* 2.3 (1973): 281–90.

Rennell, James. *Memoir of a Map of Hindoostan; or the Mogul Empire.* London: George Nicol, 1783.

Rivière, Peter. "Introduction." *The Origin of Civilisation and the Primitive Condition of Man,* by John Lubbock. Chicago: U of Chicago P, 1978.

Robbins, Bruce. "Telescopic Philanthropy: Professionalism and Responsibility in *Bleak House.*" *Nation and Narration.* Ed. Homi K. Bhabha. New York: Routledge, 1990. 213–30.

Roberts, Emma. *Scenes and Characteristics of Hindostan, with Sketches of Anglo-Indian Society.* 2 vols. Vol. 2. London: Wm. H. Allen, 1837.

Roberts, Neil. *Meredith and the Novel.* New York: St. Martin's, 1997.

Robinson, Disney. *The Law and the Gospel. A Course of Plain Sermons on the Ten Commandments.* London: R. B. Seeley and W. Burnside, 1833.

Robinson, Ronald and John Gallgher. *Africa and the Victorians: The Climax of Imperialism in the Dark Continent.* New York: St. Martin's, 1961.

——. *Africa and the Victorians: The Official Mind of Imperialism.* London: Macmillan, 1981.

Roy, Ashish. "The Fabulous Imperialist Semiotic of Wilkie Collins's *The Moonstone.*" *New Literary History* 24 (1993): 657–81.

Ruskin, John. *Praeterita.* Ed. Kenneth Clark. New York: Oxford UP, 1978.

——. "Traffic." *Unto This Last and Other Writings.* Ed. Clive Wilmer. New York: Penguin, 1985. 233–49.

Rycroft, Charles. "Detective Story: Psychoanalytic Observations." *The Psychoanalytic Quarterly.* 26.2 (1957): 229–45.

Said, Edward. *Orientalism.* New York: Pantheon, 1979.

——. *Culture and Imperialism.* New York: Alfred A. Knopf, 1993.

Schmitt, Cannon. *Alien Nation: Nineteenth-Century Gothic Fictions and English Nationality.* Philadelphia: U of Pennsylvania P, 1997.

Semmel, Bernard. *Jamaican Blood and Victorian Conscience: The Governor Eyre Controversy.* Boston: Houghton Mifflin, 1963.

Sharpe, Jenny. *Allegories of Empire: the Figure of Woman in the Colonial Text.* Minneapolis: U of Minnesota P, 1993.

Sherwood, Mary Martha. *The Indian Pilgrim; or, the Progress of the Pilgrim Nazareenee, (Formerly Called Goonah Purist, or the Slave of Sin,) From the City of the Wrath of God to the City of Mount Zion. Delivered under the Similitude of a Dream.* 7th Edn. London: Houlston and Son, 1832.

Smiles, Samuel. *Self-Help; with Illustrations of Character and Conduct.* London: John Murray, 1859.

Smith, Adam. *An Inquiry into the Nature and Causes of the Wealth of Nations.* Ed. Kathryn Sutherland. New York: Oxford UP, 1993.

Smith, Margaret, Ed. *The Letters of Charlotte Brontë.* 2 vols. to date. Oxford: Clarendon, 1995–2000.

Southey, Robert. *The Curse of Kehama.* London: Longman, 1810.

Spivak, Gayatri Chakravorty. "Three Women's Texts and a Critique of Imperialism." *Critical Inquiry* 12 (1985): 243–61.

Stalleybrass, Peter and Allon White. *The Politics and Poetics of Transgression*. Ithaca: Cornell UP, 1986.

Stanley, Brian. *The Bible and the Flag: Protestant Missions and British Imperialism in the Nineteenth and Twentieth Centuries*. Leicester: Apollos, 1990.

Stephen, Leslie. "Idolatry." *The Cornhill Magazine* 19 (1869): 690–8.

Stevenson, Lionel. *The Ordeal of George Meredith*. New York: Charles Scribner's Sons, 1953.

Stevenson, Robert Louis. *The Strange Case of Dr. Jekyll and Mr. Hyde*. Dr Jekyll and Mr Hyde *and Other Stories*. Ed. Jenni Calder. New York: Penguin, 1979. 27–97.

Stirling, A. "An Account, Geographical, Statistical and Historical of Orissa Proper, or Cuttack." *Asiatic Researches* 15 (1825): 163–338.

Stocking, George W. "From Chronology to Ethnology: James Cowles Prichard and British Anthropology 1800–1850." *Researches into the Physical History of Man*, by James Cowles Prichard. Ed. George W. Stocking. Chicago: U of Chicago P, 1973. ix–cx.

——. *Victorian Anthropology*. New York: Free Press, 1987.

——. "Colonial Situations." *Colonial Situations: Essays on the Contextualization of Ethnographic Knowledge*. Ed. George W. Stocking. Madison: U of Wisconsin P, 1991. 3–8.

Stokes, Eric. *The English Utilitarians and India*. Oxford: Clarendon, 1959.

——. *The Peasant Armed : The Indian Revolt of 1857*. Ed. C. A. Bayly. New York: Oxford UP, 1986.

Stone, Harry, ed. *Charles Dicken's Uncollected Writings from* Household Words *1850–1859*. Vol. 1. Bloomington: Indiana UP, 1968. 2 Vols. 85–96.

——. *The Night Side of Dickens: Cannibalism, Passion, Necessity*. Columbus: Ohio State UP, 1994.

Suleri, Sara. *The Rhetoric of English India*. Chicago: U of Chicago P, 1992.

Sutherland, Kathryn. "Introduction." *An Inquiry into the Nature and Causes of the Wealth of Nations*, by Adam Smith. New York: Oxford UP, 1993.

Temperley, Howard. *White Dreams, Black Africa: The Antislavery Expedition to the River Niger 1841–1842*. New Haven: Yale UP, 1991.

Thackeray, William Makepeace. *The Book of Snobs*. 1845. London: Robin Clark, 1993.

——. *Pendennis*. 1848–50. New York: Oxford UP, 1994.

——. *Vanity Fair*. 1847. New York: Oxford UP, 1998.

Thormählen, Marianne. *The Brontës and Religion*. Cambridge: Cambridge UP, 1999.

Thorne, Susan. *Congregational Missions and the Making of an Imperial Culture in Nineteenth-Century England*. Stanford: Stanford UP, 1999.

Tylor, Edward B. *Researches into the Early History of Mankind and the Development of Civilization*. 1865. Ed. Paul Bohannan. Chicago: U of Chicago P, 1964.

——. *Primitive Culture: Researches into the Development of Mythology, Philosophy, Religion, Art, and Custom*. 2 vols. London: John Murray, 1871. Rpt. in vols. 3–4 *The Collected Works of Edward Burnett Tylor*. 8 vols. London: Routledge / Thoemmes, 1994.

Vejvoda, Kathleen. "Idolatry in *Jane Eyre*." *Victorian Literature and Culture* 31. 1 (2003): 241–61.

Viswanathan, Gauri. *Masks of Conquest: Literary Study and British Rule in India*. New York: Columbia UP, 1989.

Walkowitz, Judith. *City of Dreadful Delight: Narratives of Sexual Danger in Late-Victorian London.* Chicago: U of Chicago P, 1992.

Ward, Andrew. *Our Bones are Scattered: the Cawnpore Massacre and the Indian Mutiny of 1857.* New York: H. Holt, 1996.

Warren, Max. "The Church Militant Abroad: Victorian Missionaries." *The Victorian Crisis of Faith.* Ed. Anthony Symondson. London: S. P. C. K, 1970.

Watson, Foster. "George Meredith and Education." *Nineteenth Century* 67 (1910): 305–23.

Welsh, Alexander. *The City of Dickens.* Cambridge: Harvard UP, 1986.

Wheeler, Michael. *English Fiction of the Victorian Period 1830–1890.* London: Longman, 1985.

Wilberforce, William. *A Practical View of Christianity.* 1797. Ed. Kevin Charles Belmonte. Peabody, MA: Hendrickson, 1996.

Williams, Carolyn. "Natural Selection and Narrative Form in *The Egoist.*" *Victorian Studies* 27 (1983): 53–79.

——. "Unbroken Patternes: Gender, Culture, and Voice in *The Egoist.*" *Browning Institute Studies* 13 (1985): 45–70.

Williams, Merryn. *Women in the English Novel, 1800–1900.* New York: St. Martin's Press, 1984.

Wilson, Thomas. *The Knowledge and Practice of Christianity Made Easy to the Meanest Capacities, Or, an Essay Towards an Instruction for the Indians, Which Will Be of Use to Such Christians, as Have Not Well Considered the Meaning of the Religion They Profess, Or, Who Profess to Know God, but in Works Do Deny Him.* London: J. Osborn, 1743.

Wilt, Judith. *The Readable People of George Meredith.* Princeton, NJ: Princeton UP, 1975.

Winnifrith, Tom. *The Brontës and Their Background: Romance and Reality.* London: Macmillan, 1973.

Woods, Alice. *George Meredith as Champion of Women and of Progressive Education.* Oxford: Basil Blackwell, 1937.

Wordsworth, William. "Ode: Intimations of Immortality." *Selected Poems and Prefaces.* Ed. Jack Stillinger. Boston: Riverside, 1965.

Wright, Caleb. *Lectures on India.* Boston: Caleb Wright, 1851.

Wright, William Heber. *The Teaching of the Church of England as to Church Ornaments and the Peril of Idolatry.* London: Protestant Truth Society, 1890.

Young, Robert J. C. *Colonial Desire: Hybridity in Theory, Culture and Race.* New York: Routledge, 1995.

Yule, Henry and A. C. Burnell. *Hobson-Jobson: The Anglo-Indian Dictionary.* 1886. Hertfordshire: Wordsworth Editions, 1996.

Zemka, Sue. "The Holy Books of Empire: Translations of the British and Foreign Bible Society." *Macropolitics of Nineteenth-Century Literature: Nationalism, Exoticism, Imperialism.* Ed. Jonathan Arac and Harriet Ritvo. Philadelphia: U of Pennsylvania P, 1991. 102–37.

Zonana, Joyce. "The Sultan and the Slave: Feminist Orientalism and the Structure of *Jane Eyre.*" *Signs: Journal of Women in Culture and Society* 18 (1993): 592–617.

Index